Praise for *New York Times* bestselling author Sharon Sala

"Drama *literally* invades the life of an A-list Hollywood star, and the race is on to catch a killer."

—*RT Book Reviews* on *Life of Lies*

"A wonderful romance, thriller, and delightful book. [I] recommend this book as highly as I can.... Exciting... and will keep you glued to the pages until you reach the end."

—USATODAY.com's *Happy Ever After* blog on *Life of Lies*

"In Sala's latest page-turner, staying alive is the biggest challenge of all. There are appealing characters to root for, and one slimy villain who needs to be stopped."

—*RT Book Reviews* on *Race Against Time*

Praise for *USA TODAY* bestselling author Delores Fossen

"Clear off space on your keeper shelf, Fossen has arrived."

—*New York Times* bestselling author Lori Wilde

"[*Savior in the Saddle*] takes off at full speed from the first page and doesn't surrender an iota of the chills until the end."

—*RT Book Reviews*

MISSION: IRRESISTIBLE

NEW YORK TIMES BESTSELLING AUTHOR
SHARON SALA

Recycling programs
for this product may
not exist in your area.

ISBN-13: 978-1-335-40666-8

Mission: Irresistible
First published in 2000. This edition published in 2022.
Copyright © 2000 by Harlequin Enterprises ULC

Kade
First published in 2012. This edition published in 2022.
Copyright © 2012 by Delores Fossen

Harlequin Enterprises ULC
22 Adelaide St. West, 41st Floor
Toronto, Ontario M5H 4E3, Canada
www.Harlequin.com

Printed in U.S.A.

CONTENTS

Sharon Sala is a *New York Times* bestselling author. She has 123 books published in romance, young adult, Western and women's fiction and in nonfiction. First published in 1991, she's an eight-time RITA® Award finalist. Industry awards include the following: the Janet Dailey Award; five Career Achievement Awards from *RT Book Reviews*; five National Readers' Choice Awards; five Colorado Romance Writers Awards of Excellence; the Heart of Excellence Award; the Booksellers' Best Award; the Nora Roberts Lifetime Achievement Award presented by RWA; and the Centennial Award from RWA for recognition of her 100th published novel.

Books by Sharon Sala

Secrets and Lies

Dark Hearts
Cold Hearts
Wild Hearts

Forces of Nature

Going Gone
Going Twice
Going Once

The Rebel Ridge novels

'Til Death
Don't Cry for Me
Next of Kin

Visit the Author Profile page at Harlequin.com for more titles.

MISSION: IRRESISTIBLE

Sharon Sala

Prologue

Washington, D.C.—July 4th, 2000

The American flags above the tall man's head popped smartly as the hot July breeze whipped them into a frenzy; colorful reminders of a nation's gratitude for the dedication and sacrifices of countless soldiers over the centuries who had kept the country free.

But gratitude was the last thing on the man's mind as he stood before the black, polished surface of the Vietnam War Memorial. The petals of the rose that he carried were beginning to droop, but it hardly mattered. The man for whom it was meant had long ceased to care for anything of this earth.

It wasn't the first time he'd been here on the nation's birthday, so the unusual number of visitors did not surprise him. Yet as he moved through the people, he was struck by the silence of so large a crowd.

The memorial in itself was an emotionally moving sight. A seemingly endless stretch of gleaming black marble with nothing but names etched upon its surface. Names of fathers and of sons, of brothers and of uncles, of friends and neighbors who'd given their lives because their country had asked it of them.

His heart swelled painfully as he began to scan the surface. It was here—somewhere near the center and about a third of the way down. He stepped around a small, stoop-shouldered woman, then in front of a young couple with two small children, his gaze centering on the names. The farther he walked, the harder his heart began to pound. And then suddenly he stiffened.

There it was: Frank Wilson.

He traced the letters of the name with his forefinger. By the time he got to the last letter he was looking at the world through a blur and all he could think was, *Damn you.*

His jaw clenched and a muscle jerked at the side of his temple as he dropped the rose at the base of the wall and turned to walk away. As he did, the wind gusted, causing the flags to flutter, and ruffling the streaks of gray at the temples of his short, dark hair. He squinted against the sunlight and dropped a pair of sunglasses in place as he moved toward the grassy area beyond. But the sound of the blowing flag became mixed with the memories in his mind, turning from wind and heat to the rapid fire of machine guns, the unforgettable thunder of landing helicopters and the nightmare that was Vietnam.

Saigon 1974

It had been raining off and on all day and the clothes the woman on the street corner wore were plastered to her skin until it looked as if she was wearing nothing at all. She put her hands under her breasts and lifted them toward the trio of American soldiers coming down the street.

"Hey G.I., wanna party? Good sex...hot sex..."

Private Joseph Barone of Brooklyn, New York whistled beneath his breath and elbowed his buddy.

"Oowee, Davie boy, would you look at her. You want to get yourself a little of that?"

The thought of a physical release within the warmth of a woman's arms was strong, but David Wilson had seen past her painted face and skimpy clothes. He wasn't the only one out of his element. She was doing all she knew, trying to survive in a world gone mad and adding to her hell seemed impossible to consider.

David gave her one last glance and then shook his head. "No. I'll meet you and Pete back at the barracks."

They laughed at his reticence and pivoted sharply, heading back to the woman before another one of their compatriots beat them to the offer.

David shoved his hands in his pockets and hunched his shoulders as he moved along the crowded sidewalk. An old man sat cross-legged on the ground, hawking his wares in a sing-song litany while dangling a plucked fowl above his head in an effort to catch a buyer's eye. David's nose wrinkled in protest to the smell as he passed and wondered how long the man had been trying to sell that particular bird.

He turned the corner, fully intent upon heading

for the barracks, when he heard a familiar laugh. He turned, a look of expectancy on his face. He'd know that laugh anywhere. It was his brother, Frank.

He pivoted sharply, searching the constantly moving masses for sight of his brother's face. If he could hook up with Frank, it would be a good way to pass the afternoon. His eyes were alight as he began to scan the crowd.

Frank was his elder by four years and the single reason David was in Vietnam. Lying about his age to sign up had been simple. It was the fact that he and his brother had wound up in the same company that was amazing. But David was glad. Frank had always been more than just a big brother. He'd been a substitute father—a playmate—and when he wasn't thumping on David's head himself, a bodyguard in the rough neighborhood in which they'd grown up.

The crowd in front of David parted suddenly to let a man with a pushcart pass by and as it did, he saw his brother in the distance. At that same moment, he realized Frank wasn't alone. He paused, staring curiously at the pair with whom Frank was conversing. Their heads were close together, as if they didn't want to be overheard. And when one of them straightened and turned, staring directly toward David, he found himself ducking into a doorway instead of hailing them as he'd intended. There was something about the men that he didn't trust. He watched a bit longer, trying to remember where he'd seen them, and as he did, it suddenly hit him. A few months back, one of his buddies had pointed them out in a nightclub as being Dutch. When David had asked why two men from Holland would be here in the middle of such hell, his buddy had laughed and said, *commerce, Davie-boy, commerce. It had taken a while before David realized they were suspected gunrunners.*

Now, as he watched, Frank grinned and slapped one of the men on the back, then shook his hand. When he did, David's gut began to knot. Why would Frank be talking to men like that? Like everyone else, he knew it was men like that who were responsible for selling American-made weapons to the Vietcong. Men from other countries who were in this strictly for the money, who had no allegiance to a nation, not even their own. Immediately he thought of the money Frank had been flashing during the past two months. Money he claimed he had won playing cards. But Frank was a lousy card player. Always had been. When the men began to move, David followed at a distance, desperate to assure himself that what he was thinking couldn't be true.

It started to rain again, and as it did, the streets began to clear as people took shelter inside the shops or made their way home. In an effort to remain unobserved, David had to stay far behind and twice he thought he'd lost them, only to turn a corner and see the back of Frank's head in the distance.

By the time they reached the outskirts of the city, David's gut was in knots. He'd long ago given up on this being an innocent meeting, and when they slipped into an isolated hut, David groaned inwardly. By the time he reached the hut, the rain had turned to a downpour, smothering all sound save that of the hammer of his own heartbeat and the sound of rain on the wet thatched roof.

He moved closer to the door, then shifted so that he could see inside. The interior was small and gloomy,

*yet light enough for David to see an envelope pass be-
tween Frank and the men.*

No, David thought, and held his breath, watching
as Frank counted the money then slipped it inside his
shirt before handing over a small slip of paper. Without
thinking of the consequences, he stalked into the hut.

To say Frank Wilson was stunned, would have been
an understatement, but his shock quickly turned to
anger when he realized his little brother had seen it
all. To make it worse, the other men were already draw-
ing their weapons.

"Don't!" he yelled. "He's my brother." Then he
turned to David, fear mixing with guilt. "What the hell
do you think you're doing?"

David quickly moved, putting himself between Frank
and the men and yanking the money out of Frank's shirt
and throwing it on the ground.

"Saving your stupid ass," he said. "Now let's get
out of here."

"What the hell's going on?" one of the men muttered,
and waved his gun in Frank Wilson's face.

"Leave this to me," Frank said, and shoved David
aside as he began to pick up the money.

David stepped on a wad of money just as Frank
reached for it, and in doing so, stepped on Frank's fingers instead. Pain fueled Frank's rage as he bolted to
his feet, slamming David against the wall of the hut.
Both of the gunrunners aimed their weapons as they
realized their assignation was not as secretive as they'd
wished.

Frank knew that now both he and David were in
trouble. He pulled his own weapon, aiming it at the
shorter one's head.

"Don't do it!" he yelled, and then fired off two shots before the men could answer.

Through the roar of the rain, the sounds were little more than muffled thumps. David was shaking, stunned by his brother's lack of emotion, only to find that Frank had a gun aimed at his face.

"What the hell are you doing?" David whispered.

"The question should be, what are you going to do about what you just saw?" Frank countered.

David swallowed. He'd seen that look on his brother's face before.

"What did I see?" David asked. "What did you sell them?"

Frank grinned. "A little steel. A little wood. A little lead. Just natural resources."

David's skin crawled. "Guns? You're selling our own guns to the enemy? How can you do that? How can you be a traitor to your own country?"

Frank sneered. "My own country, as you so fondly call it, sent me over here to die. And I'm not even sure I believe in what I'm fighting for. Why shouldn't I get something out of it besides a coffin?"

David held out his hand. "Please, Frank. Let's just go. No one has to know we were even here. They'll find the bodies and the money, and assume the men killed each other."

Frank's smile hardened as he dug through one of the dead men's pockets for the slip of paper with the information he'd just sold. When he found it, he wadded it into a very small ball, then popped it in his mouth like candy, chewed it and swallowed while David looked on in horror.

"I'm not leaving the money," Frank growled. "It's mine. Now the problem remains, are you gonna snitch?"

"Why? Are you going to kill me, too?"

In Frank's defense, it had to be said that he hesitated, but there was a dark gleam in his eyes when he answered.

"If I have to."

David stared into the barrel of the gun, unable to believe that his fate in life was to come all this way across the world only to be killed by his brother's hand.

"You've gone crazy," David pleaded. "Is this what you really want?"

"What I want, is to be rich," Frank said, and took aim.

Everything afterward seemed to happen in slow motion. Frank's shot searing the back of David's shoulder as he dove for a dead man's gun. Pulling the trigger as he rolled. The water leaking through the roof and falling on his left cheek at the same moment that Frank staggered and fell. The smell of gunpowder and mud as David crawled to his feet. Standing motionless beneath the leak in the roof while the raindrops mixed with tears, then throwing his head back and letting out a gut-wrenching roar of anguish.

Time passed. The rain had stopped. People were moving about and it was only a matter of time before someone found them, and yet David couldn't bring himself to move. It was the sound of a Huey flying overhead that brought him out of his trance.

He staggered to an alcove at the back of the room, dragged out a can of gasoline and began scattering it all over the walls and then the floor, making sure that the men and the money were saturated as well. Then

*he moved to the doorway, cautiously peering out. No
one was in sight. Unable to look at his dead brother's
face, he struck a match and gave it a toss, slipped out
of the hut and ran.*

He never looked back.

"Here you go, Mister."

Startled by the sound of an unfamiliar voice, David
Wilson jerked, and the memories sank back into the hell
that was his past. He looked down at the young man
before him, and at the handful of miniature American
flags he was carrying.

"You're a vet, aren't you?" the kid asked.

David hesitated, then shrugged. Admitting that much
posed no threat. He nodded.

The kid beamed. "I knew it! I can tell. My dad's a
vet. He fought in Desert Storm." Then he pulled a flag
from the bunch in his hand and thrust it into the man's
palm. "Take it, Mister. You earned it."

David's fingers curled around the small, wooden
staff as the kid disappeared. He stared at the colors so
long that they began to run together in his mind. When
he finally looked up, the glitter in his eyes was no longer moisture and the cut of his jaw was set and firm.
Earned it? He hadn't earned anything but a heartache
and a tombstone in Arlington Cemetery. To become the
man he was now, he'd had to die, presumably in the line
of duty. But nevertheless, David Wilson was dead. The
man he'd become was a solitary man. He had no one
he could call friend, no identity that mattered, no ties
to a community or church. A faceless man who, some
years back had sworn, once again, to give his life for
his country.

Now, they called him Jonah and only two people on the face of the earth knew his real identity. As the anonymous director of SPEAR, the most elite counterespionage team ever to be assembled on behalf of the United States of America, Jonah lived life in the shadows, communicating with his operatives when necessary by coded messages, a cassette delivered with an order of pizza, cryptic telegrams, and occasionally, nothing more than a voice on the phone.

SPEAR, first founded by Abraham Lincoln himself during the Civil War, was an acronym for Stealth, Perseverance, Endeavor, Attack and Rescue. It was an organization that existed in the shadows of society, and its existence, the best kept secret in the free world. Headed throughout the years by mysterious men known only as Jonah, the succession of Jonahs who had given their lives to their country were the unrecognized heroes of the past. To the world, they were dead. If they lived long enough to retire, they were given an entirely new identity and left to face their twilight years alone, without benefit of old friends or family.

In a few years, he, too, would retire and another Jonah would step into his shoes. *Dying* for his country had seemed an odd sort of justice, considering the fact that he'd taken his only brother's life.

He watched the kid running across the greens, trying to remember if he'd ever been that innocent. He then snorted beneath his breath and shoved the flag into his pocket and started toward his car. There was no place in his life for sentiment or regret.

Those years of retirement were, however, looming closer than he might have liked. Someone was trying to ruin him. Someone wanted him branded a traitor in the very worst way, and despite his access to even the most classified of records, he had been unable to find even a trace of a guilty party. It was, without doubt, the worst thing that had happened to him since Vietnam. It could be anyone, even a disgruntled operative at SPEAR who, by some stroke of fate, had discovered his identity. He was at the point of admitting he needed help, that doing this alone was no longer an option. But there was a problem. He didn't know who to trust.

Chapter 1

One week later: The Northern California coast.

A pair of seagulls perched on the railing surrounding the large, flagstone terrace of the Condor Mountain Resort and Spa. The view, like the resort, was a magnificent complement to the area overlooking the Pacific. The gulls gave an occasional flap of their wings as they squawked between themselves in bird speak while keeping watch for a dropped bit of someone's breakfast pastry. Waiters moved among the tables serving coffee and juice, while others carried freshly made foods to the hot-and-cold buffet that was set up near the door. The idle chatter of the guests as they breakfasted was diluted by the soft breeze and the wide open spaces.

It was an idyllic scene, typical for the resort, but there was nothing typical about Easton Kirby, the man who ran it. Tall and powerfully built, he looked more like a professional athlete than a business man. His shoulders strained against the soft knit texture of his white Polo shirt while navy slacks accentuated the length of leg and muscle. His hair was a shade lighter than his tan, and more than one female guest at the hotel had commented about his resemblance to the actor, Kevin Costner, although his nose had more of a Roman shape to it after having twice been broken. He often smiled, but there were shadows within the glitter of his eyes that congeniality could not disguise. He was a man who lived with secrets he would never be able to share and being a former operative for SPEAR was secondary to the fact that he considered himself a murderer.

That it had happened in the line of duty during a high-speed chase had not cleared his conscience. The teenager who'd come out of nowhere on a bicycle and right into the path of East's oncoming car had been a boy in his prime, having just won a four-year scholarship to a prestigious college, and an honor student throughout his high school years. The headphones he'd been wearing had blocked out the sound of the oncoming cars, and according to the police who'd investigated the accident, he had also bicycled across the highway from the hill above without even trying to stop, obviously trying to beat the traffic. Despite East having been cleared of wrongdoing, the guilt of the act was a hair shirt on his soul. What was done, was done. The kid was dead. End of story.

Afterward, it had been all East could do not to put a gun to his own head. Night after night he kept reliving the sight of the young man's face spotlighted in his headlights, then the impact of flesh against metal and the scent of burning rubber as he'd tried to stop.

SPEAR had sent him through counseling, then to Condor Mountain to rehabilitate. But it didn't take. For three months he had lived in the room that they'd given him, refusing to interact with anyone except on a need to basis, hiking the mountains at night and trying to purge his soul. And then one dark night during one of his nightly forays, he met Jeff. Fourteen years old and a professional runaway from the welfare system, the kid was as hard and wild as they came. East was drawn to the youth in spite of himself, recognizing the boy's sullen anger as a result of fear rather than meanness. The bond they formed was slow, but it surprised them both. Within a year, Easton Kirby had a whole new role in life. At the age of twenty-five, he became a father to a fourteen-year-old boy, and Jeff was no longer homeless.

A short while later, SPEAR named East manager of the hotel where he'd been sent to recuperate. His file at SPEAR was purged and his days as a counterespionage agent were over. But that hadn't ended his ties with the organization. Condor Mountain Resort and Spa was a part of the Monarch Hotel Chain—a legitimate corporation owned and operated by SPEAR, and available to agents on the verge of burnout.

Occasionally East saw acquaintances from his days of active duty, but only if they were sent to the Condor Resort for some R and R after the close of a particularly grueling case. Yet the tie that had bound them together before had been severed by time and distance. That part of his life was over. He existed in a come-and-go world with his adopted son as his only family and it was just the way he liked it. Only now and then was he haunted by nightmares, and when he was, he focused instead on the doctor Jeff was studying to become, rather than the horrors of his own past. It should have been enough, but the absence of a woman in his life often left him with a rootless, empty feeling. Yet how could he live his own life to the fullest when he'd taken the life of an innocent man?

The two seagulls which had been sitting on the railing took flight as a waiter walked past. A few moments later, Easton Kirby walked out on the patio, causing more than a few female hearts to flutter, as well. He nodded and smiled as he moved through the area, but his focus was on the couple at the far table. They'd checked in last night after he'd gone to bed, but his staff had informed him they were here. He made it a habit to personally greet all honeymooners, and from the way the pair was cuddling through their morning meal, their stay at Condor Mountain was off to a good start. He couldn't help thinking how blessed they were. Their whole lives were ahead of them, while his was stalled in a guilt-ridden limbo.

Before he reached their table, his cell phone rang. He moved to a guest-free area of the patio to take the call.

"Hello."

"Kirby."

It had been years since East had heard that voice, but there was no mistaking it. Instinctively, he moved off the terrace and down the steps toward the beach, putting distance between himself and the rest of the world.

"Jonah?"

"Yes."

East reached the first landing, and sat. Something

told him he needed to be immobile when he took this call.

"How have you been?" Jonah asked.

East's belly knotted. "Fine, but I'm assuming you know that, sir, or you wouldn't be calling."

A slow intake of breath was all East heard. He waited for Jonah to continue. Chit-chat was not something one did with this man. Finally, Jonah spoke.

"I need to ask a favor of you,"

East's eyes widened. Favor? Jonah didn't ask favors, he gave orders.

"Sir?"

"I have a problem—a big problem," Jonah said. "Someone is trying to destroy me."

East's heart skipped a beat and he stood abruptly, as if bracing himself for an unspeakable blow.

"Destroy you?"

"It's complicated," Jonah said. "Suffice it to say that things are surfacing within high places that make it look as if I'm a war criminal, as well as a traitor to my country." There was a moment of hesitation before he continued. "It's not true."

East's eyes narrowed. "Telling me that was unnecessary. That much I know."

Again, there was a hesitation, then Jonah spoke. "I thank you for that. But the problem still exists and despite my unlimited...uh, shall we say access...to confidential material, I have been unable to trace the source. For all I know, it could be within SPEAR itself."

East was incredulous. "No, sir! I don't believe that's possible."

"I would like to think so, too," Jonah said. "But at this point, nothing or no one can be ruled out."

East frowned. "If that's so, then why call me?"

"Because, technically, you are inactive. It's been ten years since you've been in the field. We have no axes to grind and no issues that could be a possible basis for these actions. I have to trust someone. You're it."

East's gut knotted tighter. "Sir...don't ask this of me."

Jonah's sigh whispered through East's conscience like a knife.

"It's been ten years since that incident with the kid," Jonah said.

East swallowed harshly, then closed his eyes against the glare of sunlight upon the water.

"Tell that to my psyche," he growled. "Besides, I have a family to consider."

"Yes... Jeff, isn't it? Studying to be a doctor?"

"Yes, sir. He's interning now in L.A."

"He's a man, Kirby, not a kid."

A noise on the beach below caught Kirby's attention, he opened his eyes and turned. It was a pair of sea lions sunning themselves on an outcropping of rock. For a moment, he lost himself in the spray of surf hammering against the rocks and the seabirds doing a little two-step upon the sand. The urge to take the phone and toss it into the water, disconnecting himself from both Jonah and the world was overwhelming, but it was a futile thought. He'd learned long ago that no matter how hard he'd tried, he had not been able to get away from his past.

"Kirby...are you there?"

East sighed. "Yes, sir. I was just thinking."

There was a note of eagerness in Jonah's voice. "And?"

"I have to ask you a question," East said.

"Ask."

"Is this an order?"

This time, there was no mistaking the sigh in Jonah's voice. "I can't order you to do a personal favor for me."

"I'm not the man I used to be. I've been out of the business too long. I've lost the edge needed to survive."

There was a long moment of silence, then Jonah spoke. "So...you're turning me down."

"Yes."

Again Jonah hesitated, but this time his voice was void of emotion.

"I understand. Oh, and Kirby, this call never happened."

"What call, sir?"

The line went dead and Kirby knew there would never be a traceable record of the call ever happening. A fresh wave of guilt hit him head-on.

"Damn it to hell."

He spun on his heels and headed back to the hotel.

Chapter 2

Sweat slipped from the sweatband around Alicia Corbin's head and into her right eye as she focused on a spot upon the wall in front of her, rather than the pain of burning muscles in her legs. Gripping the handlebars of the workout bike a little tighter, she glanced at the digital readout on the machine and grimaced. Only another mile to go and she could quit.

Although she was a health club regular, she hated working out. Her preference would have been to take a long, leisurely walk in a deeply wooded area with only squirrels and deer for companions rather than some of these perspiring males who kept strutting from one machine to the other, and whose sole intent was for a perfect body and some female adulation. But then Ally would be the first to admit that she was uncomfortable with her own sexuality. She didn't see herself as oth-

ers saw her. She looked in a mirror and saw a woman
on the verge of being too thin, whereas most women
would have been overjoyed to be built in her image.
Of average height, Ally's slim, finely toned body was
strong and high-breasted. The striking combination of
auburn hair and green eyes gave her youthful features
a pixie appearance, rather than that of a sultry vixen.
But there was nothing fey about Ally. No one would
ever have guessed that she was a highly-trained operative within a secret branch of the government, or that
her IQ was off the scale. She'd entered high school at
the age of ten, graduating two years later. By the time
she had turned seventeen, she had a Ph.D. in physics,
another in criminology, and was considering another
round of classes when she'd been recruited by SPEAR.
At the time, it had seemed like a good idea. Her parents, intellectuals who were more concerned with their
life paths than with hers, had left most of her upbring-
ing to hired help and higher education, so it was no jolt
for Ally to go from a college campus to the training
ground of SPEAR.

But being so much younger than her fellow students
at college had been a drawback socially. She had made
no close friends. If anyone had happened to notice that
the quiet little genius was no longer on campus, it was
so much the better. At least she wouldn't be ruining the
grading curve for anyone else.

And for Ally, joining SPEAR was all a matter of re-
adjusting priorities. There wasn't much SPEAR's in-
structors could teach her in the way of technology, but
learning about covert activities and enduring the intense
physical training put her in an entirely different world.
There had been days when she wasn't sure she would

survive, yet she had. Now it was so much a part of her life, she rarely thought about the way it had been before.

Today was only the second day of a much needed vacation and making the decision to go to the gym had come in a weak moment. Now, as she neared the end of her workout, the muscles in her legs were weak and burning. She gritted her teeth and bared down on the pedals, giving up her last bit of energy. Just as the digital readout clicked over to read twenty miles, she began to ease off, letting her muscles adjust to stopping. Finally, as she let her feet slip out of the pedals, she slumped over the handlebars with sweat pouring down her neck and between her breasts, her heart thundering in her ears.

As she sat, her cell phone began to ring. Wearily, she slid off the bicycle seat and walked toward the bench where she'd left a fresh towel and her phone, wondering as she did, who could have possibly known she was here. As she picked it up to answer, she remembered she'd left Call Forwarding on her phone.

"Hello?"

"Alicia, we haven't heard from you in a while."

The cool, almost impersonal tone in her mother's voice had long since ceased to hurt her. She draped the fresh towel around her neck and began mopping perspiration as she dropped onto the bench.

"I've been…gone," Ally said, hesitating on the last word. There was never any option about discussing the cases she worked on with anyone, parent or no. In fact, discussion about SPEAR was nonexistent, because to the general public, SPEAR did not even exist.

"We assumed as much." Then, as if it was no big deal, Mavis Corbin added, "Next week is your birthday, but your father and I are going to be out of the country. So, Happy Birthday, Alicia and many more." Ally ignored a quick surge of disappointment. It wasn't the first time this had happened. It wouldn't be the last.

"Thank you, Mother," Ally said. "Where are you going this time?"

"Egypt. A whole new burial ground has been discovered. Your father is so excited. This is very important to us, you know."

Ally grinned bitterly. She knew all too well what was important to her parents and she was low on the list. "Yes, Mother, I know. Have a good trip and thanks for calling."

"You're welcome, dear. Take care."

Before Ally could respond, the line went dead. She hung up the receiver and headed for the showers. She had a sudden urge for a milkshake and a chocolate doughnut. Instead, a half hour later she was standing in line, waiting for her order of black coffee and a plain bagel to be filled.

"Four-fifty," the clerk said, handing her a white sack with the top neatly folded and a steaming cup of coffee.

She paid, stuffed her change in the pocket of her sweatpants and headed for the door. It wasn't until she was unlocking her car and the sack bumped against the door that she realized there was something more than a bagel inside. The hair crawled on the back of her neck as she slid behind the steering wheel and locked herself in. Then she set her coffee cup in the holder on the dash and opened the sack.

The small black cassette in the bottom of the sack could only mean one thing.

"Well, hell," Ally muttered, as she slid the cassette

into the stereo on the dash. Jonah's deep, gravelly voice was familiar, as was the unusual way in which she'd been contacted. It was typical of the anonymity of SPEAR. Ordinarily she would have been excited about a new assignment, but she hadn't even been home long enough to do laundry or have an all-night session watching her favorite movies.

She started the car, listening to the tape as she drove toward home, every now and then allowing herself a frown as she pinched off bites of the bagel and poked them into her mouth.

As far as assignments went it was unusual, although she couldn't find fault with the location. She'd heard of the spa on Condor Mountain and had no problem at all taking advantage of some free R and R. And Easton Kirby, who was now the manager of the place, was a legend within the agency. Her curiosity piqued as Jonah's spare remarks began to sink in. If she understood him correctly, and she was certain she did because Jonah was not a man to leave anything to the imagination, Jonah needed Easton Kirby on active duty and Kirby had refused. The tape ended with a final order.

Ally was to change his mind—in any way that she could.

She ejected the tape and tossed it back into the sack, well aware that within thirty seconds of it having been played, it would go blank, leaving no trace of ever having been recorded upon. She pulled into the driveway of her house and punched the garage door opener. Her cheeks were flushed, her eyes snapping angrily as she waited for the garage door to go up.

"Change his mind?" she muttered, her voice dripping

with sarcasm. "And how am I supposed to do that...
drive him mad with my womanly wiles?"

Seconds later she pulled into the garage, lowered
the door and then got out, but only after the door was
completely shut. Her house key was in her hand as she
swept the garage with a casual gaze before making a
move toward the door. Once inside, she dumped her
sweaty gym clothes on the washer and the bagel sack
in the trash, then downed the last of her coffee before
adding the empty cup to the lot.

The red light on her answering machine was blinking, but her mind was on the new assignment. What
in blazes did one wear to coerce a reluctant operative
back into the fold?

Almost a week later and a year older, Ally pulled into
the parking lot of the Condor Mountain Resort and Spa,
then sat for a moment, staring at the magnificence of the
building and grounds. The four-story mixture of Gothic
and Victorian architecture seemed to fit the starkness of
the geography. Lush was not a word that described this
part of the California coast. The mountainous area of
the region had steep, and often narrow, winding roads,
and the forestation of the area was sparse, often leaving
bare spots in the rocky terrain. But there was a beauty
to the land that seemed to fit the power of the waters
that pounded the coast. Overhead, seagulls dipped and
swooped, riding the air currents while searching for
food, and she could hear the harsh, guttural barks of
sea lions coming from the beach below. From where
she was sitting, she could see the beginnings of a long,
descending series of steps leading down the side of the
hill toward the Pacific. The view was breathtaking and

the weather sunny and breezy, which was typical for this time of year. She couldn't help wishing this was going to be a "real" vacation and not another undercover assignment.

As she got out of the car and went around to the trunk to get her bags, she had to admit, her job this time was hardly on a par with what she normally did. At least she wouldn't be posing as some wayward teenager or wild child in order to infiltrate some crime syndicate. All she had to do was convince Easton Kirby to come back on active duty. How difficult could that be?

She popped the trunk on her car and leaned in to get out her bag. As she did, a large shadow suddenly passed between her and the sun and she knew she was no longer alone. She straightened and turned, expecting a bellhop, or at the least an employee of the resort.

It was a man.

He was tall, so tall, and standing close—too close. Slightly blinded from the sunlight behind him, she saw nothing but his silhouette. And then he stepped to one side to reach for her bag and she saw his face.

It was Easton Kirby himself—the man she'd come to meet.

Well, this makes it easy. At least I won't have to wangle an introduction.

"Ms. Corbin, welcome to Condor Mountain," he said, as he lifted her bag from the trunk of her car.

She thought nothing of the fact that he would know her on sight. The agency would have followed procedure and notified him ahead of time that an operative would be arriving.

"Thank you," Ally said, a little disconcerted by his height and the way he was looking at her.

She was five inches over five feet tall and he seemed a good foot taller. And, there was a look in his eyes that made her shiver. She shrugged off the thought that he would know why she'd come, telling herself that it was guilt that was making her nervous.

"This is certainly wonderful service. I only just arrived."

"I know," he said softly, then looked her straight in the eyes. "I was waiting for you."

Ally's lips parted in shock. But only a little and only for a brief moment. As she followed him up the steps and into the hotel, she couldn't shake the notion that he wasn't the only one who'd been waiting. She had a desperate feeling that she'd been waiting for him, too—all of her life.

Oh fine, she thought. *Now is not the time for my stifled hormones to kick in. Just because he's sexy, and good-looking, and I'm supposed to talk this man into something he doesn't want to do, doesn't mean I have to complicate this more than it already is.*

They reached the registration desk. Before she could speak, he was bypassing it and leading her toward the elevators.

"You're already checked in," he said. "Follow me. I'll show you to your room."

The doors opened and they stepped inside. She watched as he stuck a key into a slot and gave it a turn. Immediately the elevator car started to ascend. She grabbed on to the railing to steady herself, then noted that they had bypassed the fourth floor.

"I thought this hotel only had four floors. Where are we going? Heaven?"

For the first time since her arrival he looked at her

and grinned and her heart dropped right to her toes. *Oh lordy. I am so out of my league.*

"No, but some people tend to think the view might be similar," he said. "There's a penthouse suite on the ocean side of the hotel that's not visible from the front entrance. It's reserved for special guests such as yourself."

"Oh," she said, and then looked down at her feet so that he might not see the remorse she was feeling. He was being nice to her because he thought she was over the edge. Slipping. Burned-out. All the adjectives one might use to describe a SPEAR operative on the verge of a breakdown.

He looked at her then, reading her sudden silence as having been reminded of something terrible that must have happened to her on the job and remembered that when SPEAR operatives were ever sent here, it was usually for mental healing.

"Sorry," he said. "I didn't mean to bring up bad memories."

"No, it wasn't that," she began, but the car had stopped and the doors were opening and Easton Kirby was already on the move. She followed, kicking herself for not knowing how to draw men into casual conversation.

They exited into what appeared to be a large foyer. East punched in a series of numbers on the security panel beside the door and then turned the knob.

"Your home away from home," he said, leading the way inside. "I hope your stay will be comfortable." He set her suitcase down in the bedroom, then handed her the key and a card. "The security code is written on the back. My number is on the front. If you need any-

thing at any time of the night or day, all you have to
do is call me."

She took the key and the card and slipped them into
her pocket. "Thank you, Mr. Kirby."

"You're welcome, Ms. Corbin, and please…call me
East."

"If you'll call me Ally, it's a deal," she said, offering her hand.

When he took it, she felt as if she'd been treading
water all of her life and someone had just offered her
a line to safety. This womanly, helpless feeling was so
foreign to Ally that she didn't know how to react.

"Well then," she said, quickly releasing his hold.
"Now that we're supposed to be friends, does this mean
I don't have to tip you?"

East threw back his head and laughed. A deep-from-
the-belly kind of laugh that sent shivers up Ally's spine.
She grinned, pleased that she'd gotten some sort of positive response from him.

Still chuckling, East shook his head. "No, you don't
have to tip me and we start serving dinner around seven.
The restaurant stays open until midnight so remember,
if you need anything…"

"Yes, I know," she said, patting her pocket where
she'd put his card. "I'll use Ma Bell to reach out and
touch."

His smile stilled as he gave her a dark, unreadable
look.

"Touching is good," he said quietly, and headed for
the door, leaving Ally to put her own interpretation on
what he'd just said.

A shudder racked her as she watched him leave.
What on earth had she gotten herself into? Then she

gritted her teeth and headed for her suitcase. The least she could do was unpack. There were a good four hours of daylight left and a beach to explore.

Something told her that this operation was going to take time. Easton Kirby didn't strike her as malleable. As she went to the closet with an armful of clothes, she couldn't help wondering why Jonah hadn't just ordered this man back to active service. What sort of scenario could possibly have occurred that Jonah would allow a man's personal life to interfere with his duty?

As East was dressing for dinner, he caught himself thinking of Ally Corbin again. It wasn't the first time it had happened since her arrival, and something told him it wouldn't be the last. There was something about her that intrigued him. She was such a mixture of contradictions. Naive, yet tough. He knew what it took to become an agent for SPEAR, so he respected that her skills equaled his own. Yet there was an innocence about her that surprised him. He had no way of knowing that naivete came in not knowing herself. She was beyond book smart, but she didn't have the vaguest idea of how to live a normal life. She'd never been in love, she'd never even made love. Had he known, it might have changed his attitude completely. But all he saw was a beautiful and intriguing young woman who had endured and survived, and was here to heal.

He debated with himself about wearing a tie, then decided against it, opting for the casual look. For some reason, his mind slipped to Jonah, wondering if he'd found someone else to help him out. It had been a week since he'd gotten the call, and he hadn't slept well one night since. Then he reminded himself that was part of his past and he couldn't let it matter.

With a last glance in the mirror, he grabbed his sport coat and exited his apartment. It was time to make an appearance in the dining room.

The Condor Resort ran on schedules, not unlike those of a cruise ship, and sitting at the captain's table, or in this case the manager's, was considered an honor. It was something the previous manager had instigated and East had simply followed suit. Tonight he was actually looking forward to the event because he'd sent a note to Ally's room earlier with an invitation for her to join him. There was nothing personal about it. It wasn't as if she'd be the only one there. There would be six others, not counting himself, and a good reason for her not to eat alone. If she was as troubled as he'd been when he came, he knew she would need to focus on something besides herself. And there was no better way to achieve that than to sit at a dinner table with six perfect strangers—seven counting him—and remember that there was a world outside the realm of SPEAR.

He told himself he was just doing his job. And he believed it, all the way to the dining room and right up to the point when Ally entered the room.

It was the traditional, little black dress—simple in style, skimpy in fabric—and on Ally Corbin, pure dynamite. East knew he was staring, but he couldn't seem to stop. It wasn't as if he never saw beautiful women, because he did—daily. And it wasn't as if he didn't have opportunities to enjoy their company. It was that he usually chose not to. But this time it was different. There was an urgency within him to connect with her on something other than this ephemeral, holiday basis.

He kept thinking that if he let her leave without pursuing this desire, he would regret it for the rest of his life.

Then he shoved back the thought and stood, smiling cordially as he pulled out a chair and seated her. He needed his head examined. She was here to recuperate. Period.

He touched her shoulder briefly. "I'm so glad you felt like joining us. The food is particularly exceptional tonight." Then he added with a wink. "I know because I stole a couple of bites when the chef wasn't looking."

Everyone at the table laughed along with Ally as East took his seat at the head of the table.

"Thank you for inviting me," she said, and pretended that her heart was not in her mouth as she gave him a surreptitious glance.

Mercy, but that man certainly knew how to fill out a dinner jacket and slacks. She'd heard of clothes making the man, but in this case, it was just the opposite. There was barely time for her to be introduced to the others before a waiter appeared to take their orders.

And so the evening began.

Ally sat through one course after another, smiling and nodding and offering small bits of herself into the conversation. But her heart wasn't in it. Every time she looked at East, she fought rising panic. How could she possibly broach the subject of her mission without angering him? What could she say to convince him to go back on active duty that Jonah hadn't already said? She watched the way his mouth tilted and curved as a smile tugged at his lips and the way his eyes glittered when something moved him to a passionate response. Every time he reached for his wineglass, she caught herself staring at the way his massive hand would curl so delicately around the fragile stem.

She glanced down at the napkin she'd wadded in her lap and sighed. Never in her life had she felt so inadequate. She sighed again and looked up, only to find herself pinned under the dark, watchful stare of her host. Heat rose up her neck to her cheeks, spreading across her face like water lapping against the shore. Good Lord. She was blushing and he could see. If he grinned, she was going to have to hate him, and that thought alone made her mad.

To her relief, he was the first to look away. Soon afterward, Ally made her excuses and left, fully intent on going back to her room. She never made it past the lobby.

"Ms. Corbin… Ally…wait!"

She pivoted sharply, surprised that he'd followed her.

"Are you all right?"

The gentleness in his voice was almost her undoing. He was being so kind and when he found out why she was here, it would ruin everything. Then her shoulders slumped. Ruin everything? What was the matter with her? There wasn't anything to ruin.

"I'm fine," she said. "Just tired."

East hesitated, for some reason, still reluctant to let her go. "Would you like to take a walk? Maybe some fresh air would do you good."

Her heart skipped a beat. The perfect opportunity to establish a little one-on-one rapport. For business reasons of course.

"Yes, I believe I would," she said. "Should I get a sweater?"

His gaze raked her bare, slender arms and then up

the length of her neck, to her mouth, before he made himself focus.

"If you get cold, you can use my jacket."

"You've been far too kind already. All this personal service is going to go to my head and now you're offering your jacket? Are we still on a no-tip basis?"

He grinned. Damned if he didn't like her attitude as much as that dress she was wearing.

"Something tells me it would be hard to feed you a line," East said. "To use one of my grandfather's favorite phrases, you're a saucy little thing, aren't you?"

She frowned. "I don't know. I certainly never thought of myself as saucy. My parents always said I was forthright. Alicia is a forthright child. Not funny. Not pretty. Not even cute. Just forthright." She smiled, unaware of the poignancy in her voice. "What does it take to be saucy?"

At that moment, she reminded him of his son, Jeff. At least the way Jeff had been when they met. A little wary of East and a whole lot unsure of himself. His heart went out to her then, in a way it might never have done, otherwise.

"I don't exactly know," he said gently. "Maybe a little extra gumption and a whole lot of guts."

Suddenly, the conversation had gotten too personal for Ally and she didn't know where to go with it. Teasing with the opposite sex in any form, whether it was flirtatious or sexual, was not something she could do.

She glanced toward the door. "About that walk?"

He took off his coat and draped it around her shoulders.

The warmth of his body was still on the fabric as it

wrapped around her. She swallowed nervously. "I didn't say I was cold."

"Good. Now you won't have to," he said shortly, and took her by the elbow and led her out into the night.

Chapter 3

Despite the well-lit grounds surrounding the hotel, East headed directly for the shadows, taking Ally with him. In a way, she understood his need to walk in darkness. In their business, anonymity was often the difference between life and death, and even though East no longer put his life on the line on a daily basis, old habits obviously died hard.

"Is this the way to the beach?"

He stopped and turned, a shadowy silhouette against the night.

"No. Would you rather go down to the beach?" She started to deny his question, then convinced her—self that truth, at least as far as she could take it, would probably work better between them.

"Yes, actually I would, if it's not too much trouble?"

From the tone of his voice, she thought he smiled.

"Trouble? To walk on a beach in the moonlight with a beautiful woman? Ms. Corbin, you crush my ego."

Ally stifled a snort of disbelief. "I'm sorry, Mr. Kirby, but your reputation precedes you. From what I've been told, both your ego and reputation are indestructible."

When he answered, the smile was gone from his voice.

"If only that were so," he said, then took her by the arm. "Allow me. The steps are lit, but uneven. And when we get to the beach, I'm afraid those shoes you're wearing will be more of a hindrance than help."

Thankful for the cover of darkness, Ally rolled her eyes at her own stupidity. She'd royally botched her first opportunity to do what she'd come to do. She was supposed to talk him into returning to work for Jonah, not remind him of why he quit in the first place. When his fingers curled around the flesh of her upper arm, she swallowed nervously, picturing the way they'd looked curling around that fragile stem on his wineglass. Long. Strong. Deadly.

As they descended the well-lit steps to the beach below, the silence between them was awkward, but when they reached the sand and Ally bent down to take off her shoes, something changed. Maybe it was the sound of rolling surf, or the path of moonlight stretching upon the water. And maybe, it was just the fact that in that moment, Ally quit thinking about why she'd come and began to focus on where she was. She turned, staring in awe at the luminous majesty before her.

"How beautiful."

"Yes…beautiful," East said.

Ally was so caught up in the view, she didn't realize that he was staring at her and not the moon.

Time passed. The moon climbed higher in the night sky and the wind rose with it. A sense of sadness came upon her, knowing that this night and the spell of it all would never come again in quite the same way. Impulsively, she took a step toward the ocean, but East's grip on her arm tightened, and he held her back.

"It's too cold," he said softly.

She started to argue. All she'd wanted was to feel the pull of the ocean against her feet to see if it matched the rhythm of her heart, and then she realized that coddling a flight of fancy was not why she'd come. And, since she'd already broken the tenuous connection they'd made with her thoughtless remark earlier, she felt obliged to call it a night.

"Of course, you're right. I don't know what I was thinking. It's late and I'm sure you have more important things to do than baby-sit me." She handed him his sports coat. "Thank you for the loan. I think I'll go to bed now."

East found himself holding his jacket as Ally bolted toward the steps leading back to the hotel.

"Well, hell," East muttered, then followed her ascent, but by the time he entered the lobby, she was nowhere in sight.

East's sleepless night was exacerbated by the turmoil to which he awoke the next morning. Both a knock on his door and the frantic ringing of both his cell phone and telephone had him on his feet and grabbing for a pair of sweats before he'd barely opened his eyes. He

grabbed the cell phone on the way to the door, growling a response into the receiver as he unlocked the door.

The chef was on the cell phone yelling in his ear as
Foster Martin, the assistant manager, dashed inside his
apartment with a separate, but equally frustrating problem. He clenched his jaw, motioning for Foster to sit as
he turned his attention to the man on his cell phone.

"Please hold a moment, my other phone is ringing."

He answered the phone on the table without showing his frustration.

"This is Kirby."

"Mr. Kirby, this is Detweiler."

East flinched. The only time his head of security
called was when there was a problem.

"What's up?" he asked.

"There's a woman giving birth in Room two, one,
five."

East groaned. The last time this happened, the
woman filed a lawsuit against them for not having a
doctor on staff. She didn't win, but it was a hassle that
lasted the better part of six months. He didn't want a
repeat performance.

"You've called 9-1-1?"

"They're on the way."

"How far along is she?"

Detweiler began to stutter. "Far along? Hell if I
know. She's at the screaming stage, if that's what you
want to know."

East almost chuckled. If he remembered correctly,
Detweiler was a bachelor.

"I don't suppose there's a doctor registered?" East
asked.

Foster jumped up from where he'd been sitting, waving his hands even more in an attempt to get East's attention.

"There is, there is," Foster cried. "His name is Butcher. I remember thinking that would be a terrible name for a doctor to have."

East gave Foster a nod and then returned to his conversation with his security chief.

"Check with registration. There's a Doctor Butcher staying here. Get him to the woman's room asap. I'll be there as soon as I can."

"He's in three hundred," Foster said. "I checked him in myself yesterday."

"Did you hear that?" East asked.

"Yeah, Room three hundred," Detweiler said, and hung up.

Foster started to speak when East motioned to the cell phone he was still holding.

"Hello, Pete, you still there?" East asked.

A soft curse rolled across East's eardrum, followed by a burst of anger. "Pierre, Pierre, I told you to call me Pierre. And I do not like to be kept waiting."

East's voice lowered. "Look, Fullbright, pull that French stuff with someone who hasn't known you since sixth grade, okay?"

Pete Fullbright cursed once more, with emphasis, then sighed.

"The entire meat shipment is bad. What the hell do you suggest we serve three hundred and forty-four guests today? Hmmm?"

"Call Antonelli's Meat Market. It's just a twenty minute drive from here as opposed to the two-hour trip from L.A. Have them deliver whatever they have that's freshest, and to hell with the cost. We'll take it out of our regular shipper's hide later."

"Bien, bien," Pete said. *"Merci."*

East grinned. "Hey, Pete, you need to practice that accent a little more. It still sounds like you're saying *mercy.*"

"Go to hell," Pete muttered, then added, "…boss. Go to hell, boss."

"Been there, done that," East said, and disconnected, turning his attention to the man on his couch. "Now, what's up with you?"

Foster Martin stood abruptly, his hands fluttering about his chest like a wounded bird trying to find the strength to land.

"The computer is down. At least I think it's down. Anyway, it won't come up and we have guests waiting to check out and guests waiting to check in. I've already called our usual repair service and they're on some emergency call on the other side of L.A. Said it would be this afternoon before they can get out here."

"Then call someone else," East said, and headed for the kitchenette. Before any other disaster presented itself, he needed fortification in the form of caffeine.

"But…"

East pivoted, staring sharply at the small, pale man and tried to remind himself why he'd ever hired him. Then he frowned, remembering. He was the Attorney General's nephew and he hadn't hired him. He'd just appeared one day with a letter of recommendation written on a letterhead he couldn't ignore.

"Foster, is there a phone book in your desk?"

"Why…yes there is. Do you want to borrow it?" Foster asked, anxious to please.

East bit his lip to keep from shouting. "No, but I want you to use it. Find the yellow pages. Find someone who can work on our specific system, and get them out here, okay?"

"Yes…yes, okay," Foster said, and bolted toward the door.

"Oh, and Foster…"

He stopped and spun, his hands still fluttering. "Yes?"

"About the guests wanting to check in or out, use a pen and paper and do it like we used to before computers were ever invented."

"Yes. All right," he said, and shut the door behind him.

The ensuing silence lasted long enough for East to get his coffee made. As it was perking, he quickly dressed and made a trip to Room two hundred and fifteen to check on the expectant mother. To his relief, he found Doctor Butcher in the act of delivery and a couple of paramedics on their way down the hall, although the young woman was wailing at the top of her voice because her husband was nowhere in sight. It seems he'd gone out for his morning jog and was missing the birth of their first child. At that point, East made a quick call downstairs to send a couple of staffers in search of the man. Once he was certain that everything was under control, he dashed back to his room. After a couple of cups of coffee and a shower and shave, he headed downstairs fully expecting to find chaos at the registration desk. Instead, the desk was almost empty and only the normal ebb and flow of traffic was moving through the lobby. Mildly surprised, he moved behind the counter then into the staff room where the mainframe computer was housed.

Ally looked up from the chair in which she was sitting. "Good morning," she said, then returned her attention to the computer terminal in front of her.

East's mouth dropped. "This area is off-limits to the guests," he said, then remembered who he was talking to and changed the direction of his questions. "What are you doing?"

Her fingers paused on the keys and the look she gave him was just shy of a smirk.

"I think my security clearance is high enough that I can be trusted," she drawled, then tapped a couple more keys, hit the Save button, and leaned back in her chair with a satisfied smile. "There, that should do it."

"Do what?" East said, moving to look over her shoulder.

She stood. "Keep your system up and running for a few more years."

"You fixed it?"

She nodded as she moved toward the door. "I'm going to get some breakfast now. That's where I was going when I saw all the commotion. I offered to help and your assistant, what's his name...?"

"Foster. Foster Martin."

"Oh yes, Foster." She grinned. "He's not exactly cool under fire, is he?"

East sighed. "Was spit dribbling from the corners of his mouth?"

Her grin widened. "Only the left one."

"Great," East muttered, then shoved a hand through his hair in frustration. He glanced at the computer, which seemed to be running normally. "What did you do to it?"

Her smile stilled and she shrugged. "Oh...just dug around a little on the hard drive, punched in a few commands and gave it a new lease on life, so to speak."

"That's impossible. There are passwords."

She folded her hands in front of her like a child about to recite.

"No, it's not impossible and yes, I know."

He arched an eyebrow. "So your line of expertise for SPEAR is in computers?"

Ally shook her head. "Not really. They use me mostly for undercover work. Without makeup, I can pass for a teenager pretty easy."

"Computers are a hobby then?"

The smile on her face kept getting smaller. "No, I just know stuff," she said, and once again started toward the door. She wanted to get out before he got to the part where he found out that her IQ was bigger than his ego. It always turned men off and she didn't want to see that happen again. Not now. Not with him.

But East wasn't going to let go. He caught her by the elbow as she started to pass.

"Stuff? You call that stuff? It took three technicians two days to set up this system. It's complicated as hell and linked to Monarch's entire chain of resorts and you not only got into the system, but had it up and running within thirty minutes?"

Ally stopped, her chin lifting as she met his gaze.

"Actually it was about ten. I know things. Lots of

things, okay? Can we leave it at that?" Then she quietly pulled away from his grasp.

East hadn't realized he was still touching her and took a quick step back, aware that he'd invaded her space and even more aware that she didn't like it.

"I'm sorry," he said. "I didn't mean to be..." He sighed and started over. "Look, I guess what I should be saying is thank you."

"You're welcome."

She was all the way to the door when his voice stopped her.

"Ally."

She bit her lip, then turned. "Yes?"

"Intelligence isn't something to be ashamed of."

"Intelligence is hardly the word society uses to describe someone like me," she said, unaware of the anger in her voice.

East moved toward her, touching her shoulder, then dropping his hand. His voice was soft, his gaze compelling. She found herself unable to look away.

"Exactly what *do* they call someone like you, then?"

"Freak of nature was the favorite phrase at my alma mater."

"How old were you when you graduated?"

Her gaze turned inward, remembering how ill-equipped she'd been at ten years old to handle the social aspect of higher education.

"From high school...ten. From college...seventeen. But that was with three Ph.D.s and a minor in foreign languages, six to be exact. I was considering another semester or two when SPEAR recruited me. The rest is history."

East kept looking at her, trying to imagine what it would be like to live with so much knowledge and not go crazy at the rest of the world's ineptitude. He gave her a long, cursory stare.

"So, what you're saying is, if I asked real nice, you could do my taxes for me next year without breaking a sweat?"

Her eyes narrowed as she stared hard at his face. "Are you teasing me?"

"Yes."

"Oh." She managed a smile.

He pointed toward the door with his chin. "Still hungry?"

Her stomach grumbled. "Starving."

"Then follow me. I've got an in with the cook. He makes the best waffles this side of St. Louis."

"Who's in St. Louis?" she asked as they headed out the door.

"Aunt Dinah. Hers are the best, but don't tell Pete I said so."

"Who's Pete?"

"My fake French chef," East said. "Do you like them with whipped cream and strawberries, or are you a syrup fan?"

"Actually, I favor peanut butter and grape jelly."

East grinned. "Order it on the side or Pete will have himself a fit."

She pursed her lips primly. "Pete needs to learn to savor the finer things in life."

East laughed aloud.

As they exited the office, a frantic young man in jogging clothes came running through the lobby. He took one look at East and started yelling.

"My wife. My wife. They said she was in labor."

This would be the missing father, East thought, and took him by the shoulders, fixing him with a calm, steady gaze.

"Take it easy, Dad. She's fine. There's a doctor and a couple of paramedics with her now."

The expression on the man's face went from shock to joy.

"Dad?"

"I think I heard them say it was a boy," East said.

"Oh man, oh man. I'm a father. I'm a father," he cried.

"Yeah, so am I," East said. "Congratulations."

The man bolted for the stairs, unwilling to wait for an elevator.

East was still smiling when he turned back to Ally.

"Sorry. It isn't usually so hectic around here."

"Compared to my job, this is nothing," Ally said.

The look on her face made him hurt. He remembered all too well what that job could be like, but before he could comment, his cell phone rang again. Within moments of answering, he began to frown.

"Hang on a minute, please," he told his caller, then touched Ally's arm apologetically. "I'm sorry. I have to take this call. Why don't you head for the terrace. There's a buffet set up, or you can order for both of us. Either way, I'll be there shortly."

"Sure, but what do you want?"

"Just tell the waiter I'll have my usual." Then he

added. "Don't wait on me. I wouldn't want those waffles to get cold."

"Actually, they're better that way."

He shook his head and then chuckled. "Do you have
any other *interesting* habits I should know of?"

"I don't know," Ally said. "Exactly what do you think
you should know about me?"

East's smile slipped as his eyes suddenly darkened.
"I'm not sure, are you?"

Suddenly, his question took on a whole other meaning. She looked away, and then angry with herself for
being so gutless around this man, made herself look
at him.

"Around you, I'm not sure of anything." Then she
doubled up her fists and thumped the sides of her legs
in frustration. "And, I don't think I was supposed to
tell you something like that. Damn it all to hell, I am
not good at this stuff."

She stomped away, leaving East to make of her out-
burst what he would. Then he remembered his caller
and put the phone back to his ear.

Ally sat on the terrace with her chin in her hands,
staring out at the Pacific. This whole thing was a fiasco. Jonah must have been desperate to even consider
someone like her for this task. She kept wanting to blurt
out the reason she was here and get it over with. Sub-
terfuge was a part of her life, but she'd never used it
on one of the "good guys." Deceiving East didn't feel
right and the longer she played the part of a stressed-
out operative, the closer it came to being the truth. If
she told him now, the worst that could happen was he'd

just tell her to get lost. Then all she had to do was tell Jonah she failed.

She sighed.

Therein lay part of her problem. In all of Ally's life, she'd never failed at anything, except maybe relationships.

Her eyes narrowed thoughtfully as she continued to watch the breakers slamming against the rocks. There had to be a way to accomplish this.

A few moments later, a waiter brought her food, with the comment that he would serve East's order when he arrived.

Ally nodded.

"Will there be anything else?" he asked.

"Not right now," she said. "Thanks."

She reached for the side dish of peanut butter as he walked away and began carefully smearing each square in her waffle with an equal amount of the rich, creamy spread. Once having achieved symmetry, she did the same with the grape jelly until the waffle was all but obliterated beneath the concoction. Then, with a knife and fork, she cut into the waffle, separating a perfect three-square by three-square bite and popped it into her mouth. Her eyes rolled with appreciation as she began to chew.

East stood in the doorway leading out to the terrace, stealing a moment to watch Ally unobserved. At first glance, there wasn't anything really remarkable about her. She was of average height, without an ounce of spare flesh on her body. Her clothes were ordinary; a pair of navy slacks and a white, linen shirt hanging loose about her hips. Her hair was short and capped her head in a thicket of auburn curls and her eyes were the color of new grass. And yet as he watched her methodically preparing her food, he understood her need for control.

He could only imagine what it must have been like for a child such as she; born with an intelligence beyond understanding into a family that didn't have time for her, she must have felt like a misfit from the beginning. He didn't know, but he would guess she'd never had a "best friend" in her life and wondered if, as a child, she'd ever spent the night giggling with other girls or playing with dolls. Being a SPEAR operative wasn't conducive to gathering close friends, either. Too many secrets that couldn't be shared.

When she slowly and carefully cut another perfect square of waffle and popped it into her mouth, he was struck by an overwhelming urge to lean over her shoulder and take a great big bite out of the middle of that waffle just to see what she'd do when things went out of control.

At that moment, her waiter stopped at her table and topped off her coffee. When she lifted her head to smile and thank him, East pictured himself leaning down and tasting the peanut butter and jelly waffle on her lips. In spite of how physically resilient he knew she must be, there was something very fragile about her insecure smile and the curve of her cheek.

But he'd been too accustomed to denying himself to do anything so foolish as to get involved with a woman—especially an operative. After what he'd done, he didn't deserve happiness. It was enough that he was still alive. The kid he'd hit with his car was not.

He shoved aside his personal feelings as he strode to their table and took his seat. "Looks good," he said, pointing toward the food on her plate as the waiter filled his cup.

"Umm." She nodded, still chewing.

"Your food is ready, sir," the waiter said. "I'll be right back with it."

"Good, I'm starved," East said, taking a careful sip of the hot brew in his cup.

Suddenly, Ally gasped as a seagull swooped into their line of vision, filched a piece of left-over toast from a nearby table that had yet to be bussed and then disappeared over the roof of the hotel.

"They're pests, but this is their territory and there's little we can do about them if we choose to eat out-doors."

"I rather like them," Ally said. "I just wasn't expecting it, that's all."

East watched her pick up her knife and start to cut through her food, again sectioning off that same three-by-three square bite. Her forehead was knotted in serious concentration and she was gripping her knife and fork so hard that her knuckles were almost white. He frowned, believing that she was closer to a breakdown than he first suspected. Instinctively, his need to help her kicked in and he leaned forward.

"Why do you do that?"

She paused and looked up. "Do what?"

He pointed to the waffle. "Cut your food so precisely."

Startled, she glanced down at her plate then felt herself flushing with embarrassment. Freak. Always a freak.

"I don't know," she said. "I suppose it's just a habit." She laid down the knife and fork and then folded her hands in her lap, her enjoyment of her food suddenly gone.

"Ah, damn, I didn't mean to upset you," East muttered.

Ally made herself smile. "Don't be silly. I don't get upset."

That cold, emotionless wall had gone up between them again and East found himself resenting its presence. By God, he was going to get an emotional response from her, even if it was nothing but anger.

"Yes, you do. Everyone does at one time or another."

Ally bristled. She hadn't known this man even twenty-four hours and he thought he "knew" what she was thinking?

"Listen, Mr. Kirby, you don't know me, so how can you sit there and pretend you know my behavior patterns?"

The flush on her face had gone straight to her cheeks. They were fiery with anger, matching the glitter in her eyes. East leaned back in his chair, satisfied with what he'd done. She didn't know it yet, but she would thank him one day for putting her mind on something besides the hell that had driven her here.

"You gonna eat that?" he asked, pointing to the left-over food on her plate.

Prepared for another stinging rebuttal, his question took her off guard. "Umm… I, uh…don't suppose."

"Good," he said, and pulled the plate in front of him, then picked up the waffle like a piece of toast and took a hearty bite. As he chewed, his eyebrows arched in surprised appreciation. Then he swallowed. "Not bad," he said. "Not bad at all," and opened his mouth again.

Suddenly, Ally regained her sense of self and snatched the waffle out of his hands just in time to save it from another bite.

"I changed my mind," she said. "You eat what you ordered and I'll eat mine."

Ally stared down at her plate and the chaos he'd made of the waffle. Sighing, she reached for her fork when she heard him clear his throat. She looked up, glaring at the smug expression on his face. *Damn him. There's nothing wrong with being a little bit fussy about one's food.*

"What?" she asked.

He shrugged, as if to say he didn't know what she was asking.

"That's what I thought," she snapped. As she began trimming off the uneven spot he'd bitten into, she heard him chuckle.

"Just because I don't want to share my food, doesn't mean there's anything wrong with me," she muttered.

East's grin stilled. He leaned forward. "Ally."

"What?" she mumbled, refusing to look up.

"I was just teasing you. There isn't a damn thing wrong with you, do you hear me?"

She paused, letting an old pain resettle itself around the region of her heart. Then, just to prove she was as outrageous as the next, she set her jaw and cut a reckless swath through the chilling waffle, slashing off a diamond-shaped bite, rather than her usual, perfect square. Then she gave him a "take that" look and stuffed the bite into her mouth just as their waiter appeared with East's breakfast.

East hid a grin as the waiter set down his food. Moments later, he dug into his scrambled eggs and bacon. As he ate, he couldn't help thinking they'd never tasted so good and wondered if it was the waffle appetizer that had piqued his appetite, or the company he was in. Either way, for a day that had started off so chaotically, it was turning into something very interesting.

Chapter 4

Rain drifted in blowing sheets, hammering against the windows of the two-story cabin overlooking the gorge below. Normally the view was magnificent and the isolation well suited to Jonah's needs, but not today. The only way off the mountain was by helicopter or on foot, and until the storm passed, neither was possible.

He paced the floor between windows and walls, his anger growing at the latest news he'd just received. A courier had just been arrested at the Iranian border carrying highly classified documents. Documents that led straight back to him. And if that wasn't damning enough, there was the matter of one hundred thousand dollars recently deposited into his personal bank account that he could not explain.

"Damn, damn, damn it to hell," Jonah growled, then pivoted sharply and slammed his fist into a wall.

If it wasn't for the President's intervention, the Attorney General would already be issuing a warrant for his arrest. He didn't know how much longer he could fend off these assaults on his credibility and character. Immediately his thoughts went to Alicia Corbin. Before, he'd been willing to give her plenty of time to play on Easton Kirby's guilt, but this latest stunt with the foreign courier changed everything. Whoever was trying to ruin him was escalating the incidents. Time was no longer on his side. She'd been there almost a week and he needed to know what was happening at Condor Mountain Resort, because if East couldn't be persuaded to help, he was going to be forced to look to someone else. But to whom? The only reason he'd approached East in the first place was because he didn't know who else to trust.

A muscle jerked at the side of his jaw as he strode toward the fireplace. With a quick twist of his wrist, he turned the iron lion's head finial on the corner of the mantel. Immediately, a portion of the paneling slid into a pocket in the wall, revealing its secrets—the main communication center for SPEAR. He wasn't the first Jonah to occupy this place and he wouldn't be the last, but if he didn't resolve this mess and soon, his tenure would soon be over.

In the corner, a state-of-the-art fax hummed silently as page after page was fed into a tray, while line after line of text scrolling on a nearby computer terminal was saved for later review. Every up-to-date communication option known to man was there before him and yet with all of it at his fingertips, he still couldn't find the one man intent on ruining his life.

A flat map of the world hung at eye level from the

ceiling, imprinted on a large sheet of clear Plexiglas. The series of black intersecting marks were the locations of ongoing, world-wide investigations by SPEAR, but it was the red markings with which he was most concerned. They were the ones that pinpointed him as being involved in a subversive activity. He picked up a red dry-marker from the tray below and circled the border crossing where the courier had just been arrested, then stepped back to study the pattern. But the longer he stared, the more certain he was that there was no pattern, only a series of random incidents targeted for one purpose—to bring him down. At that point, a calm came over him. By God, he hadn't survived this long only to be brought down like this.

He moved toward his desk with purpose, then dropped into his chair, leaning forward and staring intently at the bank of phones within arm's reach. But it was the red phone on which he was focused. Within seconds, his mind had skipped through a half-dozen scenarios and chosen one best suited for this task. Without hesitation, he lifted the receiver to his ear. Two hours later, a package for Alicia Corbin was delivered to the front desk of Condor Mountain Resort.

The phone in East's office rang just as he was entering the last set of figures for his quarterly report. Grateful for the interruption, he hit the Save button on the computer keyboard and reached for the phone.

"Hello."

"Hey, Dad, it's me."

The familiar growl of Jeff's voice made him smile.

"Hey, yourself, stranger. When are you coming home for a visit?"

Jeff snorted with disbelief. "With my schedule, you've got to be kidding, right? The better question is, when are you coming to see me?"

East stood abruptly, shouldering the wave of instant guilt. "It has been a while, hasn't it, son?"

"Almost two months."

"And, so you're trying to tell me that you feel abandoned? What happened to that girlfriend you didn't want to discuss? Is she history?"

There was a brief silence, then Jeff laughed, but East thought it sounded forced.

"No, I'm not feeling abandoned. I'm just tired, and heartily sick of my own cooking. And I'm not in the mood to discuss women, period."

East chuckled. "That bad, huh?"

"Yes."

"So, let's talk about something simple then, like maybe your classes or your rotation at the hospital. Which one are you on now?"

Jeff laughed. Calling what he did "simple" was a joke and East knew it. "Pediatrics. And I'm ready for that to be over," he said, and then sighed. "Which is not to say I don't like kids, because I do, but there's something about kids and incurable illnesses that I can't get past."

East remained silent, sensing that Jeff just needed to talk, which he continued to do.

"Dad, there's this seven-year-old kid named Darcy. She's got ten of the cutest little brown freckles across her nose and the biggest blue eyes I've ever seen and she asked me yesterday if I'd marry her when she grows up." His voice broke. "Damn it, Dad, she's missing her two front teeth and all of her hair and she's dying, and there's not a goddamned thing anyone can do for her."

"I'm sorry," East said quietly. "That's got to be tough."

Jeff took a slow, shaky breath. "Sorry, it's just that sometimes this stuff gets to me...you know?"

Images flashed through East's mind—flashes of gunfire, blood splatters on his shoes from the agent who'd just died at his feet, days and nights spent in swamps with nowhere to sleep.

"Yeah, I know."

He stood abruptly and turned to the bank of windows behind his desk, staring absently through the glass without actually seeing the idyllic view of the beach below.

"Look, if you'll give me a few days to clear my calendar and make sure that my assistant can cover for me, I'll make a run to L.A. Just fax me your schedule so I won't interfere with your work or classes."

"Fantastic! I'll get the info to you sometime within the next day or two." The tone of his voice lifted. "I can already taste that steak."

East laughed. "Hungry for beef, are you? What have you been eating?"

"My cooking and everybody else's leftovers at work."

East frowned. "Are you short of money, son?"

Jeff chuckled. "No, just time."

"You sure you want to waste it on me?" East asked.

"Spending time with you is never a waste."

The unexpectedness of Jeff's remark tightened the muscles in East's throat. "Thanks," East said. "Talk to you soon."

"Yeah, right," Jeff echoed. "Talk to you soon."

The click of the receiver, then the silence that came afterward was telling. Suddenly, the distance between East and his son seemed farther than ever. He hung up the phone and started toward the door when he paused, standing for a moment in the middle of the room and contemplating the solitude in which he lived. It seemed odd to consider that a man could be lonely while living among a constant stream of people, but it was true. In that moment, the longing for a personal connection, for someone to laugh with—someone to share troubles and joys and long, lonely nights with—was overwhelming.

The image of Ally Corbin's face moved through his mind, then he sighed as he walked out of his office to relieve Foster Martin. Even if he chose to pursue her, and even if she reciprocated his feelings, there were too many reasons why it would never work.

Ally breezed into the lobby, her arms full of packages. It was the seventh day of her stay at the hotel, but the first day she'd gone exploring since her arrival. Her hair was windblown and there was a small, brown stain on the knee of her white slacks from the chocolate ice-cream cone she'd been eating on the way home. But the light in her eyes and the smile on her face were too bright to notice such a small flaw. Somewhere between midnight and daylight last night she'd made a vow to herself that unless she began to act normal, East was going to suspect her motives for being here. And there was nothing more normal than a woman shopping. Thus the packages, thanks to the small arts and crafts community based at the foot of the mountain. And while she'd started out on the shopping spree as a cover, by the time she pulled into the parking lot of the hotel and began unloading her car, she realized how badly she'd needed the break. She hadn't done anything this ordinary in over a year and couldn't wait to get to her room and relive the joy of her new finds.

"Ms. Corbin! Ms. Corbin!"

She glanced toward the desk to the young man who was waving her down.

"Yes?"

"A package came for you while you were out."

Ally swerved toward him, laughing as she tried to juggle her load to allow for another item.

"I don't know where I'm going to put it, but..."

"Allow me."

She turned to find East behind her. Before she could argue, he'd relieved her of her bags, leaving her free to retrieve the package at the desk. Suddenly aware of how she must look, she nervously smoothed her hands down the front of her blouse and managed a smile.

"Well...uh...thank you. I'll just..."

"Take your time," East said.

The clerk handed her the small package and she quickly dropped it into her bag and dug out her room key. She gave East another nervous glance. He was waiting patiently.

"You don't need to bother—"

"It's no bother," East said. "Lead the way."

All the way to the elevator she kept resisting the urge to run a comb through her hair, then discarded the thought. *What I look like doesn't matter*, she scolded herself. *He's just being helpful. It's part of his job.*

When the elevator doors opened, she stepped inside then turned, giving him a quick, nervous smile as she inserted the key into the pad that would take the elevator straight to the penthouse.

East stifled a sigh. She'd looked like a windblown

kid when she'd first entered the lobby, all pink-cheeked with flyaway hair. And that smudge on her pants. It looked like chocolate. She'd seemed so happy and now so ill at ease. Was it just him, or did all men evoke such a response from her?

"Looks like you've had quite a day," he said.

At his remark, her tension seemed to disappear.

"Oh, yes! It was wonderful. I found the most marvelous things. I can't wait to look at them all again."

He smiled. "That's good. Glad you found something enjoyable to occupy your time."

Her eyes lit up. "It was so much fun. I haven't done anything like this in ages. The only thing that could have made it better would have been sharing it with someone."

"If you'd asked, I would have been happy to—"

She blushed just as the door opened. "I wasn't fishing for an invitation," she said, and bolted into the small foyer leading to her door. With shaking hands, she punched in the security code and then opened the door and stepped aside, making room for him to enter.

"Just put them anywhere," she said. "And I really appreciate your help."

East dumped the bags on the sofa and then turned to look at her. She was still standing by the door, obviously waiting for him to leave. Despite the urge to linger, he could take a hint.

"See you at dinner tonight?" he asked.

"Yes. I'm starved already."

"Did you eat lunch?" he asked. "I can have something sent to your room."

"There's no need."

He frowned. "Have you had anything at all since breakfast?"

"Well, no, except an ice-cream cone. But I'm fine, really."

Still reluctant to leave, he glanced at the bags, curious as to what things would interest her.

"Find anything special?" he asked, pointing toward the bags.

For the first time since he'd relieved her of her bags, she gave him a genuine smile.

"Oh, yes! I collect music boxes and I found the most amazing one. It's not really a box, it's a snow globe, but it still plays music so I thought—"

"May I see?"

"Really? You really want to see?"

He nodded.

She slammed the door and bolted toward the sofa, then began digging through the bags.

As he watched, he remembered what she'd said about her parents' lack of interest in her childhood, and it occurred to him to wonder how many times in her life she had found pleasure, but had no one to share it with.

"Please, have a seat," Ally said. "It's going to take me a minute to find... No, wait, here it is."

She pulled a small box from a sack and then without thinking dropped onto the sofa next to where he'd sat down. She was so intent on unpacking the box that she didn't realize how intimate the moment had become; thighs touching, shoulders bumping as he leaned forward to see what she was digging out of the tissue.

She laughed to herself as she lifted it up, letting the light from a nearby window pierce the glass and highlight the figures within.

It was a miniature image of a cowboy on horseback with a small red and white calf lying across his lap and against the saddle horn. The cowboy was wearing blue jeans, a heavy sheepskin coat and a dark, wide-brimmed hat. He sat hunched in the saddle, leaning over the calf, as if sheltering it with his body. When she shook the globe, a sudden snowstorm appeared. Immediately, the viewer was drawn into the drama of the tender rescue of the calf from the storm.

"Isn't that the most amazing thing?" she said. Then she wound it up and tilted her head to one side, staring in fascination as the music began to play.

"What's that tune?" East asked.

She turned, her face alight with joy. "'Desperado'. It's an old Eagles song, but it fits, doesn't it?"

"Yes, it does," East said.

She looked back at the globe. "Isn't it pretty?"

"Very," he said softly, unable to take his eyes off her face.

Suddenly, aware of the brush of air against her cheek, she turned. Her eyes widened, her breath caught and then slowed. Long, endless seconds passed as they stared into each other's eyes, measuring the other's intent and the distance between their lips. The thought crossed her mind that if she leaned forward—

The music stopped.

Both of them blinked, as if startled to find themselves in such an intimate situation, but it was East who was the first to move away. Not because he wasn't tempted, because he was. But he kept remembering she was not only a guest, but had come here in a fragile condition.

"Sorry," he muttered. "I didn't mean to—"

Ally stood abruptly, the snow globe clutched to her chest like a shield.

"You didn't *do* anything, so an apology is uncalled for."

He followed her lead and got up as well. "Look, Ally, don't take me wrong. I—"

She lifted her chin and smiled. "Thank you for carrying my packages."

He fisted his hands, fighting the urge to shake that fake smile off her face.

"You're welcome," he said shortly. He walked to the door then turned, unwilling to leave her on such an uncomfortable note. "See you at dinner?"

"Of course," she said, and shut the door in his face.

"Well, hell," he muttered, and stomped toward the elevator.

"Damn, damn, damn," Ally moaned, and stomped toward the sofa, her joy in the snow globe forgotten.

It wasn't until she was changing her clothes that she remembered the package from the desk. Curious, she dug it out of her bag and began to unwrap it. But when a small black cell phone fell out of the packet with a note attached, her stomach knotted.

Jonah.

She picked up the note. As usual, Jonah's instructions were sparse and to the point.

Press the Send button. Let it ring twice then hang up.

She did as she was instructed, knowing that somewhere within the network of global communications, a chain of events was going off that would eventually alert Jonah that she'd received what he'd sent. Within a minute of her call, the small phone rang. With a sigh, she lifted it to her ear.

"This is Corbin."

The familiar rumble of Jonah's voice filled her ear.

"Are you well?"

"I'm fine, thank you. The weather here is marvelous." Then she frowned. He hadn't sent her here for a weather report. "I don't have much to tell you."

Jonah bit off an expletive. This wasn't what he wanted to hear, but it was hardly a situation he could force.

"What's the situation?"

She sighed and ran her fingers through her hair in a gesture of frustration.

"We've met, of course, even talked quite personally a couple of times. But he's not the most approachable person in the world and I'm not much good at employing feminine wiles."

Jonah almost smiled. She didn't know it, but that was exactly why he'd sent her. Easton Kirby was too shrewd a man by far to be swayed by something as sordid as impersonal sex.

"I didn't send you there to have sex with the man. You're the perfect woman for this job. You have a calm, rational approach to situations. Remember that and use it."

"Yes, sir," Ally muttered.

Jonah hesitated, but there was no need to delay the obvious.

"A situation has come up that has escalated the need for haste. Can you handle it?"

She swallowed nervously. "Yes, sir. I'll find a way. I won't let you down."

"Good. Oh, and keep the phone handy. It's pro-

grammed to contact me, and me alone. Do you understand?"

"Yes, sir."

"If it happens to fall into the wrong hands, it will
self-destruct itself when used incorrectly."

"Right."

"I'm counting on you, Corbin."

"I won't let you down."

The line went dead.

Ally disconnected, too, then put the phone in her
dresser, her joyous mood gone. She went back to the
living room and picked up the snow globe, wound it
up, then gave it a shake. Immediately, the snow and the
music began to swirl around the lone cowboy and his
mount. Her eyes narrowed as she stared, her thoughts in
as much turmoil as the snow within the globe, and she
didn't move until the music had stopped and the snow
lay dormant in the bottom of the globe. Finally, she set
it aside and started toward the bedroom to shower and
change. East didn't know it yet, but tonight, he was
going to get more on his plate than his dinner.

About a half-mile offshore, a lone yacht was dropping anchor for the evening while the staff began readying for the owner's evening meal. A man with a pair of
powerful binoculars stood aft, ostensibly enjoying the
view from the spacious white deck. But it wasn't the
rhythmic rise and fall of seagulls over the water that
captured his attention. His gaze was trained toward the
beach and the hotel that sat on the rise above it. Even
with the binoculars, he was unable to make out the faces
of the people he saw, but he didn't care. He'd already
confirmed that the people he sought were at the hotel,

and it would only be a matter of time before he introduced himself—but in his own special way.

Despite the pep talk Ally had given herself while dressing for dinner, her stomach was in knots. It wasn't so much facing East that she dreaded, as the possibility of failing Jonah. She didn't know why the need for East to return to active duty was so important to Jonah, but she knew it must be vital for him to persist in such a fashion.

The dress she was wearing was simple, as were all of her clothes; it was of a white gauzy fabric with a scoop neck and loose, three-quarter length sleeves, and a hem that brushed the tops of her ankles as she walked. Her shoes were flat and little more than three straps; one across the back of her heel, the other two across the top of her foot. Her makeup was a reflection of how she saw herself—neat, coordinated and uncomplicated.

As she exited her suite and started down the elevator, she gave herself the once-over in the mirrored interior of the car. Satisfied that nothing was smudged or smeared and that her hair was in place, she lifted her chin and prepared to do battle. The car stopped once at the third floor. An elderly man and a young couple got on. The old man nodded at her, but the young couple had eyes only for each other. Ally tried not to stare, but their affection for each other was quite compelling and impossible to ignore.

It wasn't the first time in her life that she'd wished she'd been born an ordinary child and she let herself play with the idea of "what if" all the way down to the lobby. Yet when the doors opened and it was time to get out, reality returned. She wasn't ordinary and for some reason, she'd been entrusted with a job that was very important to Jonah. The fact that she'd never seen the man in her life did not negate the loyalty she felt for him. In an odd, even pitiful way, Jonah had become the father figure she'd never had. He asked things of her that no one else would have even considered, but always with the confidence that she would do a good job, and when it was over, was forthcoming with his praise. It didn't matter to her that she'd never felt his arms around her or seen a smile on his face. It was all about trust.

She strode into the lobby with that thought in her heart, then noticed that she was a little earlier than the time she'd planned to come down. A quick glance toward the terrace was all it took to draw her outside, and as she took her place at the railing overlooking the beach below, she realized she wasn't the only one who'd had the same idea. The sun—in all its glory—was about to set.

The water burned with a radiance, reflecting the colors hovering on the horizon, and the path of the sun lay in a straight line upon the water, pointing toward the beach below the hotel. If one was prone to fancy, which of course Ally was not, one might have been tempted to step onto that path, just in case it was as firm as it appeared.

And that was how East found her, staring at the horizon with her elbows on the railing and her chin resting in her hands. The evening breeze was tugging at the hem of her skirt, as well as the loose ends of her hair, but she seemed oblivious to the taunt.

"Quite a view, isn't it?" he said softly.

Ally straightened abruptly and turned. "I didn't know you were here."

His dark eyes bore down into her face, searching for something. He didn't know what.

"Just arrived," he said, unwilling for her to know that he'd been watching her for some time before his approach. "Are you hungry?"

"Starved," she said, and was surprised to realize it was the truth. Suddenly, all her worries about facing this man faded in comparison to the beauty of what she'd just witnessed. "But before we go in, I have a question I need to ask you."

A little surprised, he hesitated, then nodded. "Of course. Ask away."

"Do you believe in repaying old debts?"

Immediately he thought of Jonah and his senses went on alert. But her face seemed so guileless, he chalked it up to guilt.

"Of course. I don't think a person can be free to go forward in life until old debts have been paid, whether monetary or emotional."

She nodded. "I agree," she said softly, then looked toward the dining room inside that was beginning to fill. "It's getting a little chilly out here. Shall we go inside?"

East offered his elbow and she accepted, as if taking the arm of a handsome man was an everyday occurrence for her. As he seated her, and then himself, it hit her how calm she was feeling, and moments later, knew why. The decision had been made and before the night was out, she would have stated her purpose and pled Jonah's case as eloquently as she possibly could. After that, it was out of her hands.

When East asked her what she wanted to eat, she laid her menu aside and blessed him with a rare smile.

"Order for me, too, will you? I'm in the mood to be surprised."

Chapter 5

Dinner was over and dessert had been ordered. The other two couples at their table had said their goodbyes and forgone the last course for a walk, instead. And although Ally wasn't really hungry for sweets, she held her ground, knowing that East would not abandon her to eat alone. It was the moment she'd been waiting for.

"The food was delicious," Ally said. "Thank you for such a fine meal."

East smiled. "Red snapper is a favorite of mine, especially when Pete serves it up Cajun by blackening the fillet as he did tonight."

She nodded, then glanced around, making sure that they were basically still isolated within the room. Satisfied that their conversation would not be overheard, she leaned forward, pinning East beneath the force of her gaze.

"Why did you refuse Jonah's request?"

East's smile froze, then disappeared. His fury was evident as his face suddenly paled.

"Son of a bitch."

Ally flinched inwardly, but she refused to let him know she was scared.

"He sent you, didn't he?"

"Yes."

It had to be said that East hadn't expected her honesty and it caught him off guard. He struggled with the need to throw something or throw her out of the hotel, but his anger landed somewhere between. He got up from the table and stalked off, leaving her behind.

It wasn't exactly the conversation Ally had hoped for, but nothing she hadn't expected. She caught up with him at the elevator and inserted herself between him and the wall.

"You didn't answer my question."

"Lady, I guarantee that right now you don't want to hear what I'm thinking, so why don't you take your little self off and mind someone else's business besides mine?"

The doors opened. Several guests got off. East got on and immediately pressed the Close Door button, unwilling to ride up with anyone else and have to deal with courtesies he wasn't feeling. But Ally was right behind him. To his dismay, he found himself enclosed in the small, mirrored car with her. Everywhere he looked, he saw a reflection of her face and the question in her eyes, still waiting to be answered.

"You told me you believed in paying back old debts. I didn't take you for a liar, Easton Kirby."

He spun, pinning her against the wall with the flat of one hand.

"You don't know what the hell you're talking about."

"I know that he saved your sanity and your butt by putting you in this job and that the one time he asked you for a favor, you refused him."

The doors opened and East pivoted, stalking off the elevator toward his personal quarters. Ally was still right behind him.

"Is that the way you repay Jonah, Mr. Kirby? For some reason known only to him, that man needs you and you've thrown up your hands and said no. Why? Because once upon a time someone died?"

He jammed his key in the lock and stormed inside. Before he could shut the door, she followed him inside.

"Shut up and get out!" he hissed. "You don't know what the hell you're talking about."

"I'll leave when I'm through," she snapped. "What I do know is that this is a war we're waging—a constant, daily war against crime and evil and all things ugly in this world and that sometimes in a war innocent people die. I know that. I've seen it firsthand, but it hasn't made me want to quit." Forgetting her earlier hesitation, she jabbed a finger against his chest. "What it has done is make me angry. And when I get angry, I want to get even. I want to take down the bad guys in a way that they will never come back. What I *don't* do is hide."

East inhaled sharply, stunned by her anger and her accusations.

"I didn't quit. I still work for SPEAR, just in another capacity. I fulfill a duty that might not be as dramatic as yours, but I am not hiding from the world."

She snorted beneath her breath. "You may have convinced yourself of that, but not me." Then she shoved her hands through her hair in frustration and started to pace. "Look, I don't mean to belittle your life. God knows it's true that you've already done your bit. You've already put yourself on the line more than most people, and what you're doing now is an important and honorable job." She stopped and turned, looking him straight in the face. "I don't know why Jonah needs you, but I suspect that you do, so can you look me in the face and tell me that whatever it is doesn't matter?"

A muscle jerked at the side of East's jaw. He knew it wasn't really her fault. She'd been following orders, just as he'd done many times before. But the thought did occur to him that for the first time in his life, he now understood what prompted the desire to kill the messenger for bringing bad news.

"Damn you," he muttered.

"No. You're damning yourself and I've done all I came here to do. The rest, Mr. Kirby, is up to you." She headed for the door.

"Where are you going?"

She stopped and turned. "To bed. Oh…and I imagine I'll be checking out sometime tomorrow so I'll tell you goodbye tonight. I can't say this trip turned out as I'd hoped, but I doubt I'll ever forget you."

Before he could answer, she'd slammed the door, leaving him with nothing but the echo of her words. With a heartfelt curse, he slumped into a nearby chair, leaned back and closed his eyes. It was going to be a hell of a long night.

It was six o'clock in the evening when Jeff Kirby unlocked the door to his apartment and then shouldered his way inside, dropping a backpack and an armful of dirty clothes on the floor by the door as he slammed it shut behind him. Although the rooms were a bit dusty and there were some dirty dishes in the sink, he'd never been so glad to be home. He'd just finished a thirty-six hour stint at the UCLA Medical Center and was so exhausted he couldn't think. It had been all he could do to navigate the traffic from the hospital to his apartment. He headed for the bathroom, shedding his clothes as he went. All he wanted was a bed and a shower. He'd worry about the rest later.

When he stepped beneath the showerhead, he braced himself against the shower stall and bent his head, closing his eyes in silent ecstasy and letting the warm jets of water knead the knotted muscles in his neck and shoulders. He stood beneath the spray until he felt himself beginning to fold, then turned off the water and got out to dry. He could see the corner of his bed from where he was standing and kept picturing himself stretching out beneath the sheets.

With droplets still clinging to his back, he tossed his wet towel toward the rack as he walked past. It missed the hook and fell on the floor, but he kept on walking. When he reached the bed, he fell face forward upon the covers, his long bare legs and arms flung out. Within seconds, he was sound asleep.

The phone began to ring, but Jeff never moved. The sun set, the moon rose, and sometime after midnight he began to stir. His belly was empty and growling and his neck was stiff from the position in which he'd been lying. With a groan, he rolled over on his back and glanced at the digital clock on the table beside his bed.

It read 12:35 a.m. Already tomorrow. He had to be back at work in five hours. Alternating between the notion of going back to sleep and getting something to eat, his empty belly won out. He crawled out of bed and put on a pair of worn-out sweats on his way to the kitchen. Halfway down the hall he froze. Someone was rattling the knob on his front door.

His mind began to race. Had he turned the dead bolt when he came in, or in his exhaustion had he only turned the lock on the knob? He entered the living room just as the door to his apartment swung inward. Three men wearing dark coveralls and caps burst into the room.

He glanced toward the phone and when one of them yanked the jack from the wall, he realized they were already ahead of him. He doubled his fists.

They came at him from all directions, leaving him with nowhere to go but through them if he was to get out the door.

With a karate kick that his dad would have been proud of, Jeff connected with the first man, sending him flying backward with a kick to the chin. He hit the wall, taking down a table, a lamp and a picture as he fell. The noise was deafening. Jeff kept expecting that at any minute, Mil and Bill, his neighbors across the hall, would hear and come to see what was happening. While that man was scrambling to get up, the other two came at him on the run, hitting him squarely in the chest and taking him down beneath the weight of their bodies. More furniture crashed. Another lamp fell, shattering upon impact. Jeff landed one punch as the third man scrambled back up on his feet. After that, they had him subdued.

Blood ran freely from a cut inside his mouth and he could already feel his right eye swelling shut.

"If you sons of bitches planned on robbing me, you picked the wrong man. I don't have anything of value except a television, a VCR and about twenty dollars to my name. Take the stuff and my car keys and just leave me the hell alone."

One of the men laughed. "A smart-mouth. Boys, we got ourselves a smart-mouth."

He yanked Jeff to his feet while the other two began wrapping duct tape around his hands and ankles. Jeff continued to struggle, but it was useless. He thought of his dad. What would he have done in such a situation? Clues. That's it, clues. He would try to leave clues. But what? My God, they hadn't exactly introduced themselves when they'd broken into his home.

As his mind was racing, one of the men bent over and began wrapping his ankles. As he did, his shirt sleeve slipped back, revealing an odd tattoo on his biceps. It was of an American flag with the initials B.O.B. above it. It made no sense to him, but it was the only anomaly he could see.

"The cops will be here any minute," he warned. "My neighbors have probably already called them."

The man looked up at Jeff and then laughed.

"Who? You mean those people across the hall? I don't think so. About ten minutes ago they got a phone call to come to UCLA Med Center and identify a body. Damn shame about the woman's mother—her dying so unexpectedly and all."

Jeff's mind stopped. "You killed an innocent woman just to get rid of witnesses to killing me?"

"Hell, no. We're not killers, boy. We just gave them a little fright. They're gonna find themselves the victims of a cruel joke. As for you, why, we're not going to kill you, either. We're just gonna take you for a little ride." Then he pointed toward the other two men.

"Straighten this place up. We wouldn't want anyone to think he went against his will."

"You bastard," Jeff snarled, and lowered his head, using it as a battering ram as he hit the man square in the belly.

They went down in a tangle of anger. Blood spurted inside Jeff's mouth upon impact, but it was nothing compared to the alarm in his heart. Unless a miracle occurred, he was about to be kidnapped, and he'd heard too many stories from his dad's past to believe that he would ever be rescued alive.

The man cursed and pushed, Jeff rolled, landing face down on the hardwood floor as the man put his boot in the middle of Jeff's back.

"Just stay put unless you want more of the same."

Jeff groaned, but did as he'd been told. He watched from the corner as they began putting the apartment back in order, dumping broken glass in the wastebaskets and then carrying them into the hall and putting them down the garbage chute while the other one set the furniture back in place.

Suddenly, one of the men cursed and yanked off his glove.

"Cut my damned finger," he muttered, and wiped the blood on the seat of his pants, then dumped the last of the glass he was holding into a wastebasket.

Meanwhile, Jeff's thoughts were in turmoil. He had to leave some kind of clue, but what? His fingers were getting numb and he flexed them painfully. As he did, he felt moisture on the floor behind him and something clicked. Blood—his blood! He could use it like ink. But what to write? Again, his gaze fell upon the man with the odd tattoo and it clicked. Quickly, before they took him away, he traced the letters *B O B* on the floor with one finger. Within seconds, they were coming toward him.

"Get the trunk," the tattooed man said.

Afraid that they would see what he'd done, Jeff pretended to make one final escape by rolling away from the wall where he'd been lying. They laughed and caught him in the middle of the room.

"Where in blazes did you think you were goin', boy?"

Before Jeff could answer, he felt a prick on his arm then his ears began to buzz.

"What did you do?" he muttered.

"Come on, boy! Get up and get yourself in the trunk before you pass out on your face."

Jeff was fading fast. "Screw you," he said, as his eyes rolled back in his head.

"Damn it, Elmore, you could have waited until we got him in the trunk. Now we're gonna have to lift dead-weight and me with a bad back."

"Just grab a leg and shut up," Elmore said. "The sooner we get back to Idaho, the better I'm gonna feel."

Somewhere between panic and pure nothing, Jeff registered what had been said, and then everything went black.

Morning came none too soon for Ally. She'd struggled all night with the urge to call Jonah and tell him she'd failed, but there was a part of her that still held out hope. The least she could do was give East until morning. If he hadn't changed his mind by the time she checked out, then would be soon enough to make the call.

Unwilling to see East again and face his bitterness and anger, she'd ordered breakfast sent up to her room, then wasted the biggest part of it, unable to eat for the pain. It was unusual for Ally to feel pain, because she had yet to suffer an injury in the field, and was rarely, if ever, ill. But the pain was there. Right around her heart. And every time she took a breath, it grabbed and tightened, squeezing until her eyes filled with tears. She kept seeing the look of disbelief on East's face turn from hurt and then to anger. She'd liked him—really liked him—and knowing she was the one who'd put this distance between them hurt even more.

With a dejected sigh, she dropped the last folded T-shirt into her bag and zipped it up, then put the cell phone Jonah had given her into her purse. It was her own fault. She'd known from the start that he wasn't going to appreciate being deceived. She grabbed a tissue from her pocket and gave her nose a quick blow. She just hadn't planned on being attracted to him. Intellectually, she knew that attraction between opposite sexes was nothing more than a secretion of pheromones. But intellect had nothing to do with her reaction to his deep, husky voice or the way his hands felt against her skin. And there was the way his eyes had turned dark when she thought he had been going to kiss her.

She dropped onto the side of the bed and covered her face with her hands. *Ah, damn. If only he'd kissed me. At least I would have had that to remember.*

The phone rang, startling her from her bout of pity. She grabbed it before it could ring a second time and then had to clear her throat of tears before she could speak.

"Hello?"

"Ms. Corbin, this is the front desk. We have a delivery for you. Shall we bring it to your room, or do you want to pick it up on your way out?"

Her heart skipped a beat. Could this be another package from Jonah? If it was, checking it out in the privacy of her room was better than in the front seat of a car.

"Bring it up, please. However, I'll be checking out soon."

"Yes, ma'am. Just let us know. We'll be happy to take care of your bags."

She set the phone back in the cradle and then went to the living room to await the delivery. A short while later, a knock sounded. She opened the door to find a bellhop holding a large manila envelope. She took it from him and then started to hand him some money when he waved it away.

"Oh no, ma'am. That's not necessary," he said, and shut the door behind him as he left.

"That's a first," she muttered, and put the money back in her pocket, then dropped the envelope on the table as if it were wired to explode before getting up the nerve to look inside. After a minute of deliberation, she dumped the contents upon the table. There were two items, a photo, which fell facedown, and a small white note card with a single phrase printed in heavy, black letters.

I know who you are.

Her heart skipped a beat. She picked up the photo and then inhaled sharply. Dear God. It was a picture of her and East standing out on the balcony last evening when they had watched the sunset.

She studied it for some time, trying to figure out what it was that bothered her, then it hit. Whoever had taken it, had done so from the water. They were being spied on, but why? It must have something to do with

Jonah. If it did, East would know. She turned toward
the window overlooking the bay. But there was nothing
in sight except whitecaps on the waves and a couple of
sea lions sunning themselves on the rocks.

I know who you are.

She shuddered. The message was a warning. There
was no mistaking that fact. And like it or not, she was
going to have to confront East with this and then tell
Jonah. She didn't relish doing either, but this note had
just changed everything.

East had spent most of the night battling his conscience. On the one hand, everything Alicia Corbin had
said to him was the truth. He did owe Jonah his sanity,
maybe even his life. After the accident that had killed
the kid, there had been many nights when he'd considered ending it all, telling himself that after what had
happened, he didn't deserve to live, either.

But then he'd met Jeff, a fourteen-year-old runaway
with no family, no roots, and no hope for a better life.
Jeff had been street-smart and angry. Looking back,
East knew that he'd subconsciously set out to save this
kid because he hadn't been able to save the other one.
But that was only at first. Within six months, his feelings for Jeff had truly changed. He cared about the boy
who was trying to become a man on his own, and to his
joy, Jeff was beginning to care for him. Somehow, Jonah
found out and gave East the opportunity he needed to
settle down by changing his status to inactive and putting him in charge of the Condor Mountain Resort. For
the first time in his adult life, Easton Kirby had a per-

manent address and someone who depended on him, while Jeff gained a father and a home.

But that was ten years ago and East knew that if he died tomorrow, Jeff would survive. He was a big, savvy young man with a bright future ahead of him, and a good part of that was thanks to Jonah's intervention.

Now Jonah was calling in the marker and East had refused. The pressure was on and he didn't know where to turn. He'd been off active duty for so long, he felt as if technology and time had passed him by. There was so much about the business he didn't know anymore. It was frightening to think about holding Jonah's future in his hands. What if he failed? What if he made another mistake? This time, it would be Jonah who took the fall and the idea was impossible. The entire safety of the free world quite often fell on the shoulders of SPEAR operatives. Destroying Jonah could prove fatal to more than just the man, himself. It could affect the lives of every citizen of the United States of America, and thinking about the burden of responsibility made him sick. But the question kept coming back to the same answer. As Ally had reminded him quite forcefully, Jonah had asked. How could he possibly refuse?

It had taken all night and into the morning before East had gotten up the nerve to call Ally's room. But before he could act upon the thought, he'd gotten a call of his own—one that had taken him out of his own problems in a heartbeat. A child had gone missing.

East exited the elevator to find Foster Martin, the assistant manager, waiting for him. East acknowledged the man with an abrupt nod.

"What do we know?" East asked. "Have you searched

the hotel? How old is he? Did you get a description of him, the clothes he was wearing?"

"I have staff searching every floor as we speak and the groundskeepers have just been alerted to search the surrounding area. The boy is almost three and wearing a pair of red swimming trunks. Nothing else."

"How do you lose a kid?" East muttered.

"Easy," Foster said. "All you have to do is blink."

East gave the man a considering look. "You sound as if you're speaking from experience."

"I lost my nephew while shopping last Christmas. I turned loose of his hand only long enough to get my wallet out of my pocket and when I reached down to get him, he was gone."

East sighed. At least he hadn't had that kind of problem with Jeff. He'd been past the hand-holding stage by the time that they'd met.

"I trust everything turned out okay?"

Foster nodded. "Thankfully, yes."

"Where had he gone?"

"Back to tell Santa to bring me a wife."

East grinned, then clapped Foster on the back. "It's too early for Santa, so let's go talk to the parents."

"They're outside right now with the bellhops who are searching the parking lot."

"Good. You stay inside and coordinate what you've already started. I'll go outside to see what I can do. Say a prayer."

"Yes, sir. Already done that, sir."

East started through the lobby, his focus on the situation at hand, and missed seeing Ally as she came off the elevator. But Ally saw him leaving and quickly followed, unaware of the unfolding drama. It wasn't until she'd exited the hotel that she realized something was amiss.

A young woman in hiking clothes came barreling around the corner of the building.

"Hey, what's going on?" Ally asked.

"Some little boy got himself lost. Everyone's helping search."

"What's he look like?" Ally asked.

The girl shrugged. "I don't know. All I heard them say is that he's little."

Ally sighed as the girl quickly left. First things first, and that meant finding the kid. But how? What would draw a child's attention in this place? There was no playground equipment, no swings, no playland via a fast-food restaurant. If he wasn't inside, then where would he be? She imagined the child being snatched, then blocked the thought out of her mind. Don't borrow trouble, she warned herself, and then took a deep breath and closed her eyes.

For a moment, all she could hear was the sound of voices calling back and forth as they searched, but she made herself block all that out and listen, instead, to the world around her.

The first thing she heard were the seagulls—the soft flapping of their wings as they rose and fell within the swells of the wind, and then their high-pitched calls. Goose bumps rose on the backs of her arms as she instinctively turned toward the sounds. She'd never really listened to the gulls before, but there was an eerie, almost otherworldly sound to their screech.

Then there was the rhythm of the waves, washing up, pulling back. A low, almost imperceptible sound came with it—a shrill, high-pitched shriek.

Her eyes flew open. Was that a gull? It came from the back of the hotel, and there was nothing there but the steep, winding steps that led down to the beach. If the child was very small, surely he would not have been able to negotiate such an obstacle alone. Again, she heard a sound, only this time it didn't sound like a bird. It was the laughter of a child. She bolted toward the back of the hotel, hoping that she was wrong. And then she saw him and her heart stopped. She paused, then turned, shouting East's name.

Immediately, she saw East freeze and then turn. She shouted again, pointing toward the beach below, and then started to run. There was no time to waste on waiting for them to catch up, because the little boy was moving toward the water without realizing the terrible danger he was in. The first wave would knock him off his feet. The second one would pull him under. After that, it would be too late.

Chapter 6

Ally started down the steps, taking them two at a time and shouting as she ran, hoping to distract the little boy, but it did no good. He kept toddling toward the lip of the ocean, unaware of the danger, and she couldn't run fast enough to catch him. She was more than halfway down when East reached the top of the steps and started after her, but she didn't know it, and it would have made no difference if she had. She didn't even hear the child's mother suddenly scream out in horror, because the thunder of her own heartbeat was pounding in her ears. Her feet made hard, slapping sounds as she ran down the steps in a jarring rhythm, taking them two and three at a time. Once she slipped and, had it not been for the fierce hold she had on the handrail, would have gone head over heels down the rest. When she reached the last step, she came off of it in a leap, shedding her shoes and her shirt as she ran and leaving her in nothing but a bra and a pair of white cotton slacks.

"Noooo!" she screamed, praying that the sound of her voice would stop the child in his tracks, but the word was lost in the shrieks of feeding gulls.

No more than fifty feet separated them when the first wave knocked the baby off his feet. He went down on his face, then came up crying. Ally saw the next wave coming and knew she was going to be too late. It rolled over him like a mother pulling a blanket over a sleeping child. There was a brief flash of red just below the surface of the water and then he was gone.

Precious seconds were wasted before Ally was in the water and running into the surf. Still focused on the last place she'd seen him, she took a deep breath and went headfirst into an oncoming wave, and then she, too, was gone.

A dozen frantic thoughts went through East's mind as he watched the water pull the baby under. But when Ally followed, too, then didn't come up, his heart nearly stopped. He was a good fifty yards behind her and time was not on their side. He knew within reason that she had to be an expert swimmer. All the SPEAR operatives were highly trained in all means of survival. But she didn't know this coast or its currents. There was a riptide about a hundred yards offshore and if she got caught in that, it would take a miracle to save her. By the time he reached the water, he had kicked off his shoes and dropped his shirt in the sand. Unsure of his direction, he started wading into the ocean when a distance away, Ally's head suddenly broke the surface of the water. Relief made him weak.

There was a collective gasp from the gathering crowd behind him and then someone shouted, "She's got him!"

But East was already up to his waist and moving fast. He dove headfirst into an oncoming wave and started swimming.

Sunlight pierced the fluid world in which Ally was swimming, and yet she could not see clearly enough to give her a direction in which to search. Treading water beneath the surface, she turned in a complete circle, searching for a flash of red or a shadow that might be the child, himself. Her lungs were burning and the salt water had all but blinded her, yet she couldn't bring herself to give up.

Then she saw something drifting down to her right and moved swiftly toward it. Suddenly, her hand brushed against flesh, then fabric. It was the little boy's shorts. With one desperate grab, she pulled, and moments later, felt the cold, lifeless impact of a tiny body against her chest. The need to inhale was overwhelming as she began to move toward the surface, ever closer toward the light and the life-giving air she knew was there. But the harder she kicked, the farther away it seemed to be. Just when she thought it was over, she broke the surface of the water, gasping for air with the child held fast against her.

Everything was a blur, but she could hear people shouting. She turned toward the sound and saw the dark, imposing shape of the coastline, took another deep breath and began to swim, pulling the little boy as she went. Suddenly, East was right before her, touching her, taking the burden of the child's lifeless body from her weary arms. She wanted to cry with relief.

"Are you all right? Can you make it back to shore?" East shouted.

She nodded.

"Are you sure?"

"Go, just go," she yelled.

East began to swim, pulling the child along like a small, deflating raft. When his feet finally touched bottom, he lifted the child into his arms and started running toward the beach. Hotel staff waded out to meet him and together, they soon had the child on the sand. He looked up at the crowd, then waved frantically toward the water at Ally.

"Help her."

A couple of men separated themselves from the crowd as East bent over the child. As he began CPR, the loud, insistent sound of an approaching siren could be heard coming up the mountain. And then his entire focus became that cold little body on the sand, and the feel of a tiny blue mouth beneath his lips.

Ally was all but dragged from the water. She managed to walk about a half-dozen steps when her legs gave way. With a low, weary groan, she waved away the men who'd helped her and dropped to her hands and knees with her head down, trying to catch her breath. Someone draped a blanket around her shoulders and murmured something in her ear, but it didn't register. She couldn't think past the sight of East bending over the baby.

"Please, God," she whispered. "Please. Don't let him die."

In the background, Ally was vaguely aware of an ambulance pulling to a stop at the top of the bluff, and then people in uniforms scrambling down the steps to get to the beach. But the silence that engulfed them was telling. There was nothing but the throb of the ocean behind them and the sun overhead. Even the seagulls seemed to sense the unfolding drama and had absented themselves from the sky in deference to the man and the child.

And then everything seemed to happen in slow motion.

There was a cough, then a gurgle, and East was turning the boy on his side as water came spilling out of his mouth. A mother's sob was undermined by a collective sigh of relief from the crowd as the child started to cry.

As the first paramedic came on the scene, East gladly relinquished the child to the expert and rocked back on his heels in exhaustion.

When the child started to cry, Ally started to shake—first from the chill, then from relief. He was alive. Thank God, he was alive. Unashamed of the tears on her cheeks, she lifted her face to the sun and began struggling to her feet. Suddenly, East was in front of her. Before she could speak, he pulled her into his arms and held her close against his chest, his voice rumbling low against her ear.

"You did it, Ally. You did it! You saved his life."

She grabbed his arms and pushed herself back.

"No," she said fiercely. "We did it."

At that moment, East couldn't bring himself to speak.

Behind them, the paramedics were strapping the little boy into a basket-like stretcher and starting toward the stairs at the base of the cliff. The crowd moved with them, leaving East and Ally alone on the beach.

She shuddered and pulled the blanket a little closer

around her, but it wasn't enough. The chill was all the way to her bones.

East saw her muscles beginning to spasm, and concern for her health shifted his focus.

"You need to get out of those wet clothes and into something warm and dry."

He took her by the hand as they started toward the steps and she let him lead her as if she were a child. Halfway there, East stopped and picked up their shoes and shirts then glanced at her, as if assuring himself she was still upright.

As they started up the steps, East took her by the elbow, bracing her weight against his body. About halfway up, Ally's legs began to shake, but she kept on climbing, afraid if she stopped, she wouldn't be able to move. Twice East felt her falter, and each time, although he remained silent, the look he gave her was filled with concern. When they reached the top, Ally breathed a shaky sigh of relief. The worst was surely over.

"Ally?"

She managed a smile. "I'm fine," she said, and made it all the way through the lobby before she suddenly stopped and clutched at her pockets. "My room key. It was in my pocket!"

"Wait here," East said, and headed for the desk, returning moments later with a duplicate.

They made it all the way to the bank of elevators before she stumbled. East cursed beneath his breath, punched the button, dumped their shoes and shirts into her hands, and then scooped her into his arms.

"Don't argue," he muttered.

"I didn't say a word," she said, and then leaned her head against his chest, grateful for his strength.

The ride up the elevator was silent. Ally took one look at their reflection in the mirrored car and closed her eyes, unable to face the expression on her own face—or on his. There were emotions she didn't know how to explore without making a fool of herself, or embarrassing him. Moments later, the doors opened and East strode out with her still in his arms.

When they entered her suite, it was impossible to mistake the meaning of the packed suitcases by the door. He stifled a frown and kept on going to the bedroom. He set her down on the side of the bed, only to stalk out, returning shortly with both bags in his hands.

"You'll be needing dry clothes," he said. "Which one are they in?" She pointed to the larger bag. He set it on the bed and then started to leave when she stopped him with one word.

"Wait."

He turned. The look on her face said it all. Seconds later she was in his arms. Pressing kisses across her forehead, then her cheeks, he began to gain sanity only after he realized she hadn't slapped his face.

"God in heaven, I thought you were both—"

Ally put her fingers across his lips. "I'm tougher than I look."

He cupped her face with the palms of his hands, looking deep into her eyes. He saw her pupils dilate, then her lips part. He sighed, then lowered his head, aware that the inevitability of this moment had been upon him since the day he'd first seen her face.

She tasted of seawater and tears, and an innocence that scared him to death. When she leaned into him and moaned, a surge of need came fast. Then she shuddered, and he became aware of her bare skin and wet clothes and he made himself move away.

"You need to get out of those clothes before you get sick," he said, and then leaned down and gave her one last kiss.

She took the kiss as if it were a life-giving drink and wondered if she would survive leaving this man after all.

When he turned her loose, she looked away, suddenly embarrassed that she'd given away too much of herself.

East sighed. He didn't know whether he'd made the situation better or worse, but he did know he would do it again.

"It's going to be okay," he said, and picked up his shirt and shoes.

What's going to be okay? You? Me? Everything? Nothing?

"Oh, sure, I know that," she said, and tried to pretend that she could kiss a man—even if it was Easton Kirby—without coming undone.

"Take a hot shower and get into some dry clothes. When you come out, I'll have something to warm you inside, as well."

She nodded.

"I'm going to go down to the lobby and check with Foster, just to make sure everything is under control. I'll be right back."

"There's no need to—"

East frowned. "I have a need," he said shortly. "So don't argue."

Ally could hardly focus on her shower for thinking about East and needs. It wasn't until she heard the door slam that she remembered the picture. She shivered again. There would be time enough later to show him the picture and the note. Right now, she needed to be warm. She dug through her suitcase, pulled out a clean pair of pants and a shirt, and some fresh underwear, then headed for the bath. It wasn't until she was completely undressed that she realized she needed her toilet articles, which were also packed and in the living room. Wrapping a bath towel around her nudity, she ran into the living room and retrieved the small bag from the floor. As she turned, she caught a flash of movement through the French doors leading out to the terrace and stopped to look, absently noting a large, and rather elegant yacht. It occurred to her then that she'd seen it before and as she watched, the skin on the back of her neck began to crawl. She glanced down at the picture on the table and then back out the window.

Taken from the water. The picture had been taken from the water. From a yacht? What if it had been that one?

"Oh man," she mumbled, and dashed back into her bedroom, frantically throwing clothes aside as she searched for the binoculars she always carried.

Moments later she ran back in the living room with the towel still clutched around her and the binoculars in her hand. Her hands were shaking as she tried to unlatch the exterior door and when it finally gave, she burst out onto the terrace and lifted the binoculars to her face.

It took several seconds before she had them adjusted to the distance, and by then, the yacht was almost around the point. She could see crew moving about, but there were no identifying flags and no name on the side of the boat. Before she could look any further, it disappeared from sight.

Muttering beneath her breath, she retreated back inside and closed the door. It seemed highly unlikely that a rich man should buy such a magnificent toy and then neglect to give it a name. And while she knew there were hundreds of boats that sailed up and down these shores in any given year, instinct told her this one had been different.

"Damn it," she muttered as she tossed the binoculars on the sofa and headed for a much-needed shower.

A short while later, she came out of the bath with the towel wrapped around her again, intent on getting into clean clothes. But she wasn't prepared for the man standing in her room, or the look on his face.

"Oh!" she gasped, clutching the towel a little tighter. "You startled me."

"What the hell is this about?" East asked, and tossed the picture and the note on the bed between them.

She sighed, then reached for her clothes. "You tell me," she said. "It was delivered to the desk this morning. A bellhop brought it up."

East thought of Jonah and his expression darkened. "This isn't good."

"Oh, I don't know," Ally drawled. "I thought they captured your best side. However, had I known, I might have worn a different dress. White rarely photographs well on me."

"Damn it, Ally, this is serious."

"It has to do with Jonah, doesn't it?"

A dark flush spread across his cheeks as he gave her a hard, angry stare.

"Just get dressed," he muttered, and stalked out of the room.

Her shoulders slumped as she dropped to the side of

the bed. "So much for the hour of the heroine. Now it's back to being the bearer of bad news."

East was pacing when Ally walked into the living room. He stopped, picked up a glass of wine from the bar and thrust it into her hands.

"The something warm that I promised you," he muttered.

"Am I to drink it, or drown myself in it?" she drawled.

East jabbed his hands through his hair in an angry gesture, then took a deep breath and made himself calm.

"Look, there are things going on that you don't understand."

"Obviously."

"The picture…it blows your cover…not just for this little job you were sent to do, but for anything else… ever."

"Not necessarily," Ally said, and sniffed the wine before taking a sip. Then she wrinkled her nose and set the glass aside. "I like it sweeter."

"Two hundred and ninety-five dollars a bottle and she wants grape juice," East muttered, then pointed. "Drink the damn stuff anyway."

Ally lifted her chin in gentle defiance. "I may not be wise in the ways of lust and seduction, but I am intelligent enough to know when I don't want to drink. I am tough. I have been in worse situations. I will not succumb to pneumonia or faint."

She moved toward him until there was little but guesswork between them, then jabbed her finger into his chest. "What I do want are some answers. My career is on the line and I don't even know why."

"Ask Jonah."

"He's not here. I'm asking you."

East spun toward the window, his shoulders hunched against the truth of her words. Silence followed, then lengthened. When he finally turned around, it gave him a measure of satisfaction to see that she hadn't moved. In a way, it was the final proof for him that she had more than her intelligence. She had staying power. It was a good trait.

"This changes everything. We need to talk to Jonah," East said.

"Are you going to help him?" Ally asked.

East frowned. "I don't know."

Ally shrugged and moved toward the front door. "Let me know when you do."

East's eyebrows rose. "Where the hell are you going?"

"To get something to eat. I'm starving. Oh, and by the way, the little boy…is he going to be all right?"

East nodded. "Yes. His parents called from the hospital. The boy is in observation, but he's not in any imminent danger."

"That's one good thing for the day, isn't it, East?"

Ally managed a smile. It wasn't much as smiles go, but there was a yearning in it that East couldn't ignore.

"Yes," he said. "It's a very good thing."

She held out her hand. "I'm going to the restaurant now. May I have my new key?"

East dug into his pocket and then handed it over. "So, does this mean you're staying?"

She gave him a slow, studied look and then dropped the key into her pocket.

"Only until you make up your mind—one way or the other."

* * *

Jeff came to in the dark just long enough to realize he couldn't move. Disoriented and sick to his stomach, he had no idea what was happening to him. Then he began to separate other sounds from the rough gasp of his own breath. He was inside a moving vehicle, and from the sound of the high-pitched whine of tires on pavement, moving at a rapid rate of speed. His stomach rolled, and he took a deep breath, willing himself to hang on. He thought about friends at school, his co-workers at the hospital, and then he thought about his dad and wondered if he'd ever see any of them again. Before he could dwell on his situation, the drug that they'd given him pulled him back under and he gratefully gave up the fight.

The next morning, Ally woke to a gray, overcast day. Just the lack of sunshine was enough to make her roll over in bed and try for another hour of sleep. But as soon as she closed her eyes, her mind began to stir. It had been almost twenty-four hours since the picture and the note had been delivered to her room and she had yet to contact Jonah, because when she did, she knew he would pull her out. And therein lay the rub. She didn't want to go. As long as she pretended to herself that East was going to change his mind, it gave her a reason to stay.

She buried her nose in the pillow and squeezed her eyes tight, trying to reclaim the memory of his mouth upon her lips and his hands centered in the middle of her back, but it wouldn't come. She rolled over on her back with a groan and stared up at the ceiling, trying to figure out what it was about the man that was making her nuts. She had seen plenty of good-looking men before and never been bothered with her emotions getting out of control. But with East, it was as if she'd lost every ounce of good sense she'd been born with. Rationally, she knew he was out of her league, but it didn't stop her from wanting, and oh, how she wanted.

Finally, she got up and stomped toward the bathroom. Maybe a hot shower and some food would put her world back on center. A short while later she stopped in the living room and gave herself the once-over before she went down to eat.

Her clothes were nondescript—a pair of well-worn jeans, a white, long-sleeved cotton sweater and her favorite pair of sandals. The only colors on her body were her red toenails and a pale peach gloss on her lips. Her gaze moved to her hair. It was its usual auburn cap of flyaway curls and nothing she could do anything about. With a shrug, she put her key in her pants pocket and slung her purse over her shoulder, then left the suite.

As she exited the elevator, she automatically looked toward the desk, hoping she might see East. He was nowhere in sight. She kept on walking, telling herself it didn't matter. When she exited the lobby onto the terrace, a sharp breeze almost took her breath away and she did a quick about-face and chose to eat indoors, instead.

She was seated at a table by the window and giving her order to a waiter, when East suddenly appeared.

"Eating alone?" he asked.

She handed the waiter her menu as he left, then focused her gaze on East. It had been more than twenty-four hours since they'd spoken and she was a little surprised by his presence.

"Not if you join me," she said.

He pulled out the chair to her left and sat with his back to the view.

"Didn't you want to order something?" she asked.

"I already did."

She arched an eyebrow. "Pretty sure of yourself, aren't you?"

He shrugged. "If I wasn't here, I'd be somewhere else. They would have found me."

Ally dropped her elbows onto the table and then rested her chin in her hands.

"Got anything you want to tell me?"

He stifled a smile as he reached for his napkin, unfolding it carefully, then draping it across his slacks.

"We're out of peanut butter."

She laughed and the sound dragged itself across East's emotions. He'd never heard her laugh before—not like this—uninhibited and all the way from her gut.

Still chuckling, she shuffled through her place setting of silverware and absently dropped her napkin in her lap.

"Okay, I get the message, but I've got one for you. I'm leaving tomorrow, with or without you."

East's heart skipped a beat. He'd gotten too used to seeing her around. The last twenty-four hours had been some of the emptiest times of his life and the thought of never seeing her again seemed impossible to consider. Within a very few days, she'd become someone special. It shouldn't have happened. He'd been so careful over the years to stay clear of emotional entanglements and now he felt ties to a woman he'd done nothing but kiss—and only once at that. If a single kiss could tie him in knots, he shuddered to think what would happen if they ever made love.

"Look, I—" In the middle of a word, his cell phone rang. "Excuse me," he said, and took the call.

"This is Kirby."

"And this is your worst nightmare," a man said.

East stiffened. "Who is this?"

"It's not my identity that matters. It's the identity of my hostage that you should be concerned with."

"What are you saying?" East muttered, then stood abruptly and walked toward the solitude of the terrace, unaware that Ally was right behind him.

"We've got your kid, and if you want to get him back alive, then you'd better do as I say."

East's mind went blank. Jeff? Someone had kidnapped Jeff? If this was so, he needed to catch them off guard. He laughed, a cold, ugly bark that ripped up his throat as he stepped out onto the terrace facing the wind.

"Look, you lying son of a bitch, I don't believe you."

"Just give your kid a call. See if he answers the phone," the man said.

East was thinking fast, laying a bet with himself that the kidnappers wouldn't have known Jeff's schedule well enough to know when East was bluffing.

"Hell, no. He's not going to answer his phone because he's backpacking up in the hills and won't be home for a good three days, so don't pull that crap on me."

Then, before he could change his mind, he disconnected, fully aware that he was gambling with Jeff's life.

"Ah, God," he groaned, and covered his face. What if he'd just signed his son's death warrant?

Ally grabbed him by the arm. "What?" she cried. "What's happening?"

East turned, then looked down at the phone in his hand as if it had become something foul.

"I think someone's kidnapped my son."

Chapter 7

Ally gasped. First the picture and the note—now this. They should have been expecting something more to occur, but how could they have guessed it would affect his son? She thought of the phone in her dresser.

"We've got to tell Jonah," she said and started to leave when East grabbed her by the arm.

"No! We wait. I just gambled my son's life on the hope that they would let me talk to him just to prove he was there."

Ally nodded as her estimation of Easton Kirby rose. That was a tough call to make, but one of the gutsiest moves she'd ever seen. And as she watched his face getting paler by the moment, she knew it was costing this man way more than he had to lose. She laid her hand in the middle of his back.

"Then we wait."

East turned toward the sea, his knuckles white from the death grip he had on the railing. "Now do you understand why I told Jonah no? This is a perfect example of why I refused him. You can't have a family and be in this business. If it doesn't kill you, it will damn sure kill them."

Ally had no answer because she knew it was the truth. And the wait continued...

Less than five minutes later, East's phone rang. The moment he answered, he accepted the fact that he was mixed up in Jonah's mess now, whether he wanted it or not.

"This is Kirby," he said shortly.

A soft chuckle rippled through his ear and sent shock waves of panic skittering through his mind.

"And a gutsy bastard, too, aren't you?"

"Who are you?" East snapped.

"I'm not important, but the people who have your son are not your usual society-page gentlemen, so I strongly suggest you don't hang up on me again."

"If they have my son as you claim, then somebody better be proving it to me, and I don't mean some recorded little bit of his voice," East snapped. "That proves nothing about his still being alive. I want to talk to him, and I want to ask questions that only he can answer, or we have nothing to discuss."

"You're not calling the shots," the man said. "I am. And it will be proven to you all too soon. However, let me outline what it is that I want from you before we hang up. That way when you get your call, you will already know where we stand."

"I'm listening," East growled.

"I want Jonah," the man whispered, and the hate in his voice was impossible for East to mistake.

"What the hell do you expect me to do about it?" East said. "I have no idea who or where he is. No one does."

"But you know how to contact him," the man said. "And I know that he's contacted you. I also know that he's sent you a pretty little helper to bring me down, but it isn't going to happen."

The information the man unwittingly gave was important, because it told East that the man wasn't as thorough as he believed himself to be. Ally hadn't come to help, she'd come to talk him into something he'd already refused.

"So what?" East said. "Just because I could talk to him means nothing. I have no way of ferreting information out of a ghost."

The man chuckled again. "Ghosts aren't as elusive as one might think. However, that's not the point. The point is, you will work with me, getting me certain information and I will take it from there."

East inhaled slowly. "You expect me to steal documents and information that would point back to Jonah as being the thief? That could take weeks, even months to set up."

"I knew you were a smart man. You catch on fast, and you don't have weeks or months to do it. I'm no longer a patient man."

"I won't do it."

"Yes, you will, if you want to see your son alive."

"I don't know that you even have him."

"You will," the man snapped, suddenly tired of the game. "And know this, I will be calling you again and when I do, you'd better have what I want."

Startled by the abruptness of the disconnect, he inhaled sharply, then turned toward Ally, his jaw set and clenched. "Son of a bitch. The sorry, son of a bitch. He shouldn't have messed with what's mine."

At that moment, Ally knew that in his mind, Easton Kirby had already vaulted the distance from hotel manager back to an agent for SPEAR. But he wasn't doing it for Jonah.

Jeff had been awake for what seemed like hours, although he couldn't be sure. Without anything to help him gauge time or distance, he had no idea how long he'd been unconscious or where the kidnappers were taking him. At first, he'd been unable to understand why he'd be anyone's target for ransom. He didn't have money and neither did his dad—at least not that kind of money. With the passing of time, the drug began to lose its control and with cognizance came clearer thinking.

It occurred to him that he might have been snatched because of what his dad used to do. East had never elaborated on it, and Jeff had known not to ask, but he did know that his father used to be a spy of sorts. He couldn't help thinking that he had become the pawn in an ugly game of payback. And while he knew the deduction was pretty far-fetched, so was the fact that he'd been abducted. However, he didn't think he was in immediate danger of being killed. At least not yet. If that had been the case, they would have done it sooner and certainly closer to home. Why take the risk of being stopped by a highway patrol and being discovered in possession of a bound man in a trunk?

A short while later, the van took a sharp turn. Unable to brace himself, the trunk slid and Jeff slid with it, slamming his face against the trunk with a thump. Stunned by the unexpectedness of the pain, he groaned as the wounds on his already swollen mouth reopened. Cursing the driver and the world in general, he spit blood and prayed for the ride to end.

The ride then became a constant series of jarring bumps, leading him to assume they were now on a dirt road. He tried to measure time in the hope he could gauge some kind of distance, but was without success. It seemed endless and he was in desperate need of water, and a bathroom.

Just when he thought his misery would never end, the van rolled to a stop, and the moment it did, Jeff's heart skipped a beat. Had he guessed wrong about them keeping him alive? Was this the end after all? When he heard their voices, and then the sound of the door sliding back on the van, he braced himself for the worst.

Thin, gray clouds scattered themselves across the sky like trailing threads from an unraveling piece of fabric, forming a dramatic backdrop for the man who strode out of the weathered frame house in the middle of the Brotherhood compound. Caleb Carpenter was tall and rangy with piercing blue eyes and hair that was as short and dark as his temper. He glared at the trio getting out of the van.

"Elmore, where the hell have you been? You're four hours late."

Elmore Todd jerked to attention. "Sir, it wasn't our fault. There was some sort of roadblock outside of Reno. We had to take another route to safeguard the target."

"Roadblock? What kind of roadblock?"

The second kidnapper, who called himself Beau, backed up Elmore's explanation.

"It had nothing to do with us, Caleb, I swear. We heard later on the radio that they were looking for some crazy carjacker who'd killed a woman and her kid."

The last one, a skinny misfit of a man who answered to the name of Phil, added his two cents to the story.

"Yeah, and can you beat it? The car he jacked was a lousy hunk of metal. You'd think if you was gonna kill for a car, you'd have the sense to pick one that was worth something."

Resisting the urge to deck Phil on general principles, Caleb pivoted sharply and motioned to the men behind him.

"Get that trunk out of the van now! I need to see what we're dealing with here." And then he fixed the three with a hard-edged stare. "And the goods better be in pristine condition as requested, or someone's going to be sorry."

Elmore paled. "He put up a hell of a fight."

Caleb's lips thinned into a grimace of a smile. "There were three of you and one of him, what the hell kind of a fight could he make?"

"Well, you said his daddy was some kind of a Fed. He must have been the one who taught him all that karate." Beau blustered, and hawked and spit just to give himself time to think. Then he added, "Besides, I never did trust a man who fought with his feet 'stead of his fists."

Caleb cursed beneath his breath as he pointed to the trunk that was now on the ground.

"Open it," he ordered.

The lid came up, revealing the man within. The first thing Caleb saw was fresh blood. He doubled his fist and pivoted sharply, nailing Elmore Todd in the nose. Blood spurted, rocking the man back on his heels. The other two took a nervous step backward, afraid they were next. To their relief, Caleb seemed to be through distributing punishment.

"Next time I send you on a mission, I expect orders to be followed."

"Yes, sir," Elmore muttered, and clamped a handkerchief over his mouth and nose to staunch the flow.

"Get him out," Caleb said, pointing toward the man in the trunk.

Moments later, Jeff Kirby found himself face-to-face with the man in charge. His legs were numb and kept threatening to fold and his throat was tight and scratchy, but he was in so much misery and pain that he was past being scared. He squinted at the man they called Caleb through a half-swollen eye.

"I want a drink of water and a bathroom, and not in that order."

Caleb Carpenter froze. The last thing he'd expected was a victim making demands. And what a pitiful victim he was—both fresh and dried blood dotted his clothing, and his face was swollen and bruised. Yet still bound, the kid was staring him straight in the eye.

A slow grin spread across Caleb's face. "The hell you say," he said softly, then pointed to the man nearest him. "You heard the man. Get that damned tape off his hands and feet and take him to the john, then get him a drink. He's thirsty."

Later, Jeff would look back on that moment and realize how fortunate he'd been in not getting himself shot. Every man there had been wearing some kind of uniform and was armed to the teeth. And the tattoo he'd seen on the man they called Elmore was on posters all over the place. Added to that, all of the vehicles in the compound had Idaho plates. At least now he knew where he was—sort of—and he knew his kidnappers' faces. But that last bit of knowledge was what worried him most. Granted he was still alive, and with a fresh meal starting to digest in his belly, but if they planned to let him go at some future date, then why had they let him see their faces?

Later, he paced the small, six-by-six room that they'd locked him in until his legs ached and the bottoms of his feet began to burn. Exhausted, he dropped onto the single piece of furniture in the room, an old army cot, and stretched out. How in hell would anyone ever find him in this godforsaken place? He might as well be on the moon.

Time passed and the air began to chill as the day turned to night. He huddled upon the cot without benefit of blankets until anger resurfaced, then he crawled off the cot and began pacing to stay warm.

Caleb Carpenter was on a mission. The phone call he'd just received left him with a rather nasty task to perform. And while it was a bit unexpected, he had not argued with the man who'd given the order. It would seem that the father of the kidnap victim wasn't being as pliable as they'd expected. He had demanded proof that his son was still alive and well, or they could all go to hell. Although they were on different sides of the war, there was a part of Caleb Carpenter that admired that kind of grit. What he had to do, however, was make sure that the kid didn't give anything away, and that was what worried him. Jeff Kirby was acting more like an unhappy guest at a cut-rate motel, rather than a victim. Caleb shook his head in disgust as he headed toward the makeshift armory where Jeff was being held. It was a shame that their need for money to fund their program had thrown them in with such a despicable despot. Kidnapping wasn't Caleb's chosen method of protesting and in his opinion, there wasn't one admirable thing about the man behind this mess. The Brotherhood of Blood operated on the age-old principles of the right to bear arms and a refusal to bow down to an oppressive government, while the man with the money seemed bent on nothing but personal revenge. It was not a trait Caleb found admirable or productive. But they'd taken the money and therefore, would do the job. He was not a man who went back on his word.

As he strode into the armory, two of the men on guard jumped to their feet.

"Morning, sir," they said, and all but stood at attention.

He nodded, then pointed toward the locked door. "Open it and bring him out."

They did as they were told, entering together, then coming out moments later with the young man clutched between them.

Caleb eyed the man's wounds, judging them to be healing, then motioned for Jeff to come forward.

"You, come here," he said.

"The name's Jeff."

Caleb's eyes narrowed thoughtfully. The kid was slick, he'd give him that. Being on a first-name basis was the first step in bonding. Maybe he thought it would make it easier to stay alive.

"You've got a phone call to make," Caleb said. "And

if you want your daddy to keep breathing, you won't try to be a smart-mouth and give away something you shouldn't, understand?"

Jeff's pulse skittered, then settled. "You want me to talk to him?"

Caleb nodded.

"It seems he doesn't trust our accommodations and wants to make sure we have clean sheets on the bed."

To Caleb's surprise, Jeff pulled his swollen lips into what passed as a grin, upping his admiration for the young man even more. Without giving away any of his thoughts, he dialed the number that had been given him, then waited for Easton Kirby to answer.

When the phone rang, East stiffened, then let it ring again.

Ally stared. "East?"

On the third ring, he answered, his voice deep and angry, his w̶   ̶d

"This is K

Caleb Ca   m-self that the   he in control.

"You wanted to speak w   t brief, and don't forget I'll be listening." Then he thrust the phone at Jeff. "Remember what I said."

Jeff took the phone. "Dad?"

East's knees buckled, but there was no other indication of how deeply he was moved.

"Did they hurt you?" he asked.

"Not enough to count."

East cursed. "Are they listening?"

"Like vultures."

East sighed. "I'm so sorry this happened to you."

"Yeah, I really crashed and burned this time, didn't I, Dad? Unlike you, I won't be able to walk out of this on my own."

East's pulse jumped. Jeff was trying to tell him something, but what?

"Don't give up on me, boy. I'll get you out. I swear to God, I'll find a way."

Caleb yanked the phone from Jeff's hand. "Sorry, Daddy, but your change just ran out. Now I suggest you do as the big man ordered if you want your son back alive."

He punched the button and disconnected.

East dropped the phone into his pocket and turned to face Ally.

"What did Jeff say?" she asked. "Is he all right? Did they hurt him?"

"I'll tell you everything later. Now we call Jonah."

She sighed. This was not how it was supposed to be. "In my room," she said shortly.

He followed her toward the elevators, while hundreds of miles away, Caleb Carpenter was putting his own set of plans into motion. He turned to his men.

"It's time," he said, pointing toward Jeff. "Put him in the hole."

The hole? Jeff spun, bracing himself for another unknown, but it was no use. He was surrounded by armed men and with nowhere to go but where he was led. They stopped about a hundred yards away from the main cluster of buildings and began moving aside a camouflage net lying across a stack of boxes. When Jeff saw the metal door beneath, he stifled a groan.

The door opened silently on well-oiled hinges, revealing a steep set of steps leading into a dark, ominous cavern.

Jeff frowned. *Another dark hole? What is it with these people and lights?*

"Get in," Elmore said, and gave Jeff a sharp push.

He staggered forward, then took his first step down.

"Hurry up. We ain't got all day."

Jeff braced himself with both hands as he started down the stairs.

"Where's the light?" he asked.

"You get a minute to orient yourself and then the door goes shut, so stop talking and start looking."

Jeff's heart skipped a beat as an old memory from his childhood suddenly surfaced. There was a man—an angry man—shoving him into a closet and slamming the door. He could remember the feel of old shoes beneath his hands and the scent of dust and leather.

Not this. God, not this.

But as Jeff reached the bottom of the steps and began to look around, it became all too obvious that this was real. There was a commode, a cot, a large water can, and a small, spindly table stacked with some sort of containers of non-perishable food inside a concrete-lined hole barely tall enough for him to stand. He caught a glimpse of a small, narrow tube poking through the ceiling and assumed it was an air vent, then saw a logo on one of the small containers just as the door began to shut. MRE—meals ready to eat. If it hadn't been so dismal, he would have laughed. Again, his creature comforts were going to be compliments of army surplus and Uncle Sam. He wondered if his dad would get the clue that he'd been trying to send, and then they closed the door and everything went black.

* * *

East shut the door abruptly as they entered Ally's room.

"How do you contact him?" he asked.

"Wait here," Ally said, and dashed toward her bedroom, coming back moments later with the phone that Jonah had sent her. She pressed the Send button as instructed, let it ring two times, then disconnected.

"Now we wait," she said.

East had worked too many years under Jonah to question the procedures. Instead, he began to pace.

"You don't tell him what's happened to Jeff."

Ally's mouth dropped. "But—"

"No!" East said, raising his voice. "If he knows, he'll put somebody else on the case because it's become too personal for me."

"But isn't it?" Ally asked.

"Hell, yes," East said. "And that's exactly why I'm doing it. Not for him. Not for Uncle Sam."

"Then what do you tell him?" she asked. "And you'd better decide quickly, because he'll be calling within the minute."

"As far as you know, I have decided to help. You tell Jonah that, then let me talk. After that, you can go on to your next assignment and leave the rest of this mess to me."

Ally's face turned a quick, angry red. "Leave? Now? What kind of a person do you think I am?"

East paused, surprised by her vehemence. "This is no longer any of—"

"You can't do this by yourself and you know it," she snapped. "You've been out of the business too long.

Besides, don't forget my intelligence. Use it. Use me. However, whenever. Just let me help."

East's expression shifted. Not much, but enough to let Ally know that she'd gotten to him. For now, it was enough. Before they could go any further, the phone suddenly rang.

"Answer it," East said. "Then tell him I want to talk."

Ally put the phone to her ear. "Hello, this is Corbin."

A deep, gravely voice rattled across Ally's eardrum. "Talk to me."

"He's in."

Ally heard a swift intake of breath, and then a moment of silence.

"Sir? Are you there? He wants to talk."

"Yes. Of course. Put him on."

She handed the phone to East.

"Jonah, you are a persuasive man."

"I'm sorry it became necessary," Jonah said.

East bit back an angry retort. "Yes, so am I," he muttered. "However, down to business. I'll need information on everything that has occurred to date. Get it to me. Also, I may need some vital information from you later. If so, I will track the transmissions in hopes of finding the source."

Jonah frowned. This wasn't what he had planned. "I don't think—"

East interrupted. "You haven't been successful so far, so why not try things my way?"

Silence lengthened into a quiet that began to make East nervous. If Jonah didn't go for this, then how could he bargain with the kidnapper to buy Jeff some time?

"Done," Jonah finally said. "But do you have the expertise to—"

"Your messenger. I'm keeping your messenger."

This time, Jonah was silent for an even longer time. Finally, he spoke. "Why her?"

"You trusted her," East said. "And so do I."

"But she doesn't know why she was sent to persuade you."

"She will before we start, or it won't work."

Jonah's hesitation was brief. "All right, but you know the drill."

A cold smile broke the somberness of East's expression, although Ally was the only one to see it.

"Oh yeah, I know the drill," East said. "If caught or captured, it's my head on a platter, not yours, because you do not exist."

"I will be in touch," Jonah said.

"By this phone?"

"Yes. Now put Agent Corbin back on the phone."

East handed the phone to Ally. "He wants to talk to you."

"Sir?"

"He needs help," Jonah said. "Whatever he asks, whatever it takes, it's his."

"And that includes me?" Ally asked.

"Yes."

Ally hid a quick sigh of relief. "I'll do what I can."

"Let it be enough," Jonah said, and hung up.

Chapter 8

East moved through the dining area, then the lobby, heading toward his office with Ally in tow.

"Now tell me what Jeff said," she demanded.

East lowered his voice as they continued to move down a hallway past a series of rooms.

"He said something odd about having crashed and burned, then added that he wouldn't be able to walk out of it like I did. I think he was trying to tell me something, but I'm not sure what."

"Crash and burn? Have you ever been in a wreck?"

"We'll talk inside," he said, as they reached his office. East opened the door, stepping aside, letting her enter first. Once the door was firmly shut, he strode toward his desk and picked up the phone.

"Stella, have all of the business calls routed to Foster's office. I don't want to be disturbed."

"Yes, sir," the operator said.

East hung up.

"Wrecks. We were talking about wrecks," Ally prompted.

East sighed in frustration. "Yes, but which one? I've been in several car wrecks, a couple of plane wrecks, and even one train wreck."

Ally stared. "What are you...your own bad luck charm? Good grief, it's not that you've endured all that so much as you're still here to tell the tale."

East shrugged. "Occupational hazard."

"So how many of those crashed and burned."

A frown creased his forehead. "Maybe three...no four, counting that chopper that went down up north."

She had confiscated a piece of paper from his desk and was furiously writing as he continued to speak.

"And of those, how many did you walk away from?" she asked.

East was beginning to appreciate the beauty of Ally Corbin's mind.

"Two."

"And they were where?"

"A car wreck in upstate New York and a chopper crash in southern Idaho."

"New York and Idaho, two possibles," Ally muttered.

"Those are far-fetched assumptions."

"There's no law against assuming," she countered. "Besides, it's more than you had five minutes ago."

He shook his head and almost smiled. "What did Jonah tell you when he sent you here?"

"My mission was to persuade you to change your status with SPEAR from inactive to active."

"He didn't tell you why, or give you any deadlines?"

"No."

East combed his fingers through his hair in frustration, then began to pace.

"Look," Ally said. "I said I'd help, and I will. In fact I want to. I feel as if, in some way, my coming here has precipitated what has happened to your son."

East shook his head. "No, it wasn't just your appearance, although it's a part of the whole. It started with the reason for Jonah's request."

"What reason?"

East hesitated, then shoved aside his reluctance to break his silence. Jonah's situation was secondary to getting Jeff back safe and he'd do whatever it took to make that happen.

"Someone is trying to take Jonah down, and if they succeed, they'll take SPEAR with him."

Ally's mouth dropped. "Oh my God, you can't be serious!" Then she gave herself a quick thump on the forehead. "That's a stupid thing to say. I'm sorry. Please continue."

"A couple of weeks ago I got a phone call from Jonah. He told me of several recent incidents of people being arrested for treason that all pointed back to him."

"Is this national or global?" Ally asked.

"I got the impression that it was global," East said. "I'll know more when I get the file on the incidents. I think it's only a matter of time before his anonymity is blown and he's arrested, unless he can find out who's trying to discredit him. Because of the nature of the things that were being done, he had reason to suspect everyone, even the people within his organization."

Ally's expression lightened as understanding

dawned. "And because you've been out of the loop, so to speak, he felt safe in assuming it wouldn't be you."

East nodded. "But I refused—for a number of reasons, not the least of which was this monkey of guilt I've had on my back for ten years. Back in my operative days, I accidentally killed a kid on a bike during a high-speed chase. It was ruled accidental, but it didn't change the fact that the kid was dead. Just thinking about returning to that life made me sick to my stomach. I didn't want to be responsible for another innocent's death."

Ally hurt for the pain she saw in his eyes and impulsively put her hand on his forearm. "I knew about that. Everyone in the department knows why you left and no one blames you. But you do know it wasn't your fault."

"Knowing and accepting are two different things. And there was Jeff. I'd adopted him after I'd taken this job. I couldn't see jeopardizing what family life I have now to go back underground. Not even for Jonah."

Ally sighed. "If I came across too militant before, I apologize. I didn't understand."

"You were only doing your job and Jonah is desperate and with good reason. But the son of a bitch who wants Jonah is obviously willing to sacrifice anyone to get the job done. Somehow he found out that Jonah had come to me, and when you showed up a short while later, I suppose he assumed we'd be working together to track him. He said as much when he called."

Ally shook her head. "That doesn't make sense. There are less than half a dozen people within the entire government that even know of SPEAR's existence. That should narrow the field."

"You're forgetting the people within the organization, itself. Add a good two hundred names to the list and we're getting close."

"But we don't even know who Jonah is. How could anyone possibly have a grudge against a man we don't know?"

"That's just it," East said. "Someone does know who he is, and that someone has a personal axe to grind. The problem is, he's willing to bury anyone, including my son, to get what he wants."

"How are you going to make this work? Won't Jonah suspect something? And even worse, what about the kidnapper? If he thinks you're trying to find Jeff…" She stopped. "You are going to look for your son, aren't you?"

"Oh, yeah," East said. "Him and him alone. If the kidnapper happens to fall into the path, then so much the better for Jonah. But I have no intention of trying to take down a faceless man to save another faceless man—not even for God and country. As for Jonah, he's given me free rein, or at least he will, whether he knows it now or not. Bottom line… I'm going after Jeff, nothing more."

Ally nodded. "Then that's what we'll do."

It was the word *we* that got to him. East hadn't had anyone at his back for so long that the simple thought of not being alone brought him up short. He looked at Ally—really looked—for the first time since she'd revealed her true self, and saw, not the young, uncertain female she'd been, but a strong, confident woman willing to go the distance. This time it was he who reached out and touched. He cupped the side of her face with his palm, feeling the thread of a steady pulse beneath his thumb.

"Thank you."

Ally's heartbeat fluttered. She had to remind herself that this wasn't a precursor to intimacy, but rather a gesture of thanks.

"I haven't done anything to help you yet," she said. "But I can promise you I will."

"You're wrong," he said softly. "You're here. That's what counts."

It came before daybreak; a fat, red, white and blue package by overnight express and East knew when he opened it that he was opening the proverbial can of worms. But what was inside was immaterial to where he was going. He'd delegated all his duties to Foster Martin the night before without a worry. Foster had shown an amazing change of character since the child's rescue from the sea, and the fact that he'd restrained from questioning East's decision to leave him in charge gave East a small measure of relief.

Afterward, East had gone to his apartment and packed for an indefinite leave of absence. But it was the knot in his gut and the gun in his suitcase that kept him awake most of the night. Every time he closed his eyes, he saw his son's face. It was all he could do to wait until dawn to head for L.A. And even though he'd tossed and turned, there was one redeeming fact that had kept him just that little bit sane; the knowledge that he wasn't facing this alone. But morning had come, and with it the packet he'd been waiting for.

Now, he tossed the file into his bag, zipped it shut, then reached for the phone. Ally answered on the first ring.

"I'm ready," she said.

"Meet you downstairs."

They hung up without saying goodbye and headed for the door, each focused on their own agenda. East was going to what he assumed would be the scene of the crime, and Ally was going to pick it apart. Between them, they would surely find something that would give them a place to start.

It was almost noon by the time they reached L.A. Traffic was jammed on the exit that East normally used, forcing him to drive on, and he muttered beneath his breath knowing that it would take longer to backtrack to Jeff's apartment.

"What a mess," Ally said.

"That's L.A."

"When I have a home, it's not going to be in a city," she muttered, and cast a wary eye out the window as they drove past a man and a woman who were standing on the shoulder of the road and screaming at each other beside a stalled car.

East gave her a curious look, then returned his attention to the traffic, but it had set a picture in his mind that he couldn't shake. Ally in a kitchen. Ally in a garden. Ally rocking babies.

He blinked. Where the hell had that last one come from? He decided to change subjects.

"What's your favorite food?" he asked. "Besides waffles with peanut butter and jelly, that is?"

"Anything, as long as it's not raw meat or made out of tofu, why?"

East grinned. "A woman after my own heart. And I asked because I'm starving. If I know Jeff, there will be nothing in his refrigerator but beer and a piece of week-old pizza." His grin faded. "I was coming up next week for a visit. He wanted steak."

Ally didn't take her eyes off the road. "We'll find him," she said. "Do you want to eat now, or go straight to Jeff's apartment?"

"Now's good, why?"

She pointed to a sign up ahead. "How about barbeque?"

He swerved into the right-hand lane and began to slow down. Moments later, they were out of the car and following the aroma of hickory-smoked meat. Ally tripped as she started to step up the curb and East grabbed her.

"You all right?" he asked, clutching her arm as he turned her to face him.

There was concern in his eyes as he waited for her answer, and all the while Ally was trying to form the word, she couldn't help thinking that once he'd looked at her with a different expression on his face.

"Ally?"

"Yes, of course. Just clumsy, I guess," and quickly pulled away before she made a fool of herself all over again.

East frowned as he followed her into the restaurant. To his surprise, they were seated almost immediately and he soon forgot the moment as they sat down.

"I hope this is a sign, because this is a first," he said.

"What's a first?"

"Since we've met, you fixed the hotel computer, saved a little boy's life and the hotel from a possible lawsuit, and now we've just walked into an L.A. eatery at noontime without a reservation and were seated without a wait. I'm thinking that you're my lucky charm."

"There's no such thing as luck."

"Excuse me?"

"It's all about the law of averages—you know, being in the right place at the right time. It has nothing to do with luck."

He leaned across the table and took her by the hand.

"It's difficult for you, isn't it?"

She looked down at her menu, pretending to study it as she spoke.

"What's difficult?"

"Accepting compliments."

"No, I don't think—"

"Ally."

She sighed, then laid her menu down and looked up.

"What?"

"This may offend you, but in my opinion, your parents need a swift kick in the butt."

It was the last thing she had expected him to say. Her eyes widened and her lips parted, but for the life of her, she couldn't think of a thing to say. All she could do was savor the knowledge that someone cared—and not about what she could do, but about the way that she felt. Struggling with her emotions, she began to scan the menu anew and found herself looking at the words through a blur.

"Do you know what you want?" East asked.

She looked up, the word *you* on the tip of her tongue, and then nodded.

"I'll have the chopped brisket in a sandwich, an order of fries and a gallon of iced tea."

"Gallon?"

She pursed her lips. "A mere figure of speech." She pointed to a small pitcher of sauce sitting between a pair of salt and pepper shakers. "I can tell by the scent of the sauce that it's hot."

"Is that okay?" he asked.

"Oh, yes, I like it hot."

East's mind went blank and he was still staring at what looked to be a small freckle on the right side of her mouth when a waiter appeared to take their order.

The closer they came to Jeff's apartment, the tighter the knot drew in East's gut. He had no idea what he'd find inside, nor was he even certain that this was where Jeff had been abducted, but it was a place to start. By the time they parked in the parking lot, he'd gone completely silent.

Ally could only imagine the fear that must be going through East's mind and when they got to the door of Jeff's apartment she knew she had to say something to break the tension between them.

"I have a forensics kit in my backpack. If need be, I can do a thorough sweep of the place."

East gave her a new look of appreciation, then nodded. "Yes, bring it in. We can't involve the police. Which reminds me, I've got to talk to someone at UCLA Medical Center, or they might put out a missing person's report on him and blow everything out of the water."

As they entered, East caught himself holding his breath as he flipped on the light switch with the end of a ballpoint pen so as not to disturb any fingerprints. He exhaled on a slow, angry breath. Even though the furniture was in place, he could see signs of destruction.

"There's broken glass beneath this chair," Ally said, squatting down and pointing to a couple of small, glistening shards. Without touching them, she gazed about the room, looking at everything from this level and then suddenly focused on a dark smudge below a desk near the wall.

"East." She pointed.

He moved in that direction, then squatted, briefly touching the edge of the smudge. It was dry and flaky, but he didn't have to test the stain for identification. He'd seen enough dried blood in his days to recognize it.

"Son of a bitch."

"It doesn't have to mean it was Jeff's," she said. "Remember, you've talked to him, so whatever happened to him was not life threatening."

He exhaled slowly, reminding himself that she was right, then stood abruptly. As he started to turn away, something about the smear caught his attention and he stepped to the side then looked at it again. Suddenly, his heart skipped a beat. There were letters traced in the blood.

"Ally, get over here. Tell me if you see what I see."

She stood, then hurried over to where East was standing.

"What?" she asked.

He shook his head. "Just look. Tell me what you see." Then he stepped aside to give her room.

Ally glanced at the smear then past it, thinking that East had seen something else, something that she'd missed. But it was quickly apparent that there was nothing beneath the desk but the smear. She stepped to one side for a different view, and almost immediately, a name appeared in the smudge.

"A name! He wrote a name in the blood!"

East nodded with satisfaction. At least he hadn't been imagining it.

"That first one is a *B* for sure," Ally said.

"And the second is definitely an *O*," East added. "But the last one isn't as clear. It looks a little bit like a *P*... no, maybe it's a—"

"It's a *B*," Ally said. "I think it's a *B*, too." Then she looked at East. "Bob? Does that make sense to you?"

"No," East said, frowning in frustration. "Who the hell is Bob? Damn, this couldn't be much more generic."

"It's still something," she said. "Don't touch anything else until I get back, okay? I'm going to get my camera and the forensics kit out of my bag."

She headed for the bag she'd dropped by the door, leaving East alone with his thoughts, and they weren't very good. As he moved about the room, he found a large amount of broken glass in a wastebasket, and the lamp sitting on the end table beside the sofa was missing a bulb. When he looked closer, he noticed that the base of a broken bulb was still screwed into the socket. Only the globe was missing. He stopped and pivoted about the room, searching walls, windows and doors. There was a blank space on the wall where a picture had once hung and what appeared to be another smear of blood on the doorjamb leading to the hall. This made no sense. Why go to all the trouble to kidnap someone and then try to clean up the place, as if it had not happened— especially when he'd already received a ransom demand?

As he stood, contemplating the oddity of the clues, it occurred to him again that the man who'd made the demands had not been the one who'd done the snatch. It was as if the people who'd physically taken Jeff had been acting under orders rather than playing it by ear. No one in the heat of the moment of a crime is going to stop and clean up the scene unless they've been told to do so, or unless they're trying to wipe away fingerprints. And, too many things had been handled in the act of cleaning up to let East believe that these criminals had not been wearing gloves. The kidnapping had been too intricately planned. No one connected with this was going to be that stupid.

Besides that, there were the phone calls he'd received—first those from the man who'd made the demands, then the one from Jeff, himself. And the time between the calls was even more proof. If Jeff was with the mastermind, then why the long lapses between calls? The longer he stood there, the more certain he became that Jeff was being held in one place, while the real man behind the crime was in another.

"Got it!" Ally announced.

She began unpacking the kit, her expression a study in concentration. Only once did she look up, and that was to ask East a question.

"Are Jeff's fingerprints on file anywhere?"

East nodded. "Unfortunately, yes. Before I found him, he'd had several run-ins with the police. Nothing serious, but very typical, homeless-kid-on-the-street stuff."

Ally nodded. "Good," she muttered, and set to work.

As East watched, the irony of it hit him. The mere fact that Jeff had ever been arrested would play an integral part in a process of elimination that might help them find his kidnappers, instead. Jeff's prints were on file. If they got lucky, maybe the other prints would belong to a known felon and they would have a place to start looking.

Several hours passed before Ally was satisfied that she'd gathered all the possible forensic evidence. She and East had worked head-to-head, speaking only in short questions and answers while taking blood samples and dusting for fingerprints on every imaginable surface, including the glass shards East had found in the wastebaskets. But now they were through. Ally had a knot in the muscles between her shoulder blades, and the beginnings of a miserable headache. The tension lines between East's eyebrows had deepened perceptibly.

East glanced at his watch, surprised to see how long they'd been working. He stepped back as Ally strode past him, heading toward the mini-lab she'd set up on the kitchen table. He saw the strain on her face before he felt his own and knew that they would have to stop, at least for a while. Burning out before they'd barely started would do no one any good, especially Jeff. He followed her into the kitchen.

"Ally…"

She laid down the evidence bags she was carrying and readjusted her microscope before reaching for a chair, unaware that East had called her name.

He smiled crookedly, wondering what it would take to get her attention.

"Ally, I'm talking to you."

She bent down to get a fresh set of slides from her carryall when East grabbed her by the shoulders and spun her around.

She'd been so deep in thought that she'd almost forgotten she wasn't alone. His touch, then that slow, husky drawl startled her enough that she gasped.

"What?"

"Sorry. I didn't mean to scare you, but you've been tuning me out for quite some time now."

She flushed and then smiled an apology. "Sorry. I get so focused when I work that I've been accused of forgetting to breathe."

"Focus is good, but there's a time for everything, and I think we both need a break."

"But the—"

He put a finger on the center of her mouth, stopping her from finishing her sentence. He'd only meant to tease, but the slight tremble of those soft, shapely lips set his own head spinning. He looked down at her face, at the startled, almost fearful expression on her face, and he groaned.

"Don't look at me like I'm going to eat you alive," he said.

"Sometimes I think I'll die if you don't." The moment she said it, she paled. "I didn't mean to say that out loud," she muttered as she tore herself free from his grasp and reached for the slides once again. "You need to leave. I can't concentrate when you're standing over my shoulder."

But East didn't move. He was still digesting the slip of her tongue. Finally, he shook his head in wonder and touched the back of her head, fingering the feathery curls at the soft nape of her neck.

"You can fuss and prickle at me all you want, Ally, but you can't ignore what you said."

She looked up, glaring. "No, but if you were a gentleman, you would."

He tilted her chin until they were looking into each other's eyes.

"What if I don't want to ignore it?"

Suddenly, the room was filled with a different sort

of tension. Her eyelids fluttered as she tried to swallow past a sudden knot in her throat.

"Then I don't know," she muttered.

"Want to learn?" he asked, his breath soft against her cheek.

"Education is a wonderful thing," Ally whispered, and lifted her lips to the kiss she saw coming.

It was a gentle coupling; founded on a new and tenuous partnership and companionable exhaustion. East wrapped his arms around her and pulled her close against his body.

Ally moaned deep in her throat as she felt her bones turn to mush.

East was the first to pull away, however reluctantly.

"You're a quick study, aren't you, Ally girl?"

Ally blinked, trying to focus on something besides the shape of his mouth. When she saw he was teasing gently, it gave her the nerve to tease back.

"I tend to absorb what I like a lot faster than the dull stuff."

He laughed. "Damn. An honest woman. I may be in more trouble than I thought."

Ally arched an eyebrow, her expression suddenly serious.

"So, you think I'm trouble?"

East's smile disappeared. "Oh, honey... I know it."

Chapter 9

Night had come to L.A., but judging from the traffic on the streets below Jeff's apartment, it seemed few, if any, people slept. Light from the streets shone in through the kitchen window, highlighting the clutter, as well as the microscope and slides that Ally had left on the table, and leaving the rest of the room in shadows. A small black bug skittered across the linoleum and slipped under a crack in the floor, from where it was unlikely to emerge, thanks to monthly visits from an exterminator service.

Down the hall, at the first door on the right, Ally lay wide-eyed and sleepless, thinking about the man on the living room sofa. What had happened between them earlier today? Was it nothing more than a symptom of shared troubles, or was something special developing between them? Afraid to hope—afraid to count on anything more than herself—she rolled over onto her side and closed her eyes.

A night wind was playing havoc with the palms outside, leaving dancing shadows on the walls opposite the sofa where East lay trying to sleep, but it wouldn't come. Tired and frustrated, he got up and headed toward the patio doors leading to the small terrace beyond. A single click sounded in the silence as he flipped open the lock. The doors slid silently aside as he moved onto the terrace overlooking the parking lot below. Compared to the view at Condor Mountain, this one left a lot to be desired, but East knew Jeff was happy here. All he could do was hope that he got to come back and enjoy it.

A siren sounded in the distance, and then another in the opposite direction, while down below an argument was in progress. He lowered his head and closed his eyes, whispering a brief but heartfelt prayer for his son's safety. When he turned around, Ally was standing in the door wearing an over-size MIT T-shirt and a pair of socks. In the dark, without makeup, she could have passed for thirteen. It made him feel like a dirty old man, because at that moment, he wanted nothing more than to take her in his arms.

"I got up to get a drink of water," she said.

"I can't sleep either," he muttered, and turned back to the skyline of L.A. "Hell of a place, isn't it?"

Ally moved to stand beside him, shoulders touching, sharing the night and the space.

"When I was little, I was afraid of people who lived their lives in the dark. Intellectually, I knew there were people like doctors and policemen, even firemen, who had to work no matter what time of day it was. But a part of me was convinced that they were really vampires who came out after the sun went down and disappeared during the day." She managed a lopsided grin. "I saw an old movie about werewolves and vampires when I was about six. I didn't grasp all the nuances, just enough to scare the bejesus out of me for a good ten years."

East laughed, and again, was surprised that he could. There was something so sweet about her lack of artifice that he couldn't help himself.

"You're good for me. Did you know that?" he asked.

Ally shook her head.

"Well, you are," he said, and gave her a quick hug. As he did, he felt her shiver. "Let's get back inside before we both get a chill."

He nodded, as he led the way back inside, and then locked the door behind them. "How about some coffee?"

"I'll pass," she said. "It would just keep me awake."

"You're already awake," East argued. "What's one cup going to hurt?"

Reluctant to admit that she was afraid of making a fool of herself again, it was all she could do to agree. She stood in the dark, watching as East walked into the kitchen and turned on the light. From the living room, she felt safe; secluded from his all-seeing eyes. Yet when he beckoned, she followed him into the light, like a moth to the flame. Morning could come none too soon. Oddly enough, after two cups of coffee, they both went to sleep. East dreamed of her laughter, and Ally dreamed of his arms, holding her tight.

Hundreds of miles away on a Colorado mountaintop, Jonah stood on the second-story balcony of his home, looking out at the darkness and the star-filled night. The emptiness of the house behind him was noth-

ing more than a reflection of his own life. Despite his
power, he had no roots—no family. If he survived this
mess he was in, his future still looked bleak. It was impossible not to think of what the last years of his life
would be like when he gave up this job to someone else.
He would be exactly what he was now, only older—a
lonely, lonely man.

A deep sigh racked his body as he looked up at the
sky. As he watched, a shooting star suddenly fell into
his line of vision, disappearing as quickly as it had appeared, and as it did, an old memory suddenly resurfaced. As a young man, he'd stood in the dark on a night
like this and watched stars falling from heaven. Only
he hadn't been alone. He shuddered, remembering the
sequence of events that had taken him to where he was
now and as he did, loneliness turned to a slow, simmering rage. He'd given up too damned much in the service
of others. And as he stood there, a certainty came to
him. After he cleared his name, he was going to resign.
There was a woman he wanted to see—just one more
time, before anonymity claimed him again. Angrily, he
turned away from the view and stalked into the house,
shutting and locking the door behind him, then moved
through the rooms without turning on the lights, confident of his path and of the decisions he'd just made.

There was another sort of darkness where Jeff was
being held; a choking blackness where, at times, the air
seemed too thick to breathe. At first, he'd been afraid
that he would eventually die from lack of oxygen, and
then he had remembered the breathing tube he'd seen in
the ceiling. As the hours passed, he also discovered that

daylight, although infinitesimal, was visible through the tiny tube and the knowledge, somehow, gave him peace.

He moved within the small enclosure, feeling his way from cot to table, fumbling his way through the packets of food, carefully sipping the water for fear this was all they would give him. Periodically, he would find his way to the steps, then go up them on his hands and knees until he got to the door, pushing hard with his hands and with his back, just on the off-chance someone had gotten careless and left it unlocked. But it was never so. Oddly enough, just the act of trying was enough to keep his spirits up—that and the hope that East would find him.

Ally raked a brush through her hair and then tossed it aside as she picked up a tube of lipstick, giving her lips a quick swipe. Her jeans were old but comfortable. Her pink and yellow, tie-dyed tank top was an alarming conglomeration of swirls and blobs, but she loved it. It was a rare concession to her youth, rather than to the austerity of her position with SPEAR.

In the other room, she could hear snatches of East's conversation with Foster Martin as he checked in with his second-in-command, making sure that all was going well at the resort. As she exited the bathroom, she looked toward the bed, trying to remember where she'd left her shoes, but they were nowhere in sight. She headed toward the living room, gathering up a file of papers as she went, anxious to get down to work.

East had already spoken with the chief of staff at the hospital where Jeff worked. Ally didn't know exactly what had been said, but she knew that East had made sure Jeff would not be penalized for missing school or work when he returned. It was a tricky situation, making certain that no one reported Jeff Kirby missing, because the last thing they needed or wanted was for the police to become involved in the search. It would drive Jeff's kidnappers even further underground and possibly anger Jonah's enemy to the point of having Jeff killed.

She entered the living room, put down her file and began looking for her shoes. East turned and waved, then quickly brought his phone call to an end. As soon as he hung up, he turned to Ally.

"What are you doing?" he asked.

"Looking for my shoes."

"They're in the kitchen under the table."

"Oh! Right! I kicked them off while I was working last night. Thanks."

She headed toward the kitchen, leaving East with a delightful view of her backside.

He shook his head, then swiped a hand over his face, as if wiping out the thoughts that kept going through his mind. It was very out of character for him, but he was having the devil of a time keeping his hands off of her.

"Found 'em," she yelled, then added a few moments later. "Want some breakfast?"

"Yes," he said. "But there's nothing here to cook. We're either going to have to shop for groceries or have food delivered."

Ally appeared in the doorway, a frown on her face. "Do they deliver breakfast?"

He shrugged. "Hell if I know. It's L.A., so probably. However, let's go find a store, buy some food for later and I'll treat you to breakfast before we get down to work."

She looked back at the microscope and the slides. "Maybe I should—"

East took her by the hand. "Look, nobody wants my son found worse than I do, but you have to eat. We won't be gone long. Besides, you said you needed a modem to hook up to your laptop."

"Oh, that's right, I do," she said. "Okay, let's go."

Just as they opened the door, a couple exited the elevator down the hall and started toward them.

"Oh, you must be our new neighbors," the woman said, offering her hand. "We're Mil and Bill. Mil is short for Millie, you know, but I like Mil better. Millie is so bourgeois."

Before East could comment, she let forth with a second burst of chatter.

"I told Bill the other night that it was too bad that nice young man was moving because he was such a good neighbor." She giggled. "Of course, part of the reason he was so good was because he was rarely here. He was a medical student, I believe. Anyway, do you and your wife have children? Bill and I don't. Not that I'm against the idea, but parenting is such a confining life-style, don't you agree?"

Ally wanted to take a deep breath for the woman because she didn't seem able to slow down long enough to breathe for herself. However, the woman had volunteered one useful bit of information, and East wasted no time in questioning her about it.

"Why did you think that Jeff had moved?" he asked.

Bill started to answer, but Mil jumped in ahead of him. "You knew him?" She rolled her eyes, then giggled. "Of course you must have, you just called him by name."

Finally, Bill interrupted. "You're Jeff's father, aren't you? I think we were introduced a year or so ago."

East nodded. "Yes, but back to my question. Why did you think Jeff had moved?"

"Oh! I remember you now. Sorry, I feel so silly, but when we came back from the hospital that night… Oh, that was just awful," Millie said, flying off in another conversational direction. "Someone called us a few nights ago…the night we saw the movers…and told us we needed to go to a hospital to identify my mother's body. Why I nearly died myself. We left immediately, of course, but the most awful thing…well, it wasn't really awful, because she wasn't there after all, and when we realized it was a hoax, we were really glad. Anyway, someone lied to us just to get us out of our apartment, Bill said. We raced home, certain that we'd come back to find we'd been robbed. Imagine our relief when everything was all right."

East glanced at Ally, but it was obvious by the look on her face that she was already on the same wavelength as him.

"So, why did you think Jeff was moving?" he repeated.

"Why…because of those three men in coveralls. They came out of your son's apartment carrying a great big trunk and after that, we didn't see him anymore so we just assumed that he had moved."

"What did they look like?" East asked.

Bill shrugged. "I didn't pay any attention."

"Oh, you know," Mil said. "Ordinary white men. One was a little taller and older than the other two and they were all wearing blue coveralls and baseball caps. Why, is something wrong?" She suddenly clapped her hands against her cheeks. "Oh, my! Was Jeff robbed instead of us? Why I never thought of that, did you, Bill?"

"No, no," East said quickly. "He wasn't robbed."

"Oh, that must have been the stuff he was shipping to you for storage," Ally said, giving East the alibi he needed to put this couple off the idea that anything was wrong.

"Right," East said.

"So Jeff hasn't moved?" Bill asked.

East shook his head. "No. He's on some sort of trade-out with a hospital in another state…specialized trauma work, or something of the sort."

The couple nodded. "Hope he does well," Bill said, and then added. "Nice to see you again."

It was all East could do to stay quiet until they were gone.

"God all mighty," he whispered. "I'd lay odds that Jeff was in that trunk and those men carried him out right under their noses."

Ally nodded. "Okay, now we know there were three men, and they had a big trunk, so it's doubtful that they were in a car or even a pickup truck. They would want some kind of an enclosed vehicle to move him away, and I'm betting on a van, although they could have had some sort of a rental truck."

"After we get back from breakfast, I'm going to question some of the people who live here. Maybe someone saw something that night that could help us."

"And maybe I'll find something in those fingerprints I lifted," Ally said. Impulsively, she gave East a quick hug. "This is wonderful," she said. "See…already we have hope because we have new clues. We'll find him, East. I just know it."

East smiled ruefully. "Where were you ten years ago? I could have used your faith and optimism then."

"Umm, I believe I was still wearing braces and working on my first Ph.D...or was it my second?"

"My God," East muttered. "I keep forgetting how young you are."

She pursed her lips in a rather puritan mode and gave him a disgusted look.

"Age is nothing but a state of mind. Personally, I can't remember a day of youthful exuberance in my entire life. I think I've always been old."

This time, it was East who reached out, pulling her close against his chest.

"I'm going to make you a promise, Ally girl. When this is over, I'm going to teach you something you don't know."

"What's that?" she asked.

"I'm going to teach you how to play."

It was late afternoon and the evening sun was coming through the kitchen window with bright persistence. Squinting against the glare, Ally shoved her chair back from the table and strode to the window, turning the slats on the shade until the room was bathed in a warm, homey glow. She tilted her head to the right, then to the left, wincing in satisfaction as her neck suddenly popped. Then she sat back down, pulled her laptop forward and resumed what she'd been doing.

It had been simple, hacking into the database at FBI headquarters. It wasn't the first time she'd done it, but never had the act been as personal to her as it was now.

During her forensic investigation, she'd found several different fingerprints, which stood to reason, since

East claimed that Jeff occasionally entertained some of his med-school buddies. And, she'd identified Jeff's and one other young man's right off. But it was the partial she'd found on a large shard of glass that interested her most. She had every chance to expect that the print could very easily have come from the man who'd cleaned up the broken glass. All she had to do was wait while the program ran, hoping she would get a match.

The blood she'd typed had been the same type as Jeff's, which virtually eliminated the possibility of linking it to someone else. Because of that, they had little else to go on, save the print. If that bombed, it left them with nothing but vague descriptions of three white men in blue coveralls. Now, she sat staring at the screen as, one after the other, it sorted through the thousands of prints on file, looking for the one with the same set of whorls and indentations as the print she'd found on the glass.

A short while later, she glanced at her watch, then got up again, this time moving toward the living room and the terrace beyond. East had gone out some time ago, intent on talking to some of the other tenants to see if they'd noticed any unusual activity the night Jeff disappeared. The file Jonah had sent him was spread out on the coffee table, and although East had remarked upon the thoroughness employed by the man who was trying to take Jonah down, he hadn't been able to find anything pertinent that might help them find Jeff.

She opened the patio door and walked out on the small, balconied terrace, then sat down to watch the comings and goings from the parking lot below. So many people, and yet no one had noticed a young man had gone missing within their midst. Within their worlds, it was as if Jeff Kirby had never existed. Yet Ally knew that he had. She'd seen pictures of him and East together—both men laughing into the camera's eye at some lost bit of nonsense: Jeff holding up a huge big-mouthed bass caught while on a Colorado fishing trip, East flipping hamburgers on an outdoor grill.

Ally sighed. East and Jeff had packed more "family" stuff into the last ten years they'd been together than she and her parents had done in her entire life. In fact, she couldn't remember a single time when her parents had gone out of their way to make her feel important. They'd left the discovery of that issue up to Ally, herself.

She kicked back in the chair and then closed her eyes, wanting so badly to give that life back to East. Mentally, she began reviewing the true facts of Jeff's disappearance, as she knew them.

There was the cryptic message from Jeff about walking away from a crash and burn.

The name Bob, written in blood on the floor of Jeff's apartment.

The three men who'd been seen carrying a trunk out of his apartment.

The so-far, unidentified fingerprint she'd found on the glass.

She opened her eyes and sat up, frustrated that they didn't know more. Again, she glanced at her watch. Almost an hour had passed since she'd come outside and she began to wonder what had happened to East. Hope began to rise as the sun began to set. Maybe he was on to something important—something that would set them on the right path to finding his son.

She stood abruptly, suddenly anxious to check on

the program that was running. Maybe a match had been made.

As she started to leave, a flash of silver caught the corner of her eye and she turned back to the parking lot, curious as to what it was that she'd seen. When she saw nothing, she shrugged, and turned again, and again, the same flash of brilliance occurred. This time she stood, looking at the light from the corner of her eye until she'd focused on the exact location.

As she turned, she realized she had been looking at something affixed to a pole in the bank parking lot across the street. When she realized what it was, her heart skipped a beat. It was one of a couple of visible security cameras. But the implications of that particular camera were impossible to ignore. Unless she was mistaken, the background images of that particular camera would most likely be the vehicles going in and out of Jeff's apartment complex.

Her first impulse was to dash across the street, flash her government badge and demand to see the tapes. But then she remembered the time and realized that the establishment had probably been closed for quite a while. It would have to wait until tomorrow.

Excited about a possible new lead, she hurried back inside, hopeful that by now the fingerprint program had found a match. To her frustration, it was still running. Shrugging off the disappointment, she began rummaging through the refrigerator for something to fix for their dinner. She was debating between the two steaks East had bought or pasta and salad when she heard the front door open. Anxious to tell him her new theory, she dumped the stuff back in the fridge and bolted for the living room.

* * *

As East exited the elevator, he was surprised by a feeling of anticipation. Not since he was a kid had he experienced a sense of excitement at coming home. But today, he found himself hurrying down the hall toward Jeff's apartment. It was a little scary to accept the fact that it was Ally to whom he was hurrying. He couldn't help thinking that this attraction he was feeling couldn't have come at a more inopportune time, but he knew that matters of the heart were not things to be scheduled. All he could do was face the truth of his feelings and try not to let them get out of hand. Yet the more time he spent in her company, the more difficult that was beginning to be.

The key was in his hand, yet when he reached the door he hesitated, putting on what Jeff would have called his game face. Then he walked inside and she was coming toward him on the run and all of his good intentions evaporated. He slammed the door shut and caught her in midair.

"A man could get used to this kind of welcome," he drawled, and kissed her soundly before he could talk himself out of it.

The kiss was sweet, and from the gasp that he heard just before they connected, obviously unexpected. But it wasn't kissing her that bothered him. It was stopping at just the one.

Ally moaned, then leaned into him, her news momentarily forgotten. When he turned her loose, she staggered, and would have bumped into the sofa had he not grabbed her first.

She could feel her cheeks getting pink, but she refused to let him know how deeply it had affected her.

"That wasn't bad," she muttered. "Want to go out and come back in again...just to see if it could get any better?"

He laughed aloud and then hugged her again, but this time it was nothing more than a friendly embrace.

"I think I'd better stop while I'm ahead," he said.

She pretended to pout. "I was afraid you'd say that." Then the moment passed as she remembered why she'd been running to meet him. "Come with me," she said, grabbing him by the hand and pulling out to the terrace. "There's something I want you to see."

He followed willingly, more than a little enchanted with the flirt she was becoming.

"So, what's the big deal?" he asked, as she pulled him to the railing, then stopped.

She waved her hand toward the street. "Look out there. What do you see?"

East looked and saw nothing but cars and people and endless tons of cement.

"Don't I get a hint?" he asked.

Her eyebrows knotted momentarily, and then she grinned and pointed. "Smile. You're on candid camera."

He looked again, and in that moment, realized he was looking across the street and straight at a pole-mounted security camera. It didn't take more than a second for the implications to dawn, and when they did, he started to grin.

"Ally, honey, I said you were going to be my lucky charm."

She gave him an exasperated look. "And I told you I'm not lucky, I'm just—"

"Smart. Yeah, I know, you're smart. And thank the good Lord that you are."

"I wasn't going to say that," she argued. "I just pay attention to details." Then she frowned. "But we have to wait until tomorrow to get the tapes. I just hope to goodness they keep at least a week's worth before taping over them."

But East wouldn't deny himself this new bit of hope.

"Grab your purse," he said. "I'm taking you out for dinner."

"But I was going to—"

"Do you want to cook?" he asked.

She shrugged. "I'm not very good at it."

He grinned. "Well, well, is there actually something you admit you don't know how to do?"

"Oh, no. I know *how* to cook, but I'm not good at it. That's one of those things where practice makes perfect, and there have been very few times, if any, that cooking has been a prerequisite for going undercover."

He shook his head and then herded her back inside.

"Go do whatever it is that women do to make themselves happy to face the world, and hurry. Suddenly, I'm starving."

"But the fingerprint ID is still running on my laptop."

He took her by the shoulders, resisting the urge to shake her.

"And it will either be running when we get back, or it will have ended. Either way, there's nothing else we can do tonight."

"Well, okay then," she said, and started toward the bedroom to change her clothes. By the time she reached the door, she was running.

Chapter 10

Ally was waiting as East came out of the bank with a stack of tapes. Flashing a United States government badge had been all it took to get an audience with the bank president. Without going into details, East had asked for the tapes by hinting that they might be valuable to an ongoing investigation. The president had jumped at the chance to cooperate and fifteen minutes later they were in East's hands, which moved him to the next step in his plans. There was a man from his past—a man named Freddie—who could work miracles with film. If there was anything to be seen on these tapes that would help them find Jeff, Freddie was the man who could find it.

"Where to now?" Ally asked.

"To visit an old friend," he said, as he scooted behind the steering wheel and dumped the tapes on the seat between them.

Forty-five minutes later, East had found the neighborhood and was now looking for a place to park.

"There's one," Ally said, pointing to an empty space in the middle of the block.

East whipped the car into the spot, then killed the engine. The neighborhood had changed, and from the amount of graffiti on the walls of the buildings, not for the better. He leaned forward, peering through the windshield to the building at the end of the block.

"From grocery store to video arcade," he muttered, eyeing the change of business below the second story of the building on the corner.

"What?" Ally asked.

"Nothing, just talking to myself," he said, then grabbed the videos. "Let's go see Freddie."

"How long has it been since you've seen him?" Ally asked.

"A little over ten years," East answered.

"How do you know he still lives here?"

"If he's still alive, he's here," East said, and opened the door.

Ally followed, slinging her purse over her shoulder as she stepped up on the curb. This place and its inhabitants could have been a clone of her last assignment. Tough places and tough people were nothing new to her, but she took comfort from the weight of the Luger in the bottom of her bag.

They entered the arcade to the mechanical sound of ringing bells and bionic beeps. Computerized roars and crashes sounded from the games that they passed, and the money the kids were feeding into the games seemed out of context in a neighborhood that appeared to have no signs of livelihood at all, save a liquor store across the street and a series of bars.

Ally walked with her hand on her bag, constantly aware that there were probably kids in this place who had killed, and who, for as little as fifty dollars, would do it again.

East moved carefully among the motley rank while keeping his eye on the archway at the end of the room. Once they moved through it to the dark hallway beyond, the noise was somewhat diminished.

"Here," he said, pointing to a series of steps leading up to the next story.

Ally moved in front of him and started up, thankful that East was at her back. Moments later, they reached the second-story landing. At East's instructions, she took a quick right.

"Good grief," she said, as they arrived at Freddie's door.

The paint on the black door was cracked and peeling, but there was no mistaking the white skull and cross-bones set dead center, nor the one word message, No, written below it.

"No, what?" Ally asked.

"No to everything," East answered.

Ally grinned. "A man of few words, I take it?"

"You have no idea," East said, and knocked.

Thirty seconds passed before East knocked again, and this time he made a fist, then pounded and yelled.

"Hey, Frederick Gene, are you home?"

Almost immediately, the door swung inward, revealing a tall, skinny man with a seventies Afro and a long, graying beard. His clothes were a reflection of his hair and the glare on his face lasted all of two seconds before he broke into a grin.

"By God, it's Easty boy! I thought you were dead!"

"Yeah, and I heard you downloaded a satellite feed off a UFO and disappeared into thin air," East said, laughing as the man drew him into a thumping embrace.

"And wouldn't that be the ultimate trip?" Freddie said, and pulled East into the room. Only then did he notice East wasn't alone. His smile stilled and his eyes narrowed. "Who's the skirt?"

"I'm not wearing a skirt," Ally said shortly, "and the name is Alicia Corbin." She held out her hand, as if daring him not to shake it.

"Go ahead," East said. "She won't bite." Then in an aside to Ally, he explained. "Freddie had a bad experience with a woman."

"Yeah, man," Freddie said. "She set her purse down on a keyboard and crashed the motherboard to one of my satellite feeds."

"When did that happen?" Ally asked.

Freddie squinted. "About ten, maybe twelve years ago. I forget."

"Holds a grudge, too," she muttered, glancing about the room at the array of computer equipment in the room behind him. Then her eyes widened and her mouth parted in a silent *O* as she walked past them in silent awe.

Ignoring a small jealous spurt that he hadn't been able to put that look on her face, East glanced at Freddie.

"I think she just fell in love."

Freddie spun and hurried after her, afraid she would touch his stuff. But he need not have worried. Ally moved about the room, gazing at one setup, then another, and another, admiring them as a patron of the arts might enjoy the great masters while strolling about the Louvre. It took a couple of minutes before Freddie settled down, and only then did he ask why they'd come.

East held up the tapes. "I need help," he said.

"What's on them?" Freddie asked.

"I hope a clue as to who's got my son."

Freddie's eyes widened as he sucked his lower lip into his mouth. Without speaking, he dropped onto a backless stool and rolled toward a VCR, shoving in the first tape and hitting Play as the castors on his stool settled into little grooves on the old hardwood floor. Images appeared immediately.

"What are we looking for?" he asked.

"Three men in coveralls carrying a large trunk. I'm not sure what they're driving…maybe a van or a rental truck."

Freddie nodded and slid a pair of Ben Franklin–style eyeglasses up the bridge of his nose then leaned forward.

"The kid… Jeff…is he all right?"

East sighed. "He was day before yesterday."

Freddie glanced up once. "Grudge?" he asked, indicating that he knew more about East's past than Ally would have imagined.

"Same as," East said, then glanced at Ally, seeing the question in her eyes. "Freddie trained me."

It all became clear. Freddie was a retired SPEAR operative, which explained everything else. East's willingness to trust him with information, the odd lifestyle, the skull and crossbones on his door, his distrust of people and his unusual expertise.

Silence filled the room as three pairs of eyes became

trained upon the black-and-white images moving on the screen. Occasional noise from the arcade below was distracting, but as time passed, they subconsciously blocked it out, much in the same way that Freddie had learned to do.

An hour passed, then another, and another. That tape played out and they inserted a second. A couple more minutes played out and then suddenly East pointed.

"That's Jeff's car."

They watched the four-wheel drive sports utility move through the apartment gates and then come to a stop near the front entrance. A vague image of a man exited and East found himself blinking back tears.

Damn, damn, damn. Don't let this be the last sight I ever have of my son.

"Is that him?" Ally asked.

East nodded as the man disappeared off-screen.

Nothing else appeared on the tape that seemed pertinent. East's nerves were on edge as Freddie slid in the last one. He'd been so confident when the day had started, and now this one was their last hope. Daylight became dark on the tape and the parking lot emptied. Despite the thirty-five mile an hour speed limit in front of the apartment building, traffic moved at a swift pace.

Suddenly Ally gasped and pointed to the right of the screen.

"There! A dark van pulling into the apartment complex!"

Freddie started to hit rewind when East touched his shoulder. "Wait," he said. "Let it play. We can always go back."

As the van turned, it moved out of camera range and

East groaned, then moments later, appeared at the right of the screen again.

"Son of a…look where they parked," East said.

Ally and Freddie peered closer. The van had parked beneath a broken street light.

"Odd choice of parking place when there are plenty of vacancies in better lighting," East muttered.

"They aren't getting out," Ally said.

East's heart skipped a beat. She was right. Something told him they were about to get lucky.

"Watch the van," he said sharply.

Within minutes, both doors opened simultaneously and three men spilled out into the shadows. Two of them were carrying something large between them, but there was no way they could get a look at their faces.

"Well, hell," East said, as the trio went in the front of the apartment. All they could see were their backs and the trunk they were carrying.

"Maybe we'll get them when they come out," Freddie said.

Instinctively, Ally moved closer to East, offering comfort in the only way that she could—by her presence.

Minutes passed—long agonizing minutes of watching cars and traffic, all the while knowing that while that camera was rolling, Jeff was most likely fighting for his life.

Suddenly, Freddie pointed. "There they come!"

Again, the trio's faces were hidden by shadows and the angle of their heads, but there was no mistaking the trunk they were carrying, or the fact that it was taking all three of them to carry it now. They moved out of camera range, appearing seconds later on the dark side of the van.

"Stop tape," East said. "Now, can you zoom in on that shot?"

"Yeah, but I don't think we're gonna see anything," Freddie said, and punched a couple of keys on his keyboard.

Immediately, the picture enlarged, then enlarged again. Freddie hit a couple more keys then moved the cursor to a specific section of the picture and clicked. At once, a specific section of the picture was separated from the whole, which he enlarged, then enlarged again.

"Can't go any higher," Freddie said. "I'm already losing clarity and density."

"Print it out," East said.

Freddie clicked the mouse and a printer to Ally's left kicked on. Seconds later, it spit out a print. She handed it to East. The men's faces were indistinct blobs of dark and light.

"Damn it," East muttered. "Play out the rest of the tape."

They watched as the van backed up, then disappeared from view, appearing seconds later as it exited the gate. As it turned into the traffic, they had a brief glimpse of a license plate before another car drove up beside the van, blocking it from the camera's view.

"Back it up," East said.

Freddie hit Rewind.

"There!" East said, pointing to the small, indistinct rectangle on the back of the van. "Can you blow up that tag?"

Freddie grinned. "Do bears…"

Ally interrupted, laughing. "I think that's a yes."

A few clicks later, they had a printout of the van's tag as well. Freddie handed it to East with a flourish, then pointed to a nearby drawer.

"There's a magnifying glass in there," he said.

Ally hurried toward it, returning with the large, round glass.

"Here," she said, thrusting it into East's hand.

He leaned forward, holding it over the pictures that he'd laid beneath the light.

"I can't make out all of the numbers, but I can make out the state."

"Idaho or New York?" Ally asked.

East straightened abruptly, his eyes round with shock.

"How did you know?"

"Crash and burn, remember?"

"Son of a bitch," he mumbled, and lifted the magnifying glass to his face one more time, reassuring himself that what he'd seen was truly there. Then he handed the glass to Ally.

"You tell me," he said.

She leaned down. When she straightened, she was smiling.

"Yippee-kiyi-yay, cowboy, it's Idaho, just like your son called it."

"He told you?" Freddie asked.

"Not exactly," East said. "It's a long story." Then he combed his fingers through his hair in frustration. "My God…if this is so…if his kidnappers have actually taken him to Idaho, how in hell do we find him?" Then he slapped the flat of his hand on the desk in frustration. "Do you know how big the state of Idaho is?"

"Actually, yes," Ally said. "It's 83,557 square miles,

including eight hundred and eighty square miles of in-
land water. It's thirteenth in size among the fifty states
and its highest elevation is Borah Peak, which is 12,662
feet above sea level."

Freddie gawked. "What is she, a walking encyclo-
pedia?"

Ally looked crestfallen. She'd blurted out the answer before she'd thought. But to her delight, East just
grinned, and ruffled her hair.

"Nope. She's my lucky charm."

His words took the sting out of Freddie's thoughtless
remark, although she would have preferred something
more from East than a pat on the head.

"I just know stuff," Ally said, and pretended great
interest in the pictures they'd printed out.

Freddie began to smile. "You know, if my last girlfriend had been half as smart as I suspect you are, we
might still be warming the sheets." He winked at East
and turned toward Ally, leaning back on his stool and
folding his arms across his chest. "Say, if you get tired
of old Easty boy, you come on back here. I've got all
kinds of toys for you to play with."

Ally laughed out loud. From anyone else, the rude,
sexual innuendo would have been insulting. But coming from this tall, skinny reject from the seventies, it
was comical, and they all knew it.

Freddie pretended to frown. "Am I to take that as
a refusal?"

"Pretty much," Ally said, "although I have to say it's
the best offer I've had all day."

Freddie pursed his lips and tugged on his beard as
he swiveled the stool around to stare at East.

"What's the matter with you, Easty boy? Looks like

your son isn't the only thing you've lost. I can remember the days when you would have—"

"Butt out," East muttered, as Ally glanced at her watch.

"The program," she said. "It has to be finished by now. Maybe we got lucky there, too."

"What program?" Freddie asked.

"I'm running a match on a fingerprint we found in Jeff's apartment."

Freddie's eyes rounded and then squinted as a wide grin began to spread.

"You hacked into the FBI system to run a print?"

Ally pursed her lips. "I didn't exactly hack," she said. "I have clearance, you know."

He grinned. "Yeah, but not from a civilian PC. I'm impressed."

She smiled primly.

East sighed and then grinned. "You're right, honey. One step at a time." He glanced at Freddie. "Old friend, you don't know what this means to me."

Freddie's smile faded. "Oh, I think I do." He hesitated, thoughtfully eyeing Ally, then added. "You're both going to Idaho, aren't you?"

East nodded.

Freddie stood abruptly and strode to a nearby cabinet, took something from a shelf, and then handed it to East.

"What's this for?" East asked, eyeing the set of keys Freddie had put in his hand.

"*Baby.* She's in storage, but I was just there last week and everything is operative, including a new battery under the hood."

"*Baby?* Who's *Baby*?" Ally asked.

"You'd have to see her to believe her," East said, then looked at Freddie. "Are you sure you want to do this?"

Freddie squinted, as if unwilling to show the emotion welling in his eyes. "Well, yes. Wouldn't have offered, otherwise. Besides, you got to get that kid back and get him through the rest of his school. Never know when I might need some free doctoring."

East clasped the key tight in his fist, then cleared his throat. "We'll take good care of her."

"It's the kid that matters most," Freddie said. "You just find him."

The two men embraced briefly then stepped apart. Freddie winked at Ally as they started to leave. "I'd give you a hug, too, except I don't think old Easty boy would appreciate my generosity."

"I field my own hugs," Ally said.

Freddie laughed and swooped.

Ally found herself momentarily nose to beard, felt a swift kiss on her forehead and then was set aside as abruptly as she'd been held. A little embarrassed, she smoothed at the front of her blouse and then patted her hair.

"Thank you," she said, primly.

Freddie laughed again. "You're welcome." Then he looked at East, who was trying not to frown. "Man, you're done for and you don't even know it."

They could still hear him laughing as he shut the door behind them. The sound of voices and videos drifted up the stairwell, mixing with the dust and gloom in which they were standing. East gave Ally a long, slow look.

"Am I?" he suddenly asked.

Her eyebrows knitted. "Are you what?"

"Done for?"

Her eyes widened, then focused on his mouth before she abruptly looked away.

"I don't know what you're talking about," she muttered. "Let's get back to the apartment. I have a good feeling about that print."

He followed her down the stairs and through the arcade, watching the sway of her hips as she strode purposefully through the crowd—so certain of her skill and intelligence, and yet so unsure of herself as a woman. Never in his life had he been more confused, or as certain that he was falling in love.

"We've got a match!" Ally shouted.

East dropped the keys onto the table and ran toward the kitchen.

Ally had dashed through the door the moment he'd unlocked it, bolting ahead of him to see if the program she'd been running was finished. From the tone of her voice, it was good news.

"Please tell me it's not one of his friends," East muttered, as he leaned over her shoulder to look at the screen.

Ally shook her head. "Not unless he's running with a crowd you don't know about." She pointed. "Elmore Todd. White male, forty-six years old, two hundred and thirty-four pounds, six feet two inches tall. Priors—assault and battery, armed robbery. Sentenced five to ten, served two and a half years in Soledad, released in 1988. Picked up for possession of an illegal weapon in 1993, but the charges were dismissed."

She kept scrolling the information, reading the arrests and dispensations without comment until she came to the bottom of the page. Suddenly, she gasped. "East! Look at this!"

He leaned closer, reading where she was pointing.

"Born in New Township, Idaho. Ties to three known militia groups within the state—America's Freemen, Sons of Glory, and the Brotherhood of Blood."

"Son of a bitch," East muttered, trying not to think of what people like that might do to his son. "But why them? What would a militia group have to do with trying to bring down a man like Jonah? Their agenda is usually broader than that."

"You've been out of the loop too long," Ally said. "It's well known within SPEAR that some of those groups are little more than mercenaries, willing to hire out to the highest bidder."

East stood abruptly. "That fits in with my theory that the man who wants Jonah is not in the same place as the people who took Jeff. If you're right…if he hired some right-wing militia group to snatch Jeff, then we're in big trouble, aren't we?"

She shook her head, disinclined to admit she was scared. "Maybe not, although there are so many off-shoots of known, organized groups that it may be very difficult to find the one that this man is connected with now." Then she added. "But not impossible."

"I've got to talk to Jonah," East said. "The kidnapper is going to call soon and when he does, I'm going to need some bargaining power."

"You're going to give the kidnapper real info?" she asked.

"No, but it's going to look that way. By the time he figures it out, I have to have Jeff safely in my possession."

"That's risky. What if we don't find him before—"

"We'll find him," East said. "We have no choice." Then he pulled Ally out of the chair and grasped her by the shoulders. "I said you were my lucky charm, and I meant it. It would have taken me days, even weeks to get this much information by myself." Then he added. "Hell, I don't even know if I would ever have gotten this far. You're right, I've been out of the loop too long."

"Actually, your instincts are still there, and you've got one thing going for you that neither Jonah or the kidnappers have."

"What's that?" he asked.

"Your love for Jeff. A parent's love for a child is stronger than any force on earth." Then she sighed and her voice dropped. "At least it should be."

East pulled her into his arms and held her close. "I wish I could change the way you were raised. There are people who should never have children, and even though your childhood was not ideal, I'm really glad you were born."

She smiled against the fabric of his shirt and closed her eyes, fighting back tears.

"Me, too," she said. "And I'll do everything I can to help you find Jeff."

He lifted her chin until their gazes met. His eyes were dark with warning.

"I'll take your help and gladly," he said. "But when this is over, prepare yourself, because I'm going to ask something more of you than just help."

She shivered suddenly, uncertain of what to say.

Then he was coming closer, blocking out her vision of everything except the want in his eyes.

Mouths merged, opening gently to the pressure, tasting the sweetness of trust and the beginnings of love.

Chapter 11

Night came to L.A. It had been eleven days since Ally had appeared at Condor Mountain, and four days since the phone call about Jeff's disappearance. East's stomach clenched. Time was running out. Tomorrow they would retrieve Freddie's *Baby* and head for Idaho. After that, the plan was vague. All he could do was hope that the threads of this mess would keep unraveling as they went, because staying stationary was no longer an option.

East came out of the bathroom wearing a pair of sweatpants and nothing else. His hair was still damp and spiky from his shower and his bare feet made soft splatting sounds as he came down the hall, intent on telling Ally that the bathroom was free. He rounded the corner with her name on his lips and ran squarely into her. She staggered backward as the stack of papers she was carrying went flying.

"Ally, honey! I'm so sorry. Are you all right?"

She rolled her eyes and pressed a hand to her midriff. "Except for the fact that you scared me senseless, I'm fine." Then she dropped to her knees and began to gather up the papers.

East knelt beside her. "Let me do that. It's my fault they fell."

"No, I'm perfectly capable of—"

He grabbed her hand, then tugged. "Ally, look at me."

She looked up, a slight flush on her face.

"I know what you're capable of, probably better than you do," he said gently. "Now go take your bath and relax. I will pick up the damned papers. Do you understand?"

Her lips pursed.

"Aren't you going to tell me to go to hell?" he teased, trying to make her smile.

She stood abruptly. "Why should I tell you something that you seem perfectly capable of figuring out for yourself?" she said, and stepped around him, striding down the hall with her head held high.

He rocked back on his heels and started to laugh. "One of these days, Ally, girl. One of these days," he called out.

The bathroom door slammed shut.

He was still chuckling as he gathered the last of her papers and put them on the dining room table, then stood in the quiet until he heard water running in the bathroom down the hall. Only then did he move to the terrace. As he did, he was surprised to feel moisture on his face. He hadn't even known it was raining. He stood for a moment in the shadows, taking shelter from the shallow overhang and listened to the sounds.

Raindrops peppered upon metal surfaces like the tinkling sounds of a player piano, clinking, dripping, running, pouring. Water fell in gushes from the downspouts onto the concrete below, mini-cascades that ran fast and free. He leaned against the wall and crossed his arms over his chest, relishing the fresh breeze and mist upon his bare arms and chest. Then he closed his eyes, wondering if it was raining where Jeff was being held—worrying if he was cold—afraid he might be hungry. Ah God, he couldn't face losing Jeff and live knowing that again, the death of an innocent would be on his shoulders; and this time his own son.

Time passed. He never knew when the rain stopped, or that Ally had been standing in the shadows of the living room for quite some time, watching the changing expressions on his face. All he knew was for the first time in years, he was scared.

He shivered, but was reluctant to go to bed and face the ghosts of his past. Finally the chill of the night got to him and he pushed away from the wall and turned to go inside when he saw Ally.

She was standing in the dark wearing that same oversize T-shirt with her hands clasped at her waist as if she was about to recite a lesson. But it was the expression on her face that stopped him flat.

Sweet heaven, hadn't anyone ever told that woman not to let a man see her vulnerability? He frowned, then moved inside, closing and locking the patio door behind him.

"It got cold."

She swallowed, trying to find something insignificant to talk about, but when he looked at her like that, she couldn't think.

"Want something to drink?" he asked, and took a step toward her.

She flinched, then shook her head.

He had to give it to her—she had guts. She looked scared to death and yet held her ground. His sigh deepened. This had to stop. If they were going to find Jeff, they had to work together, and not just during the day when there were clues to unravel, but all the time. Trust was a twenty-four hour emotion or it wasn't there at all.

"Are you afraid of me?"

She hesitated, and it stunned him to realize how much that hurt.

"Damn it, Alicia, I would never force you into anything you don't want. Don't you know that?"

It was the pain in his voice that made her find her own.

"I'm sorry, I'm sorry," she said quickly. "It's not that. It's not even you." She lowered her head. "It's me."

He moved toward her, touching her face, then tilting her chin and forcing her to look at him when she talked.

"What about you?" he asked.

"I don't know how to handle all of this."

His voice softened. "All of what, honey?"

"You. Me. Us."

He smiled gently. "Is there an us?"

She blushed. "See. That's what I mean. I don't know. I can't read the signs. I don't know the rules. All I know is when we get like this it's hard to catch my breath. Is that just lust, or is it something else?"

Her naivete and honesty shamed him. It was time

he stopped pushing her. He took her hand, then pulled her closer.

"I don't know how you feel. I can only tell you how I feel about us, okay?"

"Okay."

Her eyes were wide and fixed upon his face, and then he took her into his arms, burying his face in the soft curls at the crown of her head.

"I see your smile in my dreams. Hearing you laugh makes my stomach knot, and the trust in your eyes makes me humble. At any odd moment of the day, I wonder what it would be like to make love to you, and I don't want to think of the day we say goodbye."

"Oh, East," Ally whispered, then pulled away from his embrace and covered her face with her hands.

East's heart dropped, but he tried to make light of his disappointment.

"Dang, honey, is making love to me that hard to face?"

She shuddered, then looked up. "It's not that. Oh no, it's never that."

"Then what?"

She took a deep breath. "I've never made love. I don't know how." And before East could comment, she added. "Oh, I've read books. Lots of books. But something tells me that there's a lot more to it than the act itself."

East was stunned, and yet when he thought about it, realized he should not have been. Struggling to find the right words that wouldn't make all this worse, he smiled and cupped the side of her face.

"As always, honey girl, you're right on the money. There's a lot more to making love than the act itself. But being an expert doesn't matter. In fact, saving yourself is something to be proud of. The man you marry is going to get quite a prize when he gets you."

A slight frown appeared between her eyebrows as she considered his words. "I don't know. Do you think that maybe, when this is all over of course…that you might show me?"

East felt as if someone had just punched him in the belly.

"Show you?"

Her frown deepened. "Yes, you know…show me how to make love?"

"But I just said that being a virgin for the man you marry is a special—"

"I know all of that," she said shortly. "But I've found that experience is preferable to fumbling folly."

"Fumbling folly."

She sighed. If he kept repeating everything she said, they would get nowhere.

"Ineptitude then, if you prefer."

He started to grin. "I think I prefer."

Her eyes brightened. "Oh! Well then, is it a deal?"

He nodded. "Oh yeah, it's a deal."

She pursed her lips slightly as she considered his pledge, then folded her hands in front of her in that funny little way and smiled.

"I believe I'll go to bed now," she said, then added, "If that's all right with you."

He nodded again, all but speechless.

"Okay then," Ally said, suddenly unsure of this silent behavior. "Uh…good night."

East found his voice enough to answer. "Yes, good night."

She stood uncertainly for another moment, then finally left the room.

As East watched her go, his love went with her. She didn't know it yet, but right in the middle of her crazy reasoning, he'd fallen the rest of the way in love. Somehow, someway, he was going to make it all work between them, because there was no way in hell he was letting another man touch her.

The storage lot where Freddie kept *Baby* was huge; row after row of bunker-like buildings with identical doors and locks. The only difference between any of them were the numbers above the door.

"What number are we looking for?" Ally asked.

"Two hundred and twenty-eight."

Ally peered out the window to the nearest numbered building and rolled her eyes.

"This is stupid," she muttered.

"What's stupid?" East asked.

"They've built the entrance at the back of the lot. This is number 1420. That means we need to go south." She pointed toward the other end of the lot, past the endless stream of chain-link fence.

"South it is," East said, and accelerated slowly.

A short while later, he stopped, then turned down an aisle between the buildings and began looking for two hundred and twenty-eight.

"There it is," Ally said. "Third one down on your left."

"Leave it up to Freddie to find the cheapest method of long-term parking in L.A.," he said.

Within minutes, they had unlocked the overhead door and began pushing it up. It rolled on noisy brackets like a car driving over an old wooden bridge. East turned on the interior light, but it wasn't really necessary since the vehicle inside took up all but a narrow walking space on either side.

"Good grief," Ally said. "We aren't really going to drive this anywhere, are we?"

East had seen it before, but he still winced, picturing himself behind the wheel. The metal panels of the RV were a psychedelic swirl of greens, pinks and blues. It looked like an old whorehouse on wheels.

"Don't let me forget my sunglasses," he muttered, as he moved toward the ancient vehicle.

Ally snorted. "You aren't worried about harmful UV rays. You're just afraid someone you know will see you in this."

He laughed. "You may be right. However, wait until you see what's inside." He opened the door and then stood aside, letting her go in first. "There's a light switch to the left as you step up."

"It better be good, or—" She forgot what she'd been going to say. "Oh…my…God."

East had to push her gently to get her to move so that he could follow. Even then, Ally stood with her mouth agape, unable to believe her eyes at the array of state-of-the-art equipment inside.

"It's one of the best stake-out vehicles we ever used, and he has obviously updated it from time to time. Whatever you need is in here. Satellite feeds. Faxes. Computer systems, printers, video equipment, tracking devices…"

"Even telephone tracing systems," Ally added, running her fingers lightly over the console of one setup. Then she turned to East. "I am in heaven."

He poked the end of her nose with his forefinger and grinned.

"You just think this is heaven, honey. Wait until I expand your world and then tell me that again."

She frowned. "Expand my—?" She started to blush. "Oh. You mean when we eventually make love that I will have a lesser appreciation for technical equipment?"

East's face was a study of momentary confusion, and then he burst out laughing. Before she could take offense, he hugged her close. "Honey, don't ever let anyone tell you that you aren't sexy, because you are. In fact, you're the most desirable woman I've ever met in my life."

Ally beamed. "Why, thank you. The feeling is mutual."

He shook his head and then handed her the keys to his car. "I'm going to drive this out. As soon as I do, pull my car inside. This is a perfect place to leave it."

Thirty minutes later, they had transferred their bags and supplies into *Baby* and were on their way.

Jeff woke abruptly into the airless dark, his heartbeat pounding like a sledgehammer against his eardrums, and for one second before sanity leveled, he thought he'd gone blind.

"Have mercy," he muttered, and rolled to a seated position on the edge of his cot.

He was cold. He'd been cold for so long. Despite the triple layer of blankets he'd been sleeping under, he hadn't been warm once since they'd put him in the hole. Wearily, he rubbed his hands over his face, scratching the heavy growth of whiskers. Never in his life had he wanted a shower and a shave as badly as he did now.

He stood carefully, feeling his way along the wall until he came to the edge of the table. Using his fingers to see, he felt for the cup he kept beside the water can. When he found it, his fingers carefully curled around the handle as he dipped it into the water. As he dipped, the cup suddenly scraped along the bottom in a tinny, rasping sound. He froze. That had never happened before. Bracing himself so that he wouldn't accidentally tip anything over, he put his other hand down in the can, feeling along the side for the level of water. To his dismay, he estimated less than three inches were left.

He hesitated, weighing his thirst against the possibility that these monsters would not respond to any more demands, and then poured the water in the cup back into the can and set it aside. He could wait a little longer to quench his thirst.

His stomach rumbled, but he'd already faced the dwindling supply of field rations and cut back on his food as well. He had no way of trusting that they would replenish what was here, and no way of knowing how long it would be before his father found him.

But the moment his father's face appeared in his mind's eye, he became even more determined to survive. God in heaven, it couldn't end like this. Life had kicked him in the teeth for fourteen years and then he'd met East. He still remembered the gut-wrenching fear of rounding a corner on that high mountain path and coming face-to-face with the man. But the darkness Jeff had seen in East's eyes had quickly turned to shock, then curiosity as they stood without speaking.

It was East who'd finally broken the silence with a line that still made Jeff smile.

"Hey kid, aren't you kinda far out for pizza delivery?"

Jeff remembered grinning. It was a memorable occasion for many reasons, not the least of which was that he hadn't had anything to smile about in so long he thought he'd forgotten how.

He sighed, took four steps sideways then turned and began to pace.

Five steps forward.

Stop. Turn.

Five steps back.

Any more either way and he would hit wall.

He'd walked it so many times now that his count was subconscious, allowing him the freedom to pursue other thoughts. Periodically, he worried about his job and classes, wondering if they would let him back in, then reality would return. If East didn't find him, the concern was moot. And there were the times when a woman's face slipped through his mind. A woman with flashing brown eyes, dark, chin-length hair, who when she stretched, could look eye-to-eye with the second button down on his shirt.

His steps began to drag as the endless chill soaked deeper into his bones, yet he continued to move. Beads of sweat began to pearl on his forehead and upper lip, which when he thought about it, didn't compute. How in hell could he possibly sweat when he was cold all the way through?

Finally he stopped and looked up at the weak beam of pencil-thin light coming through the air tube. The hole was so small that the light rays seemed to disappear in midair halfway down to the floor. As he stood, something inside of him snapped, and he spun angrily and stomped toward the steps, bumping into his cot as he went. Halfway up, he tripped and fell, catching himself with outstretched hands, but not soon enough to save both knees from the impact. The pain only made his fury worse.

"Cowards! You're all a bunch of sorry cowards! I need water and some decent food. I need a bath and fresh air. Just because you people choose to live like animals, doesn't mean I will."

He hammered long and hard on the underside of the heavy metal door with his fists until they were numb and bleeding, and he still didn't stop. Finally, he gave the door a last angry blow, then moved down to the bottom of the stairs and then shouted at the top of his voice.

"You can kill me three ways to Sunday, but you won't break me. Do you hear me, you bastards? You won't break me!"

Silence was his answer. With shaking steps, he made his way back to his cot and lay down. Pulling the blankets over his bruised and shaking body, he closed his eyes and escaped the only way he knew how—in his sleep.

It was night when East crossed the California border into Nevada. *Baby*'s tires made a whining sound as they rolled along Interstate 15 into the desert stretching out before them. Ally rode silently in the passenger seat and he marveled at the woman who could be so silent for so long. The last time they'd traded words was when they'd stopped to eat, and now, her gaze stayed fixed upon the highway in front of them, as if she needed to keep watch just to keep them safe. He shook his head in silent wonder. If he'd had a partner like her before, he might not have come undone. Then he sighed. Before didn't matter. It was the hell they were in now that kept him simmering with unresolved anger.

"If you get tired, I'll drive," Ally said.

Her voice startled him, and it took him a moment to answer.

He thought of the wild colors on the outside of the vehicle and grinned. "Yeah, you wait until it's dark to get behind the wheel," he teased.

She smiled primly. "I'm no dummy."

He chuckled, then shook his head.

"Thanks, but I'm still good to go. However, when we get to the Prima Donna, I'm stopping for the night."

"Who's the Prima Donna?" she asked.

"It's not a who, it's a what," East said. "It's a casino about an hour or so west of Las Vegas."

She looked down at the map in her lap, squinting against the dim glow of the dashboard lights.

"I don't see any towns between here and there."

"There aren't."

She looked up. "You mean someone just built a casino in the middle of nowhere? Surely they don't get much business."

He shook his head. "Just wait and see."

She leaned her head against the seat, contemplating the wisdom of such folly, then settled back to wait as East said.

Sometime before midnight, Ally began to see a bright glow on the horizon. She shifted wearily in the seat and glanced at East, marveling that he showed no signs of the exhaustion she was feeling.

"We're almost there," he said.

She stood, and then walked back to the minuscule bathroom to wash her face and comb her hair. Not because she felt the need for grooming, but because she needed to do something to keep herself awake. When she came out, she took a soft drink out of the small bar-size refrigerator and carried it back to her seat. Popping the top, she took one long drink, then handed it to East without comment.

It occurred to him as he took it that, whether she knew it or not, she was becoming very comfortable with him and his presence. As he took a big drink, he wondered if she knew what she'd done; sharing the soft drink as she would with a friend.

He smiled in the dark, intrigued with the idea of her as a friend. He'd never made love to a very best friend, but something told him it was going to be special.

A short while later, he began to slow down. When he pulled into the parking lot of the Prima Donna Hotel and Casino, Ally was hanging out the window, staring in disbelief.

"They have a Ferris wheel," she muttered, pointing to the brightly lit sphere.

"Wait until you see what's inside."

Her eyes lit up. "What?"

"There's a merry-go-round on the ground floor for kids."

Her eyes widened. "They bring kids to places like this?"

"Oh honey, you have no idea."

She pointed across the highway to another large, brightly lit building. "Is that part of it, too?"

He shook his head. "No, but they share a tram of sorts."

"Amazing." Then she looked off to her right. "Look how many other people are parking here, too."

"No, those are trailer houses for the employees. We're too far out of Vegas for people to drive back and forth, so the owners just house their workers on the premises instead."

"Good grief," Ally exclaimed.

"It's an easy way to make sure that your employees show up on time."

A few minutes later, East pulled to a stop at the far edge of the parking lot.

"Now what?" Ally asked.

"We sleep. In the morning, I call Jonah. We're going to need some money, but he'll okay it. It wouldn't be the first time I had to pay for necessary information."

"What are you going to tell him?" she asked.

"As little as possible."

"When the kidnapper calls wanting information, what are you going to do?"

A muscle jerked in East's jaw. "Give it to him." Then he stood up, stretching his cramped muscles as he walked toward the back of the RV. "Are you hungry?"

"A little, but it's too late to eat. I think I'd rather sleep."

"Same here," East said. "You take the shower first, but remember, go easy on the water. We're not hooked up here, so we'll be using what's in store."

She nodded, then looked around, suddenly realizing that there were no beds in sight.

"Where do we sleep?" she asked.

"You'll see."

She shrugged, then went to clean up. A few minutes later she came out and almost stumbled on the two air mattresses in the middle of the floor. East was down on his knees, trying to put a contour sheet over the inflated pad.

"Bathroom's free. Let me," Ally said.

East stood, his cheeks red with frustration. "Have at it," he muttered, grabbed his bag and disappeared into the tiny bathroom.

By the time he came out, Ally had claimed the mattress against the wall and was sound asleep, leaving the one closest to the door for him. He stood for a moment, watching the even rise and fall of her chest beneath the covers and felt an overwhelming surge of tenderness. Another woman might have made an issue of the fact that they would be sleeping in such close quarters, or possibly tried to jump his bones. But not Ally. They were partners, therefore she'd given him her trust. Yet when he lay down beside her, it was all he could do to focus on the gift when the woman he wanted was so near and dear. Certain that he would never be able to sleep, he closed his eyes. When he opened them, sunlight was shining in his face.

Chapter 12

Ally was gone. He raised up on one elbow and wiped the sleep from his eyes, and as he did, saw the note. He leaned across the mattress and picked it up, tilting it toward the light.

> Went to get breakfast. Be back later.
> Me

He tossed the note aside as he got up and dressed, then deflated the mattresses and packed them and the linens back in the cupboard beneath one of the computer consoles. After digging through the supplies they'd brought, he found Freddie's coffeemaker and started it up. The scent of freshly brewing coffee soon filled the enclosure, making his belly growl. He glanced out the window, wondering how long Ally had been gone, and debated with himself about going to look for her, but he couldn't really afford to leave. One of them had to be by the phones at all times in case Jonah—or the kidnapper—called again. Left with no other options, he settled down to wait.

Half an hour passed and he was starting to get antsy when he saw Ally coming across the parking lot carrying a rather large, brown paper bag. He opened the door and waved. When she got closer, he called out to her.

"What did you do, buy them out?"

She handed him the sack and then climbed inside. "I didn't want to wake you."

"Something smells good," he said. "What's for breakfast?"

"A little bit of everything, so sit. I'll serve."

"We don't have any dishes or cutlery. When we go through Vegas, we need to get some disposable stuff."

"I know," she said. "I took care of the problem for today."

He grinned. "Why am I not surprised."

She handed him a paper container and a large plastic fork.

"Dig in."

He opened the lid, inhaling the food with appreciation as he forked a large bite of scrambled eggs and sausage and popped it in his mouth.

"Umm," he said, chewing around the nonverbal comment.

Ally smiled and opened her own, quickly digging in to the food.

They ate in silence until both containers were empty, then East picked them up and started to toss them in the sack she'd been carrying.

"Wait!" she cried, and jumped up, stopping him before he dropped the dirty stuff.

"What? I was going to use it for a trash container," East said.

She looked a little guilty, then took the sack and turned it upside down. Stacks of money fell out, some bundled in fives, a few in tens or twenties, the rest in one-hundred-dollar bills.

East gawked. "What the hell did you do?"

"Played a little blackjack."

He turned, staring at her in disbelief. "And you won...all this?"

"Well...yes."

"How long were you gone?"

She glanced at her watch. "Umm, about an hour, I guess." Then she added. "But it took about fifteen minutes of that time to get the food."

East kept staring at the money. "So, what you're saying is you won all of that in forty-five minutes?"

"You said we needed some money to travel on."

"Yes, but..." He stopped and started over. "How did you do that?"

She smiled. "Oh, it's quite simple, actually. It's all a matter of remembering what's been played, then figuring the ratio of what cards are left in the shoe, then taking the average—"

"Never mind," he muttered, and sat down with a thump, staring at her in disbelief.

"Exactly how *much* money did you win...in forty-five minutes, of course."

"Five thousand, four hundred and fifty dollars. There was a hundred dollars more, but I read where it's ac-

ceptable to tip the dealer if you win big, so I thought
I would—"

East started to grin and then pulled her down on
his lap.

"This is good," he said. "In fact, this is great, but
will you do me a favor?"

"Of course," she said.

"The next time you feel lucky, take me with you."

She frowned. "Oh, it's not a matter of luck. It's all
about—"

East kissed her square on the lips, stopping her explanation. When he stopped, he was breathing hard and
wishing to hell he didn't know she was a virgin.

Ally's expression was somewhere between confused
and a little bit stunned when East set her back on her
feet.

"I need to call Jonah," he said.

"You don't need his permission to make love to me,"
Ally said.

He grinned. "I don't?"

"Oh, no. Although he told me he wasn't sending me
to Condor Mountain to persuade you with sex, he did
say to do whatever it took to get you back in action."
Then she grinned.

East didn't know whether to be insulted, or glad she
was so damned honest. He decided on the latter.

"You just keep that smile on your face and see what
it gets you," he mumbled. "Now where's that phone?"

Ally went to retrieve it. As they waited for Jonah to
call, they began readying to leave.

"Where do we go from here?" Ally asked.

East pointed to the map. "We'll hit Highway 93 a

little northeast of Vegas. We're taking it straight north into Idaho."

Ally sighed. "I hope we're doing the right thing. This feels so out in left field, you know? We know some stuff, but not definite things. For instance, what about that name Jeff left on the floor? This man Bob? Is he the kidnapper, or just one of the men who took him?"

"I don't know yet, but I can promise you we will, and the first place we're heading is Elmore Todd's hometown of New Township."

Ally nodded. "You're right." Then she glanced at the bank of equipment in front of her and pulled up a small wheeled stool and sat down.

"What are you going to do?" East asked.

"Run some stuff. See if I can make connections between what we know and what we're just guessing at."

Before he could comment Ally's phone began to ring. It was Jonah.

"Do you have any information?" he asked, leaving East with no opportunity for a polite greeting of hello.

"Nothing firm, but we're on the road."

"You need money," Jonah said, as of matter of fact.

East grinned and looked at Ally. "Actually, we don't. Let's just say, I wouldn't advise anyone to play poker with my partner."

A rare chuckle echoed in East's ear.

"So," Jonah said, "if not money, then what?"

This was where it got tricky. East took a deep breath.

"I need you to really commit treason…at least in the eyes of the world."

"What the hell?" Jonah muttered.

"I have reason to believe I will be contacted shortly by someone interested in your downfall. I have no way of knowing if it's who we're looking for, or just someone who works for him. But if the call comes in, I want something incriminating."

"No," Jonah said shortly. "They can arrest me now on what they've got before I'll do that."

East had expected this. In fact, he would have been surprised if Jonah had agreed.

"I don't want anything vital sent. Just make it appear that way. Tell the President, or whoever you need to tell to get clearance, but so help me God, if you expect me to do my job, I need that much cooperation from you. I need to trace the communications that are being intercepted, and what better way than to track a piece of top security info."

There was a long stretch of silence. Finally, Jonah answered.

"I will call you back."

The line went dead.

East disconnected, his gut in a knot. If Jonah didn't cooperate, Jeff was as good as dead. And if he told Jonah what was really going on, he would be pulled immediately. Company policy was strict, and Jonah was a company man all the way.

"Is he going to cooperate?" Ally asked, without taking her eyes from the computer screen.

"I hope so," East said, and sat down in the front seat with a thump. "If he doesn't, we're screwed and Jeff's history."

A series of text suddenly popped up on the screen. With a satisfied smile, she began to scroll down the lines, scanning the text as she went.

"Maybe not," she said. "Maybe not."

"What are you into now?" East asked.

"Back in FBI files."

He frowned. "Damn, woman, don't they have any safeguards on this stuff?"

"Of course, but I sort of set this file up to begin with, so I know where the back doors are."

"Back doors?"

She glanced up at him and then smiled. "Just trust me."

He gripped her shoulders, giving them a quick squeeze. "Honey, I'm already there."

A couple of minutes passed, in which East paced and she worked. Suddenly, she laughed. He turned to see why.

"Bingo," she said softly.

He leaned over her shoulder, reading the text on the screen. "Militia groups?"

"Look at how many there are," she said.

"What exactly are you looking for here."

"I've cross-referenced the known groups with known members named Bob, and then cross-checked those names to see how many times Elmore Todd's name comes up in conjunction with them."

"Good job," East said. "What did you find?"

Her phone rang before she could answer. She pointed at East.

"You might as well answer that. It will be Jonah for you."

Saying a quick, silent prayer, he answered. "Yes?"

"Let me know when you want the information," Jonah said.

East went weak with relief. "Thanks."

"It is I who should be thanking you," Jonah said.

A dial tone sounded in East's ear. He disconnected and handed the phone to Ally.

"Buckle up, partner. We're heading north."

Jeff moaned in his sleep and woke himself up with the echo of his own voice. His head was hot and achy and it hurt to swallow. When he tried to sit up to get a drink of water, he pitched forward instead, hitting the floor headfirst.

"Son of a bitch," he mumbled, and crawled back to the cot on his hands and knees, then got back in bed.

Every muscle in his body was trembling and something wet was running from his forehead into his hair. He touched the wet spot, then put his finger to his lips and tasted it.

Blood.

A shudder racked his body as he reached for the covers, but felt nothing but air. He had enough medical experience to suspect he was on the verge of pneumonia. The constant chill, the damp, weeping walls and the lack of nourishing food and warmth were all taking their toll.

Almost twenty-four hours after they'd pulled out of the casino parking lot, they stopped at a place just outside of Boaz, Nevada. The sign on the truck stop was peeling and hanging by only one hinge, but the cafe´ was still open and they offered hookups for RVs. As tired as East was, it couldn't get much better than that.

Ally hadn't spoken in over three hours and was still in the back, doodling with the notes she'd downloaded. He stood and stretched.

"I'll go see about hookups. Be back in a bit."

She nodded without looking up.

A short while later he came back, moved the RV to the designated location and got out again to hook up the utilities. As he stepped back inside, he saw the concentration on her face, and opted to go buy some dinner. Chances were he'd be back before she ever knew he was gone.

Sometime later, Ally became aware that they'd stopped moving. She turned to look for East, but he was gone. Shoving aside the files, she stood up, and as she did, stumbled, then sat down in the floor with a thump.

"Oh, great," she mumbled, then started to laugh at herself as she took off her shoes.

East found her on the floor, barefoot and still chuckling. He set aside the food he was carrying and hurried toward her.

"Ally, are you all right?"

"I can't feel my foot. I sat there so long it went to sleep and I didn't even know it."

"Did you fall? Are you hurt?"

"Only my pride. Help me up," then added, "please."

He took her by the hands and pulled, hauling her off her butt and into his arms, then nuzzled the side of her neck before planting a kiss on the side of her cheek.

"Is this foreplay?" she asked.

Her question rocked his intentions. He looked at her and grinned.

"Do you want it to be?"

When she frowned, actually contemplating the question, he grinned.

"If you have to think about it, then your answer should be no," he said. "How about dinner, instead?"

Her eyes widened in appreciation. "Yes, please. I'm starved."

"Wash up," he said. "Hope you like what I chose, and I'll warn you, there's no money in the bottom of my sack, only napkins and ketchup."

She peeked into the sack on her way past, sniffing in appreciation.

"Mmm, hamburgers and fries. Did you put onions on mine?"

"They're loaded," he said. "You can take off whatever you want."

"I don't want to take anything off," she said, and hastened toward the bath.

East watched her go, her hips swaying to a feminine rhythm that only women can hear. He eyed her jeans and her shirt, wondering how long their food would stay hot if he followed his inclinations. She might not want anything removed, but he damn sure did.

Yet when she came back, he was the perfect gentleman, food laid out and waiting for her to dig in. It wasn't until bedtime that things began to sizzle again.

East was lying stretched out on his mattress, his eyes closed and his hands folded beneath his head. The sounds of Ally's shower were all but drowned out by the soft, country tune playing in the background from the clock radio he'd set by his bed. A woman's voice was weaving a plaintive story within the melody about a man who'd done her wrong. His conscience pricked with every note she sang. If he followed his instincts, would he do Ally wrong? He was in love with her. Flat out, deep down in his soul, forever in love. He could think of nothing better than to make a home with her, even make babies with her. But was this dream a selfish one? She was young—not even at the peak of her career with SPEAR. Maybe she didn't want to settle down. He had no idea how she felt about marriage or babies. And if she did come to love him, would she want to retire from active duty? Could he live with the knowledge that at any given time, on any operation, she might never come home.

He rolled over on his belly and gave his pillow a thump, bunching it beneath his chin and closing his eyes. The whole thing was a mess from beginning to end. He couldn't help thinking that if it hadn't been for Jonah, Jeff's life would not be in danger right now. But then, had it not been for Jonah's situation, East would never have met Ally. He thumped his pillow again just to punctuate his frustration. As he did, the song ended and so did Ally's shower. He heard the bathroom door open, then the sound of her bare feet upon the floor. He heard her hesitate, then heard her sigh. A few seconds later, the sound of shifting covers and the mattress scooting a bit on the floor told him that she'd crawled into her own bed. His gut knotted, just thinking about her lying beside him. All he had to do was turn, take her in his arms and—

"Are you asleep?"

He jumped, then stifled a wry grin before raising up on his elbows.

"Not now," he said, looking with great appreciation at the damp tendrils of her hair and her freshly scrubbed face.

Her eyebrows knotted across her forehead. "Well... *were* you asleep before?"

He couldn't find it in himself to lie, even though it would have been easier.

"No, I wasn't asleep."

"Then why pretend?"

He rolled over on his side, raised up on one elbow, and gazed down into those wide, questioning eyes.

"So I don't have to face the fact that I want to make love to you."

Ally sat up, her bare legs crossed, bracing herself with her elbows as she leaned a bit forward.

"But why?"

He sighed. "I want to ask you something. How do you feel about me?"

"I like you very much," she said promptly.

He smiled, but it wasn't what he wanted to hear.

"Thank you, honey, but that's not what I meant." He tried coming at the subject from a different way. "If the only reason you want to make love is because you're curious about the act, then I don't think I'm the man for the job."

"Oh, that's all right," she said quickly. "I think I knew all along that it wouldn't happen. I mean…why would someone like you be interested in an oddball like me…especially in that way?"

She managed a smile, but he saw the pain in her eyes before she looked away. That, above everything else, hurt his heart. He couldn't bear to think that he was causing her pain. So when she lay down with her back to him and pulled the covers up around her shoulders, he kicked his own covers aside, then crawled over to her mattress and stretched out behind her, aligning himself against her backside and then pulling her tightly against him until they were separated by nothing more than a blanket and sheet.

"What do you think you're doing?" Ally muttered.

"I think I'm falling for you," he said softly. "Now go to sleep."

There was a long moment of silence and then Ally started to cry. Not loud, ugly sobs; just quiet tears of joy and disbelief.

East felt her trembling and raised up again and leaned over her, peering intently through the shadows at her face. The glitter of tears on her cheeks made him groan.

"Ally…honey…for God's sake, don't cry. Whatever I said, I take back."

She rolled over on her back and locked her arms around his neck before he could move.

"Don't you dare," she said fiercely. "Nobody has ever said that to me before, so don't you dare take it back."

"Ah, sweetheart," East muttered, and slid his hands beneath her shoulders, lifting her close, then closer still. "You have less than ten seconds to change my mind before I show you what this is about."

"Show me," she begged, and lifted her mouth for his kiss.

He did as she asked, starting with the kiss. The covers between them came next as he tossed them aside, then her nightshirt and his gym shorts followed until they were naked to each other's sight. It was her innocence, as much as her charm, that sent his head in a spin.

"Can I touch you?" she whispered.

He grinned wryly. "Honey, you can do anything you damn well please to me and it will be okay."

"Truly?"

He pressed a kiss between her breasts and at the base of her neck, then on the center of her mouth.

"Truly," he said.

She pushed him until he was lying on his back, then splayed her hands across the middle of his chest. When those long, slender fingers began a foray across his chest, then moved lower toward his belly, he took a deep breath. As she hesitated at the juncture of his thighs then encircled him slowly, he gritted his teeth and closed his eyes. Never in his life had he experienced anything as seductive as her hesitant exploration. Within seconds, his manhood began to expand, and as it did, he heard a slight gasp, then a whispered, "Oh my."

He exhaled slowly and looked up. Her gaze was locked upon him, and then on his face. He couldn't tell if she was scared to death, or utterly fascinated by his response to her.

"My turn," he said, and rolled her onto her back before she could argue.

With a tenderness and patience he would not have believed himself capable of, he loved her to the point of insanity. Within minutes, he had her writhing beneath his caress, rocking with the rhythm of his fingers.

Ally's heart was pounding, her blood racing like flood waters toward an overflowing dam. It was at once, the most wonderful and the most frightening thing she had ever experienced. Never in her life had she been so out of control, or so bound to another's spell. The panic that came with it was almost more than she could bear, and it was instinct that made her reach for East, holding on to him to keep from dying.

"Let it go, honey," he whispered. "Just let go. I won't let you fall."

She closed her eyes and gave herself up to the ecstasy, crying aloud in the dark as the sensations shook her from her head to her toes. And when her blood was still hammering between her legs, East slipped in. She never felt the pain of his entry, or her body adjusting to his size. All she knew was that the addictive pounding of that pulse had suddenly restarted itself in a most unbelieving manner.

She opened her eyes to find him above her, looking down at her with love on his face. She lifted her arms to him, pulling him down until his weight was pressing her through the mattress to the floor, and it was still not close enough. Bits and pieces of things that she'd read began to filter through her mind as she yearned to give back to him that most wonderful thing that he'd just given her. She shifted slightly and lifted her legs, wrapping them around his waist and pulling him even closer still.

He groaned. And when she moved again, then again, then again, he groaned even more. To her joy, she could feel him coming undone and the power of his release filled her long-empty heart.

When East could talk without stuttering, he rolled, taking her with him and holding her close.

"Wow," he said. "I thought you'd never done this before."

She smiled against the warmth of his chest and snuggled a little bit closer.

"I read a book," she stated.

"Have mercy. You read all that in a book?"

She nodded.

He managed a grin, thinking to himself that he'd just possibly uncovered the mother lode.

"And what book would that have been?"

"It was actually two. One was the *Kama Sutra*, and the other was by a retired madame from the Chicken Ranch in Nevada."

East started to laugh.

Embarrassed, Ally tried to pull away, but East stopped her, holding her even closer and then smothering her face with kisses.

"What is so funny?" she finally managed to ask.

"You are the most marvelous mix of femininity I've ever encountered in my life, and all I can say is...education is a wonderful thing."

Chapter 13

"The time is seven o'clock and if you're heading out to work early, there is a wreck at the off-ramp of Interstate 80 and Highway 93. The eastbound lanes of I-80 are partially blocked, so take it slow out there, people, and keep it safe."

Ally rolled over on her back, groaning in disbelief at the cheery voice of the radio host as the clock radio East had set last night came on. When she saw him reach for the Off button without opening his eyes, she grinned and impulsively crawled around the mattress, scooting it a little farther out of his reach as the host continued his spiel with an update on the day's weather.

"On the home front today, the temperatures are predicted to reach the high seventies, with a nighttime low of forty-four."

East muttered beneath his breath and slapped toward the sound. The radio kept playing.

Ally stifled a fit of giggles as she watched him open his eyes reluctantly, in search of the offending noise.

"In national news, the Grand Jury testimony continues on Capitol Hill and members of the ATF are expected to testify before the day is out. It is rumored that certain agents of the U.S. Treasury will be called. It's difficult to say what the IRS could possibly have to add to the testimony of the ATF agents, so it looks as if it will be a case of wait and see."

Ally had been too focused on her fun with East to pay much attention to what was being broadcast until something the announcer said suddenly clicked. She sat up with a start and then bounced to her feet, dashing over East's body to the console where the hard copies of the information she'd downloaded were lying.

East opened his eyes just in time to see Ally vault over his legs. He sat up with a jerk, looking around for his gun while the radio continued to play.

"In Hollywood, insiders are saying—"

East reached for the radio, slapping the Off button and tossing it against the wall as he bolted up from where they'd been sleeping.

"What's going on? Is something wrong?"

She was slinging papers and files, moving mouse pads and pens, digging through the accumulation of information that they'd been gathering for days, all the while muttering.

"Bob…it's not really Bob after all. Where did I put those… I thought they were…never mind, here they are."

"Who's not Bob?"

Then the moment he asked it, he knew what she meant. The name Jeff had left on the floor of his apartment. If it wasn't Bob, then who?

Ally headed back to the mattress where she knelt and began sorting the pages out around her. East knelt beside her, watching and trying, without success, to figure out what she was doing.

Suddenly, she slapped her knee with the flat of her hand.

"I knew it!" she crowed, snatching a paper from one stack and adding it to the one she was holding.

"Let me in on the news."

"What if Bob isn't Bob, but an acronym?"

"For what?"

She handed him the papers in her hand.

"Read for yourself. Elmore Todd was in Jeff's house. We know that from the fingerprint. And Elmore Todd is a known militia sympathizer. We know that from his priors. And… Elmore Todd is a native of Idaho, which is where we believe Jeff is being held."

"Yes, but what does—"

"I'm getting to that," Ally said, all but clapping her hands with glee. "Bob. All this time, we thought Bob was one of the kidnapper's names, but what if it's not?"

She got to her knees and pointed to separate lines on each of the pages in East's hands.

"Elmore Todd has been tied to three different militia groups in the last twenty-one years—America's Freemen, Sons of Glory, and the Brotherhood of Blood. *B. O. B.* Bob."

East rocked back on his heels. It had been there all the time. He looked at Ally, then shook his head in disbelief.

"How did you figure this out?" Then he shook his head. "Never mind. I don't need to know. It's enough that you did."

"So you think I'm right?" she asked.

East grinned. "Honey, after last night, I'm never going to question your ability to do anything again."

She smiled prettily, blushing the least little bit as she began gathering the papers she'd scattered.

"What can we do with this information?" she asked.

"We can skip going to New Township to look for Elmore Todd. Instead, we need to find out where the Brotherhood of Blood is keeping house and find a way to pay them a visit."

She frowned. "I don't like that. We're severely outnumbered."

"So's Jeff," East growled, then grabbed her from behind and rolled, taking her with him. "And right now, so are you."

They fell in the middle of the mattresses with paper scattered all around them and began to renew the discoveries they'd made last night.

"Know any more of those tricks?" East asked.

"Oh, yes, I believe there are thirty-five chapters in the *Kama Sutra* and last night was worth only a couple of pages."

He grinned. "I have a few tricks of my own," he said. "Wanna trade?"

Three days later, they were no closer to finding Jeff. All of their leads had run into nothing and not even flashing their badges at the Idaho Bureau of Investigation had given them access to the Brotherhood of Blood. It was, according to the bureau chief, one of the few survivalist groups in the state that stayed on the move. They'd been flushed out of national park areas only to reappear months later in another area of the state. The last two reports the bureau had were over nine months old. For a group bent on revolt, they maintained a remarkably low profile, which according to the chief, made them more dangerous than most. His comment to East had been telling, and East couldn't get it out of his mind.

He'd said, "Big dogs bark and snarl and make a lot of noise, but it's those little dogs that come around behind you when you're not expecting it that will bite you in the ass."

So the Brotherhood didn't spread themselves as thinly as others. So they kept to themselves and if they were responsible for myriad dirty deeds, they kept the glory to themselves. So if this was so, how in hell was East supposed to find them?

After what seemed to be an endless drive, they parked *Baby* at a KOA campground outside of Ketchum that night and settled down to wait for the kidnapper's call. East's plan was to demand to speak to Jeff again and then try and trace the call, hoping to pinpoint the Brotherhood's location. The state was too vast and too desolate to just strike out on a mile-by-mile search. Far too many areas of the state were accessible only by boat or by air. Waiting was risky, but it was their only option. Waiting with Ally had become a risky business of its own. Day by day, they worked head-to-head—by night, they slept in each other's arms. For East, life was getting more complicated by the minute.

Ally was blossoming in a way she would have never believed. When she looked at herself in a mirror, she

saw a woman in love. Each day that she awoke beside
East was a day closer to heaven. She didn't think past
the time when this case would be over. She couldn't
let herself face what her future might be. East had said
nothing about what he was feeling, save the fact that he
loved to make love to her. That much she already knew
from the wild, crazy nights they spent in each other's
arms. What she wanted—no, needed—was to know
that he truly loved her—that when this was over, their
relationship would still exist.

Yet, as badly as she needed to hear this, pressing
him now when his son's life was at stake seemed in-
sensitive. So she laughed with him, argued with him,
and at night, made love with him and let it be enough.

The next day, at four minutes after six in the evening,
East's phone began to ring. It was what they'd been
waiting for, and yet they both stared without moving
at the small, black appliance as if it had grown fangs.
Suddenly, Ally bolted toward the equipment and hit the
controls. East grabbed the phone, then looked to see if
Ally was on the trace. When she nodded, he answered.

"This is Kirby."

"I was beginning to think you'd lost interest, my
friend."

The urge to kill was so strong East could feel it in
his bones. Instead of reacting to his rage, he took a deep
breath, then answered in a sarcastic drawl.

"I'm not your friend and where is my son?"

A low chuckle from the kidnapper rattled his poise.

"There's something you haven't realized. You're not
calling the shots. Now what do you have for me? Some-

thing special, I hope. I don't want you to disappoint me again."

East glanced at Ally. She was motioning for him to continue.

"I have what you asked for, but I want to talk to my son first. Then I'll give you the details."

There was a sharp intake of breath on the other end of the line, then an angry snarl.

"That won't do. I'm tired of playing games with you. I want my information now or your son dies."

East clenched a fist, but he kept on talking.

"I don't give you a damn thing until I know my son is still alive. You don't have to like it, buddy, but that's the way I play."

The line went dead in his ear.

"Did you get anything?" he asked.

Ally shook her head. "Nothing that will help, although I can tell you for certain that was an international call."

"You mean he's not even in the U.S.?"

"Not today," she said.

"Call Jonah, and hurry. I need the information now before the kidnapper calls back."

Seconds later, she made the call, then hung up. All they could do was wait. Within two minutes, Jonah was on the phone.

"It's going down," East said. "Give me something... fast."

Jonah rattled off a series of names and codes that made East's hair stand on end. Even though he knew this was false information, just the thought of giving away the identities of double agents abroad made him sick to his stomach.

"You're sure it's okay to use these?" he asked.

"Last week it would have meant their death. Today they've already been relocated and their codes have been changed."

"Okay," East said. "We'll see what we see."

Jonah hesitated, then added, "He's got to be stopped."

"I'm doing the best I can," East said.

Jonah disconnected.

A moment of guilt came and went, then East shook it off. Nothing mattered but Jeff. He turned to Ally, who was still on the trace.

"Out of curiosity, did you get a lock on that call?" he asked.

She grinned. "The moon."

"Hell of a scrambler he's got on that thing."

She laughed.

East's phone rang again. He pointed to Ally, counted down with his fingers; three...two...one. They picked up at the same time and the trace began.

Caleb Carpenter came out of the Brotherhood headquarters on the run with a cell phone in his hand.

"Get the hostage out of the hole! Now!" he yelled, motioning toward three nearby men.

Immediately, they dropped the guns they'd been cleaning and ran toward the hole. Within moments, the door was lifted and for the first time in many, many days, light spilled across the flat, concrete floor. One of the men leaned down and shouted.

"Hey, boy! Get yourself up here on the double!"

Nothing moved and no one answered.

By now, Caleb was at the hole and peering down.

"Hey, smart-mouth. Your old man wants to reach out and touch. Don't you want to talk to him?"

Caleb could just see the foot of the cot and thought he saw something move.

"Wake the hell up!" he shouted.

This time, they heard a distinct groan. At the sound, Caleb's heart skipped a beat. God almighty, the success of everything they were doing involved keeping him alive.

"Get down there now," he ordered. "But watch yourselves. He could be faking."

They thumped down the steps in rapid succession. But the first man had barely hit the bottom step when he stopped and turned, his expression panicky as he yelled back at Caleb.

"Sir! This doesn't look good!"

Caleb cursed beneath his breath and took the steps down, two at a time.

Jeff Kirby was almost unrecognizable. The heavy growth of whiskers on his face, along with a blood-caked forehead and lack of color beneath his skin, was proof enough to Caleb that they were all in big trouble. He felt Jeff's skin. The kid was burning with fever. A dark frown cut between Caleb's eyebrows, mirroring the lines that deepened beside his mouth. He turned.

"Where's Anderson? He was supposed to be taking care of the hostage."

They looked at each other then shrugged. "Not sure, sir. Maybe in the mess hall."

"Find him," he snapped. "Do it now."

One of the men bolted up the steps, while Caleb motioned for the others to come closer.

"Get him up and on his feet," he said. "He's got to make this call."

When a flood of light suddenly pierced the dark, Jeff thought he was dreaming. But when it persisted, and he could see vague shadows coming toward him and silhouetted against the light, he decided that he'd finally died and was on his way to heaven. It wasn't until he heard someone curse that he figured he'd made a mistake.

"Water," he mumbled.

Someone lifted a cup to his dry, cracked lips, and although the water went in his mouth, his throat was too swollen to swallow.

"Son of a bitch," someone muttered, as they dragged him to his feet.

Jeff shook his head. "Not in heaven," he mumbled.

"Not by a long shot, boy," Caleb said. "But I'll send you to hell myself if you don't do as I say."

"Already there," he muttered, as his legs gave way.

"Get him up the steps and into the sun," Caleb ordered.

The two men all but dragged Jeff up the steps. Then when he would have fallen again, Caleb ordered them to sit him on the top step instead. Gratefully, Jeff sat with his head in his hands and his eyes tightly closed, unable to bear the motion of movement, or the bright, sunlit sky.

"You're going to talk to Daddy, do you hear me?" Caleb asked. "You're going to tell him everything's fine or so help me, I'll break your stubborn neck myself."

"Go to hell," Jeff muttered and took a shaky swing at the blur before him.

Caleb dodged the feeble blow then punched in a series of numbers, waiting for the call to be answered.

East picked up on the first ring. "This is Kirby."

Caleb glanced down at Jeff, wondering how this was going to play out. All he could do was hope for the best.

"You have thirty seconds. Say what you want to your son and get it over with. The boss isn't happy with you."

"Well, hell," East drawled. "I'm not too happy with him, either. Now let me talk to Jeff."

Caleb put the phone to Jeff's ear. "Talk," he ordered.

Jeff felt the pressure of plastic against his face and moved his mouth toward the sensation.

"Dad?"

The word was barely audible, and East's heart almost stopped.

"Jeff? Jeff? Are you all right?"

East sounded so far away. Jeff reached for the phone, wanting to put it closer to his ear.

Reluctantly, Caleb released it, and he would look back on that action later with regret.

"Dad…"

Then the world started to spin. Jeff felt himself fading but couldn't find the words to speak. He pitched forward, rolling headfirst down the steps like a broken toy, and taking the phone with him. It hit the concrete a second before Jeff did, and then slid out of sight. Jeff's groan was loud and long, and then unconsciousness took him.

Caleb saw him falling and grabbed at Jeff's shirt. But it slipped through his fingers, leaving him to watch in dismay as the phone and the kid went flying.

"Grab him, damn it!"

But his order came too late. Both Jeff and the phone were gone.

East could only listen in horror, trying to imagine what was happening. Never in his life had he felt as helpless. He turned to Ally, giving her a frantic look, but she was focused on the computer terminal. The only good thing to come from it all was the phone. The line was still open. The trace was almost done.

He gripped the phone until his knuckles were white, listening intently, trying to pinpoint a recognizable sound that might help them locate Jeff, but all he could hear was a string of virulent curses, and someone named Anderson catching a large dose of hell.

A minute passed, and then suddenly Ally jumped to her feet and grabbed East, silently pointing to the screen and giving him a thumbs up.

East's shoulders slumped. Even though they'd traced the call, it didn't mean Jeff would be alive when they got there.

Suddenly, there was a breathless voice in his ear.

"Are you there? Are you there?"

"I'm here, you sorry bastard. What the hell have you done to my son?"

"We did nothing," Caleb said. "He fell. He's fine. Just confused."

"No, you're confused," East shouted. "You get nothing. Your sorry-ass boss gets nothing. Nothing goes from me to you without proof that Jeff is still alive." Then he hung up in Caleb Carpenter's ear.

"Damn," Caleb muttered. Then he pointed to Jeff.

"Get him out of the hole and into the infirmary. Have Henry take a look at him. See what he can do," then he stomped up the steps, aware that they were bound to get another call from the boss and he wouldn't be happy.

But Caleb wasn't the only one who was nervous about a call. East knew he was playing fast and loose by making demands, and he had heard Jeff's voice just before everything hit the fan. What he did know was that, sick or hurt, Jeff was in trouble and they had to get him out fast.

Within minutes, the call came that East had been waiting for. The kidnapper's fury was evident as he screamed into the phone.

"You messed up and signed your kid's death warrant."

East was shaking with an equal rage and a fast growing fear that the man was right.

"He couldn't even talk to me," East shouted back. "You don't keep your word, I have no reason to keep mine."

The kidnapper let loose with a long string of curses, promising every dire consequence to every member of East's family for the next fifty years.

East's laugh was short and bitter. "Jeff was my only family member, you stupid son of a bitch. There's no one left you can hurt."

"There's you," the kidnapper snarled.

"Come and get me," East said, and hung up.

The phone rang again within seconds.

"What?" East snapped.

It was as if East was talking to an entirely different man. The fury—the rage—the incoherence was completely gone from the kidnapper's voice.

"This is all a misunderstanding," he said. "Your son

is ill, but he's being doctored as we speak. He has not been harmed, now give me what I want."

"And if I do, when will you give me my son?"

"Well now," the man chuckled. "That's a little different. I've decided that he's a pretty good nest egg for me. I'll give you your son back, when I take Jonah down. I'll call you within a week or so for new information, and I promise you another call to your son will be forthcoming. What do you say?"

Aware that he'd played out this hand, East blurted out the information that Jonah had given him. Seconds later, a dial tone buzzed in his ear.

He disconnected, then tossed the phone aside and strode out of the RV without saying a word.

Ally followed, catching up with him at the edge of a cluster of trees. East was pale and shaking, but when she looked at his face, she saw it was rage and not fear that was holding him hostage.

She grabbed him by the forearms, making him face her—making him listen.

"Whatever he said, it doesn't matter. Turn loose of that anger and help me. I've got the location of the call. I've even got the number of the cell phone from where it was made. We can find Jeff. We can do it."

He closed his eyes and took a deep breath. When he opened them, she was still there—waiting. A calm came over him then and he knew before this went any further, she had to know what her presence meant to him.

"Come here," he said, and held out his hand, pulling her to a nearby bench where they sat.

Ally waited, unable to imagine what he must be feeling. When he palmed her hand between the breadth of his own, she looked up at him and smiled.

He leaned forward until their foreheads were touching. He kissed her cheek, then her lips. As always, the tentative blend of woman and innocence left him weak.

"The day Jeff was kidnapped was the worst and the best day of my life. I was afraid and confused, uncertain of where to start, and then I turned around and you were there. 'We'll find him,' you said, and at that moment, I knew it was true. Ever since the day you came into my life, I've been fighting an emotion I will no longer deny. I am in love with you, sweetheart…deeply and without reservation, and I am going to love you forever, whether it matters to you or not."

"Oh, East," Ally whispered, then stood up and stepped between his legs, wrapping her arms around his neck and pulling his head to her breasts. "I love you, too."

He held her there, with his cheek against the beat of her heart and knew a peace like he'd never known before.

For Ally, the last of her misgivings about herself disappeared. Safe in the assurance of East Kirby's love, she had become a confident and loving woman. Together, they could do anything—and they needed to find his son to make their family complete.

"How do you want to approach this?" Ally said.

"Geographically speaking, exactly where did the call originate?"

"The Bitterroots," she said, and then sat down on his knee as they began to make plans.

East frowned. Those mountains were desolate and unpopulated. There was no way they could come in without warning. "How close did we get?"

"I'm guessing it's about a mile radius in which we'll have to search," Ally replied.

"We'll fly the area. There's bound to be buildings of some sort that are visible from the air."

"We'll need a pilot and a—"

"I'm certified to fly just about anything shy of a jumbo jet," East said.

"I am impressed."

He gave her a lopsided smile. "And you should be," he teased. "I am an impressive kind of guy." Then he lifted her off his lap and stood. "Let's get cracking. I can't get rid of the feeling that Jeff's life hinges on how quickly we can find him."

Chapter 14

The next day they were in the air at daybreak, heading north. They'd been flying a little over two hours, and for Ally, the two-seater plane they were in was like skimming the heavens in a toy. Ally was scanning the aerial map in her lap, searching for landmarks when she suddenly tapped East's arm and then motioned for him to look down.

"Anywhere within this area. Look for rooftops. A road. Anything that indicates inhabitation."

He nodded and began to bank, taking the plane into a circle. At first they saw nothing below but the mountains, scrub brush and a vast endless canyon with a thin ribbon of reddish-brown water threaded through it. It wasn't until he began a second sweep through the area that a flash of sunlight on something below caught his eye. Unwilling to fly lower, he motioned for Ally to

use her binoculars. She could see a series of rooftops,
a couple of vehicles, and what appeared to be a single-
track road leading into the area. After one quick look,
she checked the coordinates on the map in her lap, then
looked again.

"That's got to be it," she said. "There's nothing else
out here, and these are the coordinates from which the
call was made."

He glanced at the fuel gauge, then at his watch.
"There's no place to land a plane like this. We'll need
a chopper."

"And I have an idea that might make our retrieval
easier," Ally added.

He nodded, looking down at the area one last time.
Hang in there, son. I'll be back. Then he nosed the
plane south.

East sat cross-legged on the floor of the RV, listening to the tape Ally was playing for him. Even though
he'd watched her doing it, he was stunned at the au-
thenticity of the piece.

"So, what do you think?" she asked.

"I think it's genius. Play it again, will you?"

She hit Rewind, then Play, listening along with East
to the kidnapper's voice.

*"I'm tired of playing games with you. You messed up.
I'm sending my people to retrieve my package. Have it
ready and don't disappoint me again."*

"Of course, this all hinges on our theory that the people holding Jeff did not expect him to fade out on them
or they would never have given him the phone," East
said. "It also follows that the kidnapper had to be ticked
at them, too, because it messed up his plans with me."

"I agree," Ally said. "You're sure it was Jeff's voice that you heard?"

East nodded, eyeing her with renewed respect. "You're damn good at what you do, aren't you, Ally?"

"Without tooting my own horn too loudly, I'll say yes."

"Before, I would have said our chances of rescuing Jeff without a small army were slim to none, but this could be the key to getting in and out of there without force."

She grinned. "That and a woman with attitude."

"What do you mean?"

"Well, it stands to reason that a woman who would work for this kidnapper is not going to be on any debutante list. And since you're the pilot, I will be the one ostensibly sent on retrieval detail."

A quick frown furrowed across East's forehead. "Now wait a minute, you don't think I'm going to sit in the background while you—"

"I don't think it, I know it," she said. "You're too emotionally involved in this to stay cool. Besides, the less show of force, the less the men holding Jeff will suspect."

East shook his head. "I don't like it. There are too many unknowns."

"That's what the assault rifles are for…changing people's minds. Now let's call Jonah."

A few minutes later, after going through the same procedure as always, Ally's cell phone rang. She answered.

"This is Corbin."

"Good evening, Alicia, I trust all is well?"

"Yes, sir, going quite nicely, sir. We need some supplies."

"Name them."

"An unmarked chopper, preferably a Bell Jet Ranger, two assault rifles and ammunition, camouflage gear for two, size ten women's and a man's extra large. Shoe sizes eight for me, twelve for East. Oh…and just for effect, why don't you throw in a gun and holster for me, something big, ugly and deadly."

"That's quite a list, young lady. Are you sure you've been all that good this year."

Ally's eyes widened in surprise. To hear Jonah joking about being Santa Claus, even briefly, was not in the context with which she normally dealt.

"Yes, sir, I believe that I have," she said.

He chuckled softly, then his demeanor changed. "What's going down?"

"We have reason to believe we've located some associates, although we have no way of knowing if the target will be present."

"This is good. Do you require any backup?"

Ally glanced at East. "Not at the present, although as you know, I'm not the primary on this, sir."

"Right. Let me talk to East."

"Yes, sir. I'll put him on." She handed the phone to East.

"This is Kirby."

"What's going down?"

"We've located what we believe to be known associates, and while we have no identity on your target, there is the possibility that he could be among them."

"Do what you need to do," Jonah said.

East thought of Jeff. "Yes, sir. Never doubt that is exactly what I'm doing."

"Where and when do you want the deliveries?" Jonah asked.

East gave him the time and coordinates. "It's done," Jonah said. "And good luck."

"Thank you, sir. We're going to need it."

He disconnected, then handed the phone to Ally for safekeeping.

"Hopefully, the next time we talk to Jonah, it will be with good news," Ally said.

East shook his head. "I doubt it. Not when he learns I've been deceiving him."

Ally frowned. "It's not deception in the true sense of the word. These people *are* associated with the man who's trying to ruin Jonah. Locating them will give Jonah new information. Who knows where it will go from there?"

East shrugged. "It won't be how he perceives it, but I can't let anything matter but getting my son out alive." He got to his feet and began to pace. "Waiting for daylight is going to be hell."

Ally put her hand on his shoulder, then cupped the side of his face.

"I have an idea," she said softly.

"What?"

"After dinner, I know a good way to burn off some energy."

East sighed and then smiled, thinking of that wonderful book that she'd read.

"Yeah, I could go for that," he said, and gave her a quick hug. "What sounds good to eat?"

"Oh, I don't care," she said. "It's what comes afterward that really matters."

East grunted as Ally body-slammed him onto his butt and drove to the basket with a look of glee on her face. All he could do was watch in dismay at the perfection of her layup. The basketball went through the net in a near-silent swish and she thrust her hands skyward as she laughed and turned.

"That's game!" she crowed. "I win."

"You cheated," he muttered, as she helped him to his feet.

"I did no such thing," she said. "I even offered to spot you four points but you refused."

"I didn't want to take unfair advantage of you, since I'm almost a foot taller. How was I to know you were a hustler?"

"I do not hustle," she said haughtily, and retrieved her ball before striding to a nearby bench to get her towel and bottle of water.

"Like hell," East said, as he followed her there, watching as she downed her drink.

Behind them, the dusk-to-dawn streetlights at the municipal park were just coming on and a quartet of young men was approaching the court.

"Thank God," he muttered. "Reinforcements."

She turned, eyeing the boys with curiosity. "I thought you were ready to call it quits."

"I never quit," he said shortly. "However, it would be rude to hog the only court."

She laughed. "Admit it. Their arrival saved your butt from having to play me again."

He grinned, ruefully rubbing his posterior. "No, they

arrived too late to save the butt to which you so po-
litely refer, but they did give me a good excuse to take
you home."

Impulsively, Ally threw her arms around his neck
and kissed him soundly. Just when he was getting into
the act, she withdrew.

"Not that I'm complaining," East said. "But what
was that for?"

"For being a good sport, and for offering to show
me your etchings."

He leaned forward, whispering so they wouldn't be
overheard. "I didn't say a damn thing about showing
you etchings."

She grinned. "That's right, you didn't. However,
surely you can find something of interest to show me
before the night is through."

East laughed out loud. "Woman, it's just possible
that you could be the death of me…but if that's so, then
what a way to go."

Night had come to Ketchum, Idaho, blanketing *Baby*
and her inhabitants in varying degrees of shadows. An
assortment of flying insects hammered themselves at
the blue-white night-lights of the RV park while traffic
sped by on the highway beyond. Inside the psychedelic
RV, another kind of frenzy had evolved. One born of
love and desperation, and an acceptance that tomorrow, should something go wrong, this could be their last
night on earth. And while none of these fears had been
voiced, East and Ally knew well the realities of what
they were about to do. On this night, making love was
their affirmation to each other and to the blessing of still
being alive. But long after the passion had subsided and

they lay replete and quiet in each other's arms, it was impossible for either of them to ignore the possibility that Jeff Kirby might already be beyond earthly joys.

"Around this next curve and we'll be there," East said, referring to the location he'd given Jonah last night.

Ally nodded, her mind on everything that had yet to be done. The doctored tape of the kidnapper's demand was in her pocket and a cosmetic bag with a few tricks of the trade lay on the floor beside her feet. Getting into the persona of another person was something she'd done many times now, but never had it seemed as important as it did on this day.

"Hot damn, Jonah came through with a bang," East muttered.

Ally looked up. There was a nondescript man in the clearing ahead, standing beside a gleaming black chopper. Off to his right was an older model truck with a load of feed in the bed. She suspected his innocent appearance was deceptive.

"Did you suspect that he wouldn't?" she asked.

"No, but you forget, it's been ten years since I've played this game. Some things fade with time."

She eyed him carefully, judging his state of mind. He seemed cool, almost indifferent—proper behavior for a man about to go into battle.

"And some things don't."

He nodded, unaware that she was referring to him.

After a brief identification, the man left, claiming he needed to feed his cattle, leaving East and Ally alone. She sorted through the duffle bags inside the chopper, tossing East his clothing, then began unbuttoning her own clothes. Soon, her jeans, tennis shoes and shirt had been replaced with camouflage clothing and black combat boots. Oblivious to everything now but her game plan, she reached for the makeup bag.

East was dressed and buckling his belt when he turned to check Ally's progress. He stopped short, stunned by the transformation. Her eyes had been outlined in something dark and thick, her lips a slash of red in a cold, pale face. She'd slicked some kind of gel through her hair, then combed it away from her face in a mannish style and was in the act of fastening a holster. It hung down the side of her right hip, putting the butt of the gun close at hand.

"Ally?"

She turned. "What?"

His face was expressionless. "Just wanted to see if it was you."

She smiled, and in that moment, he saw the woman he loved, and a feeling of peace settled in.

"Are you ready to make the call?"

She nodded. "Let me get the stuff."

Shuffling through her gear, she produced East's cell phone and the tape. Once more, she punched Play, just to make sure that the tape was in the correct position, then gave East a nod.

"Let 'er rip," he muttered.

Mentally thanking the technology that had allowed her to track and trace those incoming calls, she punched in the number she'd picked up from the Bitterroot area and waited for someone to answer.

Caleb Carpenter was in the middle of his second cup of coffee when his cell phone rang. He frowned and glanced at his watch. He wasn't expecting any calls, although the fit the boss had thrown yesterday after the fiasco with the hostage had given him a rather sleepless night. He cleared his throat and then answered.

"Hello?"

There was a moment of silence, then a voice came over the line that sent a cold chill up his spine.

"I'm tired of playing games with you. You messed up. I'm sending my people to retrieve my package. Have it ready and don't disappoint me again."

"But—"

The line went dead.

He cursed softly and tossed the phone on the desk. This wasn't good. This wasn't good at all. He stood abruptly and headed for the door to check on the hostage. Although they'd filled him full of antibiotics last night before they'd put him back in the hole, he couldn't help but worry. God help them all if the damn kid died.

East and Ally were in the air before eight o'clock that morning and heading north to the Bitterroots with a prayer in their hearts. Pulling this off depended upon the success of a very fragile chain of events.

The supposition that the place they'd seen yesterday was truly the stronghold of the Brotherhood of Blood and the place where Jeff was being held.

The fact that the Brotherhood had no way of communicating with the kidnapper unless he happened to call on them, therefore eliminating the possibility of anyone at the Brotherhood calling to confirm the call they had made.

The hope that Jeff would still be alive to rescue.

A faith that the Brotherhood would accept Ally's authority over their own.

It wasn't something a wise man would bet on, but it was all they had.

East pushed the chopper to its limit while steadying his anxiety with the knowledge that, one way or another, this nightmare would soon be over.

Ally sat quietly, marking time as she settled into her persona as the kidnapper's mouthpiece.

All too soon, the familiar landmarks of their appointed location began to appear. When the rooftops of the compound came into view, East circled it once, making sure that the people below were not taken by surprise.

"Here they come," he said, watching as tiny figures came spilling out of buildings like beans out of a can.

"Take it in," Ally said. "I'm ready to play dirty."

He shifted the controls and the chopper began its descent, dropping straight into the enemy's lap.

The moment Caleb heard the chopper, he knew they were here. He grabbed his gun and came out on the run, waving the other men back who had begun to assemble. The air about them swirled like a wayward twister, blasting them with debris as the chopper dropped into their midst. Caleb jammed his cap a little tighter and turned his head, shielding his eyes. When he finally turned to look, he saw a woman getting out. His eyes widened. This wasn't what he'd expected.

East grabbed Ally's arm as she reached for the door. Their gazes locked.

"I'm here if you need me."

"Oh, I need you all right. I can't fly this damned thing, so don't go and do anything crazy and get yourself hurt or killed, or we're all skunked. Understand?"

He nodded.

"There's something else," Ally added.

"What?"

"Thank you for showing me how special it is to be a woman."

East paled. This sounded too much like a goodbye. "You just keep your damned self in one piece, because I haven't even started," he warned.

"Love you, too," she said softly, then she turned, letting herself slide into that cold, hard place inside her mind. She shifted the strap on her assault rifle to a more comfortable place on her shoulder, slid a pair of sunglasses up her nose, then opened the door and jumped out.

She moved through the blowing debris with a purposeful stride, making no attempt to duck beneath the spinning rotors as people are tempted to do, nor did she turn from the dust that must have been blowing in her eyes. Her rifle was aimed at the ground in deference to propriety, but her hand was resting lightly on the place above the trigger. It was impossible to mistake her intent. When she was within a dozen yards of the silent crowd, a man separated himself and stepped forward.

Ah, the man in charge.

She strode forward with a swagger, shoving her femininity into their faces and daring them to test her.

"I came for the package," she said. "Where's it at?"

Caleb frowned. "You're not who we expected."

She slid her hand a little closer along the gun butt, making sure they saw her intent.

"Yeah, and you're not what we expected, either," she snapped. "The boss isn't happy and I didn't come here to debate this with you. I'm following orders, and if you're smart, you will, too."

"Simon still owes us the last half of the money," Caleb snapped.

Ally's heart skipped a beat. Damn. Something they hadn't counted on. But they hadn't come this far to wimp out now.

"You've got nerve," she drawled. "Screwing up a vital piece of business and expecting to still get paid."

She took a step closer, putting herself in his face. "If I were you," she said softly. "I would kiss my own ass and consider myself fortunate I still had the breath to do it."

Caleb hesitated, then turned around. "Anderson... Franklin...go get the kid."

Two men ran off to do his bidding while Ally stood in their midst. The only thing that kept her from panic was the gun on her shoulder and the man at her back. She wouldn't let herself think of what East must be feeling. Staying in this mind-set was imperative to the success of their mission.

She could not see where the two men went, but East could, and when they began dragging back a drop cloth, revealing a door in the ground, his mind went blank. All he could think was that all this time Jeff had already been buried...but buried alive.

The men disappeared in the hole then came up quickly, all but dragging a figure between them. Even though East knew it was Jeff, he would never have recognized him. His blond hair was dark and matted, he suspected with dried blood. His face was heavy with a growth of whiskers, and his features were bruised and swollen. He staggered when he walked, evidence of his weak state, and it was all East could do not to bail out of the chopper and go get him.

When the crowd parted, a muscle in Ally's eye began to twitch. It was her only concession to the shock she felt.

"Load him up," she said, motioning with the barrel of her rifle toward the waiting chopper.

Caleb hesitated, then nodded to the men, who began walking then dragging Jeff along between them.

Ally gave Caleb a last look, making sure he knew who was in charge, then, resisting the urge to run, strolled back through the thick, swirling dust as if she were going to the beach.

Blinded by the sun and swirling dust, it was all Jeff could do to keep moving. The urge to see what was happening was overwhelming, but impossible. The knowledge that he was being moved from the only place he'd told his father to look made him panic, but there was nothing he could do to stop the inevitable.

"What's happening?" he mumbled.

"Shut up, and keep moving," someone yelled in his ear.

He did as they said. Then he heard a woman's voice behind him just as they thrust him forward.

"Put another bruise on him and you'll wear one just like it," she yelled.

He didn't know who she was, but if he'd had enough spit to talk, he would have thanked her.

Suddenly, the swirl of dust was outside and he was in, lying flat on some kind of floor. He rolled over on his back and covered his eyes with his hands, shielding them from the unyielding glare of the sun.

"Scoot your butt," the woman said, and gave him a shove.

Seconds later a door slammed, shutting out dust and part of the noise. Jeff rolled again and started to shiver. His fever was up.

East wanted nothing more than to get out of his seat and take Jeff in his arms, but they weren't out of the woods yet. The crowd of men was shifting.

"Is he in?" East yelled.

Ally gave him a thumbs-up. "Yes, East, your boy is in. Now take us home."

Jeff flinched as the chopper began its ascent. He groaned beneath his breath, convinced he was hallucinating, because he could have sworn he just heard East's voice. The he felt the woman's breath on his face.

"Jeff, honey...you're going to be all right."

Honey? He opened his eyes, shading them with his hands, and looked up into an unfamiliar face.

"Who?" he whispered.

Ally tapped East on the shoulder. "He wants to know who we are."

East glanced out the side of the window to the disappearing landscape far below, then over his shoulder to the young man on the floor. For the first time in a month, he felt like crying for joy, but all he could do was grin.

"Just tell him he's going home."

Chapter 15

Guilt weighed heavily on East's conscience as he watched Jeff sleep. He wasn't the same man they'd rescued yesterday. His color was improving, as was his breathing. His body had been washed, as had his hair, and the beard was gone. Asleep, he looked like a kid again, but East knew that in surviving, Jeff had crossed a threshold into manhood that few would ever know.

He turned suddenly as the door behind him opened, but relaxed just as quickly when he saw that it was Ally.

"How's he doing?" she asked, and gave East a quick kiss on the cheek.

"Good. Still sleeping a lot, though."

"That's the medicine. He needs it. Pneumonia isn't something to scoff at, especially under those conditions."

"I know. We were lucky," he said.

"We were blessed," Ally amended, then blurted out her news before she lost her nerve. "I have another assignment."

"No," East groaned, and then caught himself. Just because he saw their lives going one way, didn't mean she agreed. He would never ask a woman to give up a career for him. "Sorry," he said gruffly. "That just slipped out."

Ally wanted to cry. "Don't apologize," she said. "It's what I said when Jonah called."

East sighed. "What did he say about all of this?"

"Not what you would expect. He seemed horrified about what had happened to your family because of him and said to tell you that he would never impose upon you like that again. Then he wished you good luck at the resort and something about a long and happy life."

East looked away. "I lied to him. It's not something I'm proud of."

"I don't think he considered it a lie, East. You were simply protecting your family the only way you knew how. Besides, don't forget that in finding Jeff, we also gave a name to the man who's trying to take him down. I would lay odds that, as we speak, something else is in the works to find this Simon character."

"You're right," East said.

"How will you get *Baby* home?" Ally asked.

"When Jeff is strong enough, we'll drive her home."

In spite of her determination not to do so, she started to cry.

"I feel like I'm losing you," she whispered.

East took her in his arms. "Never," he said softly. "You know where I am. When you're ready, just come back to me. That's all I ask."

"Oh, I'll be there," Ally said. "For as long as you'll let me."

East cupped her face, swiping at a slow stream of her tears with the balls of his thumbs.

"Forever sounds good to me," he said.

"Is that a proposal?"

"Did you by any chance happen to memorize that *Kama Sutra* thing?" he asked.

She managed to grin. "Most of it, I imagine."

"Then by the time you come back, have the rest of it put to memory. It will be something to look forward to on our wedding night."

"I love you, East."

"And I love you, too," he said softly. "Hurry home to me."

It was nightfall and the hospital sounds were far more subdued than they were during the day. East dozed in a chair by Jeff's bed, while compliments of Jonah, a guard stood watch outside the door. Until they were certain no more threats were forthcoming, they would assume nothing. All the information they'd learned about the Brotherhood's illicit activities had been given to Jonah—the rest of it was up to him.

Jeff shifted restlessly and East woke abruptly, moving to his bedside and laying his hand on Jeff's arm, then his forehead, testing for fever. To his relief, he was almost cool.

"Dad...is that you?"

East grinned. "Who did you think it would be...that woman you keep refusing to discuss?"

A faint smile slid across Jeff's face and then he closed his eyes, opening them again seconds later.

"I knew you'd come."

East curled his fingers around Jeff's forearm and gave it a quick squeeze.

"Thanks to your quick thinking. That little clue you dropped about crashing and burning was good. You know…if you ever decide to forego medical school, you'd make a hell of a good spy."

"Bite your damned tongue," Jeff mumbled.

East laughed softly.

"Did I dream it, or was there a woman with you?" Jeff asked.

Pain pierced East's composure. "No, you didn't dream her," East said. "Although I'll admit she's a dream of a lady."

The remark was so out of character for East that Jeff made himself focus.

"Sounds serious."

"Yeah," East said.

"Where is she?"

East looked away. "I don't know and that's the hell of it. Now get some sleep. I won't be far."

Jeff closed his eyes as East settled back in his chair. Just when East thought Jeff had fallen back to sleep, he slipped one last comment into the night.

"If she matters, she'll be back."

East didn't bother to open his eyes. "How do you know?"

"It's what I keep telling myself."

The loneliness in that single sentence made East sad. It was just as he'd suspected. There was, or at least there had been, someone special in his life.

As he stood, a soft knock sounded on the door. He looked up to see a nurse poke her head in the door.

"Mr. Kirby, there's a call for you in the waiting room."

He glanced at Jeff one last time, then headed for the door, leaving quick instructions with the guard that he'd be right back.

When he got to the waiting area, the phone was off the hook, and the room was empty. Hoping it was Ally, he answered.

"This is Easton Kirby."

"And a formidable opponent you were."

East's blood chilled. "You son of a bitch."

The man chuckled. "Yes, probably. However, that's not why I called."

"You leave me and my family alone, or so help me, God, I'll find you and—"

"There's no need for threats," he said sharply. "That's why I called. I misjudged you. I don't make the same mistakes twice. Rest assured that I will succeed in my mission, but that you will in no way be further involved."

"I wouldn't have been involved in the first place if you hadn't taken my son," East snapped.

"So I realized, but alas, too late. However, it's never too late to right a wrong, don't you agree?"

"There's nothing we could possibly agree upon. You won't get away with this, and I wish you straight to hell."

The man laughed again, only it was brief and bitter.

"But that's just the point, you see. I'm already there."

Epilogue

East walked out to the balcony of his apartment, eyeing the terrace below and making a mental note to have the hotel groundskeepers install some new lighting around the base of the railing. It seemed a little dim.

The television was playing in the room behind him, but he paid it no mind. It was just noise—something to keep him from thinking about how lonesome he really was. It had been a month yesterday since Jeff's rescue, and a month today since he'd last seen Ally. From the first day of his return, he'd awakened with the hope that she would call, or that he would have a letter from her in the mail. And each day that passed without that hope coming to fruition brought a deeper sense of pain to his life. He wouldn't let himself think that she'd come to harm on that last assignment. He made himself remember how cool and poised she'd been when she'd faced down the entire Brotherhood of Blood. She was a professional—and a damned smart one, he reminded himself. She wouldn't let herself get caught up in something she couldn't control.

But it had been thirty days—and thirty nights—and he hurt so deep inside his gut that he sometimes wondered if the pain would kill him after all. He missed her laughter and that prim, prissy look she got when her authority was questioned. He wanted to watch her eat waffles, one square at a time, and every hour of the day he would tell her that he loved her so that she wouldn't forget he wasn't like her parents—so she wouldn't forget the woman she'd become.

He braced his hands against the railing and leaned forward, absently watching the sunset. One moment it was there, hovering on the edge of the horizon, then disappearing so quickly that it seemed as if the ocean had suddenly opened its mouth and swallowed it whole. At once, a vivid streak of color spread upward from the horizon, painting the sky in varying shades of purple and pink.

"It's beautiful, isn't it?"

East spun. "Ally?"

"Is that offer still open?" she asked.

A wide grin split the somberness of his face. "Did you memorize the rest of that damned book?"

"Yes."

"Then yes, a thousand times yes, it's still open."

She returned the grin and then gasped as he lifted her off her feet and began kissing her over and over on every inch of her face. She closed her eyes, deciding that being loved by Easton Kirby was a little akin to flying—a little frightening, but well worth the ride.

A short while later, East was in the midst of explanations about Jeff's full recovery and return to his studies, when Ally decided it was time to share her own bit of news.

She cleared her throat and folded her hands in front of her, as if waiting for permission to speak.

When East saw her gathering herself, and then watched that beautiful mouth slightly purse, he grinned.

"Got something to say, have you?"

"How do you know?" she asked.

He shrugged, unwilling to give away the one thing he knew about her that might hold him in good stead for the next sixty or so years.

"Psychic, I guess. So what's up?"

"I brought you a present…two actually."

His grin widened. "I like presents. What are they?"

She headed for the bedroom, returning momentarily with a small, flat package and handed it to him.

East chuckled. It was a book, that much he knew. Expecting it to be a copy of that blessed *Kama Sutra*, he was taken aback by the pink and blue cover, as well as the title.

"What To Name Your Baby?"

She smiled primly. "Since it's our first, I thought you might like to choose. But if we have another, the pleasure will be mine, okay?"

The grin on his face started to slide as his eyes began to widen. Ally stared, watching in sudden fascination and wondering if one facial muscle was connected to another in such a way that what was happening was beyond East's control, or if he had gone into shock. She did a quick mental breakdown of the construction of the human form and decided upon the latter. It was definitely shock. But the longer he remained silent, the more she began to worry. Finally, she could stand the suspense no longer.

"Don't you have something to say?"

He stared at her face, then her belly, then back at her face again, blinking through a blur of quick tears.

"Actually, I think I have two," he mumbled.

This wasn't going exactly as she had planned. Her fingers knotted as she tried to offer a brief smile. It didn't come off as she'd wanted.

East saw the sudden terror in her eyes, but it was nothing to the joy in his heart.

He touched her belly, then his heart. "I don't think I've ever been so happy in my entire adult life."

Her lips parted in a quick, sweet smile.

"I'm so relieved. I mean, we hadn't discussed any of—"

"Will you marry me?"

The smile dissolved into full-fledged tears.

"Oh, East, I was hoping you would ask me that, since I've already turned in my resignation with SPEAR." She splayed her hands across the middle of her belly. "I mean… I can't be running all over the country anymore and endangering our child. I will never do to my baby, what my parents did to me. I will be there in the night when it cries. I will be there to see first steps and hear those precious first words. And I will die before I'll give this baby to someone else to raise."

He gathered her close to him, holding her as if she

was the most precious thing on this earth, which to him, she was.

Her pledge had him speechless. Finally, he managed to mutter, "Why is it that a woman always cries when she's happy?"

She sniffed, taking the handkerchief he offered as she considered the question he'd unwittingly asked.

"You know, I think it has to do with an uneven level of hormones at the moment of excitement…or fear…as the case may be. In fact, I remember reading—"

He silenced her with another kiss, and then another, and then another. It was some time later before he thought to ask her again.

"You know, you never did answer my question. *Will* you marry me, Alicia Corbin, or are you going to ask me to live in sin?"

Her eyes widened in disbelief. Just when she started to explain why she would never do that, she realized he was grinning.

"You're teasing me now, aren't you?"

"Oh, yeah," he said softly.

An answering grin tilted the corners of her lips.

"Well, since I can't have the father of my children being any kind of a sinner, then I suppose I will have to say yes."

"Ah God, Ally, you have given me something I never thought I'd have," he said.

"You mean children?"

He shook his head, thinking back to the way he'd been before Jonah had sent her—living in limbo and guilt.

"No, I'm talking about my life. You not only gave my

first son back to me, but you are giving me a future I never thought I'd have." He kissed her softly, then added, "So, thank you. Thank you so much for loving me."

Now her tears were coming in earnest. "It was easy," she said. "All I had to do was trust you enough to let go."

"I'll never let you fall," he promised.

"Oh, I know that."

East took her by the hand. "Let's go call Jeff."

She looked a little nervous.

"What will we say?"

"That he's getting a mother and a brother, all at the same time."

"I hope he doesn't resent me...us," she amended, thinking of the baby she was carrying.

"How could he resent the woman who helped save his life? Now come with me. I'm in the mood for spreading good news."

"Okay," she said. "But after that, I thought we might try out page forty-two tonight. It's a little complicated and I won't be able to do those kind of contortions once I start getting big."

East's eyes widened as he thought of her and that book all over again. Then he took her by the hand and led her toward the bedroom instead.

"We'll call Jeff tomorrow, now show me page forty-two."

It was far into the morning before East rose up on one elbow and gazed down at Ally, who lay sleeping beside him. He kept marveling at how someone could maintain such a level of naivete while filled with so much uninhibited passion. Finally, he leaned over, pressing a soft, butterfly kiss against her cheek, then whispering in her ear.

"Education is a wonderful thing."

* * * * *

Delores Fossen, a *USA TODAY* bestselling author, has written over one hundred novels, with millions of copies of her books in print worldwide. She's received a Booksellers' Best Award and an RT Reviewers' Choice Best Book Award. She was also a finalist for a prestigious RITA® Award. You can contact the author through her website at deloresfossen.com.

Books by Delores Fossen

Harlequin Intrigue

The Lawmen of McCall Canyon

Cowboy Above the Law
Finger on the Trigger
Lawman with a Cause
Under the Cowboy's Protection

HQN

Lone Star Ridge

Tangled Up in Texas
That Night in Texas (ebook novella)
Chasing Trouble in Texas

A Coldwater Texas Novel

Lone Star Christmas
Hot Texas Sunrise
Sweet Summer Sunset
A Coldwater Christmas

Visit the Author Profile page at Harlequin.com for more titles.

KADE

Delores Fossen

Chapter 1

Special Agent Kade Ryland raced up the steps of the Silver Creek hospital. Whatever was going on, it was bad. No doubt about it. The voice message from his brother had proven that.

Get to the hospital now, Grayson had ordered.

Since his brother Grayson was the sheriff of Silver Creek, it couldn't be good news. Nor was the fact that Grayson wasn't answering his phone—probably because he was in the hospital, a dead zone for reception.

Kade prayed that someone wasn't hurt or dead, but the odds were that's exactly what had happened. He had four living brothers, three sisters-in-law, two nephews and a niece. Since all his brothers were in law enforcement and one of his sisters-in-law was pregnant, there were lots of opportunities for things to go wrong.

The automatic doors swished open, and he hurried

through, only to set off the metal detector's alarm. Kade
mumbled some profanity for the delay. He'd just come
from work and was still wearing his sidearm in a shoulder holster concealed beneath his jacket. He also had
his backup weapon strapped to his boot. He didn't want
to take the time to remove either of them.

The uniformed guard practically jumped from the
chair where he was reading a battered copy of the *Silver Creek Ledger.* His name was Rowdy Dawkins, a
man that Kade had known his whole life. But then Kade
could say that about half the town.

"The sheriff's waiting for you in the emergency
room," Rowdy said, waving Kade through the metal
detector. His expression was somber. His tone dripped
with concern.

Oh, man.

Kade didn't even take the time to ask Rowdy for details, though the man no doubt knew what was going on.
He didn't just hurry—Kade ran to the E.R. that was at
the other end of the building. The hospital wasn't big by
anyone's standards, but it seemed to take him an hour
to reach the E.R. waiting room.

No sign of his brother or any other family member.

Kade's heart was pounding now, and his mind was
coming up with all sorts of bad scenarios. He'd been
an FBI agent for seven years, not nearly as long as his
brothers had been in law enforcement, but that was
more than long enough to fuel the worst sort of details
about what could be wrong.

"Your brother's in there with Dr. Mickelson," a nurse
volunteered as she pointed the way. She, too, gave him
a sympathetic look, which meant he was probably the

only person in the whole frickin' town who didn't know what the heck was going on.

Kade mumbled a thank-you to her and hurried into the doctor's office, the first door in the hall just off the waiting room. He tried to brace himself for what he might see, but he hadn't expected to find everything looking so…normal.

Well, almost.

Grayson was indeed there, standing, and looking fit as a fiddle as his granddaddy Chet would have said. He looked as he usually did in his jeans and crisp white shirt with his badge clipped to his rodeo belt.

Dr. Mickelson, the chief of staff, was there, as well, practically elbow to elbow with Grayson. Nothing looked out of the ordinary for him, either. The two had obviously been expecting him.

"I was in the middle of an arrest when you phoned," Kade started. "That's why your call went straight to voice mail, but I tried to get in touch with you after I got your message. I tried your office, too, and the dispatch clerk said her orders were for me to speak directly to you. What's wrong? Who's hurt?"

"No one's hurt," Grayson said, but then he wearily shook his head. "At least no one that we know about." He stepped closer and looked directly into Kade's eyes. Ice-gray eyes that were a genetic copy of Kade's own.

Oh, yeah. This was bad.

And downright confusing.

"What do you mean by that?" Kade asked.

Grayson and the doctor exchanged glances. "You'd better sit down. We have something to tell you." The doctor tipped his head to the chair next to his desk, which was cluttered with folders, computer equipment and papers.

The one thing Kade didn't want was to sit. "Does someone in the family have cancer or something?"

Or God forbid, had there been a suicide? It wasn't something the average person would consider high on their list of worries, but since his own mother had committed suicide when he was barely eleven, it was never far from Kade's mind.

"No one has cancer," the doctor answered. He flexed his graying eyebrows, but he didn't add more.

Like the security guard, Kade knew Dr. Mickelson. The doctor had been the one to deliver him thirty-one years ago, but Kade couldn't read the doctor as well as he could read Grayson. So, he turned to his brother.

"Tell me what happened," Kade pushed.

Grayson mumbled something under his breath. "I would if I knew where to start."

"The beginning's usually a good place." Kade's stomach was churning now, the acid blistering his throat, and he just wanted to know the truth.

"All right." Grayson took a deep breath and stepped to the side.

Kade saw it then. The clear bassinet on rollers, the kind they used in the hospital nursery.

He walked closer and looked inside. There was a baby, and it was likely a girl since there was a pink blanket snuggled around her. There was also a little pink stretchy cap on her head. She was asleep, but her mouth was puckered as if sucking a bottle.

"What does the baby have to do with this?" Kade asked.

"Everything. Two days ago someone abandoned her

in the E.R. waiting room," the doctor explained. "The person left her in an infant carrier next to one of the chairs. We don't know who did that because we don't have security cameras."

Kade was finally able to release the breath he'd been holding. So, this was job-related. They'd called him in because he was an FBI agent.

But he immediately rethought that.

"An abandoned baby isn't a federal case," Kade clarified, though Grayson already knew that. Kade reached down and brushed his index finger over a tiny dark curl that peeked out from beneath the cap. "You think she was kidnapped or something?"

When neither the doctor nor Grayson answered, Kade looked back at them. Anger began to boil through him. "Did someone hurt her?"

"No," the doctor quickly answered. "There wasn't a scratch on her. She's perfectly healthy as far as I can tell."

The anger went as quickly as it'd come. Kade had handled the worst of cases, but the one thing he couldn't stomach was anyone harming a child.

"I called Grayson as soon as she was found," the doctor went on. "There were no Amber Alerts, no reports of missing newborns. There wasn't a note in her carrier, only a bottle that had no prints, no fibers or anything else to distinguish it."

Kade lifted his hands palm up. "That's a lot of *noes*. What do you know about her?" Because he was sure this was leading somewhere.

Dr. Mickelson glanced at the baby. "We know she's about three or four days old, which means she was abandoned either the day she was born or shortly after. She's slightly underweight, barely five pounds, but there was no hospital bracelet. We had no other way to identify her so we ran a DNA test two days ago when she arrived and just got back the results." His explanation stopped cold, and his attention came back to Kade.

So did Grayson's. "Kade, she's yours."

Kade leaned in because he was certain he'd misheard what his brother said. "Excuse me?"

"The baby is your daughter," Grayson clarified.

Because that was the last thing Kade expected to come from his brother's mouth, it took several seconds to sink in. Okay, more than several, and when it finally registered in his brain, it didn't sink in well.

All the air vanished from the room.

"That's impossible," Kade practically shouted.

The baby began to squirm from the noise. Kade's reaction was just as abrupt. What the devil was going on here? He wasn't a father. Heck, he hadn't been in a real relationship in nearly two years.

Grayson groaned and tipped his eyes to the ceiling. "Not impossible according to the DNA."

Kade did some groaning, as well, and would have spit out a denial or two, but the baby started to cry. Grayson looked at Kade as if he expected him to do something, but Kade was too stunned to move. Grayson huffed, reached down, gently scooped her up and began to rock her.

"The DNA test has to be wrong," Kade concluded.

But he stared at that tiny crying face. She did have dark hair, like the Rylands. The shape of her face was familiar, too, similar to his own niece, but all babies looked pretty much the same to him.

"I had the lab run two genetic samples to make sure,"

the doctor interjected. "And then Grayson put the results through a bunch of databases. Your DNA was already in there."

Yeah. Kade knew his DNA was in the system. Most federal employees were. But that didn't mean the match had been correct.

"Who's the baby's mother?" Kade demanded.

Because whoever she was, all of this wasn't adding up. A baby who just happened to match an FBI agent's DNA.

His DNA.

A bottle with no fingerprints. And the baby had been abandoned at the hospital in his hometown, where his family owned a very successful ranch.

All of that couldn't be a coincidence.

"We don't know the identity of the child's mother," the doctor answered. "We didn't get a database match on the maternal DNA."

And that did even more to convince Kade that this was some kind of setup. But then he rethought that. Most people didn't have their DNA recorded in a law enforcement system unless they'd done something to get it there.

Like break the law.

"Since you haven't mentioned a girlfriend," Grayson continued, "you're probably looking at the result of a one-night stand. Don't bother to tell me you haven't had a few of those."

He had. Kade couldn't deny there had been one or two, but he'd always taken precautions. *Always.* The same as he had in his longer relationships.

"Think back eight to nine months ago," Grayson prompted. "I already checked the calendar you keep on the computer at the ranch, and I know you were on assignments both months."

Kade forced himself to think and do the math. He could dispel this entire notion of the baby being his if he could figure out where he'd been during that critical time. It took some doing, but he picked through the smeared recollections of assignments, reports and briefings.

The nine-month point didn't fit because he'd done surveillance in a van. Alone. But eight and a half months ago he'd been in San Antonio, days into an undercover assignment that involved the Fulbright Fertility Clinic, a facility that was into all sorts of nasty things, including genetic experiments on embryos, questionable surrogates and illegal adoptions.

Kade froze.

"What?" Grayson demanded. "You remembered something?"

Oh, yeah. He remembered *something*.

Kade squeezed his eyes shut a moment. "I teamed up with a female deep-cover agent. A Jane we call them. She already had established ties with someone who worked in the clinic so we partnered up. We posed as a married couple with fertility issues so we could infiltrate the clinic. We were literally locked in the place for four days."

Kade had been on more than a dozen assignments since the Fulbright case, the details of them all bleeding together, but there was one Texas-size detail about that assignment that stood out.

Bree.

The tough-as-nails petite brunette with the olive-green eyes. During those four days they'd worked together, she'd been closemouthed about her personal life. Heck, he knew hardly anything about her, and what he did know could have been part of the facade of a deep-cover agent.

"We didn't have sex," Kade mumbled. Though he had thought about it a time or two. Posing as a married couple, they'd been forced to sleep in the same bed and put on a show of how much they *loved* each other.

"There must be someone else, then," Grayson insisted.

"Alice Marks," Kade admitted. "But the timing is wrong. Besides, I saw Alice just a couple of months ago, and she definitely wasn't pregnant…"

Everything inside Kade went still when something else came to him. It couldn't be *that*.

Could it?

"The Jane agent and I posed as a couple with fertility problems, and the doctors at the Fulbright clinic had me provide some semen," Kade explained.

"Could the doctors have used it to impregnate the mother?" Grayson asked.

"I'm not sure. Maybe," Kade conceded. "The investigation didn't go as planned. Something went wrong. Someone at the clinic drugged us, and we had to fight our way out of there. But maybe during that time we were drugged, they used the semen to make her pregnant."

The doctor shook his head. "If the birth mother was an agent, then why wasn't her DNA in the system?"

It was Grayson who answered. "If she was in deep-cover ops, a Jane, they don't enter those agents' DNA into the normal law enforcement databases. The Bureau doesn't want anyone to know they work for the FBI."

His brother was right. The odds were slim to none that Special Agent Bree Winston's DNA would be in any database other than the classified one at FBI Headquarters in Quantico, Virginia.

Kade forced his eyes open, and his gaze immediately landed on the baby that Grayson was holding. The newborn was awake now, and she had turned her head in his direction. She was looking at him.

Kade swallowed hard.

He felt the punch, and it nearly robbed him of his breath. The doctor was right. He should have sat down for this.

The love was there. Instant and strong. Deep in his heart and his gut, he knew the test had been right.

This was his baby.

His little girl.

Even though he'd had no immediate plans for fatherhood, that all changed in an instant. He knew he loved her, would do whatever it took to be a good father to her. But he also knew she'd been abandoned. That left Kade with one big question.

Where was her mother?

Where was Bree?

And by God, if something had gone on at the clinic, why hadn't she told him? Why had she kept something like this a secret?

Kade pulled in his breath, hoping it would clear his head. It didn't, but he couldn't take the time to adjust to the bombshell that had just slammed right into him.

He leaned down and brushed a kiss on his baby girl's cheek. She blinked, and she stared at him as if trying to figure out who the heck he was.

"Take care of her for me," Kade said to his brother. "I'll be back as soon as I can."

Grayson nodded and stared at him, too. "You know where the mother is?"

He shook his head. Kade had no idea, since he hadn't heard anything from her since that assignment eight and a half months ago at the Fulbright clinic. Right now, he was sure of only one thing. If the baby was here and Bree wasn't, that meant she was either dead or in big trouble.

Kade had to find Bree *fast*.

Chapter 2

Bree heard the pitiful sound, a hoarse moan, and it took her a moment to realize that the sound had come from her own throat.

She opened her eyes and looked around for anything familiar. Anything that felt right.

Nothing did.

She was in some kind of room. A hotel maybe. A cheap one judging from the looks of things. The ceiling had moldy water stains, and those stains moved in and out of focus. Ditto for the dingy, paint-blistered walls. The place smelled like urine and other things she didn't want to identify.

What she did want to identify was where she was and why she was there. Bree was certain there was a good reason for it, but she couldn't remember what that reason was. It was hard to remember anything with a tornado going on inside her head.

She forced herself into a sitting position on the narrow bed. Beneath her the lumpy mattress creaked and shifted. She automatically reached for her gun and cell phone that should have been on the nightstand.

But they weren't there.

Something was wrong.

Everything inside her screamed for her to get out right away. She had to get to a phone. She had to call… somebody. But she couldn't remember who. Still, if she could just get to a phone, Bree was certain she'd remember.

She put her feet on the threadbare carpet and glanced down at her clothes. She had on a loose dress that was navy blue with tiny white flowers. She was wearing a pair of black flat leather shoes.

The clothing seemed as foreign to her as the hotel room and the absence of her gun and phone. She wasn't a dress person, and she didn't have to remember all the details of her life to realize that. No. She was a jeans and shirt kind of woman unless she was on the job, and then she wore whatever the assignment dictated.

Was she on some kind of assignment here?

She didn't have the answer to that, either. But the odds were, yes, this was the job. Too bad she couldn't remember exactly what this job was all about.

Bree took a deep breath and managed to stand. Not easily. She had to slap her hand on the wall just to stay upright, and she started for the door.

Just as the doorknob moved.

Oh, God. Someone was trying to get in the room,

and with her questionable circumstances, she doubted this would be a friendly encounter. Not good. She could barely stand so she certainly wasn't in any shape to fight off anyone with her bare hands. Still, she might not have a choice.

"Think," she mumbled to herself. What undercover role was she playing here? What was she supposed to say or do to the person trying to get in? She might need those answers to stay alive.

"Bree?" someone called out. It was followed by a heavy knock on the rickety door.

She didn't answer. Couldn't. The dizziness hit her hard again, and she had no choice but to sink back down onto the bed. *Great.* At this rate, she'd be dead in a minute. Maybe less.

"Bree?" the person called out again. It was a man, and his voice sounded a little familiar. "It's me, Kade Ryland. Open up."

Kade Ryland? The dizzy spell made it almost impossible to think, but his name, like his voice, was familiar. Too bad she couldn't piece that hint of familiarity with some facts. Especially one fact…

Could she trust him?

"Don't trust anyone," she heard herself mumble, and that was the most familiar thing she'd experienced since she'd first awakened in this god-awful room.

She braced herself for the man to knock again or call out her name. But there was a sharp bashing sound, and the door flew open as he kicked it in.

Bree tried to scramble away from him while she fumbled to take off her shoe and use it as a weapon. She didn't succeed at either.

The man who'd called himself Kade Ryland came

bursting into the room, along with a blast of hot, humid air from the outside.

The first thing she saw was his gun, a Glock. Since there was no way she could dodge a bullet in the tiny space or run into the adjoining bathroom, Bree just sat there and waited for him to come closer. That way, she could try to grab his gun if it became necessary.

However, he didn't shoot.

And he didn't come closer.

He just stood there and took in the room with a sweeping glance. A cop's glance that she recognized because it's what she would have done. And then he turned that intense cop's look on her.

Bree fought the dizziness so she could study his face, his expression. He was in his early thirties. Dark brown hair peeking out from a Stetson that was the same color, gray eyes, about six-two and a hundred and eighty pounds. He didn't exactly look FBI with his slightly too-long hair, day-old stubble, well-worn jeans, black T-shirt and leather jacket, but she had some vague memory that he was an agent like her.

Was that memory right?

Or was he the big bad threat that her body seemed to think he was?

"Bree?" he repeated. His gaze locked with hers, and as he eased closer, his cowboy boots thudded on the floor. "What happened to you?"

She failed at her first attempt to speak and had to clear her throat. "I, uh, was hoping you could tell me." Mercy, she sounded drunk. "I'm having trouble remembering how I got here. Or why." She glanced around the seedy room again. "Where is *here* exactly?"

He cursed. It was ripe and filled with concern. She

was right there on the same page with him—but that
didn't mean she trusted him.

"You're in a motel in one of the worst parts of San
Antonio," he told her. "It isn't safe for you to be here."

She hadn't thought for a minute that it was. Everything about it, including this man, put her on full alert.

But how had she gotten to this place?

"I was at my apartment," she mumbled. Was that
right? She thought about it a second. Yes. That part was
right. "But I don't know how I got from there to here."

Kade shut the door, though it was no longer connected to the top hinge, and he slipped his gun back into
the leather shoulder holster beneath his jacket.

"Come on," he said, catching onto her arm. He gave
a heavy sigh. "I need to get you to a doctor."

"No!" Bree couldn't say it fast enough. She didn't
want to add another person—another stranger—to this
mix. She shook off his grip. "I just need a phone. I have
to call someone right away."

"Yeah. You need to call your boss, Special Agent
Randy Cooper. Or Coop as you call him. But I can do
that for you while you're seeing the doctor."

Coop. That name was familiar, too, and it seemed
right that he was her boss. It also seemed right that she'd
get answers from him. Especially since this cowboy
agent didn't seem to be jumping to provide her with
the vital information that she needed. She had to know
if she could trust him or if she should try to escape.

Bree stared up at him. "Am I on assignment?"

Kade stared at her, too. Stared as if she'd lost her
mind. He leaned down, closer, so they were eye to eye.
"What the heck happened to you?"

She opened her mouth and realized she didn't have

an answer. "I don't know. How did I get here?" She tried to get up again. "I need to call Coop. He'll know. He'll tell me why I'm here."

"Coop doesn't have a clue what happened to you."

That got her attention and not in a good way. "What do you mean?"

Kade moved even closer. "Bree, you've been missing nearly a year."

Oh, mercy. That info somehow got through the dizziness, but it didn't make sense. Nothing about this did. What the heck was wrong with her?

Bree shook her head. "Impossible."

He shoved up the sleeve of his black leather jacket and showed her a watch. He tapped his index finger on the date. June 13.

"June 13?" she repeated. Obviously, he thought that would mean something to her. It didn't. That was because Bree had no idea what the date should be. Nor did she know the date of that last clear memory—when she'd been at her apartment.

"I didn't know you were missing at first, not until a little over a month ago," he continued. His voice trailed off to barely a whisper, but then he cleared his throat.

"What's the last thing you remember before this place?" Kade asked. But he didn't just ask. He demanded it. He seemed to be angry about something, and judging from his stare turned glare, she was at least the partial source of that anger.

But what had she done to rile him?

She cursed that question because she didn't have an answer for it or any of the others.

Bree pushed her hair from her face. That's when she

noticed her hands were trembling. Her mouth was bone dry, too. "Someone drugged me, didn't they?"

"Probably. Your pupils are dilated, and there's not a drop of color in your face," he let her know. "What's the last thing you remember?" he repeated.

She forced herself to think. "I remember you. We were on assignment together at the Fulbright Clinic. Someone figured out I was an agent, and they drugged us. We had to shoot our way out of there."

Bree glanced down at the thin scar on her left arm where a bullet had grazed her. It wasn't red and raw as it should be. It was well-healed. But that couldn't be right.

"And?" Kade prompted.

Bree shook her head. There was no *and*. "How long ago was that?"

"Nine and a half months." His jaw muscles turned to iron. She might have been dizzy, but she didn't miss the nine month reference. *Nine months.* As in just the right amount of time to have had a baby.

Her gaze flew back to him. This time Bree took a much longer and harder look at the cowboy. His face was more than just familiar. Those features. That body. Kade Ryland was drop-dead hot, and yes, she could imagine herself sleeping with him.

But had she?

She wasn't a person who engaged in casual sex or sex with a fellow agent.

"We didn't have sex, did we?" she asked.

Something shot through his ice-gray eyes. Some emotion she didn't understand. "No," he concluded. "But there was an opportunity for you to get pregnant. We were in a fertility clinic, after all."

Oh, mercy. Had the doctors in the clinic done something to her? No, Bree decided. She would have known. She would have remembered that.

Wouldn't she?

"After the shoot-out, other agents moved in to arrest the two security guards who tried to kill us," Kade continued. "But we didn't manage to apprehend everyone involved. Key evidence was missing, but the FBI decided to send in other agents to do the investigation since my identity had been compromised."

Yes. That sounded right. It wasn't an actual memory, though. None of this was, and that nearly sent Bree into a panic.

"And then you called your boss," Kade continued, his voice calm despite the thick uneasiness in the room. "You said you were taking some vacation time."

Still no memory. Bree just sat there, listening, and praying he would say something to clear the cobwebs in her head and that it would all come back to her.

"Two weeks later when you were supposed to check back in with Coop, you didn't. You disappeared." Kade caught her chin, forced it up. "Bree, I need you to think. Where have you been all these months?"

Again, she tried to think, to remember. She really tried. But nothing came. She saw flashes of herself in Kade's arms. He was naked. And with his hard muscled body pressed against hers. He'd kissed her as if they were engaged in some kind of battle—fierce, hot, relentless.

Despite the dizziness, she felt her body go warm.

Bad timing, Bree, she reminded herself.

"You, uh, have some kind of tattoo on your back? It's like a coin or something?" She phrased it as a question just in case she was getting her memories mixed up, but she doubted she could ever mix up a man like Kade with anyone else.

"A concho," he supplied. "With back to back double *R*'s, for my family's ranch. You remember that?"

A ranch. Yes, he looked like a cowboy all right. She'd bet he wasn't wearing those jeans, Stetson and boots to make a fashion statement. No, he was a cowboy to the core, and that FBI badge and standard issue Glock didn't diminish that one bit.

"We kissed," she recalled. Now, *here* was a crystal clear memory. His mouth on hers. A fake kiss with real fire. And a cowboy with an unforgettable taste. "To create the cover of a happily married couple."

"But we didn't have sex," he clarified.

No. They hadn't, and she was reasonably sure she would have remembered sleeping with Kade. She glanced at him again and took out the *reasonably* part.

She would have remembered *that*.

"How did you find me?" Bree asked. There were so many questions and that seemed a good place to start.

"I set up a missing person's hotline and plastered your picture all over the state. I didn't say anything about you working for the FBI," he added, just as she was on the verge of protesting.

The last part of his explanation caused her to breathe just a little easier. As a deep-cover agent, the last thing she wanted was her picture out there. Still, his plan had worked because here he was. He'd found her.

But why had he been looking?

Was he working for her boss, Coop?

"An hour ago, I got a tip from an anonymous caller using a prepaid cell," Kade continued. "The person disguised their voice but said I'd find you here at the Treetop Motel, room 114. The person also said you were sick and might need a doctor."

An anonymous caller using a prepaid cell. That set off alarms in her head. "Someone drugged me and dumped me here. That same someone might have been your caller."

"That's my guess." He paused, huffed and rubbed his hand over his forehead as if he had a raging headache. "Look, there's no easy way to say this, so I'm just going to put it out there so you can start dealing with it. I think someone in the fertility clinic inseminated you with the semen they got from me...."

Kade hesitated, maybe to let that sink in. But how the heck could that sink in?

Bree gasped and looked down at her stomach. "I'm not pregnant. If I were, I'd be about ready to deliver." She stretched the dress across her stomach to show him there was no baby bulge.

"You've already delivered, Bree. A baby girl. She's about seven weeks old."

She heard that sound. A hoarse moan that tore its way from her own throat. "You're lying." He *had* to be lying.

Kade didn't take back what he'd said. He just stood there, waiting.

Bree tried to figure out how she could disprove the lie, and she glanced down at her stomach again.

"Go ahead," Kade prompted. "Look at your belly. I don't know if you'll have stretch marks or not, but there'll likely be some kind of changes."

Bree frantically shook her head, but her adamant denial didn't stop her from standing. Still wobbling, she turned away from Kade and shoved up the loose dress.

She was wearing white bikini panties that she didn't recognize, but the unfamiliar underwear was only the tip of the proverbial iceberg.

Just slightly above the top of her panties was a scar.

Unlike the one on her arm, this one still had a pink tinge to it. It had healed, but the incision had happened more recently than the gunshot injury.

Probably about seven weeks ago.

Bree let go of the dress so it would drop back down. "What did you do to me?" She turned back to him. She would have pounded her fists against his chest if he hadn't caught her hands. "What did you do?"

"Nothing. It wasn't me. It was someone in the Fulbright Clinic." Now it was Kade's turn to groan, and that was her first clue that he was as stunned by this as she was.

They stood there, gazes locked. Her heart was beating so hard that she thought it might come out of her chest.

"Who did the C-section?" she demanded.

Kade shook his head, cursed. "I don't know. Until now, I didn't even know you'd had one, though the doctor in Silver Creek guessed. He said Leah's head was perfectly shaped, probably because she'd been delivered via C-section."

What little breath Bree had vanished. *"Leah?"*

"That's what I've been calling her. It was my grandmother's name."

"Leah," she mumbled. Oh, mercy. None of this was making sense. "What makes you think she's our child?"

"DNA tests," he said without hesitation. "I got your DNA from the classified database in Quantico and compared it to Leah's. It's a match."

There was so much coming at her that Bree could no longer breathe. Was this all true? Or maybe Kade and this baby story were figments of her drug-induced imagination. One thing was for certain. She needed to contact her boss. Coop was the only one she could trust right now.

And Coop had better tell her this was all some kind of misunderstanding.

"I need to use your cell phone," she insisted.

"You can use it in the truck." He took her by the arm. "Something bad obviously happened to you, and we need to find out what. That starts with a visit to the doctor so you have a tox screen."

Bree didn't dispute the fact that she might indeed need medical attention, but she had no reason to blindly trust Kade Ryland.

"I want to make that call now," she demanded.

Kade stared at her, huffed again and reached in his coat pocket. But reaching for his phone was as far as he got. There was a noise just outside the door, and despite the drug haze, it was a sound that Bree immediately recognized.

Footsteps.

Kade drew his gun, and in the same motion, he shoved her behind him.

But it was too late.

Bree heard a swishing sound. One that she also recognized. Someone had a gun rigged with a silencer.

And a bullet came tearing through the thin wooden door.

Chapter 3

Kade threw his weight against Bree to push her out of the line of fire. She landed hard against the wall, and Kade had no choice but to land hard against her.

Another bullet came through the door, splintering out a huge chunk of the already-rickety wood. No one called out for them to surrender. No one bashed in the room to hold them at gunpoint.

And that meant the gunman had one goal: to kill Bree and him.

Later, he would kick himself for coming here without backup, but he'd been in such a hurry to rescue Bree that Kade had put standard procedures aside so he could get to her before she left the motel. Or before she was killed or kidnapped again. Finding her had been critical. But now the challenge was to get her out of there alive.

It was a risk, anything was at this point, but Kade

moved from the wall so he could kick the dresser against the door. He gave it another shove to anchor it in place.

"That won't stop him for long," Bree mumbled.

No. It wouldn't. But if the gunman had wanted to get inside, he could have easily knocked down the door before he started shooting. Firing through the door had likely been his way of trying to strike first without risking a direct showdown. If so, he knew Kade was armed. Maybe he even knew that Kade was an agent.

But who was he?

And why attack them?

Kade wanted those answers, and maybe he could get them from this Bozo if he could keep the guy alive. Of course, rescuing Bree was his first priority.

Kade had to do something to keep some space between the danger and Bree, so he fired directly into the door. Unlike the gunman's shots, the one he fired was a loud thick blast that echoed through the room. He didn't wait to see if he'd hit the target. He had to get Bree out of there.

Unfortunately, their options sucked.

Kade shoved her into the bathroom, such as it was. Barely five feet across with only a toilet and what was once a shower stall.

The tile was cracked and filthy, but the room had one redeeming feature: a window that faced the back side of the motel. He knew it was there because he'd done a snapshot surveillance of the place before he ever knocked on Bree's door. The gunman would have to run around the entire length of the building to get to that window. Well, unless he had a partner with him. Kade hoped that wasn't the case. One gunman was more than enough.

Another shot came into the bedroom.

Kade returned fire, this time a double tap that would hopefully send a message—he would kill to get Bree out of there. He darn sure hadn't come this far to lose her before he got the answers to his questions.

Bree was still more than a little unsteady on her feet so Kade shoved her deeper in the bathroom, kicked the door shut and locked it. The lock was as rickety as the rest of the place, and it wouldn't give them much protection if the gunman came blasting in, but it might buy them a few critical seconds, just enough time to get out.

He hurried to the window. It popped right open, and he looked out in the thin alley that separated the motel from an equally seedy-looking bar. Both ends of the alley were open, and there were no signs of a backup gunman, but it would still be a long dangerous run to his truck.

"I'll go first to make sure it's safe," he told Bree. "You follow me. Got that?"

She gave him a look, and for a moment he thought Bree might refuse. For a good reason, too. She didn't trust him.

And why should she?

Bree was no doubt trying to absorb everything he'd just dumped on her, and Kade knew from personal experience that coming to terms with unexpected parenthood wasn't something that could happen in five minutes—especially after the trauma Bree had been through. And the trauma wasn't over.

"You have no choice," Kade told her. He moved his truck keys from his jeans pocket to his jacket so they'd be easier to reach. "If we stay here, we both die."

She shook her head as if trying to clear it, or argue

with him, but still didn't move. Not until another bullet bashed through the room.

And more.

Someone was moving the dresser that Kade had used to block the door. That *someone* was now in the motel room just a few yards away with only a paper-thin wall and equally thin bathroom door between them.

Bree's eyes widened. She obviously understood what was happening now. She caught his arm and shoved him against the window. Kade grabbed the sill, hoisting himself up and slithered through the narrow opening. He landed on his feet with his gun ready, and he looked up.

No Bree.

For one heart-stopping moment Kade thought she might have decided to take her chances with the gunman, but then he saw her hand on the sill. She was struggling to keep a grip. And Kade cursed himself again. The drugs had made her too weak to lever herself up.

While he tried to keep watch on both sides of the alley, Kade latched onto her wrist and pulled hard. She finally tumbled forward and landed with a jolt right in his arms. He didn't have time to make sure she was okay or even carry her since he had to keep his shooting hand free. Kade put her on her feet, grabbed her by the shoulder and started running in the direction of his truck.

They were already on borrowed time. By Kade's calculations, it'd been twenty seconds or longer since the gunman had fired. That meant he could have already made it into the bathroom and have seen that they weren't there. He could try to kill them by shooting through the window, or else he could be heading around the building straight toward them.

"I should have a gun," Bree mumbled.

Yeah, she should. That would be a big help right about now because Kade knew for a fact she could shoot. However, since he couldn't take the time to pull his backup weapon from his ankle holster, he ran as fast as he could with a groggy, dazed woman in tow.

Finally, he spotted his dark blue truck.

But Kade also heard something.

He glanced behind them and saw someone he didn't want to see. A guy wearing camo pants and jacket came around the far end of the building. He was also armed, and he pointed a handgun directly at Kade and Bree.

There wasn't time to get to his truck. No time to do much of anything except get out of the line of fire. So Kade shoved Bree to the ground, right against the exterior wall of the hotel, and he followed on top of her. Not a second too soon. The guy pulled the trigger.

The shot slammed into the wall.

Kade turned, took aim and returned fire.

Their attacker dived to the side but not far enough. Kade could still see him, and he wanted the SOB temporarily out of the picture so he could get Bree safely out of there. Of course, he might have to settle for killing the guy. That would mean no answers, but it was better than the alternative.

Kade sent another shot his way.

And another.

He cursed when the guy moved, causing the bullets to strafe into the ground. But the third was a charm because the gunman finally scrambled back behind the building.

Bree was trembling and as white as paper when Kade came off the ground and yanked her to her feet. She had been under fire before, but probably not while defenseless. Kade kept watch behind them, but he got them running toward the truck again. He also did some praying that a second gunman wasn't near his vehicle.

Kade fired another shot in the direction of the gunman. Maybe it would keep him pinned down long enough for them to escape.

Maybe.

He let go of Bree so he could take out his keys, and he pressed the button to unlock the doors. Thankfully, Bree ran without his help, and they made a beeline for the truck.

Kade saw the gunman again, but he didn't stop to fire. Instead, he threw open the truck door. Bree did the same on the passenger's side, and they both dived in.

"Watch out!" Bree shouted. "He's coming after us."

"I see him," Kade let her know.

He lowered the window, just enough to allow himself room to fire another shot. Just enough to keep the gunman at bay for a few more seconds.

Kade started the engine and slammed his foot on the accelerator. He didn't exactly make a silent exit out of the parking lot. The tires howled against the asphalt, but Kade figured anyone within a quarter mile had already heard the gunfight and either reported it or run away.

In this neighborhood, he was betting it was the latter.

"Keep watch," he told Bree.

While he took out his phone, he glanced around to make sure they weren't being followed. Then, he glanced at Bree.

Man, she was still way too pale, and she was sucking in air so fast she might hyperventilate. In the four days he had spent with her undercover, he'd never seen her like this, and Kade hoped she could hold herself together for just a little while longer until he could get her out of there and to a doctor.

Since he didn't want to spend a lot of time making all the calls he needed, Kade made the one that he knew would get the ball rolling. He pressed in the number for his brother, Lt. Nate Ryland, at San Antonio police headquarters. Nate answered on the first ring because he was no doubt waiting for news about Bree.

"I found her at the Treetop Motel," Kade said. That alone would be a bombshell since over the past month they'd had nine false reports of Bree's location. "But there was a gunman. Caucasian. Brown hair. About six-two. One-seventy. No distinguishing marks."

Nate cursed and mumbled something about Kade being a stubborn ass for not waiting for backup. "I'll get a team out there right away," Nate assured him, and it was the exact assurance Kade needed. "What about you? Where are you taking her?"

"The hospital. Not here in San Antonio. I'm driving her to Silver Creek." Kade didn't say that too loud, though Bree no doubt heard it, anyway. "Call me if you find anything at the hotel. I'll let you know when I have answers."

"I don't want to go to a hospital," Bree said the moment he ended the call. She was trembling, but she had her attention fastened to the side mirror, no doubt checking to see if they were being followed. "I just want to find out what happened to me."

So did Kade. But first he had to make sure the gunman wasn't on their tail. Then the hospital whether she wanted to go there or not.

While Bree was being checked out by a doctor, he could start the calls and the paperwork. It wouldn't be pretty. He would have to explain to his boss and his brothers why he hadn't waited for backup after receiving that anonymous tip about Bree's location. It probably wasn't going to fly if he told them that he had a gut feeling that she was in danger.

And he'd been right.

Still, gut instincts didn't look good on paper, and he would get his butt chewed out because of it. Kade figured it would be worth it. After all, he'd gotten Bree out of harm's way.

Well, for now.

"He's not following us," Bree concluded. She swallowed hard and looked at him.

Kade looked at her too out of the corner of his eye. She had certainly been through an ordeal. Her dark brown hair had been choppily cut and was mussed well beyond the point of making a fashion statement. And then there was the dress. It hung on her like a sack. There were dark circles under her drug-dazed eyes. Her lips were chapped raw. Still, she managed to look darn attractive.

And yeah, he was stupid enough to notice.

It was also easy to notice that Bree had passed on those cat-green eyes to their daughter.

She opened her mouth, and for a moment Kade thought she might ask about Leah. But she didn't. She snatched his phone from his hand.

"I'm calling my supervisor," Bree insisted.

Kade didn't stop her, though he knew Randy Cooper

didn't have the answers that Bree wanted. That's because Kade had spent a lot of time with the agent over the past month and a half.

She must have remembered the number because she pressed it in without hesitation and put the call on speaker. "Coop," she said when the man answered.

"Bree," he said just as quickly. "Are you all right?"

"No." With that single word, her breath broke, and tears sprang to her eyes. She tried to blink them back, but more just came.

"The last lead paid off," Kade informed Coop. "She was at the Treetop Motel here in San Antonio, but so was a gunman. The informant could have set us up to be killed."

Coop cursed. "Either of you hurt?"

"I'm fine," Kade assured him. "Not so sure about Bree—"

"Where have I been all these months?" she interrupted.

"I don't know," Coop answered. He gave a weary sigh. "But trust me, we'll find out."

Yeah. They would. Step one was done. Kade had located Bree, and now that he had her, he could start unraveling this crazy puzzle that had resulted in the birth of their daughter.

"I need to see you ASAP," Coop told her. "How soon can you get her here, Kade?"

"Not soon," Kade let him know. "Someone drugged her, and even though it looks as if it's wearing off, she needs to see a doctor."

"I can arrange that," Coop insisted.

Of course Coop could, but if Kade took Bree to FBI headquarters, she'd be sucked into the system. Exams, interviews, paperwork. That had to wait because the FBI wouldn't put Leah first.

Kade would.

He had to find out if the gunman meant Leah was now in danger, too. Kade had a hard time just stomaching that thought, but it wouldn't do him any good to bury his head in the sand.

"Is it true, Coop?" Bree asked. "Did I really have a baby?"

Coop took some time answering. "Yes," was all he said.

Bree groaned, squeezed her eyes shut and the phone dropped into her lap. She buried her face in her hands. She wasn't hyperventilating yet, but she was about to fall apart.

"Coop, we'll call you back. In the meantime, my brother Lt. Nate Ryland is on his way to the hotel crime scene and is trying to track down this gunman. We need to find this guy," Kade emphasized, though Coop already knew that.

Because the gunman could be the key to unraveling this. Well, unless he was just a hired gun. But even then, that was a start since they could find out who'd paid him to kill them.

Coop began to argue with Kade's refusal of his order to bring Bree in, but Kade took the phone from her lap and ended the call. He also made another turn so he could check to make sure they weren't being followed. Things looked good in that department but not with Bree. She kept her hands over her face. Clamped her teeth over her bottom lip. And then she made that sound. Half groan, half sob.

Hell. That did it.

Kade hooked his arm around her and dragged her across the seat toward him. Much to his surprise, she didn't fight him. She dropped her head on his shoulder.

For a moment, anyway.

Just a moment.

Her head whipped up, and she met his gaze. She blinked. Shook her head and got a strange look in her eyes.

"I have to keep watch," she insisted. Bree moved back across the seat and glanced at the mirror. Her breathing got faster again. "There's a black sedan behind us."

"Yeah." Kade was fully aware of that. "But I don't think it's following us. It just exited onto this road." To prove his point, he made another turn, and the car didn't follow.

That didn't settle Bree's breathing much. She started to chew on her bottom lip. "You told Coop that your brother was helping us. He's a cop?"

Kade nodded. "San Antonio PD. All four of my brothers are in law enforcement. We've been working to find you ever since someone abandoned Leah at the hospital."

"Leah," Bree repeated, and she slid her hand over her stomach. "We didn't have sex," she tossed out there.

"No. But someone in the fertility clinic obviously inseminated you."

"Hector McClendon," Bree said, and it wasn't exactly a question.

Kade suspected the man, as well. Hector McClendon had been head of the Fulbright Fertility Clinic and was the main target of their undercover investigation that had started all of this.

"McClendon said he wasn't aware of the illegal activity going on at his own clinic," Kade reminded her.

"Right," she mumbled, sarcasm dripping from her voice. "Stored embryos were being sold without the owners' permission or knowledge. Illegal immigrants were being used as surrogates and kept in deplorable conditions. Babies were being auctioned to the highest bidder. We were pretty sure McClendon knew what was going on." Bree looked at Kade. "Please tell me he's behind bars."

Kade hated to be the bearer of more bad news. "No. None of the evidence we got from the clinic implicated McClendon in any of the serious crimes."

And it hadn't been for Kade or the FBI's lack of trying.

"But McClendon ordered those two security guards to kill us," Bree pointed out.

"No proof of that, either. The guards are in custody, but they're insisting they acted alone, because they thought we were a threat to the other patients. They claim they had no idea we were agents."

"Right," she repeated.

Kade had to agree with that, too. But the guards weren't spilling anything, probably because they knew it would be impossible to prove their intent to murder without corroboration from someone else. So far, that hadn't happened, and Kade suspected the guards would ultimately accept a plea deal for much lesser charges.

"The only two people arrested so far have been McClendon's son, Anthony, who was a doctor at the clinic and a nurse named Jamie Greer," he explained. "They're both out on bond, awaiting trial."

Bree repeated the names. "Just because there's no

evidence, it doesn't mean McClendon's innocent of kidnapping and doing God knows what to me."

Kade tried to keep his voice calm. "True, but if he did it, he's not confessing. Still, he has the money and the resources to have held you all this time."

She shook her head. "But why?"

Now it was Kade's turn to shake his head. "I don't know. There were no ransom demands for you. Leah wasn't hurt. In fact, she was dropped off at the hospital probably less than a day after she was born."

She shuddered, maybe at the thought of her kidnapping. Maybe at the way Leah had been abandoned.

"And if McClendon had wanted me dead," Bree finished, "then why not kill me after the C-section? Heck, why not just kill me after taking me from my apartment?"

This is where Kade's theory came to an end. "I was hoping you'd have those answers."

Bree groaned. "I don't! I don't remember any of that."

He reached over and touched her arm. Rubbed lightly. Hoping it would soothe her. "But you can with help. That's why I'm taking you to the hospital."

She opened her mouth, probably to repeat that she didn't want to go, but she stopped. And gasped. "What if the gunman goes after the baby?"

"He won't." Kade hoped. "She's at my family's ranch with my brother. He's a deputy sheriff and can protect her."

Bree frantically shook her head and pushed his hand away so she could latch onto his arm. "Hurry. You have to get to her now."

There's no way Kade could stay calm after that. "Why?"

"Hurry," Bree repeated. Tears spilled down her cheeks. "Because I remember. Oh, God. I remember."

Chapter 4

The memories flooded back into Bree's mind. They came so fast, so hard, that she had trouble latching onto all of them. But the one memory that was first and foremost was the danger to the baby.

Her baby.

Even though that didn't seem real, Bree had no more doubts about the child. She had indeed given birth, and at the moment that was the clearest memory she had.

"You have to get to the baby," Bree insisted.

"I'm headed there now," Kade assured her. His voice sounded more frantic than hers. "What's wrong?" he demanded. "What do you remember?"

"Pretty much everything." And Bree tested that by starting with the first thing she could recall. "The night after the botched assignment at Fulbright Fertility Clinic, I was kidnapped by a person wearing a mask."

"How did that happen?" Kade wanted to know. "And what does it have to do with Leah?"

"It has everything to do with Leah." Because it was the start of her becoming pregnant. "I came out of my apartment that night, and the person was waiting for me just outside the door. He popped me on the neck with a stun gun. I went down like a rock before I could even fight back. Then, the guy used chloroform." Yes, definitely. She recalled the sickly sweet smell of the drug.

"Chloroform," he repeated, but there was impatience in his voice now. Concern, too. "Did you get a good look at the person before you lost consciousness?"

"No." In fact, not a look at all, good or otherwise. The guy never took off his mask. "When I finally came to, I was at a house in the middle of nowhere, and the guy wasn't alone. A masked woman was with him." Bree had to pause and regroup. "You were right—they inseminated me with your baby."

He had a death grip on the steering wheel and was flying through traffic. "Why did they do that, and why do we have to hurry to get to Leah?"

Oh, this was crystal clear. Well, part of it, anyway. "More than once they said that the baby was to get me and you to *cooperate*."

"Cooperate?" he questioned. "With what?"

"I don't know. And it's not that I don't remember. They didn't say how they would use the child. But I'm figuring they'll go after her, especially now that they no longer have me."

Kade cursed, snatched up his phone and made a call. Hopefully to one of those brothers he'd mentioned that were in law enforcement.

"Lock down the ranch," Kade instructed to whomever was on the other end of the line. "There could be trouble. I'll be there in about twenty minutes."

He jabbed the end call button so hard that she was surprised the phone didn't break. "Who held you captive, and if they planned to use Leah to get to you and me, then why abandon her at the hospital?"

That part wasn't so crystal clear, but Bree had a theory about it. "Something must have gone wrong. Not at the beginning, but later."

Much later.

The memories came again. Like bullets, slamming into her. "I woke up after the delivery and heard my kidnappers talking," she continued. "The man told the woman he didn't get the money they'd been promised. He was furious. He was going to kill me right then and there." A shiver went through her. "Maybe the baby, too."

Kade's jaw muscles turned to iron. "What stopped them?"

Bree had to take a moment because she was reliving that horrible fear as if it were happening all over again. "The woman talked the man out of it. She said she'd take care of the baby." Bree had to choke back the emotions she'd felt then. And now. "I thought that meant..."

She couldn't finish, but she'd thought she would never see her baby alive.

"This woman must have been the one who dropped Leah off at the hospital," Kade said through clenched teeth. He turned off the interstate at the Silver Creek exit. "Leah wasn't harmed."

Relief flooded through Bree. But it didn't last long. "If the man who kidnapped me knows that she's alive..." She couldn't finish that, either.

"No one will get onto the ranch without my brothers being alerted," he promised. He didn't say anything else for several moments. "How did you escape?"

"The woman helped me again. She had on a prosthetic mask, one of those latex things that makes it impossible to see any of her real features. And she used a voice scrambler so I never heard her speak normally. But a few hours after she disappeared with the baby, she came back and got me."

Now, here's where her memory failed. No more bullets. Only bits and pieces of images and conversations that Bree wasn't sure she could trust. Were they real or part of the nightmare she'd had all these months?

"She drugged me then and I don't know how many times after. A lot," Bree settled on saying. "The woman moved me, too. Usually to and from hotels, but a time or two, she took me to a house. I think she was trying to save me."

"Sure. And she might have made that call to let me know you were at the motel," he suggested. "The person who contacted me used a voice scrambler, too."

If so, then Bree owed that woman her life many times over. Not just for saving her, but for delivering Leah to Kade.

Except the woman had also been one of Bree's kidnappers.

If she hadn't helped keep Bree captive, then maybe none of this would have happened. And since Kade and she had come darn close to dying today, Bree wasn't ready to give the woman a free pass just yet.

"This has to go back to the Fulbright clinic," Kade said. "Hector McClendon could have masterminded all of it. His son, Anthony, and that clinic nurse, Jamie

Greer, could have helped with the kidnapping. And with the delivery since Anthony is a doctor."

She couldn't argue with that. Plus, she'd seen what they really were at the clinic—criminals—and believed them capable of murder. After all, someone had tried hard to cover up everything that had gone on there.

"You said Anthony and Jamie were out on bond awaiting trial?" Bree asked.

"Yeah. And their lawyers have been stonewalling the investigation and the trials."

Great. So, not only were they suspects, both had the means and opportunity to have done this to her. In fact, they could be working as a team.

"Maybe they were looking for another way to get some leverage over us," Kade went on, "since we're the only two people who could or would testify against them. That could be why the kidnappers said they would use the baby for leverage."

True, and McClendon could have done the same, as well. Of course, if she remembered correctly, there wasn't any hard evidence against him except for some minor charges that wouldn't warrant much jail time, if any at all.

Not so far, anyway.

Nor could Kade and she testify that they'd seen him do anything illegal because they hadn't. McClendon had stayed away from the dirt, and even though Bree had tried, she hadn't been able to make a direct connection between him and the crimes.

Still, McClendon could have feared that some evidence would surface that would support their testimony. After all, Kade and she had failed to find the missing disks to the clinic's surveillance systems. Those systems were dated and still did hardcopy backups. If they'd found those, then McClendon might be in jail right now, and he couldn't have kidnapped her.

If he had been the one to honcho the kidnapping.

The agent in her reminded her to look at all the angles. To examine the evidence and situation with an unbiased eye. But it was hard to do that when someone had made Kade and her involuntary parents, and might now be placing their daughter in danger.

"You heard your male kidnapper speak," Kade continued. He took a turn off the main highway and turned onto Ryland Ranch Road. "Was it Anthony or McClendon?"

Bree had to shake her head. "Maybe. The man also used a voice scrambler whenever he was around me." Which wasn't very often. He always kept his distance from her and only came into the room after she'd been given a heavy dose of drugs. "But if I could hear interviews with Jamie and Anthony, I might be able to pick up on speech patterns."

Kade didn't respond except to pull in a long hard breath. And Bree soon realized why. He stopped directly in front of the sprawling three-story house that was surrounded by acres and acres of pasture and outbuildings.

It looked serene. Inviting. Like pictures of ranches that she'd seen in glossy Western magazines. There definitely wasn't any sign of kidnappers, gunmen or danger, but Bree still felt panic crawl through her.

The baby was inside.

Oh, mercy. She wasn't ready for this. Maybe she'd never be ready. But she especially wasn't ready with her mind in this foggy haze.

"I need a minute," she managed to say. A minute to

get her breath and heartbeat tamped down. Her composure was unraveling fast. "For the record, I'd never planned on having children."

When Kade didn't say anything, Bree looked at him. She didn't exactly see empathy there. Well, not at first. But then he gave a heavy sigh and slipped his arm around her. As he'd done before, he pulled her across the seat until she was cradled against him. It felt better than it should.

Far better.

Bree knew she should be backing away. She should be trying to stay objective and focused on what had happened. Besides, she'd learned the hard way that taking this kind of comfort from a man, any man, could be a bad mistake. Especially since she could feel this steamy attraction for Kade simmering inside her. It'd been there from the first moment she'd laid eyes on him.

And it was still there now.

Getting worse, too. The comforting shoulder was getting all mixed up with the confusion, the attraction and the fact that he'd just saved her life.

Bree took another deep breath and gathered her composure. "Let's do this," she said, pushing herself away from him.

Kade lifted his eyebrow but didn't question her. Not verbally, anyway. He got out of the truck and started toward the porch. Bree followed him, and with each step she tried to steady her nerves.

She finally gave up.

Nothing could help in that department.

But then, Kade reached out and took her hand.

It was such a simple gesture. And much to her surprise and concern, she felt herself calm down. It lasted just a few seconds until Kade threw open the front door, and Bree spotted the armed dark-haired man.

Kade's brother, no doubt.

But this Ryland had a hard dangerous look that had her wanting to take a step back. She didn't. However, she did pull her hand from Kade's.

"This is my brother Mason," Kade explained. He took off his Stetson, put it on a wall hook where there were two similar ones, and he glanced around the massive foyer.

Bree glanced around, too, looking for any threats, any gunmen. Anything other than the brother that might set off alarms in her head.

Like the house's exterior, this place screamed *home*. It looked well lived in and loved with its warm weathered wood floors and paintings of horses and cattle. There were more pictures and framed family shots in the massive living room off to her left.

"Where are the others?" Kade asked when he'd finished looking around.

"Dade's in his office watching the security cameras. After you called, I had a couple of the ranch hands take Kayla, Darcy, Eve and the kids to Grayson in town. They'll stay at the sheriff's office for a while."

Since Bree didn't recognize those names, she looked at Kade.

"Dade's another brother," he clarified. "He's a deputy sheriff like Mason here. Kayla, Darcy and Eve are all my sisters-in-law." He turned his attention to Mason but didn't say anything.

Something passed between them. A look. And Mason tipped his head to the room off the left side of the foyer. Kade caught Bree's arm and led her in that direction.

For one horrifying moment she wondered if she'd been a fool to trust Kade. After all, someone had kidnapped her and done heaven knows what to her. But that horrifying moment passed and settled like a rock-hard knot in her stomach when they walked into the living room and Bree saw the petite woman with reddish graying hair.

The woman was holding a bundle in a pink blanket.

"This is Grace Borden, one of the nannies here at the ranch," Kade said. "Grace, this is Bree Winston."

Grace offered Bree a tentative smile and then walked toward her. As she got closer, Bree saw the tiny hand as it fluttered out from the blanket. The knot in Bree's stomach got worse. It got even tighter when Grace stopped in front of her, and Bree could see the baby nestled inside all that pink.

"This is Leah Marie Ryland," Kade volunteered. He led Bree to the sofa and had her sit down, probably because she didn't look too steady on her feet. And she wasn't. "The names of both my grandmothers."

A lot of family tradition for such a tiny little thing. "You said she's healthy?"

Kade nodded. "She just had her checkup, and she's nearly eight pounds now."

Bree had no idea if that was good or bad. And the terrifying feeling returned in spades when Grace came closer and held out the baby for Bree to take. The nanny must have picked up on Bree's uneasiness because she shot Kade a questioning glance. The moment he gave another nod, Grace eased the baby into Bree's arms.

It probably wasn't a normal reaction, but Bree gasped.

She'd never held any living thing this tiny, and Leah felt too fragile for Bree to trust her hands. Her breath stalled in her throat. In fact, everything seemed to stop.

"I'll be in the kitchen if you need me," Grace whispered.

"I need you to call Dr. Mickelson," Kade told her. "If he can, have him come out to the ranch right away to give Bree a checkup. Explain that she'll need lab work done."

That made sense. Maybe they could learn what she'd been drugged with. Considering the female kidnapper had seemingly tried to keep Bree alive, maybe the drug wasn't addictive or harmful. Ditto for the drugs they'd given her when she was pregnant.

Grace verified that she would indeed call the doctor and walked out of the room. The silence came immediately. Awkward and long. Bree couldn't say anything. She could only stare at the baby's face.

"She's got my hair and coloring," Kade said. "Your green eyes, though."

Yes, those curls were indeed dark brown, and there were lots of them. Bree couldn't see the baby's eyes because she was sound asleep. But she could see the shape of her face. That was Kade's, too.

Until Bree had seen the baby, she'd been about to question the DNA test that Kade said he'd run. She had figured to ask him to repeat it, just to be sure. But a repeat wasn't necessary. Kade was right: Leah was a genetic mix of Ryland and Winston blood.

And that required a deep breath.

Because she knew this baby was indeed hers.

Oh, mercy. Not good. She had lousy DNA, and that's why she'd never intended on passing it on to a helpless little baby.

"Here," Bree managed to say, and she quickly handed Leah to Kade. Despite her wobbly legs, she got up so she could put some distance between Kade and her.

Kade cuddled the baby closer to him, brushed a kiss on her cheek. The gesture was so loving. But the glare he aimed at her wasn't. Far from it. She'd obviously riled him again, and he had no trouble showing it.

"I don't have a normal life," Bree blurted out. "I'm always deep undercover. Always living a lie."

That didn't ease his scowl.

"Besides, I'm no good with kids." Even though looking at that tiny face made her wish that she was. There was something about that face that made her want to do what Kade had done—brush a kiss on her cheek.

Kade's scowl ended only because Leah made a sound. Not a cry exactly, more like a whimper. And he began to rock her gently as if it were the most natural thing in the world.

"I was raised in foster care," she added. Heaven knows why she'd volunteered that. Maybe to stop him from scowling at her again. Yes, it was true, and it was also true that her childhood had been so nightmarish that she'd vowed never to have children of her own.

And technically she hadn't broken that vow.

But someone had overridden her decision, and Kade was holding the proof in his arms.

Kade kissed the baby again, stood and placed her in a white carrier seat that was on the coffee table just inches away. Leah stirred a little, but she didn't wake up. He put his hands on his hips and stared at Bree.

"It's all right." His jaw was tight again, and his gray eyes had turned frosty. "I don't expect anything from you."

It felt as if he'd slugged her, and it took Bree several moments to recover and gather her breath. "What the heck does that mean?"

Kade shrugged. Not easily. The muscles were obviously locked tight there, too. "It's clear you're not comfortable with this."

"And you were?" Bree fired back.

"I am now. She's my daughter, and I'll raise her." He started to turn away, but Bree caught his arm and whirled him back around to face her.

"Now, just a minute. I didn't say I wouldn't raise her. I just need time. You've had seven weeks to adjust to being a dad," she reminded him. "I've had an hour, and for a good part of that time we've been ducking bullets and nearly getting killed."

The mini tirade drained her, but Bree stayed on her feet so she could face him. They weren't exactly eye to eye since she was a good seven inches shorter than he was, but she held his gaze.

And she saw the exact moment he backed down.

Kade mumbled some profanity and scrubbed his hand over his face. "I'm sorry. It's just that I love Leah, and I figured you'd feel the same."

"I do!" The words came flying out of her, and so did the heart-stopping realization that followed.

Bree looked at that tiny face again. Her daughter. The baby she'd carried for all those months while being held captive. She felt the tears burn her eyes, and Bree cursed them and tried to blink them back.

"I tried not to think of her as a real baby," Bree said,

her voice barely a whisper. "Because I wasn't sure we would make it out of that place alive."

Oh, mercy. The confession brought on more blasted tears. Bree hated them because she wasn't a whiner, and she darn sure didn't want Kade to think she was trying to milk some sympathy from him.

Kade cursed again and called himself a bad name before he moved toward her. Bree wanted to tell him it wasn't a good time to offer her a shoulder to cry on. She was too weak and vulnerable. But Kade pulled her into his arms before she could protest.

And then she was glad he had.

Bree dropped her head on Kade's shoulder and let his strong arms support her. She felt that strength, and the equally strong attraction.

Good grief.

Didn't she have enough on her plate without adding lust to the mix? Of course, maybe it was a little more than lust since Kade and she had this whole parenthood bond going on.

She pulled back, looked up at him. "This holding is nice, but it's not a good idea."

His left eyebrow cocked. "Considering what you've been through, you've earned the right to lean on somebody."

But not you.

She kept that to herself, but it was best if she kept Kade out of this emotionally charged equation. There was still so much to figure out. So many questions…

First though, she wanted to get acquainted with her daughter.

Bree eased out of Kade's grip and walked to the carrier seat that was lined with pale pink fabric and frilly lace. She touched her finger to Leah's cheek, and Bree was more than a little surprised when the baby's eyes opened.

Yes, they were green like hers.

Leah stared at her. Studying Bree, as if trying to figure out who she was.

"I'm your mother, little one," Bree whispered. "Your mom," she corrected. Less formal. Even though both felt foreign to Bree's vocabulary. "And you're the one who kicked me all those months. With all those hard kicks, I thought you'd be a lot bigger."

The corner of Leah's mouth lifted. A smile! It warmed Bree from head to toe. Yes. Now she knew what Kade meant when he said he loved this baby. How could he not? It was something so strong, so deep that if Bree had been standing, she wouldn't have managed to stay on her feet for long.

"This is potent stuff," she mumbled.

"Oh, yeah," Kade agreed. "Wait until she coos."

Bree wasn't sure she could wait. She stood, reached into the basket and brought her baby back into her arms. Bree drew in her scent. Something that stirred feelings she thought she'd never have.

Magic. Pure magic.

It hit Bree then. This was the only person she had ever truly loved. Someone she would die to protect.

Of course, that brought back on the blasted tears, but rather than curse them, Bree sank down on the sofa and gave her daughter a good looking over. She pulled back the blanket.

"Ten fingers, ten toes," Bree mumbled.

"And a strong set of lungs," Kade supplied. He sank

down next to her. "You'll hear just how loud she can be when she wants her bottle at 2:00 a.m."

Bree turned to him. "Will I be here at 2:00 a.m.?"

Kade nodded, but it wasn't exactly a wholehearted one. Yes, he'd given her that hug and some much-needed empathy, but he was holding back. And Bree didn't blame him. She was holding back, too. The problem was she didn't want to be separated from Leah.

Correction: she couldn't be.

Yes, she'd just laid eyes on her for the first time, but Bree felt like something she'd thought she would never feel.

She felt like a mother.

An incompetent one but a mother nonetheless.

"You can stay while we sort things out," Kade finally said.

Again, it wasn't a resounding yes, but Bree would take it. At this point, she would take anything she could get that would allow her to stay with this precious child.

"Things," she repeated. A lot fell under that umbrella. The danger. And the custody, of course. Living arrangements, too. She probably no longer had an apartment since she'd been gone all this time and hadn't paid rent.

Heck, did she even have a job?

"Take one thing at a time," Kade said, his Texas drawl dancing off each word.

She returned the nod. "So, what's first?"

But Kade didn't get a chance to answer. That's because Bree and he turned toward the footsteps. A moment later, Mason appeared in the doorway.

One look at his face, and Bree knew something was

wrong. *No.* Not again. She automatically pulled Leah closer to her.

"We got trouble," Mason announced, and he drew his gun.

Chapter 5

Trouble. Kade was positive they'd already had enough of their share of that today.

"What's wrong?" Kade asked his brother.

Mason tipped his head toward the front of the house. "About a minute ago, a strange car turned onto the ranch road, and Dade ran the plates. The vehicle is registered to none other than Hector McClendon."

Beside him, Bree gasped. Kade knew how she felt because McClendon shouldn't be here at the ranch. After all, he was their lead suspect in too many crimes to list—including Bree's own kidnapping that had led to Leah's birth.

That stirred some strong conflicting feelings in Kade.

He loved Leah so much that he couldn't imagine life without her, but someone would pay for what had happened. His baby didn't deserve the rough start she'd gotten in life.

Kade got to his feet, the questions already forming in his head. He hadn't wanted this meeting with Mc-Clendon, but maybe they could learn something from it. Right now, he'd take any answers he could get—as long as he got them while keeping Leah safe.

Bree, too, he mentally added.

Yes, she was a trained federal agent, but she was in no shape right now to face down a snake like Mc-Clendon.

"Wait here," he told Bree. "I'll deal with this."

But she stood, anyway, and eased Leah back into the carrier. "You're not letting him near the baby."

"Not a chance. I'm not letting him in the house, period. But I do want to talk to him and see why he came. He's never been out here to see me before now, and I don't like the timing."

It was past being suspicious since it'd been less than an hour and a half since Kade had rescued Bree from that motel. Was McClendon here to finish off the job that the hired gunman had failed to do?

Kade drew his gun and headed toward the front door.

Of course, Bree didn't stay put as he'd ordered. She was right behind him.

"Have Dade keep monitoring the security feed," Kade instructed Mason. This could be a ruse that someone could use to get gunmen onto the ranch, but Mason probably already knew that. "And take Leah to Grace. I want them to stay at the back of the house until Mc-Clendon is off the grounds."

Mason hesitated, glancing first at Leah in her carrier seat and then out the front window at the approaching silver Jaguar. His brother was probably trying to decide if he should stay and play backup, but Mason thankfully picked up the carrier and hurried out of the room.

Good. That was one less thing to worry about. One less *big* thing.

Kade gave Bree one last try so he could take another worrisome issue off his list. "McClendon could be dangerous, and you're still feeling the effects of that drug."

Her chin came up, and even though he didn't know her that well, Kade recognized the attitude. Bree wouldn't back down. Something he understood since he would have reacted the same in her position. However, because she wasn't duty ready, he eased her behind him when he headed for the door.

Kade paused at the security system so he could open the door without setting off the alarms. By the time he'd done that, McClendon was already out of his car and walking up the porch steps. His driver—aka his armed goon bodyguard, no doubt—stayed by the open car door.

Even though it'd been months since Kade had seen the man, he hadn't changed much. The same salt-and-pepper hair styled to perfection. A pricey foreign suit. Pricey shoes, too. The man was all flash. Or rather all facade. McClendon appeared to be a highly successful businessman, but at the moment he was basically unemployed and living off the millions he'd inherited from parents. Old money.

The man was also old slime.

And Kade was going to have to hang on to every bit of his composure to keep from ripping McClendon's face off. If this arrogant SOB was behind Bree's kidnapping and the insemination, then he would pay for it.

Kade positioned himself in the center of the door, blocking the way so that McClendon couldn't enter. He also blocked Bree so she couldn't get any closer. She was already way too close for Kade's comfort.

"Why are you here?" Kade demanded.

McClendon ignored the question and looked past Kade. His attention went directly to Bree, who was on her tiptoes and peering over Kade's shoulder.

"I got a call about her." McClendon jabbed his index finger in Bree's direction. "I thought I was rid of you. Guess not. But if you're back to make more accusations about me, then you'd better think twice."

Despite Kade's attempts to block her, Bree worked her way around him, stepping to his side, and she faced McClendon head-on. "Who called you?"

McClendon's face stayed tight with anger, but he shook his head. "It was an anonymous tipster. The person used some kind of machine to alter his voice so I couldn't tell who it was. I couldn't even tell if it was a *he*. Could have been anybody for all I know."

Like the call Kade had gotten about Bree. "This person told you Bree was here? Because I only found her myself a little while ago."

"No, the person didn't say she was here, only that she was with you. I figured out the ranch part all by myself since this, after all, is your family home," McClendon smugly added.

"It's a long drive out here just to talk to Bree," Kade remarked.

The man made a sound of agreement. "Let's just say the anonymous caller piqued my interest. Plus, I wanted to make sure Agent Winston here wasn't trying to pin more bogus charges on me."

Kade wished he had a charge, any charge, he could pin on the man. Maybe he could arrest him for trespassing, but that wouldn't get him behind bars.

"So, why do you look like death warmed over?" McClendon asked Bree.

"Because I've had a bad day. A bad year," she corrected in a snarl. "Someone kidnapped me. Maybe you? Or maybe someone working for you? Maybe even the Neanderthal standing by your car." Bree aimed her own finger at him, though unlike McClendon's, hers was shaky. "And that someone had me inseminated. What do you know about that, huh?"

McClendon flexed his eyebrows. Maybe from surprise, but Kade seriously doubted it. In fact, McClendon might have personal knowledge of every detail of this investigation.

"I know nothing about it," the man insisted. "And it's accusations like that I'm here to warn you against. I have plans to open a new clinic in the next few months. One that will help infertile couples. *Real couples.* Not FBI agents hell-bent on trying to ruin me and my reputation."

"Your own shady dealings ruined you," Kade fired back. "You used illegal immigrants as gestational carriers and surrogates. Hell, you didn't even pay them. Just room, board and minimal medical care." And for each of those women, McClendon and the clinic had collected plenty of money.

"Prove it," McClendon challenged.

"Give me time and I will. And while you're here, you could just go ahead and make a confession." Though Kade knew that wasn't going to happen.

McClendon looked ready to jump in with a smug answer, but instead, he pulled in a long breath. "I knew nothing about the illegal activity that went on." No more flexed eyebrows or surprise, feigned or otherwise. Fire went through McClendon's dust-gray eyes. "That was my son's doing and that idiot nurse, Jamie Greer. They'll be tried, and both will pay for their wrongdoings."

"Yes, they will," Kade assured him. "But that doesn't mean there won't be more charges. Ones that involve you spending a lot time in jail."

Now, the venom returned. "I'm not responsible for those two losers' actions, and I refuse to have any of Anthony and Jamie's mud slung on me. Got that?"

McClendon didn't wait for Kade or Bree to respond to that. He turned and started off the porch.

"If you did this to Bree…to *us*," Kade corrected, calling out to the man. "I'll bring you down the hard way."

McClendon stopped and spared them a glance from over his shoulder. "Careful, Agent Ryland. You just might bite off more than you can chew. Trying to bring me down will be hazardous to your health. And anyone else who happens to get in my way."

Bree started after him, probably to rip him to shreds as Kade had wanted to do, but Kade caught her arm. She wasn't in any shape to take on a man like McClendon, and besides, assaulting an unarmed civilian wouldn't be good for the investigation.

And there would be an investigation.

That's how Kade could wipe that smug look off this rat's face. He didn't believe for one second that McClendon had stayed clean from all the illegal junk that went on at the clinic.

"An anonymous tipster," Bree mumbled. Her mind, too, was obviously on the investigation. Good. Because they needed answers and they needed them fast. That was the only way to make sure Leah remained safe.

Bree, too.

Even though Kade doubted she'd agree to let him protect her. Still, he had to do something to make things as safe as he could. McClendon had just thrown down the gauntlet, and it could be the start of another round of danger.

Kade's phone buzzed, and on the screen he could see it was from his brother, Dade. "Make sure McClendon leaves the grounds," Kade said to him as he watched the Jaguar speed away.

"I will," Dade assured. "But someone else is coming up the driveway. It's Dr. Mickelson, and he should be there any minute. Who's sick?"

Kade looked at Bree, who was still glaring at McClendon's retreating Jag, and he hoped that she didn't fall into that sick category. Heaven knows what her kidnappers had done to her these past ten and a half months. Hopefully nothing permanent, but he doubted they'd had her health and best interest at heart. There were a lot of nasty addictive drugs they could have used to force her to cooperate.

"The doc's here for Bree," Kade told his brother, and he ended the call just as he saw the doctor's vehicle approaching. Not a sleek luxury car. Dr. Mickelson was driving a blue pickup truck.

"This checkup is just for starters," Kade reminded Bree, just in case she planned to fight it. "Once we're sure Leah is safe, I want you at the hospital for a thorough exam."

She opened her mouth, probably to argue like he'd anticipated, but her fight was somewhat diminished by the dizzy glaze that came over her eyes. No doubt a residual effect of the drugs, or maybe crashing from the adrenaline that kept her going through the gunfight.

Kade caught her to keep her from falling. When she wobbled again, Kade cursed, holstered his gun and scooped her up in his arms.

Of course, she tried to wiggle out of his grip. "I'm not weak," Bree mumbled.

"You are now," Kade mumbled back. "Thanks for coming," he said to the doctor.

"This is Leah's birth mother?" the doctor asked.

Unlike their previous visitor, the doctor had concern all over his expression and in his body language. With his medical bag gripped in his hand, he hurried up the steps toward them.

"Yep, the birth mother," Kade verified.

The sterile title worked for him, but he didn't know if it would work for Bree. Especially not for long. He'd seen the way she had looked at Leah right before Mc-Clendon had interrupted them, and that was not the look of a *birth mother,* but rather a mother who loved her baby and had no plans to give her up.

"This way," Kade instructed the doctor, and he carried Bree up the stairs toward his living quarters.

There was probably a guest room clean and ready. There were three guest suites in the house, but Kade didn't want to take the time to call Bessie, the woman who managed the house. And she also managed the Rylands. Bessie was as close to a mother as he had these days. Heck, for most of his life, since his mother had passed away when he was barely eleven.

"I can walk," Bree insisted.

Kade ignored her again, used his boot to nudge open

his door, and he walked through the sitting-office area
to his bedroom. He deposited her on his king-size bed.

Funny, he'd thought about getting Bree into his bed
from the moment he first met her on the undercover
assignment, but he hadn't figured it would happen this
way. Or ever. After Bree and he had escaped that clinic,
he hadn't thought he would see her again. Now her life
was permanently interlinked with his.

"She'll need blood drawn for a tox screen," Kade
reminded Dr. Mickelson.

"Will do. Any possibility there's something going
on other than drugs?" the doctor asked. "Maybe an in-
fection or something?"

Kade could only shake his head. "I'm not sure. She's
been held captive for months. I have no idea what all
they did to her. And neither does she."

"I'll run a couple of tests," Dr. Michelson assured
him, and he motioned for Kade to wait outside.

That made sense, of course, because Dr. Mickelson
would want to check Bree's C-section incision. Maybe
other parts of her, too. Kade didn't want to be there for
that, especially since Bree had already had her privacy
violated in every way possible.

Kade eased the bedroom door shut, leaned against
the wall. And waited. It didn't take long for the bad
thoughts to fly right at him.

What the devil was he going to do?

McClendon's visit was a hard reminder that he hadn't
left the danger at the motel in San Antonio. It could and
maybe would follow them here to the ranch, the one
place he considered safe.

He couldn't bear the thought of his baby girl being
in harm's way, though she had been from the moment

of her conception. What a heck of a way to start her life. But there was a silver lining in all of this. Leah was too young to know anything about her beginnings. She knew nothing of the danger.

Nothing of a mother who wasn't totally acting like a mother.

Yeah. That was unfair, and it caused Kade to wince a little. Bree needed to get her footing, and when she did…

Kade's thoughts went in a really bad direction.

When Bree got that inevitable footing, what if she wanted full custody of Leah? Until now, Kade hadn't thought beyond the next step of his investigation—and that step was to find Bree. Well, he'd found her all right.

Now what?

It sent a jab of fear through him to even consider it, but could he lose custody of his baby?

He shook his head. That couldn't happen. He wouldn't let it happen. Besides, Bree was a Jane and by her own admission not motherhood material. She worked impossible hours on assignments that sometimes lasted months. Then there was that whole confession about her being raised in foster care and never having planned to be a mother.

But Kade hadn't thought he was ready to be a father until he had seen Leah's face. Just the sight of her had caused something to switch in his head, and in that moment Leah became the most important person in his life.

He would die to protect his little girl. But his best chance of protecting Leah was to stay alive. And keep Bree alive, as well. There were probably some much-needed answers trapped in Bree's drug-hazed memories, and this exam by the doctor was the first step in retrieving those memories.

Kade's phone buzzed, and he saw on the screen that the call was from Mason. Mercy, he hoped nothing else had gone wrong. He'd had his *gone wrong* quota filled for the day.

"I've got news," Mason answered. As usual, there was no hint of emotion in his brother's voice. Mason definitely wasn't the sort of man to overreact, even when all hell was breaking loose. "I just got off the phone with Nate."

Kade breathed a little easier. Well, at first. Nate was handling the situation at the Treetop Motel in San Antonio where the gunman had tried to kill Bree and him. "Please tell me nothing's wrong," Kade commented.

"Not that I know of. But then all I got was a thirty-second update. Nate wanted me to tell you that he has his CSI folks out at the motel. They're going through the room where Bree was. His detectives also plan to comb the area to look for anyone who might have seen Bree come in."

That was a good start. "Any chance of surveillance cameras?"

"Slim to none. That neighborhood isn't big on that sort of thing."

Probably because it was a haven for drug dealers, prostitutes and a whole host of illegal activity. Still, they might get lucky. CSI could maybe find something that would help him identify Bree's kidnappers. That was step two. Then, once he had the culprits behind bars, he could think about this potential custody problem.

And Bree.

There was something stirring between them. Or

maybe that was just lust or the uneasiness over what could turn out to be a potentially nasty custody dispute. Kade hoped that was all because lust and uneasiness were a lot easier to deal with than other things that could arise.

"I want to talk to Anthony McClendon and Jamie Greer again," Kade insisted. Both were suspects, just like Anthony's father, and he hadn't officially questioned them in months. "Can you set up the interviews and get them to the Silver Creek sheriff's office?"

That way, his brothers could assist, and he wouldn't have to be too far away from Leah or Bree. Though judging from her earlier behavior, Bree might want to get far away from here. He couldn't blame her after McClendon's threats. The man hadn't named Leah specifically, but it had certainly sounded as if he were threatening the baby.

"Sure, I can get Anthony and Jamie out here. McClendon, too. But you have a couple of other fires to put out first. Special Agent Randy Cooper just called and demanded to see Bree. I take it he's her FBI handler or whatever it is you feds call your boss?"

"Yeah." Kade couldn't blame the man for wanting to see Bree, but the timing sucked.

"He seems kind of possessive if you ask me," Mason went on. "You sure he's just her handler?"

No. Kade wasn't sure of that. In fact, he didn't know if Leah had a boyfriend stashed somewhere. The only thing he knew about her was what he'd managed to read in her files. Which wasn't much. There wasn't a lot of paperwork and reports on undercover FBI Janes, and sometimes the files were nothing but cover fronts.

"Tell Coop he'll have to wait until tomorrow to see

Bree," Kade said. "After the doctor finishes the exam, she'll need some rest."

That was the next step in his *for starters*. Maybe there wouldn't be anything that rest and time couldn't fix. Kade really needed her to recall more details of her captivity.

Mason made a sound of agreement. "Don't worry. I'll stall Coop." He paused. "Hold on a second. I just got a text from Nate. Might be important."

Kade could only hope this wasn't more bad news.

"There's another problem, little brother," Mason said. *"A big one."*

Chapter 6

Bree woke up to the sound of voices. Voices that she didn't immediately recognize.

She reached for her gun and phone. Not there. And an uneasy sense of déjà vu slammed through her. She sprang from the bed, her feet ready to start running when they landed on the thickly carpeted floor. Bree stopped cold.

Where the heck was she? And why hadn't there been a gun on the nightstand?

She glanced around the massive sun-washed bedroom, decorated in varying shades of blue and gray. At the king-size bed. The antique pine furniture. And it took her a moment to remember that she was at the Ryland ranch in Silver Creek.

More specifically, she'd been in Kade's bed.

She looked around again, first in the bathroom

through the open door, then the massive dressing room. No sign of Kade.

So, she'd been in that bed alone.

And was apparently safe and sound since she had slept hard and long. After the ordeal she'd been through, she was thankful for that. Well, maybe. She was thankful *if* she hadn't missed anything important.

Which was possible.

After all, Leah was in her life now, and Kade and she were in the middle of a full-scale investigation. Yes, the potential for missing something important was sky-high, and she had to find Kade.

After she got dressed, that is.

Bree glanced down at the pink cotton pjs. They weren't familiar, either, but she did remember the doctor helping her change into them before he insisted that she sleep off the effects of the drugs her kidnapper had given her. She hadn't had a choice about that sleep, either. The fatigue and drugs had mixed with the adrenaline crash, and Bree hadn't been able to keep her eyes open at the end of the exam the doctor had given her.

Another glance, this time at the clock on the nightstand.

Oh, sheez.

It was nine, and she doubted that was p.m. because light was peeking through the curtains. It was nine in the morning, and that meant she'd been asleep at the ranch for heaven knows how many hours. Not good. She was certain she had plenty of things to do. But first, she needed to locate some clothes, the source of those voices and then see if she could scrounge up a phone and a strong cup of black coffee to clear the rest of the cobwebs from her head.

She hurried to the bathroom to wash up, but since she couldn't find a change of clothes, Bree gave up on the notion of getting dressed, and instead, she headed to the sitting room wearing the girlie pink pjs. She prayed nothing was wrong and that's why Kade had let her sleep so long. Too bad the thoughts of ugly scenarios kept going through her mind.

Bree threw open the door that separated the rooms in the suite and saw Kade. That was one voice. He was holding Leah and talking to someone. The other voice belonged to an attractive brunette that had her arm slung around Kade's waist.

The pang of jealousy hit Bree before she could see it coming.

"Oh," the woman said, her voice a classy purr.

Actually, everything about her was classy including her slim rose-colored top and skirt. Her hair was so shiny, so perfect, that Bree raked her hand through her own messy locks before she could stop herself. What was wrong with her? With everything else going on, the last thing she should care about was her appearance.

The woman smiled and walked toward her. "You must be Bree." Her smile stayed in place even when she eyed the pajamas. "I'm glad they fit."

"They're yours?" Bree asked.

The woman nodded.

Of course, they were. This woman was girlie, and she was also everything that Bree wasn't. Bree could see the love for her in Kade's eyes.

Another pang of jealousy.

Bree smoothed her hair down again before she could stop herself.

"I'm Darcy Ryland." The woman extended her hand for Bree to shake.

"Darcy is Nate's wife," Kade supplied. "He's the cop at SAPD who's helping us with the investigation."

Kade had a funny expression on his face as if he knew that Bree had been jealous.

Bree tossed him a scowl.

He gave her another funny look.

"I'm also the Silver Creek assistant D.A. and the mother of two toddlers who are waiting for me to bring them their favorite books and toys." Darcy checked her watch. "And that means I should have already been out of here. Good to meet you, Bree. We'll chat more when things settle down."

"Good to meet you, too," Bree mumbled.

Darcy tipped her head to the plush sofa. "I left you some other clothes—ones that aren't pink. Toiletries, too. And if you need anything else, just help yourself to my closet. Nate's and my quarters are in the west wing of the house. Just be careful not to trip over the toys if you go over there."

Bree added a thanks and felt guilty about the unflattering girlie thoughts and jealousy pangs. So, Kade's sister-in-law was, well, nice despite her picture-perfect looks.

Darcy walked back to Kade and picked up her purse from the table. In the same motion, she kissed him on the cheek and then kissed Leah. Using her purse, she waved goodbye to Bree and glided out of the room on gray heels that looked like torture devices to Bree.

Bree didn't waste any time going to Leah. No blanket this morning. The baby was wearing a one-piece green outfit that was nearly the same color as her eyes.

She was also wide-awake and had those eyes aimed at Kade. Leah seemed to be studying his every move.

"I slept too long," Bree commented, and she touched her fingers to Leah's cheek. The baby automatically turned in her direction. "You should have woken me up sooner."

Bree wondered if there was a time when that wouldn't seem like such a huge deal. She hoped not. Because now everything seemed like a miracle, and just looking at her baby washed away all her dark thoughts and mood.

"You needed sleep," Kade insisted.

When he didn't continue, Bree looked up at him. And she waited. Clearly, he had something on his mind, and thankfully he didn't make her wait long to deliver the news.

"The doctor got back your lab results."

That hung in the air like deadweight. Bree couldn't speak, couldn't ask the question that put her breath in a vise—had the drugs permanently harmed Leah or her?

"You had a large amount of Valium in your system. It caused the grogginess and the temporary memory loss." He paused. "It was temporary, right?"

She nodded and felt relief. Well, partly. "Any chance they gave me Valium when I was pregnant?"

"It's hard to tell, but Leah is perfectly healthy," Kade assured her. "I suspect because they wanted to use the baby for leverage that they didn't do anything that would risk harming her."

Good. That was something, at least. And with that concern out of the way, Bree could turn her full attention back to Leah.

"The doctor said any gaps in your memory should

return," Kade explained. "So, it's possible you'll re-member other details about your kidnappers."

She had a dozen or more questions to ask Kade about the test results and an update on the case, but Bree couldn't get her attention off Leah. She had to be the most beautiful baby ever born.

Or else Bree's brain had turned to mush.

"How is she this morning?" Bree asked.

"Fine. She just had her bottle." He motioned toward the empty one on the table.

She felt a pang of a different kind. Bree wished she'd been awake to feed her, and she cursed the long sleep session that had caused her to miss all these incred-ible moments.

"How long before she'll want another bottle?" Bree asked.

"Around one or two." He paused again. "There's a problem," Kade said.

Bree's gaze flew to his because she thought he was going to say that something was wrong with Leah, after all. She held her breath, praying it wasn't that.

"Late yesterday, Nate's detectives at SAPD found the gunman who shot at us," Kade finished. "He's dead."

Bree groaned. So, the problem wasn't with Leah, but it was still a big one.

"Please tell me he managed to make a confession before he died?" Bree asked.

"Afraid not. His name was Clyde Cummings. We ID'd him from his prints since he had a long rap sheet. In and out of trouble with the law most of his life." An-other pause. "Word on the street is he was a hired gun."

That didn't surprise Bree. Whoever had master-minded her kidnapping had no doubt hired this goon.

A goon who would have succeeded in killing her if Kade hadn't arrived in time to save her.

"Cummings didn't die in a shoot-out with the cops," Kade continued. "When Nate's men found him, he was already dead." Kade paused again. "He died from a single gunshot wound to the back of the head."

Oh, mercy. An execution-style hit on a hit man. That meant someone didn't want Cummings talking to the cops, or maybe this had been punishment for allowing Kade and her to get away. It didn't matter which. The bottom line was this case was far from being over.

Bree looked at Leah and hated that Kade and she had to have a conversation like this in front of her. A baby deserved better, even if Leah was too young to know what they were saying. Still, she might be able to sense the tension in the room. Bree could certainly feel it, and it had her stomach turning and twisting.

"Since we don't know who hired Cummings," Kade went on, "my sisters-in-law and the kids are leaving town for a while. Darcy came back to pack some things."

That gave Bree something else to be frustrated about. The monster after her had now managed to disrupt the entire Ryland family. Now, all of them were in possible danger, and that included Kade's nephews and niece.

Kade ducked down a little so that they were eye to eye. "I think it's a good idea if Leah goes with Darcy and the others."

"No," flew out of her mouth before Bree could stop it. But she immediately hated her response and hated even more that she might have to take it back.

"I'm just getting to know her," Bree mumbled, and she kissed Leah's cheek as she'd seen Kade do. Each kiss, each moment was a gift that she didn't deserve but would take, anyway.

Bree pulled in a long breath and tried to push away the ache. But no, it was still there. It hurt her to the core to think of her daughter being whisked away when she'd only had a few real moments with her. It hurt even more though to know that Leah was in danger and would continue to be until Kade and she put an end to it.

"Whoever killed Cummings could hire someone else," Bree said, more to herself than Kade. She had to make her heart understand what her brain and instincts already knew. Her training and experience forced her to see scenarios and outcomes that ripped away at her.

"Just where exactly is this safe place that the others and Leah could go?" she asked.

"My other sister-in-law, Kayla, has a house in San Antonio. It's an estate with a high wrought-iron fence and security system surrounding the entire grounds and house. SAPD will provide additional protection. Plus, Dade and Nate would be with them."

It sounded like a fortress. Ideal for keeping her baby safe. But Bree knew that bad guys might still try to get through all those security measures.

"You could go, too," Kade quietly added.

"No." And this time, Bree wouldn't take back her response. Just the opposite. It was the only answer that made sense. "Wherever I go, the danger will follow. I'm the one this person wants dead, and I don't want Leah anywhere around if and when he hires another hit man to come after me."

Kade didn't argue. Because he knew it was the truth. The more distance between her baby and her, the better.

Still, that didn't ease the ache that was quickly turning into a raw, throbbing pain.

"This is much harder than I thought it would be," Bree whispered.

Kade only nodded, and she could see the agony in his icy gray eyes. So much emotion that it prompted Bree to touch her fingertips to his arm. She wasn't big on providing comfort, and her job had required her not to sympathize with anything or anybody, but she and Kade shared this heartbreak.

"When would Leah have to go to Kayla's house?" she asked.

Kade lifted his shoulder and sank down on the sofa. "Soon. This morning," he clarified. "But maybe it wouldn't be for long."

Maybe.

And maybe it would be far longer than Bree's heart could handle.

An uncomfortable silence settled between them, and Bree eased down on the sofa right next to him. She waited. Hoping. And it wasn't long before Kade sighed and placed the baby in her arms.

It was far better than anything else he could have done.

It soothed her. And frightened her. It filled her with a hundred emotions that she didn't understand. But even that seemed trivial.

She was holding her baby.

And it was breaking her into pieces.

Until this moment she hadn't realized she could love someone this much. Or hurt this much because she might lose her, even for only a day or two.

"What are we going to do?" Bree said under her breath.

When Kade didn't answer, she looked at him and saw his jaw muscles set in iron.

Handsome iron, she amended.

Because his good looks weren't diminished by a surly expression or the possible impending danger. Again, she blamed it on their shared situation. And on the close contact between them. After all, they were arm to arm. Hip to hip. Breath to breath. Except she doubted Kade was thinking about the close contact in a good way.

That expression let her know that he hadn't told her everything, and the part that he had left out would be something that would only add to the pain she was already feeling.

"Okay, what's wrong?" Bree demanded.

He didn't answer right away. He'd mulled over his answer. "I'm not giving up Leah."

For a moment she thought he meant that he'd changed his mind about the baby going to the San Antonio estate, but then she got it.

Oh, yeah.

She got it all right.

Kade had physical custody of Leah since she was just a few days old. Plus, he had something that Bree didn't—a home, a supportive family and money from the looks of it. There was also the fact that he had strong ties in the community. That meant ties with people who could help him keep custody of their child.

Still, that was just one side of it.

"I'm her mother," Bree said when she couldn't think of another argument. It certainly wasn't a good one, and it didn't mean she had what it took to raise a child. But the other side was that she loved this child with all her heart.

Kade nodded. "And I'm her father."

Frustrated, she stared at him. "Does this mean we're at some kind of stalemate?"

"No." And that's all he said for several moments. "It means we have some things to work out. Things that will be in Leah's best interest."

Bree could see where this was going, and she didn't like the direction one bit. "You think you can be a better parent than me."

He didn't deny it.

She couldn't deny it, either. He certainly looked at ease with Leah. So did the other members of his family that she'd met. Leah was a Ryland.

But she was Bree's baby, too.

Bree huffed. "I'm not just giving her up, either." Even though it didn't make logical sense, it made sense to her. As a mother. Yes, it was a new role, new feelings. New everything. But it was a role she would embrace with as much devotion and love as she had her badge.

Kade didn't huff, but he mumbled something under his breath. "Be reasonable about this. You're a Jane for heaven's sake."

Bree jumped right on that. "And I could become a regular agent. Like you."

In the past that would have caused her to wince. Or laugh because she had thought a regular job would be a boring death sentence. But she wasn't wincing or laughing now. In fact, she was on the verge of crying at the thought of losing this child that she hardly knew.

With those iron jaw muscles still in place, Kade

leaned forward and picked up the little silver object from the table. Bree recognized the design. It was the same as the tattoo on his shoulder. He began to roll it like a coin across his fingers. Maybe as a stress reliever. Maybe so he wouldn't have to look at her. Whatever, it was working.

Well, for Kade.

Bree didn't think anything could relieve her stress, but she shoved that aside and tried to reach a solution. Even a temporary one. She sure needed something to get her through this morning.

"We only have a few hours to spend with Leah before she leaves," Bree conceded. "We can table this discussion until after...well, after," she settled for saying.

Because she refused to admit this could end badly. The stakes were too high for that.

"Later, then," Kade agreed, and he looked back at her. His expression let her know that *later, then,* wasn't going to happen immediately.

"There aren't a lot of rules for situations like this. And we don't know each other very well." He kept rolling the concho. "In fact, I don't know much about you at all."

It wasn't a gruff or barked observation. It was conversation, that's all, and he had genuine concern in his voice. Bree knew this could turn ugly, but since he was trying to make nice, she tried, too.

"Bree is my real name. Bree Ann Winston. I'm twenty-nine." She paused. Frowned. "Wait. What's the date?"

He glanced at his watch. "June 14."

That required a deep breath. "Okay, I'm thirty." She'd missed a pivotal birthday by two months.

Ironically, it had been a birthday that she'd been dreading since many Janes didn't last long after their mid-thirties. They were either dead or moved to a regular agent position. However, after the ordeal she'd just been through, turning thirty didn't seem so bad, after all.

"Both of my parents are dead," she continued, addressing another touchy subject. "They were killed in a meth lab explosion when I was nine. Let's just say they weren't stellar parents and leave it at that. I spent the rest of my so-called childhood in foster care."

Hellish foster care that she didn't discuss. Ever. With anyone.

Bree took another deep breath. She hadn't intended to confess all of that dirty laundry, but she figured this wasn't a good time to keep secrets. Besides, if it came down to a custody fight with Kade, he'd find out, anyway. Kade would learn that prior to becoming an FBI agent, she'd been a mess. A juvenile record for underage drinking. Truancy. And running away from foster care. Especially that. Bree had lost count of how many times she'd run. In fact, she always ran when things got tough.

Or rather she had.

She wouldn't run now.

"So, there's the dirt on me," she concluded. "Nothing like your life, I'm sure."

He made a sound that could have meant anything and followed it with a deep breath to indicate it was his turn to spill his guts. "I'm Kade Jason Ryland. Age thirty-one. And I've lived here at this ranch my entire life. Wouldn't want to live anywhere else."

She could see him here as a little boy. Learning to ride those magnificent horses that she'd seen in the

painting in the foyer. Running through this sprawling
house surrounded by older brothers and other family
who loved him the way Bree loved Leah. It was so far
from what she'd experienced as a kid that it seemed
like a fantasy.

Kade's next deep breath came with a change of expression. His forehead bunched up, and he dodged her
gaze. "When I was ten, my grandfather was murdered.
He was the sheriff then, and well, I was close to him.
All of us were. He was gunned down by an unknown
assailant, and the case has never been solved."

"I'm sorry." And that was genuine. An injustice like
that ate away at you. Obviously, that's what it'd done
to Kade. She could see the hurt still there in his eyes.

He shrugged, and she saw the shield come down. He
was guarding himself now. Bree knew, because she was
a master of doing it.

"A few days after my grandfather was murdered, my
father gave me and my five brothers a custom-made silver concho." He held it up for her to see.

"That was nice of him." Though there was something
about his tone that said differently.

"It was a guilt gift." Kade didn't continue until he'd
taken Leah from her and put the baby in the carrier
seat on the table in front of them. "After that, my father
walked out on us. My mother killed herself because she
was severely depressed, and my older brother, Grayson,
had to forgo college, life and everything else so he could
raise all of us and keep the ranch going."

Kade met her gaze. "So, there's the dirt on me."

Okay. Bree hadn't expected anything other than a
fairy tale family story to do with the idyllic family
ranch, but that was more a nightmare. The sympathy

came, and it didn't feel as foreign to her as she thought it would.

"I'm sorry," she repeated.

He waved her off. "Yeah. I'm sorry about your life, too."

It was the first time she ever remembered anyone saying that and really meaning it. And much to her surprise, it felt good. Too good. And it set off more warnings in her head. Her motto of *don't trust anyone* was slowly being chipped away.

By Kade.

She looked up at him, to thank him, not just for the reciprocal sympathy but also for taking care of their baby when she hadn't been around to do it.

Kade looked at her, too. And her *thank you* died on her lips when he put his arms around her and pulled her to him.

"We have to be together on this," he whispered.

It wasn't exactly the kiss that she'd braced herself for. Just the opposite. He was holding her as if trying to comfort her.

His arms were warm and strong. So welcoming. Of course, she'd been in his arms before at the fertility clinic. She'd been naked then. Kade had, too. And his body had definitely given her dreams and food for thought.

Not now, of course.

And Bree wanted to believe that.

Too bad those memories warmed her far more than they should have. It'd been a job, she reminded herself. And that job was over now. Kade's naked body was just a memory, and it had to stay that way.

Bree wanted to believe that, too.

He pulled back, met her gaze. His breath was warm, as well, and he moved closer. Closer. Until his mouth brushed against hers. Bree tried to brace herself again, but what she didn't do was move away.

"I'd kiss you," he drawled, "but we both know that'd be a bad idea."

She was about to agree with him, but Kade leaned in and touched his mouth to hers again. Still not a kiss, but it heated her as thoroughly as if it had been one.

"A bad idea," she repeated. Mercy. She sounded like a wimp. And she still wasn't moving. Bree could see what was happening. Like a big train wreck. Except this was a wreck that her body was aching to experience.

What would a real kiss feel like with Kade?

The fake ones had been amazingly potent, and she figured a real one would pretty much melt her into a puddle.

"Bad," he mumbled without taking his eyes off her.

Bree could see a kiss coming. Could feel it. And she heard herself say *uh-oh* a split second before Kade snapped away from her.

Okay.

No kiss, after all. She didn't know who looked more disappointed or more confused—Kade or her.

He cursed. Some really bad words. And Bree thought that was it. The end of the possible lethal kiss. But then he came back at her. He grabbed her and put his mouth on hers. And it wasn't for just a peck this time.

This was a Kade Ryland kiss.

Yes, this was so different from the fake ones, and they weren't even naked to enjoy the full benefits. Still, there were benefits. His mouth moved over hers as if he'd been born to kiss her like this.

The heat washed through her, head to toe. It cleared the haze and fogginess from her mind while it created some haze of a different kind. Her body was suddenly on fire.

From one blasted kiss!

How could he do that to her body? How could he dissolve all her defenses and make her want him like this?

Bree wasn't sure she wanted to know the answer. But she was certain that she wanted the kiss to continue. And it couldn't. For one thing, Leah was in the room. For another, neither Kade nor she was in a good place for this to be happening.

Still, she wasn't the one to stop. Kade did. Later, much later, after her body cooled down, she might actually thank him for it.

He pulled back, dragged his tongue over his bottom lip and made a sound of approval. Or something. Whatever the sound, it went through her as fiery hot as the kiss.

Bree didn't ask for clarification on what that sound meant. She didn't need it. That kiss had held up to the fantasies she'd had after those naked fake kisses at the clinic.

"I'm sorry," Kade said.

She didn't have time to repeat that lie to him because someone cleared their throat and both Bree and Kade turned toward the open doorway. It was Mason, and he obviously hadn't missed the close contact between them. He didn't look too pleased about it, either, but then he hadn't looked pleased about much since her arrival.

"You got a visitor," Mason said, his attention landing on her. "SA Randy Cooper."

Coop. The very person that she should have called

by now. Sheez. How could she have forgotten that? But then Bree remembered.

Sleep, baby and kisses.

Yes. That had really eaten into her time, but she had to get her mind back on track. She had to think like an agent because that was the best way to keep her baby safe.

"I had him wait on the front porch," Mason explained. "Just in case you didn't want to see him."

Oh, she wanted to see him all right. She turned to Kade. "I need to change my clothes. Best if I don't talk to my boss while wearing these pink pjs."

He nodded and picked up Leah in the infant carrier. "Mason can watch Leah. Meet me downstairs in the living room after you've changed."

"There's more," Mason said, and that stopped both Kade and her midstep. "Somebody else called the sheriff's office and left a message for you. And it's a call I think you'll need to return before you speak to Agent Cooper."

Bree shook her head, not understanding that remark. "Who wants to talk to us?" she asked cautiously.

"To *you,*" Mason corrected, staring right at her. "It's Anthony McClendon."

One of their suspects. She glanced at Kade, wondering if he knew why Anthony would be calling her, but he only lifted his shoulder.

"What does he want?" Kade demanded.

"Apparently a lot. He's either lying through his teeth or else you should rethink seeing Agent Cooper. That's why I left him on the porch and locked the front door. I reset the security alarm, too."

Bree lifted her shoulders. "Why would you take

those kinds of measures for a federal officer?" she added. "And why would you listen to a piece of scum like Anthony McClendon?"

It was Mason's turn to shrug. "Because he says he has proof that Cooper is dirty."

"Proof?" Kade challenged.

Mason nodded. "Oh, yeah. And he says he's also got evidence that Cooper is the one who wants Bree dead."

Chapter 7

"Proof," Kade mumbled while he waited for Bree to change her clothes.

He was eager to hear exactly what that would be or if such a thing even existed. Kade had already tried to return Anthony's call, but it had gone straight to voice mail.

"So-called proof coming from a confirmed suspect awaiting trial," Mason interjected. He dropped down on the sofa and gave Leah's foot a little wiggle. His brother didn't smile, but it was as close to a loving expression as Mason ever managed. "Anthony could be just blowing smoke."

Under normal circumstances that reminder would have been enough to calm some of Kade's concerns. But it wasn't enough now.

His daughter was in the house.

The very house that Coop was waiting to get inside. Yeah, Mason would protect Leah, and Kade could do the same to Bree, but he hated the possibility of danger being so close. Bree already had enough danger dumped on her, and judging from her still-sleepy eyes and unfocused expression, she wasn't anywhere near ready to face down someone who might not be on their side.

Especially when it was someone she thought was on their side.

"I'm ready," Bree announced, hurrying out of the bathroom. No more cotton candy pajamas. She wore loose black pants and a pale purple top. Darcy's colors. But they didn't look so bad on Bree, either.

Kade also saw the change in her body language. No more lack of focus. Hers was the expression of an agent who wanted some answers. Or maybe she just wanted to throttle Anthony for making that accusation against her boss.

"I know, I know," she mumbled when she followed his gaze. She went to Leah and kissed her forehead. "The clothes aren't my usual style."

"You look good," he settled for saying.

Bree glanced down at the outfit and grumbled a distracted thanks. Her mind was obviously locked on seeing their visitor.

Kade aimed for the same mind lock. He pushed her clothes, Leah, the kiss and this attraction for her aside so he could deal with something potentially dangerous.

"You trust Coop?" he came right out and asked.

"Of course." She answered without hesitation, but she stopped on her way to the door. Now, she paused and shook her head. *"Of course,"* she repeated it and slowly turned back around to face him. "What did Anthony have to say about Coop wanting me dead?"

"I wasn't able to reach him, but I left a message and told him to call my cell."

"Well, I'm sure whatever comes from Anthony's mouth will be a lie," she added and headed out of the room. "Coop's not the enemy. I can't say the same for Anthony, especially since he's facing criminal charges."

Kade hoped she was right about Coop, but just in case, he kept his hand over his gun. He also moved ahead of Bree, hoping that he could keep himself between Coop and her until he could determine if there was a shred of truth to Anthony's allegations.

The maneuver earned him a huff from Bree.

He gave her a huff right back.

Kade disarmed the security system and looked out the side window. It was Coop all right. Kade had had many conversations with the lanky blond-haired man while he'd been searching for Bree. Conversations where Kade had been sure that Coop's actions were the right ones.

He hoped he continued to feel that way when he opened the door.

"Bree," Coop said on a rise of breath as if he truly hadn't expected to see her. The man stepped forward, and Kade had to make a split-second decision about letting him in.

But Bree made the decision for him. She stepped around Kade and pulled Coop into her arms for a hug. The man hugged back and kept repeating her name. It was a regular warm and fuzzy reunion.

"I never thought I'd see you again," Coop whispered, though it was plenty loud enough for Kade to hear.

"It was touch-and-go yesterday," Kade offered.

"Yes." Coop eased away from Bree and had the decency to look a little uncomfortable with his public display of affection for his subordinate.

Coop then turned his attention to Kade. "I heard about the shooting in San Antonio. About the dead gunman, too. You should have called me the second you got that anonymous tip."

That would have been protocol, yes, but Kade hadn't exactly been operating on a logical level. "No time for calls," Kade answered. "As it was, I barely had time to get her out of there alive."

Coop still seemed annoyed that he hadn't been looped in. "Thanks for getting her out."

"I didn't do it for you." Kade should have probably kept that to himself, but there was something about this reunion that riled him. Hopefully, it was Anthony's accusation and not the possessive way Coop was holding on to Bree.

Coop took something from his pocket and handed it to her. Her badge. Bree closed her fingers around it, then slipped it into her pocket. "Thanks."

"I got it from your apartment after you went missing," Coop explained. "I figured you'd want it back right away. You always said you felt naked without it."

Coop smiled.

Kade didn't.

And he hated that at a critical time like this the naked comment had an effect on him. A bad one. The kiss had been a huge mistake, and worse, he wanted to make that mistake again. He hoped he didn't feel that way because of the shot of jealousy he'd just experienced.

"I talked to the doctor who examined you," Coop

volunteered, dropping the smile. "He wouldn't tell me much, other than you were okay. He did say there'd be no lasting complications from the delivery or your ordeal."

"Other than the threat to her life," Kade spoke up. He looked at Bree to give her a chance to ask Coop about what was on both their minds.

She flexed her eyebrows and sucked in a quick breath. "Anthony McClendon called the ranch. He made some, uh, accusations against you."

Coop's eyes widened, and he tossed his concerned gaze first to Kade and then back to Bree. "What kind of accusations?"

"Anthony said you were *dirty*," Bree explained, then paused. "And that you're the one who's trying to kill me." She waved it off before he could say anything. "He's lying, of course."

"But he said he had proof," Kade added.

"Then he's lying about that, too," Coop said as gospel.

Coop caught Bree's arm and turned her to face him. "Anthony's guilty of a lot of things that went on at the Fulbright clinic. It was pure luck on his part that we didn't get those missing surveillance backups that would have no doubt proven that he's guilty of even more serious charges. If he's trying to put a spin on this, it's because he knows I'm going to put his sorry butt in jail."

Kade agreed that Anthony was likely guilty of something more than harboring illegal immigrants, theft and embezzlement, but he still wanted to hear what the man had to say. Especially what he had to say about Coop.

"What's the status of the Fulbright investigation?" Bree asked.

"It's still active," Coop said. "Kade and you gave us a good start with your undercover work, and I'm still digging. Trying to connect the dots. I do know that Anthony was skimming money from the clinic, and that's why father and son are now at odds."

Kade had learned the same thing, but realized that he hadn't brought Bree up to speed on the case. Of course, there hadn't been much time for that between dodging bullets and sleeping off the Valium.

"And what about the shooting yesterday?" Bree pressed. "Any word on who might have hired a hit man to come after me?"

"Nothing yet. It's SAPD's jurisdiction. For now. But I've requested that the FBI take over, since the shots were fired at two agents."

Yeah, but moving it to the FBI would take Nate out of the investigative loop. Kade preferred his brother in on this. Nate had an objective eye, and Kade needed that right now. Clearly, his objectivity had taken a hike. First the kiss. Now the jealousy.

He wasn't on a good track here.

Bree blew out a long, weary breath. "Is there any evidence about why someone would have kidnapped me in the first place?"

Coop shook his head and gave her arm a gentle squeeze. "I'm sorry. I'm trying hard, but I haven't been able to prove anything. Of course, my theory is that McClendon did all of this so he'd have some leverage over the investigation."

"But he hasn't contacted Bree, me or you to try to tamper with evidence or anything." Kade tried not to make it sound like a question. He also tried not to be so suspicious of a fellow agent.

Oh, man. He couldn't let a suspect like Anthony play these kinds of mind games.

"McClendon hasn't contacted me *yet*," Coop verified. "I figured it would happen as Anthony's and Jamie's trial dates got closer. But since Bree managed to escape and since the baby is here and safe, the person responsible has lost their leverage."

Kade wanted to believe that, because if it were true, then that meant the danger to Bree and Leah had lessened. Well, maybe. That didn't mean the person wouldn't try to kidnap them again. But at least both were safe now.

And it had to stay that way.

Even if he had to check out Anthony's crazy allegation. Kade would do that and anything else that it took. He made a mental note to recheck all the security measures at the ranch. And to try to convince Bree to take him up on his offer to send her to a safe house.

"So, what are your immediate plans?" Coop asked Bree. But he didn't wait for her to answer that. "How soon are you returning to work?"

She glanced at Kade, and he was certain that he looked as surprised as she did. The timing was all off, but Kade didn't jump to answer for her.

"I'm not sure," she finally said. Not an answer, but it appeared that was all she was going to give him. She fluttered her hand toward the stairs. "I want to spend some time with my daughter. Get to know her."

Coop's forehead bunched up. "I thought you'd want to figure out who kidnapped you right away."

"I will." But then she paused. "I just need some time."

Coop's gaze shifted to Kade, and the man instantly frowned. "Not too much time, I hope. Bree, you haven't worked in nearly a year."

"That wasn't exactly her fault," Kade pointed out.

Coop's frown deepened, and he moved even closer to Bree. "Officially, you were listed as missing in the line of duty, but we both know your Jane identity was compromised when things went wrong at the Fulbright clinic. Your face was on those surveillance videos, and your cover was blown."

Kade couldn't deny any of that. But what he still didn't know was how their cover had been blown. It was definitely something he wanted to learn, but for now, he had other things that were much higher priority.

"What are you saying?" Bree asked Coop. "That I can no longer be a Jane? Well, that's okay. It would have been hard to pull off deep-cover assignments now that I have Leah."

Coop looked as if she'd slugged him. "I didn't think you'd ever give that up without a fight." He shook his head and stared at her as if she'd lost her mind. Or as if Kade had brainwashed her. "But that's not the only problem we have here. Bree, there are people in the Justice Department who feel you brought this kidnapping on yourself. That you didn't take the proper security precautions."

Kade tamped down the rush of anger and stepped by Bree's side. "They're blaming the victim?"

Coop huffed. "No. I'm not saying that—"

But he didn't get to finish because Mason appeared at the top of the stairs. He had Leah's carrier in his left hand, and he had the baby positioned behind him in a protective stance.

"We have another problem," Mason called down to Kade. "The ranch hand that I've got watching the security cameras just called, and we have some more visitors. He's running the plates, but it looks like Anthony McClendon and Jamie Greer."

"Good," Coop spat out, and he drew his gun. "Because I can confront the SOB about the lies he's spreading about me."

Kade look at Bree, and her expression verified how he felt. This wasn't *good*. Far from it. Two of their suspects were way too close for comfort, and they had a riled agent with his gun drawn.

"Keep your gun down," Kade ordered Coop. "And you need to stay with Leah," he added to his brother. "Call a couple of the ranch hands to the front in case I need backup."

"I'm your backup," Coop snarled, and with his gun ready, he stormed out onto the porch.

Kade caught Bree's arm to stop her from following. "I know you won't wait upstairs with Mason." He reached down and pulled the Colt .38 from his ankle holster. Kade had no idea if she had a steady aim yet, but even if she didn't, he preferred Bree to be armed.

"Thanks," she mumbled, but her attention was on the stairs where Mason had just left with Leah. "He's a good cop?" she asked.

"Yeah. And we're not letting anyone get past us."

She nodded, licked her lips and looked a little shakier than Kade wanted. However, he couldn't take the time to soothe her because he didn't want bullets to start flying this close to Leah. Even though Coop was a well-trained agent, he seemed to be working on a short fuse when it came to Anthony.

Kade stepped onto the porch, with Bree behind him, just as the white Lexus stopped next to Coop's car. It was Anthony and Jamie all right. Kade had interviewed them enough to recognize them from a distance.

Anthony got out first. He definitely didn't look like a killer or even a formidable opponent. The man was lanky to the point of being skinny, and his black hair was pretty thin for a man in his early thirties. But Kade knew that Anthony had some strength. During their undercover assignment, Kade had watched Anthony get into a shoving match with an irate illegal immigrant father who was looking for his daughter. Anthony had some martial arts skills to make up for all that lankiness.

The man wore no scrubs today, as he'd worn in all his interviews with Kade. He was dressed in khakis and a white shirt. He looked like a nerd. If he was carrying a concealed weapon, Kade didn't see any signs of it. That didn't mean Kade would let down his guard. Neither would Coop. Or Bree.

"No reason for those guns," Anthony called out. "I'm just here to talk."

"You mean you're here to lie," Coop shouted back.

Oh, yeah. This could turn ugly fast, and Kade was thankful when he spotted the three armed ranch hands round the east corner of the house. The men stopped Anthony in his tracks, probably because they were armed with rifles that no amount of martial arts could match.

But those rifles didn't stop Jamie from getting out of the car.

Jamie spared the ranch hands a cool, indifferent glance before she slid on a pair of dark sunglasses and strolled toward them as if this were a planned social visit. No nerd status for her. Jamie was tall and lean, and she had her long auburn hair gathered into a sleek ponytail. Kade had always thought Jamie looked more like a socialite than a nurse.

"How did you know I was here?" Coop demanded.

"I didn't." Anthony looked past him and put his attention on Bree. "I came here to see you. It's all over the news about the shooting, and since Agent Ryland wasn't at his office in San Antonio, I thought he might bring you here. Obviously, I guessed right."

Kade hoped it was a guess, and that Anthony didn't have any insider knowledge. Of course, Anthony could have learned Bree's location from his father, but Kade didn't think the two were on speaking terms.

"Why'd you want to see Bree?" Kade demanded while Anthony and Coop started another glaring contest with each other.

"Because SAPD has been hassling us again," Jamie calmly provided. "And Anthony and I thought we'd better nip this in the bud."

"What are you planning to nip?" Kade asked, and he didn't bother trying to sound friendly. He wanted all three of these people off his porch and off his family's property.

"You, if necessary." Jamie turned toward Kade, though with those dark shades, he couldn't tell exactly where she was looking. "You had your shot at investigating us, and you found nothing on me other than a few charges that you can't make stick."

"Not yet. But at least you'll do some time in jail.

That'll be enough for now." Kade knew it sounded like a threat, and he was glad of it. "Bree's been through hell and back, and someone will pay for that."

Anthony pointed toward Coop. "What about him? He should be the one paying."

"I warned you about those lies." There was a dark, dangerous edge to Coop's voice.

Still, Anthony came closer, but he pleaded his case to Bree, not Coop or Kade. "Did Agent Cooper tell you that he provided *security* to the Fulbright clinic and that he was paid a hefty amount for his services?"

"Security?" Kade repeated over Coop's profanity-punctuated shouts that this was all a crock.

Anthony nodded, and Jamie strolled closer until she was near the bottom step and standing next to Anthony. "It's true. Anthony's father told me that Agent Cooper kept the local cops from digging too deeply into what was going on."

Coop turned that profanity tirade to Jamie, but it didn't stop the woman from continuing.

"Hector said Cooper was stunned when he realized Bree, one of his own agents, had been sneaked into the undercover assignment at the clinic that could ultimately land him in jail." Jamie paused, a trace of a smile on her dark red lips. "And Anthony here has proof."

Anthony had a bit of a smile going on, as well. Kade could understand why—*if* there was proof. And it was that possibility of proof that kept Kade from latching onto them and giving them the boot.

"Anthony and you have nothing on me," Coop fired back. "Neither does Hector McClendon."

But Jamie only shrugged. "You're investigating the

wrong people, Agent Ryland. You need to be looking closer to home. You need to investigate Agent Cooper."

Bree huffed and stepped around Kade, between Coop and him. But she didn't say anything. She just studied Jamie from head to toe, and Kade had to wait just like the others to hear Bree's take on all of this.

"Are you the woman who held me captive all those months?" Bree asked.

With all the other accusations flying around about Coop, Kade certainly hadn't expected such a direct question from Bree. But he waited for Jamie's answer and watched her expression. He wished he could strip those glasses off her so he could see her eyes because he was certain that question had hit some kind of nerve.

Jamie shifted her posture and folded her arms over her chest. "I did nothing wrong," she insisted.

Kade looked at Bree to see if she believed Jamie, but Bree only shook her head. It made sense. After all, Bree had said her kidnappers had kept on prosthetic masks, but he'd hoped that she would recognize something about Jamie or Anthony.

Of course, maybe there was nothing to recognize because they hadn't been the ones to hold her captive.

"Did. You. Hold. Me. Captive?" Bree repeated. Her anger came through loud and clear.

Jamie shifted again. "No." She paused. "Are you accusing me so you can protect your boss? My advice? Don't. Because accusing me won't do anything for your safety. Or your baby's safety." Jamie leaned in and lowered her voice as if telling a secret. "Investigate him, and you'll learn the truth, even if it's not what you want to hear."

That got Coop started again. "I want to see this so-called proof of my guilt," Coop demanded.

Anthony lifted his hands, palms up. "You think I'm stupid enough to bring it with me? *Right.* Then you just kill me and take it."

"I'm an FBI agent," Coop fired back, "and I'm not in the habit of killing people just because they're telling lies about me."

"I'm not lying, and you know it." Anthony turned to Kade and Bree. "I have an eyewitness who'll testify that Agent Cooper here had a meeting with my father at the clinic, less than an hour before your cover was blown."

Oh, that was not what Kade wanted to hear, and by God, it had better not be true. If so, Coop would pay and pay hard.

"That witness will also tell you that Cooper took money from my father," Anthony smugly added.

It took a moment for Kade to get his teeth unclenched. Bree had a similar reaction. She was hurling daggers at Anthony with a cold glare, but she wasn't exactly giving Coop a resounding vote of confidence, either.

"Sounds like I need to talk to this witness," Bree commented.

"No, you don't." Coop walked toward Jamie and Anthony with his finger pointing at the man who'd just accused him of assorted felonies. "I'm not going to let you get away with this."

Because Kade didn't want Coop to do something they'd both regret, he grabbed his fellow agent. He held on until he was sure Coop would stay put.

"We're not dealing with this here at the ranch," Kade informed Anthony, Jamie and Coop. He shifted his at-

tention to Anthony. "Bring the witness to the Silver
Creek sheriff's office. And while you're at it, both of
you come prepared to answer some more questions because this investigation is just getting started."

Jamie groaned softly and mumbled something. "I've
had enough questions to last me a lifetime."

Kade tossed her a glare. "Then you'll get a few more.
Be there when Anthony brings in this secret witness."

Much to Kade's surprise, Anthony nodded, and his
smile wasn't so little now. The man was smirking when
he headed back to his car. "Come on, Jamie. We're finished here, for the moment."

But Jamie paused a moment and glanced over her
shoulder at Anthony before she spoke. "I don't trust
Anthony," she said in a whisper. "And neither should
you. The man is dangerous."

Bree and Kade exchanged a glance, and she was no
doubt thinking the same thing—what the heck was this
all about? One minute ago Jamie had been ice-cold and
unruffled. Now she looked on the verge of panicking.

"If Anthony is dangerous, then why did you come
here with him?" Bree asked.

Jamie didn't answer right away. She glanced over her
shoulder again as if to make sure Anthony wasn't close
enough to hear. "Because sometimes the only choice
you have is to cooperate." And with that, she turned
and followed Anthony to the car.

"They're liars," Coop repeated before Anthony even
started the engine. "It's a mistake to give them an audience for whatever it is they're trying to pull."

Kade shrugged. "I have to start somewhere to get to
the bottom of what happened to Bree."

"What happened to Bree is *my* concern," Coop snapped.

That was *not* the right thing to say, especially after those heated accusations that Anthony had just made. Kade had to fight once more to hang on to his temper, but Bree beat him to the punch.

"Kade and I became parents," she reminded him. And there was a bite to her voice. "What happened is most definitely his concern."

That didn't cool down the anger in Coop's face. He opened his mouth, no doubt ready to argue, but there was no argument he could give that would make Kade back off from this investigation. His baby girl's safety was at stake.

Coop gave her a look that could have frozen hell. "Be careful who you cast your lot with, Bree. It could come back to bite you."

Bree faced him head-on. "I'm always careful."

That obviously didn't please him because he cursed. "I'm giving you forty-eight hours." Coop's voice had that dangerous edge to it again. "If you're not at headquarters by then, you'll never see your badge again."

Chapter 8

Bree watched Leah sleep and hoped the baby would wake up before Kade's brother Grayson arrived to take her to the house in San Antonio. These last minutes with her daughter were precious time, and she needed every second to count.

"Grayson will be here in about a half hour," Kade informed her when he got off the phone.

Bree had listened in on the flurry of calls that Kade had made after their guests' departures, but her main focus had been on Leah.

And her badge.

It was hard to push that aside completely, even though that's exactly what Bree wanted to do.

She'd been an agent for five years now, after she'd slogged her way through college night classes at the University of Texas and cruddy jobs so she could get her degree. And Coop had helped with that. In fact, he'd helped with a lot of things to put her on track and keep her there. He hadn't just been her boss but also her mentor and friend.

"All three of the nannies will be at the estate in San Antonio," Kade explained. "So, Leah will have lots of attention from them and her three aunts."

Still, it hurt that she wouldn't be there to share it. "I've never thought of family as being a good thing," she mumbled. "But I'm glad Leah has yours."

"So am I." He walked back to the sofa where she was seated. "It's not too late, you know. You can go to San Antonio with them."

Mercy, that was tempting, just so she wouldn't have to leave Leah, but Bree had to shake her head. "Too big of a risk, especially since all of our suspects know I'm with you."

Bree's gaze whipped to his. "Please tell me that Grayson will take precautions when driving Leah to San Antonio. McClendon and the others can't follow him."

"They won't follow," Kade promised. "Grayson's a good lawman. And besides, his pregnant wife is at the house. He wouldn't put her or any of the rest of the family at risk."

Further risk, Bree mentally corrected. Because the risk was already there.

He sank down on the sofa next to her and touched Leah's cheek. The baby stirred a little but went straight back to sleep. Bree repeated what Kade had done and got the same results.

"Don't worry," Kade said. "You'll have time with her after this is over."

Yes, and that was another unsettled issue to go with

the others. Leah. A custody arrangement. And the man next to her.

Her mind was already spinning with some possibilities. "Maybe I can move to Silver Creek. And get a regular job with the FBI." Those were things she'd considered *before* Coop's visit. "If I still have a badge, that is."

"You will," Kade promised. "Coop was just, well, I think he was pissed that you didn't jump to go back with him. He's pretty territorial when it comes to you."

That sent her gaze back to his. "There's nothing personal between Coop and me."

"Didn't think there was on your part, but Coop's reaction could be because of guilt. He failed to protect you, and now he's trying to make sure nothing else goes wrong."

She stared at him. "Or?"

Kade shrugged. "Or Anthony's accusations could be true. We have to at least consider that Coop might be in on this. I'm having someone check his financials to see if there's a money trail that leads to the Fulbright clinic or any of our suspects."

Before today, Bree would have jumped to defend her boss. But that was before someone tried to kill her. "What about this witness that Anthony claims he has?"

Another head shake. "Anthony won't give names, but both Jamie and he are supposed to show up at the sheriff's office tomorrow. Grayson told them they'd better have proof and the witness."

That caused her stomach to churn, because she didn't want to believe that Coop could have endangered her this way. But it also gave her some relief. If Anthony maybe had proof that could lead to an arrest, then Bree wouldn't have to be away from Leah very long.

Of course, that might not end the danger.

Coop could be just a small piece in all of this. An insignificant piece. But Bree still didn't like that he could have kept a secret that would have an impact on the investigation. Not just for the Fulbright clinic but for the aftermath and what had happened to her.

"When are Anthony's and Jamie's trial dates?" she asked Kade.

"Two more weeks. I'll testify. They'll want you to do the same."

Yes, because their testimony was what would convict them of the worst of the charges since there wasn't a lot of hard evidence.

"Nothing else on those missing surveillance backups?" she pressed.

"No. We have agents looking for them, though. Agents who don't work for Coop," he added before she could voice her concern. "Even if we don't find them before the trial dates, our testimony should be enough to convict Jamie and Anthony of at least some of the charges. The security guards, too."

Because those guards had tried to kill Kade and her on that undercover assignment. Plus, she could testify about the two illegal immigrant surrogates she'd ferreted out while there. The women had said both Jamie and Anthony were responsible for them being at the clinic. Of course, the women had also since disappeared and hopefully were alive somewhere, but Bree's testimony should be sufficient.

Unless…

"McClendon's lawyers could use my ordeal to question how reliable my memories are." That didn't help with the acid in her stomach. "And we don't have proof that McClendon, Anthony or Jamie was the one who had me kidnapped."

Kade nodded and eased his arm around her. He also eased her to him. "Two weeks is a long time, Bree. Anthony's witness could pan out."

And if so, that meant Coop would be arrested or implicated in something bad. It was a long shot and one she hoped she didn't have to face.

"What if an arrest doesn't end the threat against us?" she asked.

"Then, we keep looking."

Kade pulled in a deep breath and brushed a kiss on her forehead. He didn't look at her, and it didn't seem as if he'd noticed what he had done. That made it even more scary. Had they become so comfortable with each other that a benign peck was standard?

Apparently so.

The danger was responsible for that. And Leah. Kade and she were joined at the hip now, and that wasn't likely to end anytime soon. Their situation was bringing them closer together and keeping them there. For now. But Bree knew that bubbles often burst.

"I know you're uncomfortable with all of this," Kade said. He glanced at his arm slung around her and then at the spot where he'd kissed her.

So, he had been aware of what he'd done.

"I'm comfortable," she corrected. "And that's what makes me most uncomfortable."

He laughed. It was smoky and thick. All male. And she realized it was the first time she'd heard him do that. It made her smile in spite of the mess they were in. And then the easy way she'd smiled only added to the discomfort.

Sheez.

She was in trouble here in more ways than one.

"If you take the danger out of the situation," he continued, "then what's happening between us might not be a bad thing. I mean, I'm attracted to you, and I'm pretty sure you're attracted to me. That's better than having us at each other's throats."

That created an image that she tried to push aside. Fast. Of Kade kissing her throat. Her, kissing his. Heck, she was just fantasizing about kissing him, period.

"The attraction isn't going to make this easier," she reminded him.

He paused, made a sound of agreement. Then, made another sound that could have meant anything. "Not easier, but I can't seem to stop it. I dreamed about you."

She risked looking at him, even though that put them face-to-face with their mouths too close together. Another kiss wouldn't send them into a wild scramble to have sex on the sofa. Because Leah was there. But if the baby hadn't been, then all bets were off.

And Grayson would arrive soon to take Leah.

What then?

More dreams, no doubt.

She didn't question Kade about his dream. Didn't need to hear the details. She'd had enough hot dreams about him when they'd played under the covers at the clinic. She doubted his dreams about her could be as hot as the ones she'd had about him.

The corner of his mouth lifted, and a dimple flashed in his cheek. That smile no doubt caused many women to melt into a puddle.

And it was doing the same to her.

But the puddle cooled down when she heard the sound. It was slight. Like a little squeak. However, it was enough to send Kade and her looking down at Leah. The baby squirmed, made another of those sounds.

And her eyes finally opened.

"About time you woke up," Kade told her, and he kissed the baby on her cheek.

Bree did the same. A puddle of a different kind. How could she possibly love someone this much?

"I'll miss her," Bree whispered. And that was a huge understatement. It would kill a piece of her to see Grayson take her baby out that door.

"Yeah," Kade agreed. It sounded as if he had a lump in his throat. He opened his mouth to say more, but another sound stopped him.

Footsteps.

And that meant Grayson had likely arrived to take Leah away. Bree instantly had to blink back tears.

However, it was Mason who appeared in the doorway, and while he wasn't exactly out of breath, he had obviously hurried. He was also carrying a laptop. "We have another problem," he told them.

Bree groaned. "Not another visitor?"

"Of sorts," Mason verified. "You guys are real popular today. Someone just scaled over the fence. And that someone is armed."

Kade cursed and drew his gun. He didn't want a confrontation with a gunman. Especially not with Leah still in the house. Not with Bree there, either.

Mason put the laptop on the table in front of them. The screen was split into six frames, each of them showing the feed from the various security cameras positioned around the grounds. Mason pointed to the top right where Kade could see an armed man behind a tree. He was armed all right.

A rifle with a scope.

Bree pulled Leah even closer to her. "How far away is he from the house?"

"Half mile," Mason answered.

But the moment Mason spoke, the guy darted out and raced for cover behind another tree. He was moving closer to the house. Closer to Leah.

"I've alerted the ranch hands," Mason continued. He drew his gun. "And I'm about to head out there myself."

Kade wanted to go with him. He wanted to be the one to confront this SOB and one way or another get some answers from him.

But that would mean leaving Bree and Leah alone.

He couldn't do that. Too big of a risk.

"I'll watch the surveillance and call you if there's a problem," Kade assured his brother.

Mason nodded, switched his phone to the vibrate mode so that it wouldn't be heard, and he hurried out of the room.

Bree moved closer to the laptop screen, her attention fastened on the man who was wearing dark camouflage pants and shirt. He had a black cap that obscured the upper part of his face.

"How tall do you think he is?" Bree asked.

"Six feet, maybe." He glanced at her. "Why? Do you recognize him?"

She kept studying him. "Maybe. I think it could be the man who kidnapped me. There's something about the way he's holding that rifle that looks familiar."

Then Kade wanted the man alive. Of course, his brother already knew that. Because this goon could give them answers. Kade wasn't sure if he could keep his temper in check if this was the man who'd put Bree through hell and back.

"Your captor held a rifle on you?" Kade wanted to know.

Bree nodded, and that only added to the anger he'd felt. Each little piece of information only worsened the description of hell that she'd been put through.

The gunman moved again, going behind another tree. The shift in position only highlighted more of his face. Kade couldn't see the guy's eyes, but they had a clearer image of his mouth and chin.

"Recognize him?" Kade pressed.

Bree shook her head. "I never saw his face," she reminded him. "Nor the woman's."

Still, it was obvious that she thought this could be the guy, and that was enough for Kade.

Kade looked at Leah to make sure she was okay, and thankfully she'd fallen back asleep. His baby girl didn't have a clue what was going on, but he didn't want her sensing any of Bree's fear. Except maybe it wasn't fear because Bree was staring at the man as if she wanted to rip him limb from limb.

Good.

Fear was natural, but it was determination and some luck that would get them through this.

"There aren't any more trees between that part of the pasture and the house," Kade let her know. "So, if he wants to get closer to fire that rifle, he'll have to do it out in the open."

Where Mason and the ranch hands could spot him.

And hopefully stop him. But just in case the guy managed to get off a shot, Kade needed to take some more precautions.

He grabbed the laptop and took it toward the other side of the room. Toward the front of the house and far away from the windows on the rear where the gunman would no doubt be approaching. Kade helped Bree onto the floor behind the sofa. The bathtub would have been safer if it weren't for the two windows in there.

Kade kept his gun ready, and he watched. On one screen he could see Mason and three ranch hands. All armed, all headed toward the gunman. The gunman stayed put behind the tree, but he took a small device from his jacket pocket and aimed it toward the house.

"The gunman has infrared," Kade mumbled along with some profanity.

Kade fired off a text message to let Mason know that the gunman now had a way to get a visual of who was in the house. He wouldn't be able to see actual images, but he could tell from the heat blobs on his screen where they were.

"He came here to kill us." Bree's voice was barely a whisper, and Kade heard the fear now.

She turned so that her body was between Leah and the gunman. She was protecting their child, and Kade moved in front of them to do the same.

Kade braced himself for the gunman to come closer, especially now that he no doubt knew where they were.

But the man didn't do that.

He dropped the infrared device and fired. Not at the house. He fired in the direction of Mason and the ranch hands. They all dived to the ground as the bullets pelted around them.

"They're pinned down." The fear in Bree's voice went up a notch.

Kade felt his own fear rise, too, and he frantically searched the screen to see if any other ranch hands were close enough to respond and provide Mason and the others with some backup.

They weren't.

Probably because Mason had ordered everyone to stay away from possible gunfire. And they were doing just that. At least a dozen of them were guarding the house, but it wouldn't do Mason and the others any good.

"I have to go out there," Kade told Bree. He hated to tell her this, but he had no choice. "I can approach him from this direction." He tapped the screen to the gunman's right. "While he's keeping my brother pinned down, I can sneak up on him."

Bree shook her head, but then she groaned and squeezed her eyes shut a second. She knew this had to happen.

"Be careful," she said.

"That's the plan." Kade gave Leah and her one last look. Hopefully, a reassuring one, and he grabbed the Colt .38 from the table so he could put it by Bree's side. Things would have to have gone to hell in a handbasket if she had to use it, but Kade didn't want to leave her defenseless.

He raced out of the room, barreling down the steps and out the front door. He stopped just long enough to holster his handgun and grab a rifle from the weapons' safe just off the foyer.

"Text Mason for me," Kade instructed the ranch hand

guarding the front of the house. "Tell him I'm approaching the shooter from the west side."

The shots kept coming. Not rapid fire any longer, probably because the guy wanted to conserve ammunition, but the bullets were spaced out just at the right pace to keep Mason and the others on the ground.

Kade ran to the side of the house and peered around, but the angle was wrong for him to see the gunman. He headed toward the first outbuilding—the stables—and he raced along the side until he reached the back.

Now, he had the right angle.

The shooter was still a good distance away, but the guy wasn't looking in Kade's direction. Or, thankfully, the direction of the house.

Kade took aim. Not for a kill shot. But for the man's right arm.

And he fired.

The shot blasted through the air. Kade saw the man's body snap back when the bullet slammed into his shoulder.

But the shooter didn't drop the rifle.

Despite the bullet wound, the guy pivoted, lightning fast, aimed at Kade. And he fired.

Kade ducked behind the stables in the nick of time. The shot slammed into the exterior wall in the exact spot where his head had just been.

Whoever this guy was, he wasn't an amateur.

Kade stayed low, glanced around the stables, but before he could get a good look, another shot came at him.

Then another.

Kade tried to see this as a good thing. This way, Mason might be able to return fire, but it was hard to see the good side of things with the bullets coming at him.

He got even lower to the ground and looked out again. The man had taken aim but not at Kade.

At the house.

His heart went to his knees. Yes, Bree and Leah were somewhat protected, but this guy could maybe get off a lucky shot.

Kade couldn't risk that.

He came out from the stables, his rifle already aimed at the intended target. No arm shot this time. He went for the kill.

And Kade pulled the trigger.

Even from this distance, he heard the sickening thud of the bullet tearing into the shooter's body. The man's rifle dropped to the ground.

Seconds later, so did the man.

Kade started running toward him.

Maybe, just maybe, he could get to him in time, before he took his last breath. And then Kade could learn the identity of the person who'd sent this monster after Bree and his baby.

Chapter 9

Bree almost wished the latest adrenaline crash would numb her to the fear and desperation that she was feeling. Not for herself.

But for Leah.

Their situation wasn't getting better, and judging from Kade's stark expression, he felt the same way. He sat across from her, his elbows on his knees and his face in his hands.

"I'm sorry," he repeated to her.

"You had no choice but to kill him." Bree knew that was true because she'd watched the nightmarish ordeal play out in front of her on the laptop screen.

First, she'd been terrified that Kade, his brother or one of the others would be killed. Then, her terror had skyrocketed when the shooter took aim at the house. For a couple of horrifying moments, Bree had thought he might shoot. That a bullet could tear through the walls and reach Leah.

But Kade had made sure that didn't happen. The gunman hadn't even had time to pull the trigger again before Kade shot him.

And killed him.

She'd watched that, too, while she'd held her baby close and prayed that nothing else bad would happen. Leah was okay, thank God. But the shooter hadn't been able to say anything before Kade got to him. No dying confession to clear his conscience, and that meant they were right back at square one.

Well, almost.

Kade's brother Grayson had arrived just minutes after the fatal shooting and immediately taken over the necessary mop-up of an inevitable investigation. Grayson was pacing their suite while talking on the phone, and from what Bree could glean from the conversation, he was within minutes of turning over the investigation to one of his deputies so he could leave for San Antonio.

With Leah, of course.

That was good, Bree kept reminding herself. However, in this case *good* felt like something beyond bad.

"We're doing the right thing sending Leah with Grayson," she whispered. She tried not to make it sound like a question, but it did, anyway. She prayed she wasn't sending her baby from the frying pan into the fire.

Kade eased down his hands, looked at her. Then looked at Leah, who was in Bree's lap. "Yeah." He no doubt knew everything Bree was feeling because he was feeling it, too. He paused. "I also need to make arrangements for you."

Bree shook her head. "Once Leah is away from the

danger, what I'd really like is a showdown with who-ever's responsible for this."

That sent another jolt of anger through her. She wanted to find this person fast and be the one to put them in jail or do what Kade had just done. End it with a bullet.

"You're up for that?" Kade questioned.

Probably not. Her hands were still shaky, and she felt years removed from her FBI training. Right now, she felt like a mother with a child who'd just been placed in harm's way. And that was a far stronger motivation than she'd ever had to bring down a criminal.

Bree touched her daughter's cheek, and even though Leah's eyes were closed, she gave Bree one of those baby smiles. The feeling of warmth replaced the anger. But not the determination for Bree to keep her safe.

However, Leah wasn't the only person for her to be concerned about.

"Are you okay?" she asked Kade. "And before you give me a blanket *I'm fine* answer, I'd like the truth."

Kade stayed quiet a moment. "Ever killed a man in the line of duty?"

"Once." A cut-and-dried case of defending herself, just as Kade had done.

"It doesn't get easier," Kade mumbled.

Bree rubbed his arm and hoped that would help. But how could it? He'd done what he had to do, but he'd also have to come to terms with taking a life.

Yet something else they had in common.

As if they needed more.

Sometimes, like now, Bree felt that Kade and she were speeding headfirst, no helmets, into a brick wall. One of them, or both, would get hurt, but there didn't seem to be anything that would stop it. She didn't know whether to fight it or just save her energy and surrender.

Grayson ended his call, and when he didn't make another one, both Kade and Bree looked at him.

"The dead shooter's name is Tim Kirk," Grayson explained. "He worked as a security guard at the Fulbright clinic during your undercover investigation."

Maybe that's why he'd seemed familiar to Bree. "Kirk's connected to one of our suspects?" And she didn't include Coop in that list, despite what Anthony had told them during his visit to the ranch.

"He is. And he's also connected to the man who tried to kill you at the motel. Mason checked Kirk's cell, and yesterday morning he called the prepaid phone of the triggerman who turned up dead." Grayson paused. "However, the last person he called was Anthony."

Anthony, who'd accused Coop of wrongdoing. Of course, that accusation hadn't gotten Anthony's name off their suspect list. Now he was at the top of it.

"SAPD is sending someone over to Tim Kirk's apartment to check it out now. There might be more evidence linking him to Anthony. Or one of the others," Grayson added.

Maybe Coop, judging from Grayson's tone. Well, good. Bree wanted them to look, but she was sure they wouldn't find anything.

"While they're at Kirk's place, I hope they'll search for those surveillance backups that went missing from the Fulbright clinic," Kade reminded him.

"They will." Grayson shrugged. "But unless Kirk was planning to use them to pin the blame on someone else, those backups might have been destroyed."

Yes, Bree had considered that. She had also considered if that had happened, they might never have enough evidence to convict any of their suspects to long jail sentences. Heck, it was possible that even with a conviction Anthony and Jamie would get as little as probation.

Kade and she needed more evidence.

Grayson looked at Bree. "Any luck remembering where you were held during your pregnancy? Because there might still be some evidence there we can use."

Bree pushed her hair from her face and forced herself to think. "It was a house in the country." Which she'd already told them. "High brick fence with guard dogs. Dobermans." She shook her head. "I can remember the rooms clearly now, but I can't tell you what was past that fence."

If that disappointed Grayson, he didn't show it. "When one of the kidnappers helped you escape, do you have any idea how long it took you to get from the fenced house to the motel?"

Those images weren't so clear. In fact, they were nonexistent.

"I don't have a clue about the time frame, but I do know we didn't go directly from the house to the Tree-top motel. We went to another hotel first. In Austin, I think. And she gave me a heavy dose of drugs before we left." Bree stopped a moment. "But she was in a hurry. The man wasn't there, and she said we had to get out before he came back because he was going to kill me."

Since Kade's leg was touching her, she felt him tense. "Why did he want to kill you?" Kade asked. "Leah was gone by then. Why did he or his boss feel you were no longer of any use to them?"

Again, Bree forced herself to think. "Maybe I saw

something. Or maybe something changed in his situation. His boss might have found a different kind of leverage to tamper with the investigation."

But what?

Bree drew a blank on all counts.

"It sounds as if you were around the female kidnapper a lot," Grayson commented. "Any chance it was Jamie Greer?"

"A good chance," Bree admitted. "The height and body build are a match." Still, she had to shake her head. "But she certainly didn't dress like Jamie, and the prosthetic mask was very good. I couldn't see any of her features behind it." She shrugged. "Of course, the drugs probably helped with that. Hard to see a person's features when they're swimming in and out of focus."

"Keep trying to remember," Grayson insisted after a nod. He checked the time and blew out a weary breath. "McClendon, Anthony and Jamie are all on their way to my office. Or they sure as heck better be. If not, I warned them they'd all be arrested."

Good. Maybe they would defy that order, and that would get them tossed in jail. A temporary stay was better than nothing.

"I need you to help Mason question them," Grayson added, his attention on Kade. "Are you up to it?"

"Absolutely." Kade got to his feet. "Anthony accused Bree's boss of being a dirty agent, said he had a witness. Maybe he'll bring that witness with him."

Bree adjusted the baby to the crook of her arm and stood, too. "I'd like to get in on this."

The brothers exchanged glances and were no doubt thinking she wasn't mentally or physically ready for this. She wasn't, but that wouldn't stop her. "When I hear what they have to say, it might help me remember where I was held captive."

Grayson finally nodded. "Tape the interviews and follow the rules. If one of them is guilty, I don't want them slipping through the cracks on a technicality."

Bree was on the same page with that. Someone would pay for what had happened. Hopefully, it wouldn't be Kade, her or Leah.

"It's time," Grayson said, and with those two little words, Bree knew exactly what he meant.

Kade did, as well, because he leaned over and kissed Leah's cheek. "This won't be for long," he promised the baby in a whisper.

Bree kissed her, as well, but she didn't trust her voice to speak. Oh, mercy. This was much harder than she'd imagined it would be; something she hadn't thought possible.

"Three of the ranch hands are making the drive with us," Grayson let them know. He picked up the diaper bag, looped it over his shoulder and then walked closer.

Waiting for Bree to hand Leah over.

Bree gave her baby one last kiss. Kade did the same. And she eased Leah into Grayson's waiting arms.

"I'll take good care of her," Grayson promised. And just like that, he hurried out of the room.

Bree's heart went with him.

Tears stung her eyes, and she blinked them back when Kade slipped his arm around her.

"Everything will be okay," he said, his voice clogged with emotion. He cleared his throat. "And the sooner we question our suspects, the sooner we can maybe end this."

So that Leah could come home.

Well, come to the ranch, anyway. It was her home, of course, but Bree knew that might change when Kade and she worked out some sort of custody arrangement.

"Let's go to the sheriff's office," he insisted, and with his arm still around her, he led her to the door where Grayson had just exited.

Kade stopped.

He looked down at her and opened his mouth. Closed it. Then shook his head. "Later," he mumbled.

Bree nearly pressed him for an answer, but she wasn't sure she wanted to open any cans of worms with Kade right now. One thing at a time, and the first thing was to get through these interrogations.

By the time they made it outside to Kade's truck, Grayson had already driven away. *To safety,* Bree reminded herself again. And if Kade and she could do their jobs and make an arrest, their time apart from Leah would be minimized. That was all the motivation she needed to end this quickly.

"What if Anthony produces a witness who says that Coop is dirty?" Kade asked her. He started his truck and headed for town.

"Then, I'll assume Anthony paid off the person to lie." Bree figured this wasn't the answer Kade wanted to hear. She stared at him. "Why are you so willing to believe Coop worked for McClendon?"

He stayed quiet a moment, mumbled something she didn't quite catch. "For the worst of reasons." Another pause. "I think I might be jealous of him."

"What?" Bree couldn't get that out there fast enough.

"This is hard for me to admit, but Coop seems possessive of you."

"In a boss to employee sort of way," she clarified. "There has never been anything personal between Coop and me."

"You're sure he knows that?"

Again, she jumped to answer, but then stopped. And Bree remembered something that'd happened over a year ago. "Coop kissed me."

"He did what?" Kade volleyed glances between the road and her.

"He'd had too much to drink. And he apologized."

Kade made a *yeah-right* sound.

"Hey, you kissed me, and you apologized," Bree reminded him.

"The apology was a lie. I'm attracted to you and so is Coop." He cursed. "But that attraction probably means he wouldn't betray you."

Bree felt relieved. For a moment. However, the uneasy feeling came. "I pushed him away that night," she recalled. "I told him I didn't feel that way about him."

She waited for Kade to say something about a scorned man seeking revenge, but he only shrugged. "If you hadn't been kidnapped, he probably would have tried again. I would have," Kade added in a mumble.

Bree stared at him. Yes, he would have. "If you hadn't, I would have," she confessed. "And if you think that pleases me, think again."

Despite the seriousness of the conversation, the corner of his mouth lifted, and she got a hint of that killer smile once more. "I just don't want you to think that the attraction I feel for you has anything to do with Leah."

She'd been on the verge of smiling herself, but that stopped it. Bree shook her head.

"I'm not trying to work out custody issues with you in bed," he clarified.

Oh.

At first there was a jolt of anger, that maybe Kade would think that's what she was trying to do. But she kept staring at him and didn't see any sign of it.

The only sign she saw was the confirmation that what she felt for him had zilch to do with Leah. Or with the danger. It had to do with the fact that he was, well, hot.

She groaned and leaned her head against the window. "Sex should be the last thing on my mind right now."

"Yeah," Kade agreed.

That didn't make it true.

Both of them knew that.

"I'm thinking when you're a hundred percent, we just get it over," he continued. "I mean, we worked ourselves up on the assignment. Now the close contact is steaming things up again. If we could just find the time to jump into bed, that might cool us down."

Her smile came, anyway. "Is that some kind of invitation to your bed?" Oh, yes. Headfirst into that brick wall.

He took her hand, lifted it and brought it to his mouth to kiss. "I already have you in my bed, but you're not in any shape for sex."

Her mind agreed.

Her body didn't.

And Bree was about to blurt that out when Kade's phone buzzed. He answered it but said little so she couldn't tell if the caller was Grayson. Soon, she'd want to contact Kade's brother and make sure the trip to San Antonio had gone smoothly.

Bree prayed it had.

"Let me know if you find anything," Kade said to the caller, and he hung up. "That was Nate, my brother at SAPD. It's not about Leah," he quickly added.

Good thing, too. Her mind wasn't going in a good direction on this.

"Nate sent one of his detectives to Tim Kirk's apartment, but it's been ransacked. His wall safe had been opened, and it was empty."

Definitely not good. Any potential evidence had probably been destroyed or contaminated. Still, Bree had a gut feeling that Kirk was the person who'd kidnapped her. Proving it, though, would be a bear.

But then, as Kade was pulling into the parking lot of the sheriff's office, she saw someone who could maybe clear all of this up.

Anthony.

He was heading inside the front door of the building. For the interview no doubt, but he clearly wasn't happy about being there. And he was alone.

No witness.

However, that wasn't the only thing Bree wanted to question Anthony about. It was that phone call that Kirk had made to him.

Kade and she got out of the truck, and both checked their surroundings. Old habits. Plus, the events of the morning still had her on edge. Bree wished that she'd at least brought a firearm with her just in case someone had already hired another hit man, but she'd given Kade back the little Colt that he carried in his ankle holster.

They stepped inside the back entrance, but the sound of the voice stopped them. A voice that Bree recognized.

Hector McClendon.

And whomever he was talking to, it wasn't a friendly conversation. McClendon was speaking in whispers, but the anger in his tone came through loud and clear.

Kade pointed to the last room on the right and put his finger to his mouth in a stay-quiet gesture. Bree did, and she listened.

"I don't know what game you're trying to play," McClendon snarled. "But I'm warning you to keep your mouth shut. If you don't, Bree Winston isn't the only person who'll be on the business end of a rifle."

Chapter 10

Kade couldn't wait to see the face of the person that Hector McClendon had just threatened. He stepped into the doorway.

And saw Jamie Greer.

Both McClendon and Jamie snapped toward Kade and Bree. Jamie's eyes were wide, and she appeared to be shaken. Not McClendon, though. He just cursed. It was ripe, raw and aimed at Kade and Bree.

Especially Bree.

The venomous look the man gave her made Kade want to punch his lights out. *Great.* No objectivity left, and while punching McClendon might make him feel a little better, it wouldn't do anything to help their investigation.

"Eavesdropping," McClendon barked. "Figures."

Kade shrugged. "If you want your death threats to

be more private, maybe you shouldn't do them in a sheriff's office."

"It wasn't a death threat. It was a warning."

"Sounded like a death threat to me," Bree spoke up.

Kade waited, gauging Jamie's reaction, but the woman didn't have much of one other than the obvious fear.

"Deputy Garza is waiting to interview me," Jamie said, and she stepped around the three of them and headed up the hall.

Deputy Melissa Garza, known as Mel, would no doubt fill in Kade later if Jamie volunteered more about the threat.

"And your brother is waiting to interview me," McClendon informed them.

Bree blocked the man's path when he started out of the room. "Just to let you know, your intimidation tactics won't work. I'm testifying against Anthony and Jamie, and I'll testify against you too the second charges are filed. And they will be filed."

"Really?" McClendon stayed calm and cool. "You'd testify against me? You think a jury will listen to a woman who has gaps the size of Texas in her memory?"

Bree looked ready to demand how he knew about her memory issues, but she stepped back. The man was on a fishing expedition, probably, and Kade didn't want Bree to provide him with anything that he could in turn feed to his team of attorneys.

Well, McClendon couldn't have known about the memory gaps unless Coop had told him. But Kade had enough on his plate without looking for another angle on this. And the biggest thing on his plate came walking up the hall toward him.

Hector McClendon's son, Anthony.

He spared his father a glance. The two didn't speak. The senior McClendon walked off and disappeared into one of the interview rooms where his attorneys and Mason were no doubt waiting for him.

"I told you that Coop would try to silence you," Anthony said to Bree the moment they were alone.

Kade didn't respond, but he did step into the interview room across the hall, and he motioned for Anthony and Bree to join him. Once they were inside, Kade made a show of hitting the record button on the camera that was mounted in the corner.

Anthony's eyes narrowed, first at the camera, then at Bree.

"I stand by what I said," Anthony insisted. He sank down into one of the chairs.

Bree leaned against the wall. "But yet you didn't bring the witness who could corroborate your allegation."

His eyes narrowed even more. "The witness wasn't available at such short notice. Tomorrow."

Kade wouldn't hold his breath. He took the chair across the table from Anthony, whirled it around and sat with the chair back facing Anthony.

"Today, we'll talk about Tim Kirk," Kade started. "Oh, and for the record, you do know you have the right to remain silent and the right to have an attorney present—"

"You're reading me my rights? Well, I already know them." He paused only to draw breath. "You planning to take me back in into custody, Agent Ryland? Because I have to tell you that I'll press to have your badge removed for an illegal detainment."

"Won't be illegal if I have cause," Kade tossed back.

"Tim Kirk," Bree prompted. She moved closer, propped her hip on the edge of the table and put on her best law enforcement face. "He tried to kill us earlier."

Anthony couldn't have looked more disinterested. "So?"

"So, guess who was the last person Kirk called before the attempted murder of two federal agents, a deputy sheriff, multiple civilians and a seven-week-old baby?"

Now Anthony was interested, and those once-narrowed eyes widened. "He didn't call me."

Kade nodded. "Yeah. He did. And unlike your mystery witness, I have real proof of it. I have Kirk's cell phone."

"Well, I don't have mine. It went missing yesterday." Anthony stopped and groaned. "I thought I'd lost it, but it's obvious someone stole it so they could set me up."

Kade huffed. Of course the man would come up with something. "Who would do that to you?" Kade pressed. And he would bet his next paycheck that Coop's name was going to roll off Anthony's tongue.

But it's a bet he would have lost.

"My father," Anthony answered.

Bree flexed her eyebrows. "And why would he do that?"

"To make me look guilty, of course. Don't you see? He's desperate, especially since his overpriced lawyers haven't been able to stop the investigation. Now that you're back in the picture, he's got to be thinking he's just days away from being arrested on something more serious than misdemeanors."

Bree and Kade exchanged glances, and she was probably thinking about the encounter they'd just overheard between McClendon and Jamie. Anthony was right about one thing—his father was indeed desperate.

"You have any proof that your father stole your phone?" Kade asked.

Anthony shook his head. "But he had the opportunity because he came to see me last night. He could have taken it when I stepped out of the room to take a call on my house phone."

Bree stared at the man, probably trying to determine if everything coming out of his mouth was a pack of lies.

Or the truth that made his father look very guilty.

"Why did he visit you?" Bree questioned.

"Probably to steal my phone," Anthony practically yelled, but he settled down almost immediately. "He said he was worried about you, that the person who kidnapped you probably wasn't done. That he or she would want you dead because you might remember something that would get the person arrested."

"Persons," Bree corrected. "Two people held me captive, and I think one of them was Tim Kirk. He's linked to you with that phone call."

"Keep digging. He's linked to my father, too, because dear ol' dad is the one who hired Kirk to work at the clinic. Security," he added with a smirk. "The man was as dirty as they came, and my father hired him."

That may be, but it still didn't mean McClendon had paid Kirk to kidnap Bree or to try to kill her.

"Go ahead, access my cell phone records," Anthony insisted. "Maybe you'll be able to see that the phone wasn't at my house. I tell you, my father stole it."

Kade wasn't sure he could get that kind of info from

the records, but he'd try. After all, he was pretty sure McClendon was a criminal for the things that had gone on at the clinic, and it wasn't much of a stretch for the man to try to put the blame on someone else.

Including his own son.

Anthony stood. "I think I should consult my lawyer now. Because it's clear I'm not making any headway with you two. Believe what you will. But watch your backs when you're around my father or any of his cronies. That includes Agent Cooper."

Kade considered stopping Anthony. Maybe putting him in lockup for a few hours until his lawyer could arrive. But that wouldn't accomplish much other than to give Kade some satisfaction that someone was paying for what'd happened to Bree. The problem was, he wasn't sure Anthony was the right someone.

So he let the man walk.

Kade stood, turned off the camera just as Bree huffed.

"How soon can you get someone on Anthony's cell records?" she asked.

"I can do that with a phone call." Kade paused. "And while I'm doing that, I can see what's happening with the search into Coop's financials."

That hit a nerve. Bree dodged his gaze, huffed again. "I'm guessing the agents have found nothing or they would have called."

"Yeah, that's my guess, too." Another pause. "That doesn't mean they won't find something eventually."

"I know." She nodded. "I know. But unless they do, McClendon and Anthony are looking better and better for this. Is there a chance we can get Anthony's bond revoked, or bring some charges, any charges, against McClendon?"

"It's possible." And Kade would try. "There were some financial irregularities at the clinic that we could use to arrest McClendon. But either of them could still try to get to you even if they're behind bars."

He ran his hand down the length of her arm. Felt her shudder. She was no doubt reliving the worst of the moments of the attacks that had led up to this.

"Let's go back to the ranch. Mason and the other deputies can handle these interviews, and I'll see about setting up a video call with Grayson."

Her eyes lit up. "So we can see Leah."

Yeah. Seeing images of their baby would have to do for now. And maybe it wouldn't be long before they had the real thing.

Kade led her into the hall, but they'd made it just a few steps before Jamie stepped into the hall, as well.

"I have to speak to you," she mouthed. And she looked all around as if she expected them to be ambushed.

That put Kade on full alert, and he eased Bree behind him. He put his hand on the gun in his holster.

"What do you want?" Kade asked, and he didn't use his polite voice. He was sick and tired of all the suspects and just wanted to get Bree out of there.

Jamie looked over her shoulder again and reached into her purse. That had Kade tightening the grip on his gun, but Jamie didn't draw a firearm. She pulled out a small folded piece of paper and handed it to Bree.

"Read it," Jamie instructed. "Not here. And don't let anyone else know that I gave it to you. If anyone else is involved, I'll call the whole thing off."

Kade had no idea what Jamie was talking about. Apparently neither did Bree because she started to unfold the note.

"Not here," Jamie repeated, her voice still barely above a whisper. "It's not safe for anyone else to know."

And with that cryptic warning hanging in the air, Jamie turned and walked back into the interview room.

Bree looked at Jamie's note again, even though she already knew what it said. The message was simple:

I'll call you to arrange a meeting for tomorrow.
By then, I'll have the answers you need.

"Answers," Bree mumbled.

Well, Kade and she were certainly short of those, but she wasn't sure that Jamie would be the one to provide them.

Neither was Kade.

"It could be a trap," Kade said, glancing at the note while he drove them back to the ranch.

Yes, it could be. Plus, there was another question. "Why didn't Jamie just give us these *answers* while we were at the sheriff's office?"

Kade lifted his shoulder. "Maybe because McClendon was there. Or maybe she doesn't have them *yet*."

Well, McClendon had threatened her just minutes earlier, so Jamie could be afraid of him. Still, something didn't add up. Bree wanted to suggest that they go back to the office and demand information, but that might cause Jamie to take back her offer.

Right now, that offer was pretty much all they had.

"So, what? We just wait for Jamie's call?" she asked.

He nodded though he didn't seem very eager to walk into a trap. Of course, doing nothing was just as dangerous. Bree was willing to do whatever it took to speed up the investigation and get Leah back.

Kade parked his truck directly in front of the ranch house porch, and even though there were several ranch hands there for their protection, Kade didn't dawdle. He held on to Bree and practically raced inside. Once he had the door shut, he armed the security system.

Bree stood there a moment to catch her breath and try to absorb everything that'd happened. Kade must have needed the same thing because he leaned against the door and drew in a long breath. But the breath-taking moment was over quickly.

"Our cook is at the estate in San Antonio, but I'll fix you some lunch," he said.

However, Kade had barely made it a step when his phone rang.

Kade mumbled something and pushed the button to answer the call on speaker.

"You're having me investigated," Coop immediately said. "You had someone dig into my financials."

"I did," Kade readily admitted. "It's standard procedure. Anthony McClendon made an accusation about you providing security to the clinic, and I had to check it out. Just as I've done with all leads."

"It's a witch hunt, and you know it." Coop's voice was so strained with anger that Bree barely recognized it.

She thought of the conversation earlier when Kade had admitted that he might be jealous of Coop. Bree was still trying to wrap her mind around that, but she didn't think for one second that jealousy was what had motivated Kade to investigate Coop.

"This had to be done, Coop," Bree spoke up. "We had to rule you out as a suspect. Standard procedure. You would have done the same thing if you were in my place."

Silence.

Her heart skipped a beat. "The investigation will rule you out, right?" And Bree hated that it was a question.

More silence, followed by more profanity. "It'll only muddy the waters more than they already are."

When Coop didn't add more, Bree glanced at Kade. And then she tried to brace herself for whatever they were about to hear from a man she'd been positive she could trust.

"I take security jobs on the side," Coop finally said. "It helps with the child support and my old college loans."

Oh, mercy. "Did you work for McClendon at the Fulbright clinic?" Bree demanded.

"Not in the way you think," Coop snapped. But he paused again. "A friend of a friend put me in contact with McClendon about eighteen months ago. McClendon said he thought he had some employees skimming profits, and he wanted me to set up a secret security system in addition to the basic one they already had. So I did."

Each word was like a slap to the face, and Bree reached for the wall to steady her suddenly weak legs.

"Give me details," Kade ordered.

"McClendon paid me ten grand to set up equipment in his son's and Jamie Greer's offices. I monitored the surveillance for a couple of months, and then he said my services were no longer needed. That happened weeks *before* the two of you were sent in there undercover."

That wasn't exactly comforting, but it was something.

If it was true.

Bree just didn't know anymore.

"Why didn't you tell anyone this before now?" Bree asked, and she held her breath.

"Because I knew it would look bad. And I also knew it didn't have anything to do with the case. Like I said, this just muddies the waters. The whole time I was monitoring those phone taps and hidden cameras, I didn't see anything illegal going on."

Kade groaned softly and shook his head. "Are you telling me that during all of this, you didn't hear anything about the FBI's investigation of that clinic?"

"Not a word," Coop insisted.

That was possible because the investigation had been kept close to the vest, but Coop still should have come forward when he finally had heard about it.

And that brought Bree to another question that she didn't want to ask. But she had to.

"When did you learn about Kade's and my undercover operation?"

Another stretch of silence. "Three days into it," Coop answered.

Her legs got even shakier. "The day our cover was blown and someone tried to kill us."

"I had nothing to do with that!" Coop snapped. "And I want all of this talk and accusations to go away. I've told my boss all about it, and it's the end of it. *Period.*"

Maybe the official end as far as the FBI was concerned, but it gave Bree some major doubts. Still, she couldn't believe that Coop would have known about her kidnapping and not tried to do something to stop it.

"Are you satisfied, Ryland?" The anger in Coop's voice went up a notch.

"No," Kade readily answered. "Not even close. If I find out you did something to endanger Bree and our daughter—"

"I didn't," Coop interrupted. "And everyone at the Bureau believes me. They know I'm a good agent." He paused again. "Bree, I need to see you. We need to talk alone. Say the word, and I'll drive out to see you right now."

Yes, they did need to talk, but it couldn't happen *right now.* "I'll call you when I can," she let him know.

Bree gave Kade a nod, and he pressed the end call button. They both stood there, silent, while Bree tried to absorb what she'd just learned. But that wasn't possible.

"Coop's the reason I have a badge," she managed to say.

Kade just nodded and pulled her into his arms. Until he did that, Bree hadn't known just how much she needed to be held.

This hurt, bad.

"Just wait until all the evidence is in, and we'll see where this goes," Kade said, and he pressed a kiss on her forehead. "It might not even lead back to Coop."

She eased back, looked up at him. "Even if Coop isn't dirty, he still should have said something about having worked for McClendon."

Kade could only make a sound of agreement.

And Bree felt as if her world had fallen apart.

The soft sobbing sound left her mouth before she could stop it, and it caused Kade to pull her back into his arms.

"Shhh," he whispered, his breath brushing over her face. "It'll be okay."

Bree wasn't sure she believed that and looked up to tell him, but everything seemed to stop. Not the pain. That was still there. So was the ache at being separated from Leah. But the whirlwind of thoughts about Coop and the investigation came to a grinding halt. She was instantly aware of Kade. Of his arms. Of the way he made her feel.

Without thinking, she came up on her toes and kissed Kade.

He made a sound, too. A low rumble that came from deep within his throat, and he snapped her to him until her body was pressed against his.

And he kissed her right back.

But he did more than that. Oh, yeah. More. Kade took control of things. His mouth moved over hers, and he parted the seam of her lips with his tongue.

The taste of him roared through every inch of her. She'd known the attraction was there. Had felt it. But this was more. It was a burning fire that the kiss fanned until it seemed more like a need.

His fingers dived into her hair, anchoring her head so that he controlled the movement. He didn't stop there. He turned her and put her back against the wall. And he put himself against her.

The sensations hit her hard. Not just the heat and the need, but the feel of his body on hers. It didn't help when he took that kiss to her neck.

Bree fought to get in a different position so that she

could feel more of him, and she got it finally. The alignment brought his sex against her, and the intimate contact along with his lips and tongue on her neck were making her insane. She was within seconds of dragging him to the floor so they could do this the right way.

Or the wrong way.

She caught his chin and lifted it, forcing eye contact. "Are we ready for this?" she asked.

It no doubt sounded like a joke, but there was nothing humorous in Kade's eyes. That icy gray had turned fiery hot, and it was clear that he wanted her as much as she wanted him.

"Ready?" he repeated as if it were painful just to ask the question. He dropped back an inch.

"Sex will complicate things," she settled for saying.

He thought about that a few seconds. "Yeah." And he put another inch of space between them.

Bree hated the loss of his touch and the heat, but she was also aware that both could return in a snap. What she felt for Kade wasn't just going to disappear.

"When we have sex," he said, "it probably shouldn't happen on the foyer floor."

For some reason that made her smile. "The place is optional," she let him know. "But the timing isn't."

Almost reluctantly, he nodded. "Soon, then." And he came back at her with a kiss that could melt metal.

He pulled away, leaving her breathless and making her rethink her decision to delay this, just as Kade's phone buzzed again. She groaned because she thought it might be Coop, but this time it was Jamie.

As he'd done with Coop's call, Kade took the call on

speaker. "We read your note," Kade greeted. "You have answers? Well, I'd like to hear them *now*."

"Not yet," Jamie answered, her voice strained with fear.

Or something.

Bree wasn't about to take anything this woman said at face value.

"Meet me tomorrow morning, both of you," Jamie explained. "Nine a.m. at the pond that's in the park on the edge of town. If you bring anyone else with you, the meeting is off. You'll never learn the truth."

Bree got a very uneasy feeling about this.

Apparently, so did Kade. "What truth?" he demanded.

Jamie groaned softly. "The truth about what *really* happened to Bree after she was kidnapped."

Chapter 11

Kade wasn't at all sure this meeting should happen, and Jamie's one condition had made him even more concerned.

They were supposed to come alone, or the meeting was off.

Kade understood Jamie's fear—feigned or otherwise—but he had a greater need to keep Bree safe. That's why he was taking precautions without violating Jamie's *come alone* command.

He ended the call with Mason and glanced over at Bree on the passenger's seat beside him. Her attention was fastened to the rearview mirror, no doubt making sure no one was following them. She also had her hand on the gun in the shoulder holster that he'd lent her.

After all, they could be driving into a trap, and he hadn't wanted her unarmed. Since he couldn't tuck her away safely, the next best thing was to use her agent's training to get them out of this.

"Mason's in place at the park," Kade relayed to her. "He's across from the pond and hidden in some trees. Jamie arrived a few minutes ago."

"Good." She paused. "Was Mason able to secure the area before Jamie got there?"

"More or less." It was the *less* part that was giving Kade some second and third thoughts about this, and it wasn't too late to turn his truck around and head back to the ranch.

But then, they wouldn't be any closer to ending this investigation.

"Mason is armed with a rifle in case something goes wrong, and he has one of the ranch hands with him," Kade explained. "But there are a lot of places to hide in that park. Jamie could already have someone in place."

And by someone, he meant another hit man.

"You could wait at the sheriff's office," he suggested. After looking at her, he didn't want her in danger. So much for relying on her training. "I'll call Jamie and renegotiate another meeting place. A safer one."

"She'll just say no, and one restless night away from Leah has been enough. I want this to end."

Yeah. He couldn't disagree with that. Being away from Leah had sucked, but this meeting and Bree had also contributed to his lack of sleep.

Kade blamed himself for the Bree part.

The kissing session had left his body burning for her, and even though she'd slept in the guest room just up the hall from him, that brainless part of him below the waist hadn't let him forget that Bree was nearby.

Brainless had also reminded him repeatedly that if he pushed, he could have Bree in his bed.

But it was wrong to push.

Even if he wanted to badly.

No, this was one of those situations where he had to leave the decision making to his brain.

Kade kept driving, through town and past the sheriff's office. Deputy Melissa Garza was inside and monitoring the lone security camera at the park. It wasn't at the best angle, but if she saw someone approaching the pond area, she had instructions to call Mason.

Not a foolproof plan, but maybe they'd get lucky.

He took the turn into the park and was thankful to see it practically deserted. Probably because it was a weekday, and it was still a little too early for an outing. Kade drove to the pond that was on the back side of the twenty-acre area, and he parked as close to it as he could. He had no trouble spotting Jamie.

The woman was seated at a picnic table and was wearing a dark green pants outfit that blended in with the summer grass and the leafy trees. She had on her usual sunshades and a baseball cap—probably her attempt at a disguise. Hard to disguise that bright auburn hair. She stood the moment Kade and Bree stepped from his truck.

"You came," she said on a rise of breath. Her skeptical tone let Kade know that she hadn't expected him to follow through.

Or else she was acting.

"You didn't give us much choice," Bree informed her. Like Kade, she kept watch on their surroundings. And on Jamie. Bree kept studying the woman to make sure she didn't draw a weapon on them.

"Let's make this quick," Kade told her right off the bat. "Give us the *answers* so we can get the hell out of here."

Jamie nodded, swallowed hard. "I want to make a deal. Immunity from prosecution in exchange for information."

Interesting. But somewhat predictable. Jamie was facing some jail time. "What information?"

But Jamie shook her head. "I need your word that you'll help me work a deal with the D.A."

Kade didn't jump to answer but finally said, "Sure." It was a lie. Maybe. If Jamie did help them end this, then he would see what he could do.

Jamie didn't jump to answer, either, and she sank back down on the table's bench. "About ten months ago I got a call from Tim Kirk, and he said there was a security problem that had to do with something going on at the clinic. He gave me an address to a house in the Hill Country, and when I got there, he was holding Bree captive. She'd been heavily drugged."

Bree pulled in a quick breath, and Kade figured she'd be taking a lot of those in the next few minutes.

"Why didn't you call the police or the FBI?" Bree asked.

Jamie glanced around again. "Because Kirk was blackmailing me. I signed off on one of the questionable surrogate deals."

"You mean an illegal deal," Kade corrected.

"Yes," Jamie said, her mouth tight now. "I didn't want to go to jail, and I thought he was only going to hold Bree long enough to try to influence the investigation."

"Influence?" Bree repeated. She cursed. "You let him inseminate me."

"I also helped you!" But the burst of energy seemed to drain her, and Jamie groaned. She turned that shaded gaze in Kade's direction. "I don't know who was paying Kirk, but the plan was to force you to destroy all the evidence that could incriminate anyone. Including me."

Ah, he got it now. "That's why you went along with it." So that there would be no evidence against her. But there was a problem. "The FBI doesn't have all the possible evidence so there's no way Bree or I could have destroyed it all. There are missing surveillance backups."

Jamie shook her head. "I have the backups."

Kade didn't know who looked more shocked—Bree or him. Now, this was something he hadn't expected to hear in the meeting.

"Where are they?" he demanded.

"Hidden safely away. They're my insurance that Kirk's boss won't come after me. He knows there's enough incriminating evidence on them to put him in jail for years. McClendon knows I have them, too."

Well, that explained the threat McClendon had made at the sheriff's office.

"McClendon knows you're trying to cut a deal with us?" Bree asked her.

"I don't think so." But Jamie didn't sound at all convinced of that. "McClendon threatens me a lot, but I've told him that if something happens to me, then those backups will find their way to the FBI."

Kade gave that some thought. If what Jamie was saying was true, this gave McClendon motive for trying to use Bree. Of course, maybe those backups showed someone else engaged in criminal activity.

Like Coop.

Anthony.

Or even Jamie herself.

"You can give us a copy of the backups," Kade suggested. "And that way you'd still have the originals to keep yourself safe."

"The backups can't be copied," Jamie explained. "It's the way McClendon set up the system. The backups have an embedded code to wipe them clean if anyone tries to burn a copy."

Well, hell. Now Kade had to figure out a way to get the originals from Jamie. If the woman really had them, that is.

He wasn't sure she was telling the truth. About this. Or about anything else.

"I wasn't there when Kirk or whomever did the insemination on Bree," Jamie went on. "I wasn't there for the C-section, either. But later Kirk told me that the obstetrician had been killed." Jamie shivered. "He even showed me a picture of a mutilated body and said the same thing would happen to me if I didn't keep my mouth shut."

Kade huffed. "You're an accessory to murder."

Jamie frantically shook her head. "No. I swear, I didn't know until afterward, and that's when I knew I had to do something. Kirk was saying they didn't need Bree anymore, that the baby was leverage enough to get you to cooperate."

Yes, and it might have worked. Kade would have done anything to protect Leah.

"So, how did you talk Kirk into keeping me instead of Leah?" Bree asked.

"I didn't. Couldn't," Jamie corrected. "He ordered

me to take the baby to a house in San Antonio where a nanny was waiting and when I returned he was going to kill you. Instead, I drove the baby to the Silver Creek hospital and left her there."

Because Bree didn't look too steady on her feet, Kade moved closer to her. Not too close, though, because he wanted them both to have room to draw their guns if something went wrong. There was still a chance of that happening. Whoever had hired Kirk wouldn't want Jamie to spill this.

"Kirk couldn't have been pleased about you not delivering the baby to San Antonio." Kade made a circling motion for Jamie to continue.

Jamie touched her hand to her lips. Her fingers and mouth were trembling. "He wasn't. I told him someone had run me off the road and kidnapped her. He was furious and said he had to see his boss immediately. I knew I had to get Bree out of there, too."

"But you didn't, not right away," Bree reminded her. "Why?"

"Because Kirk kept watching me. He didn't trust me after what happened with the baby. Then one night I slipped him a drug, and that's when I went on the run with you. When I was sure I wasn't being followed, I left you at that motel and then made the anonymous call so Kade could come and get you. Before Kirk did."

Well, it had worked. So far. Bree and Leah were both alive, and the man partly responsible for what had happened—Kirk—was now dead.

Kade moved closer to Jamie, hoping it would make her nervous enough to tell them whatever else she was keeping from them. "Who was Kirk's boss?"

"I don't know." She answered without hesitation.

"Kirk used to call him, but I never heard him say the person's name. I always assumed it was McClendon."

Good assumption.

But it could be a bad one.

Kade glanced at Bree and realized she was no doubt thinking the same thing.

Bree cleared her throat. "Did Kirk do anything else to me?"

Jamie looked in her direction for a moment. "No. Nothing like rape or torture. He just kept you drugged as much as he could. More so after the C-section."

Kade was relieved that other horrible things hadn't been done to Bree, but Jamie was wrong about the torture. Being held captive while pregnant was the stuff of nightmares, and he figured those nightmares would be with Bree for the rest of her life.

And someone would pay for that.

Kade took out the small notepad he kept in his pocket and dropped it on the table by Jamie. "Write down the address of the house where Bree was held."

Jamie shook her head. "They burned the place to the ground. Kirk told me that when he called to threaten me to stay silent."

Hell. But still a burned-out house was better than nothing. "I want the address, anyway," Kade insisted. He'd get a CSI team out there ASAP. Maybe they could find something that would give them clues about the identity of Kirk's boss.

Of course, the biggest clue might be sitting in front of them.

When Jamie finished writing the address, he took the note paper but kept staring at her. "I want those surveillance backups."

"I can't. I told you they're my insurance so that Kirk's boss won't kill me." Jamie yanked off her glasses, and he could see that her eyes were red. Maybe from crying. Kade had to consider that she was truly afraid, but he couldn't put that above Leah's and Bree's safety.

"You can give them to us." Bree also moved closer to the woman. "And you will. In exchange we'll provide you with protection."

Jamie jumped to her feet. "You can't protect me. No one can. My advice is for both of you to leave town for a while. Get lost somewhere and enjoy the time with your baby. Because as long as you continue this investigation, the danger will be there for all of us."

She turned as if to walk away, but Kade stepped in front of her. "The backups," he reminded her. "I won't let you leave until you tell us where they are."

The threat was real and had no sooner left his mouth when he caught the movement out of the corner of his eye. Something in the trees. And it wasn't the spot where Mason had said he would be. This was farther down by the end of the pond.

Bree must have noticed it, too, because her head turned in that direction. "Get down!" she yelled.

But Kade was already moving. He latched onto Bree and Jamie and dragged them down with him. It wasn't a second too soon.

A bullet sliced across the top of the wooden table above them.

Chapter 12

Bree didn't take the time to berate herself for coming to this meeting in such an open place, but she might do that later. However, the bullet meant Kade and she were in a fight for their lives.

Again.

Since Kade was already holding Jamie and her, Bree drew her weapon and scrambled forward, using the table for cover. It wasn't much, but it was the nearest thing. The trees and their vehicles were yards away.

Mason, too.

Though maybe Mason was already trying to figure out how to stop what was happening.

Another bullet bashed into the table. Then another, until they were coming nonstop. Jamie screamed with each one and covered her head with her hands.

Kade turned, took aim in the direction of the shooter and fired.

Bree was ready to do the same, but Jamie's screams got louder, and the woman tried to bolt from the table. She probably thought she could make it to her car that was parked nearby. But Bree knew that once Jamie was out in the open, she'd become an easy target.

"The shots are going over us," Kade mumbled.

Somehow, Bree managed to hear him over the noise of the shots, Jamie's screams and the sound of her own heartbeat pounding in her ears. She listened and watched.

Kade was right.

The first two shots had gone into the table, but these were much higher.

Bree kept a grip on Jamie's arm, and she looked where the bullets were landing. In the trees near Kade's truck and Jamie's car.

"He's not shooting at us," Bree said. If Jamie heard her, it didn't stop the woman from struggling.

There was another shot. Different from the others. From the sound of it, it had come from a rifle.

Mason.

Thank heaven. Because the shooter stopped firing.

Bree shifted so she could try to see what was going on, but in the shift, Jamie threw off Bree's grip. She reached for the woman again, but Jamie bolted out from beneath the table.

"Get down!" Bree yelled to her.

Jamie didn't listen to that, either. She got to her feet and started running to her car.

She didn't make it far.

Another shot tore through the air, and Bree watched

in horror as it smacked into Jamie. The woman screamed and fell to the ground.

Bree didn't think. She started toward Jamie, but she felt Kade put a hard grip on her shoulder.

"No. You can't," he insisted.

And Bree knew he was right. If she went out there, she'd be shot, too. In fact, that was probably what the shooter wanted her to do.

Bree waited and watched while Jamie squirmed on the ground and clutched her left arm. There was blood, but thankfully it didn't appear to be too much. And the wound seemed to be limited to her arm. Still, she needed medical attention.

"I need your phone," Bree told Kade.

With his attention fastened on the area around the shooter, he retrieved it from his pocket and handed it to her. She called the emergency dispatcher to request backup and an ambulance.

"Stay down," Bree called out to Jamie the second she finished the call. Maybe, just maybe, Jamie would listen this time.

"No more shots," Bree heard Kade say.

He was right. There hadn't been another shot since the one that injured Jamie. And that meant either Mason had managed to neutralize the shooter or...

The thought had no sooner crossed her mind when Kade's phone buzzed. "It's Mason," Bree said.

"Answer it," Kade instructed since he was still keeping watch.

Bree pressed the answer button.

"He's getting away," Mason said. "I'm in pursuit through the east side of the park."

Oh, God.

This wasn't over.

"I heard," Kade let her know, and he moved out from beneath the table. "Stay with Jamie. I'm going after this SOB."

Kade kept low, starting away from Bree and Jamie, and he headed for the area around the pond where Mason had said he was in pursuit.

It was a risk.

And he had to do this in such a way that he could still keep watch to make sure the shooter didn't double back and come after them again.

Specifically Jamie, since she seemed to be the target this time around.

He hoped her injuries weren't life-threatening, and while he was hoping, he added that the ambulance would be there soon. Backup, too.

Kade didn't want to leave Bree and her without as much protection as possible, but if Mason and he could catch this gunman then that could put them one step closer to making an arrest.

Behind him, Jamie was still yelling, and he could also hear sirens in the distance. Thank God. Kade threw a quick glance over his shoulder. Bree had stayed put under cover of the table, and she had her gun aimed and ready.

Good.

Kade followed along the edge of the pond. It wouldn't save him, but if the gunman started firing again, at least he could dive into the water. He hoped it wouldn't come down to that. Bree had already had enough shots fired near her today. Jamie, too.

He saw movement in the trees but didn't fire. Good thing, because it was Mason. His brother motioned to his right and then disappeared into the trees.

Kade hurried.

Mason was a good cop, but he didn't want him facing down a professional hit man on his own.

If that's what the shooter was.

Something wasn't right about all of this, but Kade couldn't put his finger on exactly what was wrong.

Kade heard the ambulance come to a stop behind him so that meant Jamie would soon have the medical care she needed. Added to that, the gunman hadn't fired in minutes so he was probably trying to get out of the area. Not stopping to take aim.

Neither did Kade.

He broke into a full run to the spot where he'd seen Mason. No sign of him yet, but he zigzagged his way through the trees and underbrush. Kade knew what was on the other side of the trees.

The back parking lot.

He listened for the sound of a car engine, but Kade couldn't hear anything over his own heavy breath and the sirens from both the ambulance and a deputy's car. Kade shoved aside some low hanging branches and ran out into a clearing that led to a hill.

Mason was there.

He had his left hand bracing his right wrist, and his gun was aimed at the parking lot.

His brother fired.

That made Kade run even faster. He barreled up the hill and caught just a glimpse of the black car before it disappeared around a bend in the road.

Mason cursed.

Kade did the same.

"Did you get a look at him?" Kade asked.

Mason cursed again and shook his head. "He was wearing a ski mask." He pulled out his phone and hit a button. A moment later, Kade heard the emergency dispatcher answer. "The assailant is driving a late model black Chevy on Elmore Road. He's armed and dangerous."

Kade knew the dispatcher would send out all available deputies to track down this guy, but he also knew it would only be a matter of minutes before the shooter reached the interstate. Once there, he'd be much harder to find.

"I'll do everything I can to catch up with him," Mason promised, and he started running toward the road where he'd no doubt left his truck.

Kade would have liked to go in pursuit, as well, but with the shooter already out of sight, he had to check on Bree and Jamie. He could still see through the trees, but he wouldn't breathe easier until he'd talked to Bree.

He made his way back through the wooded area and came out at the pond. There was a lot of activity already going on. An ambulance and two cruisers, one of which was speeding away—hopefully out to search for the shooter.

But Kade picked through all the chaos to find Bree.

She was there, next to the medics who were lifting Jamie onto a stretcher. Bree spotted him, and she hurried toward Kade, meeting him halfway. She went straight into his arms.

Right where Kade needed her to be.

"Are you okay?" she asked in a whisper.

He nodded. "You?"

"Okay."

But he checked her just in case. No signs of injury, thank goodness.

Kade automatically brushed a kiss on her forehead, looped his arm around her and went to the medic, Tommy Watters, who was strapping Jamie onto the stretcher.

Jamie's face was paper-white, and she was shaking from head to toe. "Did you catch him?" she asked Kade.

"No. But Mason is after him. We might get lucky."

Jamie groaned, and tears spilled down her cheeks. "You can't rely on luck. You have to catch him because he nearly killed me."

Kade assured her they would do everything to find the shooter, and he turned to Tommy. "How is she?" Kade asked.

"Not bad. Looks like a flesh wound to me." The young medic followed Kade's gaze to those straps that Tommy was adjusting. "All this is just safety procedures. I'll take her straight to the hospital and have the E.R. doc check her."

"We need to be there in case the doctor releases her," Kade whispered to Bree.

She nodded, and they hurried to his truck. Later, there'd be a ton of paperwork to do—there always was when it came to a shooting—but it could wait. Jamie had said a lot of things, made a lot of accusations, and Kade didn't want her slipping away before she told them the whereabouts of those missing surveillance backups.

They got into his truck and followed right behind the ambulance as the siren wailed.

"You're sure you're okay?" Kade asked when Bree didn't say anything. She kept checking the area all around them. "Because I think that gunman is long gone."

"I agree." She squeezed her eyes shut a moment. "But I also think something about this wasn't right. The gunman wasn't really shooting at us. He kept the shots high despite the fact Jamie was under that table with us."

Yeah. Kade's thoughts were going in the same direction. "What are you thinking?"

"I hope I'm wrong, but maybe Jamie set all of this up to make herself look innocent."

Again, his thoughts were right there with Bree. "If so, it was working. Still is. After all, she got shot. That's a way to take blame off yourself."

Bree nodded. "But I watched her when you were running after the shooter, and she was stunned. And angry. I know people have a lot of reactions to being wounded, but something about this felt like a setup."

Kade made a sound of agreement. "Maybe we can press her for more info while she's at the hospital."

If her injuries were as minor as the medic seemed to think. If they weren't, then Bree and he would have to rethink their theory about this being a setup.

Kade stopped his truck in the hospital parking lot and got out, but he'd hardly made it a step when he saw the man walking toward them.

Anthony.

Kade stepped in front of Bree and slapped his hand on his gun.

Anthony held up his hands in mock surrender, but didn't stop until he was only a few feet away. He hitched his thumb to the ambulance that had stopped directly in front of the E.R. doors.

"I was at the sheriff's office when the call came in about the shooting," Anthony said. "Who's hurt?"

Kade considered being petty and not answering, but Anthony would learn it sooner or later. "It's Jamie. She was shot."

Anthony made a sound of stark surprise and dropped back a step. He looked at the medics as they lifted Jamie out of the ambulance and whisked her into E.R.

"Is she alive?" Anthony asked.

"Yes," Kade and Bree answered in unison.

It was Bree who continued. "In fact, according to the medic she'll pull through just fine." She stared at Anthony. "Bet you're all torn up about that."

His stark surprise turned to narrowed eyes. "I don't wish Jamie any harm, but she was a fool to think she could trust my father. Or Agent Cooper."

Bree huffed and folded her arms over her chest. "And you think one of them is responsible for this?"

"Who else?"

"You," Kade quickly provided. And he silently added Jamie's name to that list of possibilities.

"You're wasting your time trying to pin any of this on me." Anthony tapped his chest. "I've told you who's behind all of this, and yet both are still out on the streets. How many more shootings will it take for you to haul my father and his lackey FBI friend in for questioning?"

Right now, speaking to Jamie was his priority.

"Come on." Kade slipped his arm around Bree and started for the E.R. entrance.

"Jamie accused me of all of this, didn't she?" Anthony called out. "I'll bet she said she had some kind of proof of my wrongdoing. But let me guess, she didn't have that proof with her."

Kade and Bree stopped, and Kade eased back around to face him. Not because he wanted to see Anthony, but he wanted to make sure the man wasn't about to pull a gun on them.

"She doesn't have proof of anything," Anthony went on, "unless it's crimes she committed."

"I thought Jamie and you were friends of sorts," Kade reminded him.

"No. She's a viper. My advice? Watch your back around her, and don't believe a word she says."

Kade didn't intend to believe any of them, and this conversation was over. Even though Anthony continued to bark out warnings, Kade and Bree went to the E.R. and entered through the automatic doors.

The first person Kade saw was Tommy Watters, and he made a beeline toward them. "The shooting victim is in the examining room."

Good. Maybe it wouldn't take long, and then Kade could get Bree out of there. Even though she'd been stellar under fire, the spent adrenaline was obviously getting to her. It was getting to him, too. Besides, he needed to call Grayson and check on Leah.

Kade didn't stay in the waiting area since he wanted to keep an eye on Jamie and talk to the doctor about her injury. He led Bree past the reception desk and into the hall where there were examining rooms on each side. The first was empty. The second had a sick-looking kid with some very worried parents by his bedside.

Bree walked ahead of him, checking the rooms on the other side of the hall. She made it to the last one and whirled around.

"Where's Jamie?" she asked.

That was not a question Kade wanted to hear, and he started his own frantic search of the room. He cursed. Because Jamie was nowhere in sight.

Chapter 13

Bree had no idea what to think about this latest mess. Had Jamie left on her own, or had she been coerced into leaving the hospital?

Unfortunately, Kade and she didn't know the answer.

But after a thorough search of the area and the entire hospital, they hadn't been able to find the woman. Heck, they hadn't even been able to find anyone who'd even seen her. Jamie had simply vanished.

And without her, they couldn't get those backups.

Bree had pinned her hopes on the backups. Kade's latest phone call was to his brother Mason, who still was at the hospital reviewing the surveillance feed of the two newly installed cameras. One in the hospital parking lot. The other, fixed at the E.R. entrance where just weeks earlier someone had left Leah. It was because of Leah's abandonment that the city had put the cameras in place.

Kade was seated at Mason's desk at the sheriff's office, the phone sandwiched between his ear and shoulder, while he fired off messages to the rangers that he'd asked to assist in the search for Jamie. That's because all the deputies were tied up either providing protection for Leah and the others or investigating the shooting.

Bree had personally verified the protecting Leah part because, despite the need to find Jamie, she had an even greater need to make sure her baby was okay. Grayson, his wife and both sisters-in-law had assured Bree that all was well, but she wouldn't be convinced of that until she held Leah in her own arms.

Kade hung up the phone and shook his head.

Bree's hopes went south for a quick end to this.

"Nothing," Kade verified. "The camera angles are wrong to film someone leaving out the side exits."

Which Jamie had no doubt done since one of those side exits was very close to the examining room where the EMT had left her to wait for the doctor.

"What about the backups?" Bree asked. "Has SAPD had time to search her house for them?"

"They're there now, but they haven't found anything so far."

She groaned even though the search had been a long shot. Her house was probably the last place Jamie would have left them. But where could they be?

"The rangers and deputies will keep looking for Jamie and the shooter," Kade continued. "And we'll look for a money trail. If she's going into hiding, she'll need cash."

Bree rubbed the back of her neck and the pain that

was starting to make its way to her head. "She'll need money if she left voluntarily."

Kade nodded, stood and went to her. He took over the neck massage. At first, it felt too intimate for his brother's office—for any place—but after a few strokes of those clever fingers, Bree heard herself sigh.

"Thanks," she mumbled.

"Why don't we get out of here so you can get some rest? Maybe we can do another video call to Grayson and check on Leah."

Until he added that last part, Bree had been about to say no, that they needed to stay and assist with the search and investigation. But she was tired, and more than that, she wanted to see her daughter's face.

Bree walked into the hall, but the sound of footsteps had her turning in the direction of the dispatcher's desk.

Coop was there.

And judging from his expression, he was not a happy man.

Great. Something else to add to her already nightmare of a day.

"The dispatcher's trying to stop me from seeing you," Coop called out. He nudged the woman aside, flashing his badge, and he headed right for Bree.

"I heard about the shooting," Coop said. "Are you both all right?"

"Fine," Kade said and stayed right by her side. "The deputies have things under control so Bree and I were about to leave."

"I have to talk to Bree first." Coop's tone was definitely all FBI. Oh, yes. This would not be fun.

"About what?" she asked. Bree didn't even try to take the impatience out of her tone. She really wanted out of there now and didn't want to go another round of pressure from Coop.

Coop, however, didn't budge. "You haven't called, and I thought I made it clear that you had a decision to make."

Oh, that.

Bree hadn't forgotten that Coop had ordered her into work, but there hadn't been time. "Put me on unpaid leave," she suggested.

But Coop only shook his head. "I've been keeping the powers that be off your back, but I can't do it any longer, Bree. They want you in for some evaluations— both physical and mental. You have to come with me *now*."

"Now?" Kade and she asked in unison.

Coop lifted his shoulder. "I warned you this could happen."

"Did you tell those powers that be that Bree is assisting with an investigation?" Kade fired back. "And that she's in danger?"

"Part of the reason she's in danger is because she's here with you." Coop's mouth tightened. "If she'd come into headquarters when I asked, she wouldn't have had shots fired at her."

When Kade tried to maneuver himself in front of her, maybe to take a verbal swing at Coop, Bree positioned herself so that she was face-to-face with Coop. There was no need for Kade's career to suffer from this.

"My daughter is in danger," Bree stated as clearly as she could to Coop. "I don't have time to go to headquarters for evals."

"Then you leave me no choice." Coop held out his

hand. "Surrender your badge. Because if you don't come with me, you're no longer an FBI agent."

Bree's breath stalled in her lungs. Those were words she'd certainly never expected to hear. Not from Coop, not from anyone. The badge and her job had been her life for so long now that they were *her*.

"You can't do this to her," Kade insisted.

Coop shook his head. "She's given me no choice. But Bree can fix it all just by coming with me now."

If she went to headquarters, she'd get caught in the whirlwind of paperwork and evals. There wouldn't be time to search for Jamie or those backups. There wouldn't be time for a video call to see Leah.

Bree suddenly felt drained and overwhelmed, but she knew exactly what she had to do. She took her badge from her pocket.

And handed it to Coop.

Coop's tight jaw went slack, and he just stared at her. Kade didn't say anything, either, but he gave her a questioning look.

"I'm sure," she said to Kade. "Let's go."

"You can't just go!" Coop practically shouted. He latched onto her arm, his grip hard and punishing. "You can't throw your life away like this."

Kade moved to do something about that grip, but Bree didn't want a fight to start, so she glared first at the grip and then at Coop.

"You asked for my badge and you got it. You're no longer my boss, and you'd better get your hand off me."

Coop let go of her, shook his head and stepped back. He added some raw profanity, too, and turned that profanity on Kade. "You've brainwashed her. Or else she's still too high on drugs to know what she's saying."

Bree had to fight not to slap him. "I'm not high. I'm tired—of you and this conversation." She headed for the back door and hoped Kade would follow rather than slug Coop.

With his voice low and dangerous, Kade said something to Coop, and she finally heard Kade's footsteps behind her. Thank goodness. She'd had enough violence for today. For the rest of her life.

"I'm sorry," Kade said, catching up with her. He hooked his arm around her waist. "I'll call my boss at headquarters and have him intervene. You'll get your badge back."

"Thanks, but I'm not sure I want it back." And Bree was surprised to realize that was true.

"You're a good agent," Kade pointed out.

"I *was*." She didn't say more until they had gone outside and were in Kade's truck. "But I can't go back to being a Jane. You said it yourself—motherhood and being a deep-cover operative aren't compatible."

"I said that because I didn't want to lose custody of Leah." He groaned, started his truck and headed toward the ranch.

"It's true," Bree insisted. "Besides, I'd like to take some time off and work out things in my head. And with you."

His eyebrow slid up.

"Not that way," she answered. But then she shrugged. Yes, maybe that way. "I have some savings," Bree went on. "I'm thinking about finding an apartment or a small house to rent in Silver Creek. That way I can be close to Leah." And Kade. But she kept that last part to herself.

Kade stayed quiet several moments. "You could stay at the ranch."

It was a generous offer but one she couldn't take. "Probably not a good idea while we're trying to work things out."

Several more quiet moments. "You could marry me."

Bree turned her head toward him so quickly that her neck popped. "What?"

"It makes sense. You could live at the ranch, and you wouldn't have to work. We could raise Leah together."

Bree just stared at him. "A marriage of convenience?" She shook her head. "Or more like a kept woman." Because in all of that, Kade darn sure hadn't mentioned anything about a real marriage.

"Just think about it," he snarled.

She didn't have to think about it. There was only one reason she would ever marry, and it was for love. Period. And Kade obviously didn't love her because there'd been no mention of it.

Bree didn't love him, either.

But she was falling hard for him in spite of his making stupid, generous offers like the one he'd just made.

She mentally cursed herself. Falling for Kade would only make this more complicated. She didn't need a broken heart on top of everything else.

With the snarl still tightening his mouth, Kade took the turn toward the ranch. Where they'd likely be *alone* inside the house. Bree hadn't given that much thought, but she thought about it now—after his offer. She didn't want a fake marriage from Kade, but she did want *him*. And that meant being alone under the same roof with him wouldn't be easy.

His phone buzzed, and he put the call on speaker as he pulled to a stop in front of the house.

"This is Sgt. Garrett O'Malley at SAPD. Your brother asked me to call you."

"You found Jamie Greer?" Kade immediately asked.

"No. But we searched a storage facility that Ms. Greer had rented, and we got lucky. We found the surveillance backups that were missing from the Fulbright Clinic investigation."

Chapter 14

Kade sat on the foot of his bed and waited for Bree to finish her shower. She'd been in there awhile, and he figured she wouldn't end it anytime soon.

Probably because she was trying to work out what had happened.

Kade could still see the look on Bree's face when Coop had demanded her badge and when she'd handed it to him. Coop had given her no choice, but that didn't mean Bree wasn't hurting. And Kade was hurting for her. The badge was a big part of who they were, and it had no doubt cost her big-time to surrender it.

Kade could also still see Bree's face when he'd suggested they get married. The timing had sucked, of course. And he hadn't meant to blurt it out like that. But it was something that had been on his mind since she'd first arrived at the ranch. While a marriage of convenience didn't sound ideal, it was a way for both of them to raise Leah and not have to deal with split custody.

Still, he'd made it seem more like a business merger rather than a proposal.

The question was—would Bree take him up on it?

He groaned, moved his laptop to the nightstand and dropped back on the bed. Kade was too afraid to close his eyes even for a minute because as tired as he was, he might fall asleep. To say the day had been long was a massive understatement.

It wasn't just the proposal. There'd been the meeting with Jamie. The shooting and her disappearance from the hospital. The confrontations with both Anthony and Coop. Followed by SAPD recovering those backups. They were in the process of reviewing them, and the sergeant had told Kade that once they finished the initial review, the backups would be delivered to the ranch by courier in a couple of hours.

It would take more than a couple of hours to go through them.

Maybe all night.

That's why Bree and he had gone ahead with the video call to Grayson and Leah before her shower. Their daughter had slept through the entire call, but it'd been good to see her precious little face.

When the bathroom door opened, Kade snapped back up and tried to look alert. Suddenly, it wasn't that hard to do when he caught sight of Bree. Fresh from her shower, her hair was damp. Her face, too. And the heat and steam had put color back in her cheeks.

No pink pjs but she was wearing a pink bathrobe that hit well above her knees.

"Darcy must have a thing for pink clothes," Bree said apologetically.

Obviously. And even though it wasn't Bree's usual color, it looked good on her. Too good. Especially the parts of her that the robe didn't cover. Those parts were the ones that latched onto his attention.

"Darcy said it was okay to check her closet." Bree fluttered her hand toward the doorway. "So, I thought I'd look for a pair of jeans."

She took a step but then stopped. Stared at him. "Is something wrong? Is there a problem with the back-ups?"

"No problem." He stood, and to give his hands something to do, he crammed them into his jeans pockets. "They should be here in a couple of hours."

Hours, as in plenty of time to do something about whatever it was that was happening between them.

Bree nodded.

Kade figured the best thing to do would be to keep his distance from Bree. The air between them was changing. Heating up from warm to hot. He blamed it in part on the clingy bathrobe, but the truth was, Bree could be wearing anything and he would have had the same reaction.

Heck, he'd reacted to her while they were under-cover.

She stood there, staring at him. Waiting, maybe. Kade didn't make her wait long. He started toward her just as Bree started toward him.

He pulled her into his arms.

The kiss was instant, hungry, as if they were starved

for each other. That wasn't too far from the truth. Kade had wanted her for a long time now.

He eased back just a fraction to make sure she wasn't planning to stop this. She wasn't. Bree hooked her arms around him and pulled Kade right back to her.

The fire slammed through him. The need, too. And he knew he had lost any chance of looking at this with reason and consequences. Sex wasn't about reason. It was about the burning need to take this woman that had turned him inside out.

"Kade," she whispered with her mouth against his. It wasn't a soft romantic purr, either. There was an urgency to it.

Something Kade understood because he felt the same urgency.

They fell backward onto the bed, and the kiss continued. So did the fight to get closer. Body to body.

Kade took those kisses to her neck. And lower. He snapped open the robe and kissed her breasts. Bree arched her back, moving closer, and she made a sound of pure feminine pleasure.

A sound that kicked up the urgency a notch.

"Now," Bree insisted.

She meant it, too. She went after his shirt, pulling the buttons from their holes and shoving it off his shoulders. It was easier for Kade. All he had to do was pull off that robe, and underneath was a naked woman.

Well, almost.

Bree wore just a pair of white panties, and Kade would have quickly rid her of those if she hadn't played dirty. She ran her hand down his bare chest. To his stomach.

And below.

That crazy frantic touch let him know exactly what she wanted.

Kade turned her, rolling on top of her so he could work his way out of his jeans. Bree didn't help with that, either. She kept kissing him. Kept touching. Until he was certain he'd go crazy. But somehow, he managed to get off his boots and Wrangler jeans.

"Hold that thought," he mumbled when she dropped some kisses on his chest.

He leaned across to the nightstand and took out a condom. Good thing he remembered. With the fire burning his mind and body, and with Bree pulling him closer and closer, he was surprised he could remember anything, including his name.

Bree pulled him back to her the moment he had the condom on, and Kade landed with his body on hers. Perfect. Or not. Bree maneuvered herself on top, and in the same motion she took him inside her.

No more frantic touches or kisses.

Both stilled a moment, and their gazes met.

Kade saw the surprise in her eyes and figured she saw it in his. He'd expected this to be good. But not this good. This felt like a lot more than sex.

She started to move, rocking against him and creating the contact they needed to make that fire inside him flame high. The need built. Little by little. With each of the strokes inside her. However, even through his sex-hazed mind, Kade took a moment to savor the view.

Oh, man.

Bree was beautiful.

He'd known that, of course, but this was like a fantasy come true.

She pushed herself against him. Harder and faster. Until Kade felt her shatter. His own body was on the edge, begging for release, but still he watched her. He watched as Bree went right over the edge.

"Kade," she said. This time, it was a purr.

And he gathered her in his arms, pushed into her one last time and let himself go.

Bree couldn't catch her breath, and she wasn't sure she cared about such things as breathing.

Every part of her was on fire but yet slack and sated.

At peace.

Strange. She'd thought that sex with Kade would cause immense pleasure followed by the feeling that they'd just screwed things up worse than they already were.

Well, the pleasure had been immense all right.

Maybe it would take a while for the screwed-up feeling to set in.

But for now, she would just pretend that all was right with the world while they lay there naked and in each other's arms.

Kade made a lazy, satisfied sound. A rumble deep within his throat, and as if it were something they did all the time, he pulled her against him and kissed her. The moment was magic. Perfect. And even though Bree tried to keep the doubts and demons at bay, she couldn't stop the thoughts from coming. Well, one thought, anyway.

What now?

She couldn't accept his marriage proposal. Yes, she cared for Kade. Was hotly attracted to him and vice versa. But that wasn't the basis for a real marriage. For that matter, neither was the fact that they had a child together.

Kade made another of those sounds, gave her another kiss. "I'll be right back." And he headed into the bathroom.

The walk there was interesting, and she got a good look at his backside. Oh, yeah. The man was hot, and that body appealed to her in a down-and-dirty kind of way. Too bad the rest of him appealed to her, as well.

Because this could lead to a crushed heart for her.

With that miserable idea now in her head, Bree got up, located her bathrobe and slipped it on. She was trying to locate her panties when the bathroom door opened, and Kade came back in the room.

Naked.

She got a good frontal view this time and went all hot again. Mercy. She'd just had him. How could she want him this much again so soon?

His eyebrow lifted in not an approving way at the bathrobe.

"The backups will arrive soon," she reminded him. It was the truth, but it was that fear of a crushed heart that had her putting on the terry cloth armor.

He frowned, walked to her and pulled her back onto the bed. Kade also slipped his hand into the robe and cupped her breast. "We have at least another hour," he drawled. "My suggestion? We stay naked."

Bree laughed before she could stop herself.

And just like that, the moment was perfect again. No

doubts. No worries of hearts. Kade sealed the moment with another of those searing, mind-draining kisses that reminded her that yes, they were indeed naked. Or almost. He shoved open the robe and kissed his way down from her mouth to her stomach.

At first Bree thought the sound was the buzzing in her head, but when Kade cursed, she realized it was his phone.

He rolled off the bed, grabbed his jeans from the floor and jerked out his phone. He glanced at the screen and shook his head.

"The caller blocked the number," Kade mumbled, and he put the call on speaker. "Special Agent Ryland."

"Agent Ryland," the person answered.

And with just those two words, Bree's blood turned to ice. Because it wasn't a normal voice. The caller was speaking through a voice scrambler.

"Who is this?" Kade demanded.

"Someone you're going to meet in an hour at the Fulbright Clinic in San Antonio."

The voice sounded like a cartoon character, making it impossible to recognize the speaker. But that didn't mean she couldn't figure out who it was. After all, there weren't many people who would make a demand like that.

"The Fulbright is closed," Kade reminded the caller. "It's an abandoned building now."

"Yes." The caller paused. "And that's exactly why it's a good place for us to meet. Show up in one hour alone. Just you and Bree. And when you come, bring those missing surveillance backups with you."

Kade glanced back at her and groaned softly. This

was no doubt one of their suspects. But which one? Mc-Clendon, Anthony, Jamie?

Or heaven forbid, Coop?

"We don't have the backups," Kade said.

"Yes, but you can get them from SAPD. And trust me, it'll be in your best interest to get them and bring them to me at the clinic."

The caller didn't raise his voice, didn't change his inflection, but the threat slammed through her.

"Leah," she mouthed.

Kade shook his head, pulled her down to him and whispered in her ear, "Grayson would have called if something had gone wrong with Leah."

True. If something hadn't gone wrong with Grayson, too. Maybe the missing shooter or one of the suspects had gotten into the estate and was holding them all captive.

"Call him," Kade whispered, and he pointed to the house phone on the nightstand next to Kade's laptop. And he mouthed the number.

"It won't do any good to try to trace this call," the voice on the phone said. "Prepaid cell. And I'll toss it once we're done here."

Bree kept one ear tuned to what was being said, but she grabbed the house phone and went to the other side of the room. Grayson answered on the first ring.

"Is Leah okay?" she whispered.

"Of course. Why? What's wrong?"

The breath swooshed out of Bree, and the relief nearly brought her to her knees. "Are you all okay? Is anyone there threatening you?"

"Not a chance. I have this place locked up tight with Nate and Dade standing guard. Why?"

Bree couldn't get into details, mainly because she had to figure out what exactly the details were. "We might have a problem. Kade will call you when he can." And she hung up so they could finish this puzzling call.

"Leah's okay," she relayed in a whisper to Kade.

The relief was quick and obvious.

"Give me one reason," he said to the caller, "why Bree and I would meet you and give you evidence?"

"One reason?" the person repeated. "Oh, I have a big one reason. Well, actually a small one, but I think it'll be a very big reason to Bree and you. Check your email."

Bree's heart was still pounding like crazy, and she wanted to dismiss all of this as some kind of ploy, but that didn't stop Kade and her from moving toward his laptop. It was already on so he clicked into his email and found a new one with an attachment.

"Click onto the link in the attachment," the caller ordered.

Kade did, and the link took them to an online video. One with very poor quality. It appeared to be a dark room, so dark that Bree couldn't make out anything in it.

"Let me move closer to the camera," the caller said.

There was the sound of footsteps. Still no light. But as the footsteps got louder, she could just make out the image of someone. An adult. The person was cloaked in black. Maybe a cape with a hood. And the person was seated in a chair.

He or she was holding something.

Bree drew in her breath. Waited. And zoomed in on whatever was in the person's arms.

Oh, God.

It was a baby.

"Leah!" she practically screamed when she saw the baby's face.

"It's not her," Kade said, but he didn't sound convinced. "It's some kind of trick."

Yes. Bree forced herself to remember that Grayson had just told her that Leah was all right. Kade's brother wouldn't have lied, and he hadn't sounded under duress when he'd answered her.

"No trick," the caller assured them, the cartoon voice sounding smug. "But the baby isn't Leah."

Bree shook her head. It was a real baby all right. Dressed in a pink dress and wrapped in a pink blanket, she was asleep, but Bree could see the face.

A face identical to Leah's.

"Confused?" the caller mocked. "Well, I've been keeping a little secret. And the secret is the reason you'll both come alone to the clinic and bring me those tapes."

"Who's baby is that?" Kade demanded.

The caller laughed. "Yours. Yours and Bree's," he corrected.

"What?" Bree managed to say. She had no choice but to drop down onto the bed.

Kade didn't look too steady, either. "What do you mean?"

"I mean seven weeks ago, Bree gave birth to identical twin girls."

"Oh, God," Bree mumbled, and because she didn't know what else to do, she kept repeating it.

She stared at the face, at the shadows, and could only shake her head. What was going on?

"Here's the bottom line," the caller continued, the horrible voice pouring through the room. "If you don't want your second daughter to be sold on the black market, then you'll be here alone at the clinic in one hour. I'll trade the baby for the backups."

Chapter 15

"Wait!" Kade shouted into the phone.

But it was too late. The caller had already hung up. And his computer screen went blank. Someone had pulled the plug on the video feed.

Behind him, Bree was gasping and shaking her head.

"It is possible?" Kade asked. "Could you really have had twins?"

She looked at him, her eyes filled to the brim with tears. "I suppose so. They sedated me for the C-section."

Kade cursed. Yes, it was possible this could be some kind of elaborate hoax, but it was too big of a risk to take to ignore it.

He wiped away her tears. "Get dressed. We're going after the baby."

Bree nodded, and even though she was shaky, she

hurried to the bathroom where she'd left her clothes. Kade dressed, too, and he called his brother Grayson.

"We have a problem," Kade said when Grayson answered. "I don't have time to sugarcoat this or explain it other than to say I need those surveillance backups from SAPD. Someone called and wants the backups in exchange for a baby. A twin girl that Bree might have delivered when she had Leah."

"What?" Grayson snapped.

Kade ignored his brother's shock and the questions Grayson likely wanted answered now. "Just have an SAPD officer, one you can trust, meet us at the intersection of Dalton and Reyes in San Antonio."

"The Fulbright Clinic is near there. Kade, you're not thinking—"

"Bree and I have to go in alone. That's the condition."

Grayson cursed. "But it could be dangerous. It could be a trap."

Both of those were true. "What would you do if it were your child?" Kade fired back.

Grayson cursed again. "At least let me arrange to have some backup in the area."

"Only if they stay far away and out of sight. I'm figuring this guy has already set up some kind of perimeter surveillance. They'll know if we have someone with us."

"Who did this?" Grayson pressed.

"When I know, I'll you let know. For now, just get me those backups."

Kade ended the call, knowing his brother would make it happen. After all, his other brother Nate, was an SAPD lieutenant, and he could do whatever it took to have those backups ready and waiting for them.

He hurried, dressing as fast as he could, and by the time he'd finished, Bree ran out of the bathroom. Dressed and looking ready to panic.

"We can do this," he promised her and hoped it wasn't a lie.

Kade put on his shoulder holster and ankle strap, filled both with guns and extra ammunition, and he took his backup weapon from the nightstand and handed it to Bree. She also grabbed some extra magazines of bullets and stuffed them into her pockets. They couldn't go in there with guns blazing, not with a baby's safety at stake, but Kade had no plans to go in unarmed, either.

They both ran down the stairs, but Kade used the security monitor by the door to make sure no one had sneaked onto the ranch. When he was sure it was safe, they hurried outside to his truck, and he drove away fast.

"What about the backups?" she asked.

"Grayson will get them."

She nodded and made what sounded to be a breath of relief. But Kade knew neither of them would be in the relief mode until they figured out what the heck was going on.

"Think back," he told her. He flew down the ranch road and onto the route that would take them to the interstate. "When you were pregnant, did you have any indications there was more than one baby?"

"Maybe." Her forehead bunched up. "There was a lot of movement from the baby, a lot of kicking and moving around and I felt huge. But I figured plenty of pregnant women felt that way."

"They do." He'd gone through his sister-in-law's pregnancy and now Grayson's wife, and both had complained about their size. "What about an ultrasound?"

"They did one, but they didn't let me see the monitor."

Hell, probably because they hadn't wanted her to know that it was twins.

But why keep that from her?

One baby or two, Bree wasn't going to fight them back for fear of harming the child. Her captors had her exactly where they wanted her.

"The second baby is their ace in the hole," Bree mumbled. And she groaned. "I remember Kirk using that term, but I thought he was talking about me. Or Leah. I had no idea he was talking about another baby."

Kade mentally groaned, too. "What did Kirk say exactly?"

She lifted her hand in a gesture to indicate she was thinking about it. "He said it wouldn't do any good for me to escape, that he had an ace in the hole." Her gaze rifled to him. "But why would Kirk's boss wait all these weeks to tell us about the other baby?"

Unfortunately, Kade had a theory about that. "Maybe the boss thought you were dead and if so, you couldn't testify against him. When you resurfaced, that meant you became a threat."

She turned in the seat toward him. "But Jamie's the real threat because she's the one who had those backups."

He shook his head. "She wasn't a threat as long as she kept the backups hidden. After all, those backups implicated her in a crime, too. She didn't want the cops or us to have them. She wanted to hang on to them as her own ace in the hole."

Bree pulled in her breath, nodded. "Then SAPD found the backups and now all of this has come to a showdown."

A showdown where his baby could be in danger.

"Twins," he said under his breath. He had to accept that it was possible. And that meant he had to do everything humanly possible to save his child.

"I'm sorry," Bree whispered, her voice shaking hard. "I should have put all the little things together to know there was a second baby."

"You couldn't have known. This was all part of some sick plan, and keeping you in the dark was essential." He took the ramp to the interstate. "But Jamie should have known. Even if she wasn't there for your C-section, she must have heard Kirk talking to someone about it."

"Yes," Bree agreed. "So, why didn't she say anything at the park?"

Kade could think of a reason. A bad one. Maybe Jamie was the person behind all of this. Those backups could have been her protection from Kirk's boss.

Or Jamie could be the boss.

"This might be Jamie's way of getting the backups back," Kade pointed out.

Bree stayed quiet a moment and then nodded. "That would explain why we're just now getting the news of the other baby." Another pause. "There must be something incriminating that we don't know about on those backups."

Kade agreed. And the bad flip side to that was SAPD hadn't had time to review them. Neither had Kade and Bree.

"It's too big of a risk to take in fake backups," Bree

said. "And we can't give him or her just one or two. This person knows how many backups there are."

She took the words right out of his mouth. No, the person would almost certainly verify they were real before he or she handed over the baby.

And then what?

Kade didn't like the scenarios that came to mind. But there was a possible good outcome.

Well, semigood.

"The person disguised his or her voice," Kade explained, playing this through in his mind. "So, it's possible we can do a safe exchange. The backups for the baby."

"And we just walk out of there," Bree added in a mumble.

Yeah. That was the best-case scenario. Kade didn't want to do any bargaining with this SOB while the baby was still in the picture. Later, once they were all out of there, he'd move Bree, the twin and Leah to another safe location.

Then, he'd go after the person who'd orchestrated this.

Of course, that was just the beginning. If the second baby was real, then he had another child. To love and raise. To protect. Another custody issue to work out with Bree.

Since all of that was only clouding his mind, he pushed it aside and focused just on now. And *now* started with getting the backups.

Kade drove into San Antonio and kept an eye on both Bree and the clock. The caller had given them only an hour to deliver the backups, and half that time was already gone. He hated to think of what would happen if they were late.

He slowed down when he reached the intersection of Dalton and Reyes, and Kade's heart nearly stopped when he didn't see anyone waiting for them. But then, his brother Nate stepped from the side of a gas station. Kade mumbled a prayer of thanks and pulled in, stopping right next to Nate.

"The backups," Nate said. He handed the evidence envelope to Kade when he lowered the window.

"Thanks." Kade dropped the envelope on the seat between Bree and him. "Did this put your badge on the line?"

Nate shrugged. Meaning, it had.

"I'm sorry," Kade told him. And he was. He knew how much the badge meant to Nate, but he also knew how much family meant to him. "Grayson told you about the baby?"

"Yeah." Nate looked over his shoulder in the direction of the Fulbright clinic only a block away. "I put some SWAT guys on the roof." He hitched his thumb to the three-story building not far from where they stood. "And I have six others waiting to respond. We haven't seen anyone outside the clinic, but we've only been here about ten minutes."

Kade mumbled another thanks, took out his phone and set it so that he could reach Nate with just the touch of one button. "What about using infrared to get a glimpse of who's inside?"

Nate shook his head. "We tried. No luck. The place used to be a radiology clinic, and infrared won't penetrate the walls."

Bree made a frustrated sound, and even though the

timing sucked, Kade remembered that he hadn't introduced Bree to this particular brother. But it would have to wait.

"Be careful," Nate said, and he stepped back from the truck.

Kade nodded and drove away, making his way toward the clinic. Less than a year ago, Bree and he had to battle their way out of here and had run along this very street.

Maybe they wouldn't have to do that again.

The thought of trying to escape with a baby under those circumstances sickened him.

Bree pulled in a hard breath when Kade came to a stop in the clinic's parking lot. It was empty. Not another vehicle in sight. No lights, either. Even the ones in the parking lot were out—maybe because the caller had disabled them.

There was also a problem with the windows. Each one facing the parking lot had burglar bars. Thick metal rods jutting down the entire length of the glass. It would be impossible to use those to escape.

The moment Kade turned off the engine, his phone buzzed. The caller's info had been blocked, just like before.

"Agent Ryland," the scrambled voice greeted him when Kade answered. "So glad you made it. Do you have the backups?"

"I do," Kade hesitantly answered.

"Excellent. Both of you enter the clinic through the front door. I've already unlocked it. You're to put all your weapons and the backups on the floor—"

"I'll give you the backups when you give us the baby," Kade interrupted.

There was silence for several heart-stopping moments. "All right," the caller finally said. "Then, let's get this show on the road."

The person ended the call, and Kade looked at Bree to make sure she was up to doing this. She was. Yes, she'd cried earlier, but there weren't tears now. Just the determined face of a well-trained federal agent who would do anything to get her baby out of harm's way.

"If something goes wrong," Kade whispered, "I want you to take the baby and get out of there. I'll run interference."

She shook her head, and the agent facade waivered a bit, but she couldn't argue. The baby had to come first.

"We're all coming out of there alive," Bree whispered back. And she leaned over and kissed him.

Kade wanted to hold on to that kiss, on to her and that promise, but there wasn't time. "Stay behind me," he added, "and hide your gun in the back waist of your pants."

After she'd done that, he stepped from his truck. He waited until Bree was indeed behind him before they walked to the double front doors. He wished they were glass so he could see inside but no such luck. They were thick wood. Kade said another prayer and tested the knob.

The door opened.

Like the exterior of the building and the parking lot, the entrance was pitch-black, and he could barely make out what appeared to be a desk and some chairs. This was the reception area, and if anyone was there, he couldn't see, hear or sense them.

"Here's my gun," Kade called out, and he took his

weapon and one of the extra magazines and put them on the floor.

"Now, the other weapons." The voice boomed over an intercom. The same scrambled voice as the caller.

"Weapon," Kade corrected. And he motioned for Bree to surrender her gun, as well.

Kade could feel her hesitation, but she finally did it. That only left them with the small gun in his ankle holster, and he hoped like the devil that the SOB on the intercom didn't know about it.

Behind them, there was a sharp click. Not someone cocking a gun. But maybe just as dangerous.

Someone had locked the door. That someone had no doubt used a remote control because Nate wouldn't have let anyone get close to the exterior side of the door.

"Kick the weapons down the hall," the voice ordered.

Kade did it, the sound of metal scraping across the tiled floor.

"Here," Kade whispered to Bree, and he handed her his cell so if necessary she could make that emergency call to Nate. It would also free up his hands in case he had to go for the ankle holster.

"Where's the baby?" Kade asked, holding up the envelope with the backups.

"I'll have to verify the backups first. Walk forward, down the hall. Keep your hands in the air so I can see them at all times."

The *dark* hall. Where they could be ambushed and the backups taken from them.

"How about you meet us halfway?" Kade asked.

"How about you follow orders?" the person snapped.

"Because your orders could get us killed. Either meet us halfway, or show us the baby now."

More silence. And with each passing second, Kade's heartbeat revved up. Bree's breathing, too. Since her arm was against his back, he could feel how tense she was.

"Okay," the person finally said. "Start walking. I'll do the same."

It was a huge risk, but staying put was a risk, too.

Kade took the first step, then waited and listened. He heard some movement at the end of that dark hall, and he took another step. Then another. Bree was right behind him and hopefully would stay there.

If this goon sent in someone from behind, through those front doors, Nate's men would stop them. The same if a gunman tried to shoot through one of the windows.

So, the danger was ahead.

"There are two rooms ahead off the hall," Bree whispered. "One on the left. The other on the right."

Kade hadn't remembered that about the clinic layout, but he was thankful that Bree had. He would need to make sure no one came out of those rooms to ambush them.

Another step.

The person at the end of the hall did the same.

Now that Kade's eyes were adjusting a little to the darkness, he could see the shadowy figure better. Well, the outline of the person, anyway. He couldn't make out any feature and couldn't tell if it was a man or woman. The person seemed to be wearing some kind of dark cloak.

"When you get to the spot where the reception area meets the hall," the voice instructed, "take the backups from the envelope and hold them up so I can see them."

Kade made several more steps to get to that spot, and with his attention fastened on the figure ahead of him, he took out the backups and lifted them in the air.

Overhead on the hall ceiling, a camera whirred around, the lens angling toward Kade's hand. Either this guy had backup inside the building or else he was using a remote control device.

Kade was betting he had backup.

Behind him, he heard a buzzing sound. His phone. And Kade mentally cursed. "Answer it," he whispered to Bree, hoping that the person at the end of the hall hadn't heard.

She didn't say anything, but she pressed a button and put the phone to her ear. A moment later, she froze.

"What's wrong?" Kade asked, still trying to keep his voice low.

"You're sure?" she asked.

Kade was about to repeat his *what's wrong* question, but Bree latched onto his arm.

"It's a trap," she said. And Bree started to pull him to the floor.

But it was already too late.

The shot slammed through the air.

Chapter 16

Bree pulled Kade to the right, out of the line of fire of the person in the hall.

Just as the bullet slammed into the locked door.

Kade and she slammed onto the floor. Hard. It knocked the breath right out of her, but Bree fought to regain it so she could get them out of harm's way.

If that was even possible now.

Thankfully, Kade could breathe and react because he grabbed her by the shoulder and dragged her onto the other side of the desk. He also drew the small Colt .38 from his ankle holster. It wasn't much firepower considering their situation.

And their situation was *bad*.

"Stop shooting!" Kade yelled. He shoved the back-ups inside his shirt. "You could hit the baby."

The person laughed, that cartoony voice echoing

through the dark clinic. Bree knew the reason for the sickening laughter.

"There's no second baby?" Kade whispered to her on a rise of breath.

"Not here. That was Mason on the phone. About ten minutes ago a woman dropped off a baby at the Silver Creek hospital. A baby who looks exactly like Leah. She's all right. She hadn't been harmed."

The sound that Kade made deep in his throat was a mixture of relief and dread. Relief because their baby was all right, away from the monster who'd fired that shot at them. But the danger for Kade and she was just starting.

"Thank you for cooperating with my plan," the figure called out. "And see? I'm not such a bad person, after all. The woman I hired to take the baby to the hospital did exactly as I asked. So, all is well."

Kade cursed. "If all is truly well as you say, then you'll let us go."

"Can't do that."

Another bullet blasted into the door.

Kade's brother Nate would likely have heard the shots. He no doubt knew about the baby being dropped off at the hospital. But there was no way Nate could come in with guns blazing. Still, if Kade and she could make it to the window, they might be able to figure out a way through those burglar bars. Then Nate might be able to provide enough cover for them to get out of there.

Later, when this was over, she'd try to come to terms with the fact that the second baby was real. That she'd delivered twins. But right now, she had to focus on keeping Kade and her alive.

"You can have the backups," Bree told the shooter. She latched onto Kade and inched toward the window. "And we don't know who you are. There's no reason for you to kill us."

"Oh, there's a reason." And that's all the person said for several moments. "You both know too much. Especially you, Bree. You're too big of a risk because I have no idea what you might have overheard when Kirk was holding you. You might know who I am, and I can't risk you testifying against me."

Bree tried to figure out who was speaking. All of their suspects probably thought Kade and she knew *too much*. Especially since all their suspects were tied in some way or another to this clinic.

"I didn't overhear anything that would identify Kirk's boss," she explained, hoping the sound of her voice would cover Kade's and her movement toward the window.

"Can't take that chance," the shooter fired back.

He also fired another shot into the door.

"Oh, and if I were you, I wouldn't try to get out through the window—they're locked up tight and they have thick metal security bars. So, you might as well stop where you are. Well, unless you want his brother to die."

Oh, mercy.

Kade and she froze. The shooter must have a camera in place so that they were watching their every move.

"What the hell does my brother have to do with this?" Kade shouted.

"A lot actually. Before your cop brother arrived to put some of his men on the roof near here, I already had a gunman in place. In the catbird seat, you might say."

Kade cursed. "He could be lying," he whispered to Bree.

But it didn't sound like a lie. This person had had plenty of time to set all of this up.

"My hired gun has a rifle trained on your brother right now," the person added.

That didn't sound like a lie, either, and even if it was, it was too big a risk to take. Nate had come to help them, and she didn't want him dying.

Bree knew what she had to do. Now it was just a matter of convincing Kade to let her do it.

"I'm the threat to your identity," she shouted, levering herself up a little so that she could peer over the desk. "Not Kade. Let him go. So he can raise our daughters," Bree added so that it would remind Kade of what was at stake here.

If both of them died in this clinic, their twins would become orphans.

"You're not doing this," Kade immediately said, and he pulled her back down behind the desk.

The shooter laughed. "I'm not looking for a sacrificial lamb. I'm afraid both of you have to die."

Her stomach twisted, but Bree wasn't about to give up. There had to be some kind of argument she could use to get at least Kade out of this alive.

There was a sound. Some kind of movement at the end of the hall. And Bree tried to brace herself for the person to come closer.

Where Kade could shoot to kill.

"These are copies of the backups," she tried. "Not the originals. Those are in a safe place."

"Liar," the shooter answered.

Was it her imagination or did the person sound farther away than before?

"The backups can't be copied," the voice continued. "And I should know because it's a security check that I put in place. Didn't want anyone copying them to use them for blackmail."

"They're not coming closer," Kade whispered.

She'd been right about the moving away part. But why would the person do that?

Unless he or she was trying to escape?

But that didn't make sense, either. Kade and she had the backups.

"I'm afraid I have to say goodbye now." And footsteps followed that puzzling comment.

Was the person just leaving them there?

No, her gut told her that wouldn't happen and that something was terribly wrong.

Kade must have realized it, too, because he got to his feet and hurried to the door. He rammed his shoulder against it, but it didn't budge.

And then he cursed.

Bree stood, trying to figure out what had caused his reaction, and she spotted the tiny blinking red light on the wall. Except it wasn't just a light.

The blinks were numbers.

Ticking down.

Seven, six, five...

"It's a bomb!" Kade shouted.

He grabbed Bree and they started to run.

Kade had to make a split-second decision because a few seconds were all they had left.

The door behind them was locked. No way out there.

It was the same with the windows. He could risk pulling Bree behind the desk, but he could see the fistful of explosives attached to the timing device. The reception area and the desk were going to take the brunt of the impact.

So, with his left hand vised around Bree's arm, he raced down that dark hall.

Yeah, it was a risk. The shooter could be waiting for them to do just that, but at the moment the bomb was a bigger risk, especially since the shooter had also made a run for it.

"Hurry!" Kade shouted to Bree, though she no doubt understood the urgency.

They raced down the hall, past the first two rooms that were nearest to the lobby, and he pulled her into the next door. He dived toward a desk, pulling her underneath it with him. Kade also put his body over hers.

The blast tore through the building.

The sound was deafening, and the blast sent debris slamming into the desk and a chunk of the wall slammed into Kade's back. He'd have a heck of a bruise, but Bree was tucked safely beneath him.

He got his gun ready, in case he had to shoot their way out of there, but the sound made him realize they had bigger things to worry about than the shooter.

The ceiling groaned, threatening to give way.

"Run!" Bree shouted.

She fought to get up, just as Kade fought to get the debris off him. They finally made it to their feet and raced out of the room. What was left of it, anyway. It was the same for the hall. Walls had collapsed, and there was junk and rubble everywhere.

Bree hurdled over some of the mess and continued

down the hall. Cursing, Kade caught up with her, and shoved her behind him. Of course, that might not be any safer, what with the ceiling about to come down, but there were other rooms ahead. An exit, too. And he didn't want that shooter jumping out from the shadows.

After all, Kade still had the backups.

Maybe the guy thought the blast would destroy them, along with Bree and him. Especially Bree, since the bozo clearly thought she was the biggest threat. Still, this could be all part of some warped plan to get them out and into the open so he could gun them down.

Behind them, another chunk of the ceiling fell. It slammed into the tile floor and sent a new spray of debris their way. They kept on running until they reached the back exit. Kade hit the handle to open it.

Hell.

It was locked.

He cursed, grabbed Bree again and ducked into the room to their left. He couldn't be sure, but he thought this would lead them to the quarters where the infertile couples stayed. As Bree and he had done. There were more exits back in that area. Maybe, just maybe, not all of them would be locked.

His phone buzzed, and since Bree was still holding it, she pressed the button to put the call on speaker.

"Are you okay?" the person asked.

Not the shooter. It was Nate.

"Barely," Kade answered. "Did you see anyone leave the building?"

"No."

Kade cursed again and kept watch around them. "Bree and I are trying to make our way to an east side exit."

"Good. My men and I are converging on the building now."

Kade wanted to ask about the baby, how she was doing after being dropped off at the hospital, but it would have to wait. Right now, he had to get Bree out of there. Bree closed the phone and they started running as fast as they could.

Her breath was gusting. His, too. They meandered their way through the maze of rooms and furniture until they came to another hall. There were more windows in this part of the building. Good thing because it allowed him to see.

There was a door ahead.

"Stay behind me," Kade reminded her once again.

He lifted his gun and made a beeline to the door.

They were still a good ten feet away when the second blast ripped through the hall.

Chapter 17

Bree didn't have time to get down. The blast came right at them, and she felt herself flying backward. Everything seemed in slow motion but fast, too.

Her back collided with the wall.

Kade hit the concrete block wall beside her, and despite the bone-jarring impact, he managed to hang on to his gun. He also yanked her to her feet. Kade didn't have to warn her that they had to get out of there.

She knew.

Because there had already been two explosions, and that meant there could be another.

So far Kade and she had either gotten lucky or this was all some kind of elaborate trap.

"This way," Kade said, and he led her away from the part of the hall where the door had once been. It was now just a heap of rubble—a mix of concrete, wood and metal—and it was dangerous to try to get through it.

They hurried in the other direction, back through the rooms where Kade and she had stayed nearly a year ago when they were undercover.

Each step spiked her heartbeat and tightened the knot in her stomach. Because each step could lead them straight into another explosion. For that matter, the entire place could be rigged to go up.

Kade and she made their way into another hall, one with windows. And it was the thin white moonlight stabbing its way through the glass that allowed Bree to see the movement just ahead of them.

Kade pulled her into the room.

Just as a shot zinged through the air.

There was another jolt to her body when Kade and she landed on the floor. Another shot, too. But it slammed into the doorjamb and thankfully not them.

Despite the hard fall, Kade got her out of the doorway, and they scrambled to the far side of the room.

She glanced around. More windows, all with security bars, and there were two doors, feeding off in both directions. The doors were closed, but that didn't mean someone couldn't be waiting on the other side.

Since she no longer had a gun, Bree grabbed the first thing she could reach—a metal wire wastebasket. It wasn't much of a weapon, but if she got close enough, she could use it to bash someone.

Another shot.

This one also took a chunk out of the doorjamb.

As unnerving at those shots were, it did give Bree some good news. Well, temporary good news, anyway.

There likely wasn't about to be another explosion in this area. Not with their assailant so close.

Close enough to gun them down.

"You're like cats with nine lives!" the person shouted, still using the voice scrambler. "You should have been dead by now."

Yes, Bree was painfully aware of that. And so was her body. She was aching and stinging from all the cuts, nicks and bruises. Beside her, Kade was no doubt feeling the same.

"Why don't you come in here and try to finish the job?" Kade shouted back.

Bree prayed the guy would take Kade up on the offer. Because Kade was still armed. But she didn't hear any movement in the hall or outside the building.

Were Nate and the other officers there, waiting to respond?

She hoped so because Bree didn't want this monster to escape. If that happened, the danger would start all over again. The threats to Kade and her would hang over their heads. The heads of their babies, too.

That couldn't happen.

This had to end now, tonight.

"Are you too scared to face us?" Bree yelled. Yeah, it might be a stupid move to goad their assailant, but it could work.

Maybe.

"Not scared. And I'm not stupid, either. This can only end one way—with your deaths."

"Or yours!" Bree fired back.

Kade nodded, motioned for her to keep it up, and while he kept low, he began to inch toward the hall door.

"You know, I think I do remember some things Tim

Kirk said," Bree continued, keeping her voice loud to cover Kade's movement. "He wasn't very good at keeping secrets, was he?"

Silence.

Kade stopped. Waited.

"All right," their assailant finally said. "If Kirk told secrets, then who am I?" The person didn't wait for her to answer. "You don't know. You can only guess. And guessing won't help you or Agent Ryland."

Kade moved closer to the door but crouched down so that he was practically on the floor.

"What if it's not a guess?" Bree lied. "What if I've already left a sworn statement with the district attorney? Think about it—I wouldn't have risked coming here if I didn't have an ace in the hole."

She nearly choked on those words, the same ones that Kirk had used to describe her child. Maybe their attacker would recognize them and panic. Mercy, did she want panic. Maybe then the person would make a mistake, and Kade could get off that shot.

"Well?" Bree called out when she didn't get an answer. "Should I call the district attorney and tell him to release my statement?"

She waited, her heart in her throat.

Kade waited, too, his attention fastened on the hall and doorway.

Bree was so focused on what she could say to draw out this monster that she barely heard the sound. Not from the hall or the doorway.

But from behind her.

She turned and saw the shadowy figure in the now-open doorway on the right side of the room.

Oh, God.

The person lifted his arm, ready to fire. Not at her. But at Kade.

Bree didn't think. She dropped the trash can and dived at the person who was about to shoot Kade.

Kade whirled around just in time to see Bree launch herself at the gunman. And there was no mistaking that this was a gunman because Kade spotted the guy's weapon.

He also saw that weapon ram into Bree when she collided with their attacker. But it wasn't just the collision and the gun that latched onto his attention.

Kade's heart went to his knees when the sound of the bullet tore through the room.

"Bree!" Kade heard himself yell.

She had to be all right. If this SOB had shot her... but he couldn't go there. Couldn't bear to think of what might be. He just ran toward her.

And then he had to come to a quick stop.

Their attacker hooked an arm around Bree's throat and snapped her toward him. In the same motion, the person jammed a gun against Bree's head.

Now that Kade's eyes had adjusted to the darkness, he had no trouble seeing the stark fear on her face. Her eyes were wide, and her chest was pumping for air.

"Run!" she told Kade.

But the person ground the barrel of the gun into her temple. "If you run, she dies right now," her captor warned. "Drop your gun and give me the backups."

Kade tried to give Bree a steadying look, and then his gaze went behind her to the figure wearing the dark clothes and black ski mask. Kade also didn't miss the object in the gunman's left hand. But he or she didn't hold on to it for long.

It clattered to the floor.

The voice scrambler, Kade realized.

Their attacker had dropped it, no doubt so that both hands could be used to contain Bree. And it was working. Bree couldn't move without the risk of being either choked or shot.

"I said drop your gun and give me the backups," the man repeated.

And it was a man all right. Kade knew that now that the scrambler was no longer being used. It was a man whose voice Kade recognized.

Anthony.

So, they had the identity of the person who'd made their lives a living hell and had endangered not just them but their newborn daughters.

The anger slammed through Kade, but he tried to tamp it down because he had to figure out a way to get that gun away from Bree's head. He wasn't sure Anthony was capable of cold-blooded, close-contact murder, but considering everything else he'd likely done, it was a risk that Kade couldn't take.

"Why are you doing this, Anthony?" Bree asked, but she kept her attention fastened on Kade. Her left eyebrow was slightly cocked as if asking what she should do.

Kade didn't have an answer to that yet.

"You know why I'm doing this," Anthony assured her.

Kade heard it, but the words hardly registered. That's because he got a better look at the grip Anthony had on the gun. Oh, mercy. Anthony's hand was shaking.

Not good. He was probably scared spitless despite the cocky demeanor he'd had earlier, and Kade knew from experience that scared people usually made bad decisions in situations like these.

"Put down the gun." Kade tried to keep calm. Normally, it would be a piece of cake. All those years of training and experience had taught him to disguise the fear he felt crawling through him. But this wasn't normal. Bree was on the other end of that gun.

"You don't want murder added to the list of charges," Kade pressed.

"No." And that's all Anthony said for several moments. "But I'll be charged with murder and other things if the cops see the surveillance backups."

Hell. So, that's what was on them. *Murder.* Kade figured it was bad if Anthony was willing to go through all of this to get the backups, but he'd hoped for some lesser charges. Murder meant Anthony had no way out.

This was not going to end well.

"I didn't know my father and Coop had set up the extra cameras," Anthony said, his voice shaking. "And I did some things."

Bree pulled in a hard breath, and Kade knew she'd come to the same conclusion as he had. Anthony couldn't let them out of there alive, not with those backups that could get him the death penalty.

He was a desperate man.

But Kade was even more desperate.

"I didn't know about the backups at first," Anthony went on. "I thought you and Bree were the only two people who could send me to jail."

"So you kidnapped me," Bree provided. She glanced around as if looking for a way to escape. Kade hoped she wouldn't try until he had a better shot. At the moment, he had no shot at all.

"The kidnapping worked." Anthony paused again. "Until Jamie decided to do something stupid like leaving the baby at the hospital and letting you escape." He said the woman's name like venom. "Jamie's dead now. I don't have to worry about her or her stupidity anymore."

Hell. That was not what Kade wanted to hear. Yet another confession to murder to go along with the ones on the surveillance backups.

"The cops are outside," Kade reminded him just in case Anthony had forgotten that he wasn't just going to shoot and stroll out of here.

"Yes, and so is the gunman I hired."

There was an edge in Anthony's voice. Not the edge of someone who was a hundred percent confident in this plan. So Kade decided to see if he could push a button or two.

"You mean the incompetent gunman who was supposed to kill Jamie in the park?" Kade asked.

Anthony stammered out a few syllables before he managed some full-blown profanity. Clearly the gunman was a button, and Kade had indeed managed to push it. Now he could only hope that it didn't put Bree in more danger. Kade needed Anthony distracted, not just fuming mad.

Anthony ripped off his ski mask. "Yes! That's the idiot. But he won't fail me this time. He knows it'll cost him his life if he doesn't succeed."

Kade made an *I-doubt-that* sound in his throat.

Another button push. Every muscle in Anthony's face tightened. "Give me the backups," he demanded.

"And put down that gun. If I have to tell you again, you're a dead man."

Despite the *dead man* warning, Kade didn't move until he saw Antony's hand tense. He was going to pull the trigger if Kade didn't do something fast.

"Here's the gun," Kade said. He stooped down and eased it onto the floor.

Kade looked at Bree, just a split-second glance, so that she'd know he was about to try to get them out of this, and she gave a slight nod.

"Now, I want the backups," Anthony ordered.

When he was still in a crouched position, Kade reached into his shirt. But he didn't get the backups. It was now or never. He said a quick prayer and launched himself at Anthony.

Kade rammed into the man before Anthony could pull the trigger. That was the good news. But the bad news was that Bree was still in danger.

Between them.

Where Anthony could kill her.

Anthony no longer had the gun aimed at her head, but he wasn't ready to surrender. Far from it.

Kade tried to shove Bree to the side, but Anthony held on to her, choking her with the crook of his arm. She clawed at his arm while Kade caught the man's shooting hand and bashed it against the floor.

Anthony cursed, but he still didn't stop fighting.

Neither did Bree or Kade. Bree rammed her elbow against Anthony's stomach, and he sputtered out a cough.

It was the break that Kade needed.

For just that split second, Anthony was distracted while he tried to catch his breath. Kade shoved Bree away from the man, and he brought down his fist into Anthony's jaw. His head flopped back.

And he dropped the gun.

Bree hurried to pick it up, and she put it right to Anthony's head.

"Give me a reason to kill you," she said. "Any reason will do."

Maybe she was bluffing, but after everything Anthony had put her through, maybe not.

Either way, Anthony believed her. He stopped struggling and his hands dropped limply by his sides.

Chapter 18

"Can you drive any faster?" Kade asked his brother Nate.

It was exactly the question Bree had wanted to ask. She was more than grateful that Nate had stepped up to rush them to the Silver Creek hospital, but Bree wanted an emphasis on the *rush* part.

It was torture waiting to see their other daughter.

"I could drive faster," Nate drawled. "But I'd rather get there in one piece. Well, what's left of one piece. You do know you're both bleeding, right?"

Bree swiped at her lip again with the back of her hand. Yep. Still bleeding. She dabbed at the cut on Kade's forehead. She hated seeing the injuries there on his otherwise drop-dead gorgeous face, but the injuries were superficial and could wait. The baby couldn't.

Well, she could, but Bree thought she might burst if she couldn't see her and make sure she was all right.

Nate's phone buzzed, and he answered it while he took the final turn to Silver Creek. The seconds and miles were just crawling by, even though it had only been twenty minutes or so since they'd left the Fulbright Clinic. When she'd looked back in the rearview mirror at the place, the SAPD officers had been stuffing a handcuffed Anthony McClendon into a patrol car.

Bree hoped he'd rot in jail.

It wasn't a forgive-and-forget sort of attitude to have, but she never wanted the man near her, Kade or their children again. Anthony was slime and had done everything in his power to destroy them.

Thank God, he hadn't succeeded.

"You're still bleeding," Kade let her know when she made another unsuccessful swipe at her mouth. He caught her chin, turned her head to face him and touched his fingers to her lip. "Does it hurt?"

She shook her head. There was probably pain, but she couldn't feel it right now. In fact, Bree couldn't feel much physically, only the concern she still had for Kade and their daughters.

"Does that hurt?" She glanced up at the bump and cut on his forehead.

"No." He kept his fingers on her mouth and his gaze connected with hers. He replaced his fingers with his lips and kissed her gently.

It stung a little, but Bree didn't care. The kiss warmed her and took away some of the ice that Anthony had put there. In fact, it even took some of the edge off her impatience and reminded her of something very important.

She smiled. "We won." With all the turmoil going on inside her and the hatred she had for Anthony, Bree hadn't had time to put things in perspective. Leave it to Kade's kiss to do exactly that. They'd won, and the prize was huge.

Kade smiled, too. "Yeah. And we're the parents of twin girls."

For just a moment that terrified her as she imagined trying to be a mother to both of them. *Twins*. Before Leah, she'd never even held a baby, and now she had two.

"You look like you're about to panic," Kade whispered.

Bree chuckled and winced as it pinched at her busted lip. "So do you."

He nodded. "Maybe a little. I'm thinking about how we can get through those 2:00 a.m. feedings with both of them."

"And the diapers." But suddenly that didn't seem so bad. It even seemed doable. Maybe because Kade had said *we*.

"You mean that?" Bree asked before she could stop herself.

He flexed his eyebrows and made a face from the tug it no doubt gave that knot on his head. "Mean what?"

Bree froze for a moment and considered, well, everything. Kade and she had known each other such a short time, and most of that time they'd been working undercover or getting shot at. Hardly the foundation for a relationship.

But somehow they'd managed just that—a relationship.

Of sorts.

Bree was still a little hazy on Kade's thoughts and feelings. However, hers were clearer now. Maybe because they'd come so close to dying tonight. That had certainly put things in perspective. So, she decided to go for it. She would question that *we,* and then she would tell him it was what she wanted, too. She wanted them to do this family thing together.

Whatever that entailed.

But before Bree could answer, Nate ended his call and looked back at them.

"They found Jamie's body," he let them know.

And just like that, Bree was pulled back into the nightmarish memories that Anthony had given Kade and her. Enough nightmares to last a lifetime or two, and now Anthony had another victim—Jamie. Even though Bree didn't care for the woman's criminal activity, Jamie had tried to help her, and now she was dead because of it.

"Anthony confessed that he killed her," Kade explained.

"Yes, he confessed it to my men, too," Nate verified. "He'll be booked on capital murder changes, and he's not just looking at jail time but the death penalty."

Bree remembered something else he'd said. "Anthony murdered someone else. It's on the surveillance backups."

Nate nodded. "Kade gave them back to us, and we'll give them a thorough review. Trust me, we'll add any and all charges to make sure Anthony is never back on the streets again. His father, too, because Anthony said there'd be plenty enough on the backups to bring charges against Hector McClendon."

Good. After everything that had gone on at the clinic, McClendon certainly deserved to be punished.

Kade glanced at her first before looking at his brother. "Did Anthony say anything about Coop?"

"No, and from the sound of it, Anthony is blabbing about anyone who can be arrested for anything. A misery loves company sort of thing."

Bree felt the relief wash over her. So, her former boss and mentor wasn't dirty. That was something, at least, even though Kade's and her lives would never be the same.

And part of that wasn't all bad.

In fact, part of it was nothing short of a miracle. She might never have become a parent by choice, and it broke her heart to think of all the things she would have missed. She couldn't imagine life without Kade and the babies.

Except she might not have Kade.

And she didn't know what she would do if that happened.

Bree saw the Silver Creek hospital just ahead and knew her baby was inside. Just like that, the jitters and impatience returned with a vengeance. Her breath started to pound, her mouth went dry. She felt a little queasy.

And then Kade caught her hand in his and gave it a gentle squeeze. That squeeze was a reminder that she didn't want to do this alone.

No, that wasn't it.

She wanted to do this with Kade.

Bree looked at him to ask him about that *we* remark, but again she lost her chance when Nate stopped directly in front of the hospital doors. A discussion that would have to wait.

Kade and she barreled out, leaving Nate behind to park his SUV, and they rushed through the automatic doors. Her heart was in her throat by the time they made it to the lobby.

And then Bree saw them.

Mason was standing near the reception desk, and he was holding a baby who did indeed look exactly like Leah.

Kade's and her baby.

Bree knew that after just a glimpse.

The baby was crying, and Mason was trying to soothe her by rocking her. It wasn't working, and Mason looked more than a little uncomfortable with his baby-holding duties. Bree went to him, took the little girl and pulled her into her arms.

Yes, this child was theirs. Just holding her warmed every bit of Bree's heart.

Kade came closer, sliding his arm around both her and the baby. Leah's twin looked up at them as if trying to figure out if she was going to start crying again. She didn't. She just studied them.

Bree pulled back her blanket and studied her, too. Ten fingers, ten toes. There didn't appear to be a scratch on her, thank God.

"She's okay?" Bree asked Mason.

He nodded. "She's got a healthy set of lungs. And she peed on me." Mason frowned when he looked down at the wet spot on his shirt.

Bree smiled. Laughed. And then the tears came just as quickly. Her emotions were a mess right now, but the one thing she felt the most was the unconditional love. She pulled the baby closer and held on tight.

"It'll be okay," Kade whispered to her.

"Yes," Bree managed to say. "These are happy tears."

Kade smiled too. Kissed her, and then he kissed their daughter.

"The doc did a DNA test," Mason let them know. "But I don't think it's necessary."

"Neither do I," Kade agreed. "She's ours."

Behind them, the doors swished open, and because of the events of the night, Bree automatically pulled her daughter into a protective stance. Kade moved, too, to position himself in front of them.

But all their posturing wasn't necessary.

Grayson came through the doors, and he was carrying Leah in the crook of his arm. He stopped a moment, looking at the baby Bree was holding, and he smiled.

"Yeah, she's a Ryland all right." Grayson came closer and handed Leah to Kade.

"She's got a healthy set of lungs," Mason repeated in a mumble. He glanced at both babies. "Hope you don't expect me to babysit."

His tone was gruff, but Bree thought she saw the start of a smile. So this was what it felt like to be surrounded by family?

By love.

The *l*-word stopped her for a moment, and she looked up at Kade. No stop this time.

She was in love with him.

Bree wasn't sure why it'd taken her so long to come to that conclusion. It felt as if she'd loved him forever. Just like the babies.

Of course, that didn't mean he felt the same way

about her. Yes, they had the twins, but that only meant they were parents. Not a couple in love. And it tore at her heart to realize she wanted it all, but she might not get it.

Kade might not love her.

"Why don't I get all you back to the ranch?" Grayson suggested. He gave the other twin's toes a jiggle. "What are you going to name her?"

"I've been calling her Mia," Mason volunteered and then looked uncomfortable with the admission. "Well, I had to call her something other than *kid,* and it rhymes with Leah."

Bree shrugged and looked up at Kade. He shrugged, too. "It works for me."

It worked for Bree, too.

So, they had Leah and Mia. The girls might hate the rhyming names when they got older, but they fit.

Everything about this moment fit.

Except for the person who came through the hospital doors.

Coop.

Everyone's attention went to him, and judging from Grayson's and Kade's scowls, they weren't any happier to see the man than she was. Bree wanted to spend this time with Kade and the girls. She definitely didn't want to go another round with her former boss.

"We were about to leave," Bree *greeted* him. And she hoped he understood there was nothing he had to say that she wanted to hear. She only wanted to leave.

Coop nodded. Glanced at the babies. There was no smile, only concern on his face. "I heard what happened, and I wanted to say how sorry I am."

There was no anger in his eyes or tone. The apology

sounded heartfelt, and Bree was glad they were mending some fences, but her mind could hardly stay on the conversation.

"I came here to give you back your badge," Coop added. "I was wrong to put that kind of pressure on you."

"Yes, you were," Kade agreed.

Coop reached in his pocket and held out her badge.

Bree stared it a moment and then looked at each of her daughters. Then, at Kade. She had a decision to make and was surprised that it wasn't that hard to do.

"No, thanks," Bree said. And there wasn't a shred of doubt about this. "I can't go back to that life. It wouldn't give me much time for the girls."

Or Kade.

Coop's eyes widened. "You're serious?"

"Completely," she verified. "I want a job that'll keep me closer to Silver Creek."

Grayson shrugged. "I've got a deputy position open in the Silver Creek sheriff's office. It's yours if you want it. After you've taken some maternity leave, that is."

Bree nodded and managed to whisper a thanks around the sudden lump in her throat. Later, she would tell him how much she appreciated that. The deputy position would keep her in law enforcement. And Silver Creek.

"But an FBI agent isn't just your job. It's who you are," Coop argued.

Bree looked him straight in the eye. "Not anymore. Goodbye, Coop."

Keeping a firm grip on the baby, Bree extended her hand for him to shake, but for a moment, she thought he might refuse. Finally, Coop accepted and shook her hand. He also hugged her.

"Have a good life, Bree." And he turned and walked back out.

Bree expected to feel some kind of pangs of…whatever, but she didn't. She looked up at Kade and didn't feel pangs there, either.

She just saw the man she loved.

Mason cleared his throat. "I'll bring the car to the door."

Grayson gave both Kade and her a look, too. "I'll help."

Clearly, Kade's brothers realized that this might become a private discussion. The *we* talk.

But Kade didn't exactly launch into a discussion. He leaned in and kissed her. Not a peck. A real kiss. It lasted so long that a nurse passing by cleared her throat.

Kade broke the intimate contact with a smile on his face. "No regrets about giving up your badge?"

"Not a one." And this was a do-or-die moment. A moment Bree couldn't let slip away again. "The only thing I regret is not telling you that I'm in love with you."

Kade froze in midkiss, and he eased back so they were eye to eye. Between them, both babies were wide-awake and playing footsies with each other. They both had their eyes fastened to their parents.

Then, Kade smiled. Really smiled. "Good." He hooked his left arm around Bree's waist and got as close to her as he could. "Because I'm in love with you, too."

Bree's breath vanished, and the relief she felt nearly brought her to her knees.

Kade was right there to catch her.

And kiss her.

This one melted her.

"Of course, that I-love-you comes with a marriage proposal," Kade said.

The melting turned to heat, and Bree wished they were somewhere private so she could haul him off to bed. Well, after the babies were asleep, anyway. She wasn't sure how they would work such things into their crazy schedule, but with this fierce attraction, they'd find a way.

Kade took Bree by her free hand. "Will you marry me, Bree?"

She didn't even have to think of her answer. "In a heartbeat."

Kade let out a whoop that startled both babies and had several members of the hospital staff staring at them. Bree ignored the stares. Kissed both babies.

And then she kissed Kade.

She didn't stop until the babies' kicking became an issue, but Bree ended the kiss knowing there would be plenty of others in her future.

"Want to go home?" Kade asked.

Another easy answer. "Yes," she whispered.

Going home with Kade and their daughters was exactly what Bree wanted.

* * * * *

*Rancher Johnny King thought he'd moved on since
Chelsea Black broke their engagement and shattered
his heart. But with his emotions still raw following
his father's murder, Chelsea's return to town and her
vulnerability touches Johnny's heart. And when a
mysterious stalker threatens Chelsea's life, protecting
her means risking his heart again for the woman
who abandoned him.*

Read on for a sneak preview of
Closing in on the Cowboy,
the first installment of the
Kings of Coyote Creek miniseries
by New York Times *bestselling author Carla Cassidy!*

"CHELSEA, WHAT'S GOING ON?" Johnny clutched his cell
phone to his ear and at the same time he sat up and turned
on the lamp on his nightstand.

"That man…that man is here. He tried to b-break in."
The words came amid sobs. "He…he was at my back
d-door and breaking the gl-glass to get in."

"Hang up and call Lane," he instructed as he got out
of bed.

"I…already called, but n-nobody is here yet."

Johnny could hear the abject terror in her voice, and an
icy fear shot through him. "Where are you now?"

"I'm in the kitchen."

"Get to the bathroom and lock yourself in. Do you hear me? Lock yourself in the bathroom, and I'll be there as quickly as I can," he instructed.

"Please hurry. I don't know where he is now, and I'm so scared."

"Just get to the bathroom. Lock the door and don't open it for anyone but me or the police." He hung up and quickly dressed. He then strapped on his gun and left his cabin. Any residual sleepiness he might have felt was instantly gone, replaced by a sharp edge of tension that tightened his chest.

Don't miss
Closing in on the Cowboy *by Carla Cassidy,*
available July 2022 wherever
Harlequin Intrigue books and ebooks are sold.

Harlequin.com

Love Harlequin romance?

DISCOVER.

Be the first to find out about promotions, news and exclusive content!

f Facebook.com/HarlequinBooks

y Twitter.com/HarlequinBooks

◉ Instagram.com/HarlequinBooks

P Pinterest.com/HarlequinBooks

You Tube YouTube.com/HarlequinBooks

ReaderService.com

EXPLORE.

Sign up for the Harlequin e-newsletter and download a free book from any series at **TryHarlequin.com**

CONNECT.

Join our Harlequin community to share your thoughts and connect with other romance readers! **Facebook.com/groups/HarlequinConnection**

HSOCIAL2021

HARLEQUIN

Heartfelt or thrilling, passionate or uplifting—Harlequin is more than just happily-ever-after.

With twelve different series to choose from and new books available every month, you are sure to find stories that will move you, uplift you, inspire and delight you.

SIGN UP FOR THE HARLEQUIN NEWSLETTER

Be the first to hear about great new reads and exciting offers!

Harlequin.com/newsletters